It began as an early winter Maine snowstorm before
Dan and Kathy Simmons found themselves . . .

STRANDED

Norman R. Kalloch, Jr.

Cover photo by Wesley Kalloch

Designed and produced by:
Maine Authors Publishing
12 High Street, Thomaston, Maine
www.maineauthorspublishing.com

Printed in the United States of America

Dedicated to our children,
Rebecca McNerney and Wesley Kalloch

CONTENTS

MAJOR CHARACTERS

Kathy Simmons

Dan Simmons

Hazel Martin: Kathy and Dan's daughter

Tom Martin: Hazel's husband

Frank Bartlett Sr.: founder of Bartlett Haven

Louise Bartlett: Frank's former wife,
and mother to Frankie, Dick, and Josh

Frankie (Frank Bartlett Jr.)

Beatrice: Frankie's live-in

Darlene: Dick's live-in

Wendy: Josh's live-in

INTRODUCTION

New England has had its share of devastating winter storms. The most severe have monikers like the Ice Storm of 1998 and the Great Blizzard of 1952, which dumped three feet of snow on northern Maine. Then there was the Great New England Blizzard of 1978, with winds up to 110 miles per hour, which killed about a hundred people. As disastrous as these storms were, their disruption of daily life was generally short-lived, lasting only a few days. Even the effects of the most catastrophic storms rarely last a week before life slowly returns to normal.

Fortunately, many New Englanders have not had to live through such calamities. For most people, the closest brush with a winter-weather-related disaster is a brief power outage caused by high winds or heavy wet snow breaking electrical wires and snapping power poles. The usual consequence of such temporary blackouts is sitting in the dark, gripping a flashlight, and occasionally peeking out the window to see if the neighbors have power.

If the electricity is off for several hours, concern mounts about the two pounds of bacon that's been in the freezer for the last six months thawing before the power is restored. However, before anyone freezes to death or dies of starvation, the lights snap on and the refrigerator starts to hum. The minor disruption soon becomes a distant memory. Although an inconvenience, these brief outages do not qualify as life-changing events.

At the extreme, consider a storm of epic proportions lasting weeks, even months, a storm so devastating that the region's economy crumbles, with roads closed and businesses shuttered. Millions of people are isolated at home without heat, with only the food in the kitchen cupboard separating young and old from starvation. A catastrophic storm that strikes so suddenly, it is as if people are being ripped from their twenty-first century lifestyle and dropped into a candlelit farmhouse of the 1800s. Except this imaginary farmhouse has a food reserve in the root cellar and a well-stocked woodshed for heat. Would neighbor help neighbor? Or would everyone fend for themselves as marauding gangs try to make others' possessions theirs?

The story of Kathy and Dan Simmons's struggle to survive their calamity is not so different from what any of us might face in a similar situation. The difference is in the details and the choices made, including whether to fight through such a disaster or to hunker down and hope to be rescued.

PROLOGUE

Defense Intelligence Analysis Center
Joint Base Anacostia-Bolling
Washington, D.C.

"Mr. Henderson, I need to speak to you for a minute!" Russ Hall hollered as he ran down the hall of the massive intelligence-gathering building, eighteen minutes from the White House. "Please, just a minute, sir," he called again as Ronald Henderson, assistant to the director for electronic data coordination, opened the door to conference room 501.

Henderson checked his watch. He closed the conference room door and waited for Hall to reach him. "What is it, Russ? I've only got a couple of minutes, so make it fast."

"Can we talk in your office? There's something I need to show you."

Henderson motioned to his private office across the hall.

"Okay. Give it to me. Larry Eagleton in the Spatial Data Division is retiring Friday. The staff is having a little send-off party for him. And of course they want me to say a few words."

"Of course, sir." Hall slid six twelve-by-eighteen-inch black-and-white images from an oversized manila envelope stamped "Top Secret, Confidential" in large red letters. He laid one beside the other on Henderson's desk. Before Hall could explain, Henderson gave each satellite photo a cursory look and then looked up.

"All I see is a North Korean locomotive pulling four flatbed rail cars, each carrying something covered. They're likely moving missiles or equipment into one of their underground storage sites. That's nothing new, Hall. We've known for years the DPRK keeps its intermediate-range missiles hidden inside a half dozen mountains in the Nangnim range."

"That's right, we do know that. However, each photo shows a train at a different underground storage facility. Moreover, the six images were taken within the same forty-eight hours."

"So? They're likely having maneuvers to keep the army busy. Something other than marching in parades celebrating their beloved, caring leader," Henderson scoffed.

"Look at the flatcars and the coverings over the missiles," Hall said.

Hall pulled six more photos from a second envelope and laid each beside its corresponding image. "These are the same trains as they exited the underground facilities. Now compare the size of the shrouded missiles being hauled by each engine." Without waiting for Henderson to study the six pairs of digitally enhanced prints, Hall continued, "Each of those missiles is twenty feet shorter than those that went into the mountains."

Now Hall had Henderson's attention. His eyes jumped from image to image. "Do you know what's under those coverings?" Henderson asked, taking off his reading glasses and looking up at the remote sensing analyst standing over the desk.

"I do. My analysis of the images tells me that what went into the mountains is the new and improved Hwasong-17 ICBM and what came out was the smaller Hwasong-14. You'll have to ask the boys at Defense Intelligence why they removed the Hwasong-14s. Although I suspect the underground storage area isn't large enough to accommodate both missiles."

"How can we be sure those are missiles under the coverings? Maybe the North Koreans are just playing mind games, knowing our satellites are watching their every move. Perhaps they're just trying to rattle our cage. You know, hoping that the Big Satan will make an ass out of itself by panicking over a bunch of cardboard boxes they stacked under that canvas to look like ICBMs. Besides, the experts at the CIA said it would be at least three years before

North Korea perfected a guidance system for their new bird and another two before the Hwasong-17 went into production, giving us plenty of time to mess up their plans."

"You can thank the Chinese for lending them a hand on that one. However, that's another story. I know that the Hwasong-17 missiles went inside those mountains. We have photos taken by our enhanced-radar AQUADE satellite of the H-17 being rolled onto the Mayang-Do Naval Base launch pad six weeks ago. From that image, I was able to calculate its exact dimensions. The measurements of what's under those coverings are identical to the Hwasong-17."

Henderson knew that if Hall was correct in his analysis, the twenty-four ICBMs seen going into the mountains had a range of ninety-three hundred miles. That would place the entire United States mainland within striking distance.

Russ Hall had worked as a satellite interpretation and analysis expert for eight years at the National Geospatial-Intelligence Agency (NGIA). There was none better at it than Hall. He had pinpointed the Abbottabad, Pakistan, compound, the hideout of Osama bin Laden. After his discovery, Hall became a hot commodity. All the federal security agencies wanted him on their staff. Trying to lure Washington's top remote-image analyst to another intelligence-gathering agency isn't different from a professional football team attempting to convince a great quarterback to leave his team and play for another. Everyone wants an edge over the competition, even intelligence agencies charged with protecting the United States from its enemies.

Finally, an unknown higher-up in the State Department told Hall to report to the Defense Intelligence Analysis Center. The NGIA tried to block Hall's reassignment, not wanting to lose its best analyst, who just happened to be the one who located the hideout of one of the world's most wanted terrorists and the bragging rights it had brought to one of the more obscure Washington intelligence agencies. A techie superstar on the staff can't hurt when you compete with sixteen other power-hungry intelligence agencies for a piece of the annual $60 billion intelligence community budget.

"Good work, Russ. Let me know if you learn anything else," Henderson said, picking up the phone to call Edgar Davis, who, as director of national intelligence, coordinated intelligence collection and sharing among U.S. intelligence agencies.

After his conversation with Henderson, Davis set up a meeting with representatives of the seventeen intelligence agencies for the next day. The nine o'clock meeting would be in the Eisenhower Conference Room at the Office of National Intelligence in McLean.

The following morning, waiting for the agency heads to arrive, the various staff huddled in separate groups, quietly discussing the seriousness of what appeared to be the deployment of the DPRK's newest and most potent long-range ballistic missile.

"So what do you think? Are those missiles for real or part of another stunt by the North Koreans?" asked one of the aids to Major General Gerald Simpson, head of Air Force Intelligence.

"With that little despot, you never know what's up. He could have had a breakthrough in developing the Hwasong-17. And if he did, it's serious, or it could be an elaborate hoax to twist the U.S.'s tail just to watch us squirm."

"Well, he's doing that all right," another answered, looking around the room at the thirty staffers waiting for their bosses to enter the room.

"No matter how you cut it, it's a bad scene having that scumbag Jeong whacked out on fentanyl, binging on *Dr. Strangelove* on Netflix, in bed with two hookers, with his finger on the launch button." The six men broke out into a muffled chuckle but not muted enough to avoid the questioning stares from those close enough to hear.

The door to the conference room opened, and the representatives of the United States intelligence agencies paraded into the room. The staffers broke from their groups and sat behind their respective bosses, ready to provide any documentation if asked. There would be no more office gossip, at least not until the workday ended and they hit the bars on Fourteenth Street.

Director Davis entered the room last, an attractive middle-aged woman no one recognized at his side. The two looked somber as they approached the oversized conference table. The woman, wearing a stylish gray business suit, sat beside the director. The staffs of the various agencies glanced at one another. This woman and her reason for being there would undoubtedly be on the evening's agenda over whiskey sours.

"Before we get started, I want to introduce Dr. Susan Vogel. Dr. Vogel is joining our discussions on the latest developments in North Korea. Dr. Vogel has done groundbreaking research on climate change resulting from nuclear war." Davis stopped and looked around the oval table. "I can tell by the look on everyone's faces that you are wondering where we're going with today's meeting. Don't worry—there's no plan to start World War Three. As the discussion progresses, you will hear from Dr. Vogel and understand why she is here.

"Now, I expect two outcomes from this meeting. One is to assess the threat from the supposed deployment of the H-17s by the North Koreans. The second is to formulate options for responding to that threat that I will present to the National Security Council meeting on Thursday.

"Ron Henderson, assistant to the director for electronic data coordination, will show us the satellite imagery that has brought us here today."

At that, a large screen dropped from the ceiling. Henderson momentarily fumbled with the laptop's keyboard, trying to locate the correct key to cast the image onto the monitor. After several embarrassing seconds, the first satellite image appeared—one of the images Hall had shown Henderson twenty-four hours earlier, now enhanced with labels and arrows pointing to the shrouded missiles and the entrance to the underground silo. Henderson went through the comparisons almost word for word as Hall had explained to him. Fifteen minutes later, the stage was set for the remainder of the meeting.

Davis thanked Henderson for his exemplary work identifying the clandestine missiles. He then called on Harold Carson for the Central Intelligence Agency's assessment of North Korea's sudden buildup of long-range missiles.

"In one word, Director Davis, it's *food*, at least the shortage of it. Agricultural crops have failed miserably for the last three years in North Korea as a result of extreme drought, mismanagement, and reduced imports of grains from China. Combined, these issues have stifled agricultural production. The DPRK has no maize, rice, or any other grain stockpiles.

"People are starving, at least the ones who aren't well connected to Jeong's inner circle. When people are hungry, they get desperate. We have intercepted government and military cell calls and emails that food riots are happening in all nine North Korean provinces. Uprisings are unheard of in the DPRK, and Jeong is scared. Usually he throws dissidents into concentration camps or makes an example out of them by lining them up in the town square and shooting them. That's always been Jeong's permanent solution to a temporary problem, but not this time. The only way Jeong and his generals know how to deal with this situation is to shift the population's focus from empty stomachs to the Great Satan. Convince the masses that national survival is far more important than missing a few meals.

"The saber-rattling of recent months and the deployment of the H-17s are all for public consumption. Jeong wants to convince his people that America and Japan are in cahoots planning an attack on the homeland. His people are bombarded with propaganda on nearly every street corner from Pyongyang to the smallest hamlets along the North's border with China."

"But how can we be sure he won't launch those missiles? Maybe he's using the famine as a cover-up to go on the offensive," Davis asked.

"Why would he do that? He knows we could wipe him off the map and send him and his buddies back to the Stone Age," the CIA director responded.

"Send him *back* to the Stone Age? That country has been in the Stone Age since DoYoon Jeong, the former Dear Leader, arrived on the scene in nineteen-ninety-four," Colonel Aubrey of army intelligence scoffed. Davis ignored the colonel's remark.

"There's another possibility for deploying advanced missiles. Jeong has long believed North Korea needs to modernize and refine its nuclear capability for added leverage in future arms reduction talks with the U.S. For the past five years, they've demanded to be treated as an equal by the United States. The development of ever-more-advanced nuclear and missile capabilities is one way to earn that respect," interjected Dr. Ronald Williams, representing the Strategy and Security Institute at Stanford University.

"That may be, but we don't want to underestimate Jeong's intentions," Davis responded. "Admiral Lee, how many nuclear warheads has North Korea stockpiled?"

"We cannot know for certain, but we estimate twenty to sixty. He's constantly shuffling them around the countryside in plain view of our satellites. Still, we doubt if all of them are actually bombs. Some could be empty cylinders shaped to look like nuclear devices."

"The explosive yield of each bomb, Admiral?"

"If the size of the one tested six months ago at the underground Punggye-ri test site is accurate, each warhead can deliver one hundred fifty thousand tons of explosives. Sixty nuclear devices are equivalent to about nine million tons of TNT. Enough power to destroy eight cities the size of St. Louis," Lee answered.

"As an exercise, let's assume Jeong has sixty atomic bombs capable of being carried atop the H-17s. He attempts to launch all sixty simultaneously. We'll assume that five rockets malfunction and never leave the launchpad and, for whatever reason, another five crash harmlessly into the ocean. For argument's sake, our anti-missile defense system shoots down twenty-five of the remaining ICBMs. Still, twenty-five get through and hit their targets.

We counterattack with sixty of our own missiles loaded with the same size megaton bombs. Assume five of our missiles malfunction. As North Korea lacks a credible anti-missile shield, the other fifty-five missiles hit their intended target. Combined, eighty nuclear warheads, each carrying a hundred fifty kilotons of explosives, detonate during our hypothetical twelve-hour confrontation. This, of course, assumes the Chinese and the Russians don't feel obligated to join in and ensure mutual destruction." Davis paused and looked at each of the representatives of the intelligence agencies. "Do any of you disagree that this is a plausible scenario?" No one spoke.

"Okay. We win the war, and Supreme Leader Jeong and his cronies are history. However, what are the ramifications of permanently wiping out North Korea's nuclear capability? We know that each of the hypothetical twenty-five atomic bombs dropped on the U.S. would have ten times the power as the bomb that flattened Hiroshima. There will be tens of thousands of Americans killed, homes and businesses destroyed, along with roads and water supplies, everything that makes a society function. Add the fifty-five bombs we deliver to North Korea, and we have a worldwide calamity. Beyond the mass destruction, what effect will such a nuclear war have on the world's climate?

"This is why I asked Dr. Vogel to join us. Dr. Vogel will lay out what will happen to the world's weather patterns if the scenario I just outlined were to play out."

"Thank you, Director Davis. The short answer to your question is that nobody knows. And the answer is the same whether it's a regional exchange or an all-out nuclear slugfest among China, Russia, the United States, and its allies. Although in the final analysis, the latter would undoubtedly mean the end of civilization. A regional nuclear conflict would also significantly alter our world, although it's likely that its effects would be temporary.

"A 2010 research paper by Dr. Harold Barnes and Jeffery Coburn comes closest to predicting the outcome of a limited nuclear exchange. In that study, they analyzed the effects of an atomic war between India and Pakistan, where one hundred devices explode over two days. The one hundred fifty kiloton bombs represent the entire nuclear arsenal of both countries."

A graphic popped up on the screen. Dr. Vogel held the red dot of her laser pointer for several seconds on each of the seven bullets, giving those in the room time to read each one.

- *As many as two million killed by the blasts*
- *Another two million killed by fires*
- *Eight million tons of soot and ash into stratosphere, blocking sun*
- *Temperature drop of 3–6 degrees*
- *Agricultural production reduced by one-third*
- *Two million die of starvation*
- *Negative effects last up to 3 years*

After Dr. Vogel discussed each item in detail, an image of a tangled mass of cells appeared on the screen. She then set the image into motion, and the attendees watched the cells twist and turn as one cell bumped into another as they flowed erratically around the flattened facsimile of the globe. Dr. Vogel explained that the graphic demonstrates how the eighty detonated nuclear devices in a hypothetical North Korea–United States confrontation could alter the earth's weather patterns.

Director Davis interrupted. "Dr. Vogel, can you be more specific about how these climatic abnormalities will affect the weather patterns in the United States?"

"I'll try. As I stated at the beginning of my talk, nobody knows the outcome of a limited nuclear war. There are just too many variables. However, my colleagues at Stanford are working closely with the Climate and Weather Prediction Center at the National Weather Service to develop a predictive model that will help answer that very question. As you learned in your first experimental design course as a freshman in college, models are as reliable as the assumptions that go into them. So what I'm about to tell you is subject to revision." Dr. Vogel then skipped ahead in her visuals and stopped at a slide of the United States.

"The blue lines represent the normal oscillations of the jet stream during a calendar year. The red line is the jet stream's location after a nuclear exchange. The reasons they are different are not necessary to understand, only the effects. The jet stream in the western part of the country will remain essentially stationary as long as the atmosphere remains unstable. Our model tells us that its fixed position will block moisture from the Pacific from reaching the coast. This means that the western United States will face a prolonged drought, lasting one to five years depending on the number of nuclear devices that explode and the payload size.

"The jet stream in the eastern part of the country, represented by the green line, will set up along the eastern seaboard, and it too will become stationary. Unlike the jet stream in the west, it will pull water from the tropics like a humongous sponge, carrying it north as an atmospheric river of moisture. This overabundance of moisture will fuel fierce random storms from about the mid-Atlantic states north through New England. Also, remember that the temperature is three to five degrees cooler than normal and as much as ten degrees cooler in the highlands of northern New England. There, most of this precipitation will fall as snow. It will mean disastrous flooding along much of the coast and a snowfall Armageddon in the northeastern states. It doesn't take much imagination to realize the havoc the prolonged extreme weather would have on the region's people and the economy." She then concluded her presentation and turned the meeting back over to the director.

"Thank you, Dr. Vogel." Davis paused for a moment, then addressed the room. "So as you can all see, we have quite the conundrum. If the DPRK should use what we suppose is their new super-rocket to attack the United States, the ramifications of a counterattack will be disastrous—for the rest of the world as well as us. Yet the United States must defend itself from this pariah state.

"Before I go any further, I ask that all the staffs be excused from the meeting. What I'm about to say is only intended to be heard by the representatives of the intelligence agencies." Once all the staff members had left the room and the conference room door was shut, Davis resumed his remarks.

"Unless any of you have anything to add, the following will be my recommendations to the National Security Council." Davis took a folded sheet of paper from his jacket pocket. Since the previous day's conversation with Henderson, he had known what he would recommend to the president. He essentially used the meeting to validate his reasoning for reaching this decision.

"There is strong, though not yet verified, evidence that North Korea has deployed its advanced long-range H-17 ICBM. I will recommend not launching a preemptive strike at this time out of concern about an overreaction from China and Russia. Instead, we must convey our suspicions directly to Supreme Leader Jeong. I will recommend that the president of the United States do this. The president will warn Jeong of dire consequences for him and his military if it is proven that the H-17 has been deployed armed with nuclear warheads. And that any firing of a long-range ballistic missile over Japan's territorial waters will be considered an attack on the United States, and we will act accordingly."

After he finished reading his statement, Davis removed his glasses, then added, "I will also apprise the National Security Council of the associated climatological risks of a limited nuclear exchange with North Korea, as described by Dr. Vogel. It is the president's decision as to how we will proceed. Let's hope Jeong gets the message and doesn't do anything that he or the rest of the planet will regret."

RETIREMENT

*Just Right Engineering
Bangor, Maine*

"Good morning, Dan. How was the weekend?" Nate Simcock asked, sticking his head over the faded red office partition.

"Great! We went up to camp Friday after work and got back last night. We had a little rain, but I still got about a cord of wood split. Kathy cleaned her flower garden and painted the trim on the storage shed."

"Wow, now that sounds like a fun time was had by all. Do you ever do anything at camp besides work?"

"I don't consider it work. I'm a lot like Ronald Reagan. I remember reading how relaxing it was for him to split wood at Rancho del Cielo after escaping from Washington for a few days. So how was your weekend?" Dan asked, knowing Nate wasn't a ball of fire on or off the job.

"Well, I didn't split wood, but I did saw a little. Saturday I slept until almost noon. After that, I picked up a pizza and spent the evening watching a World War Two documentary on PBS," Nate said, thinking of his weekend activities as a major accomplishment.

"Oh, then you did have a much more enjoyable time than we did."

"Anyway, Dan, I was wondering if you had looked over the design for the proposed expansion to the Hanson building. The architect called me Friday afternoon. He needs a cost estimate by Wednesday; can you have it done by then?"

"You told me Friday that the new Bangor parking garage was a top priority."

"It is. And so is the Hanson building. See what you can do, okay?" He gave Dan a big smile and a grating two-thumbs-up, then continued his Monday morning walk through the engineering section. A minute later, he returned to Dan's cubicle.

"Oh, I almost forgot, there will be a staff meeting at one with the vice president in the conference room."

"What's that about? We just had one Wednesday."

"No idea. Willard told me to ask a few of the staff to attend, so that's what I'm doing. Just be there at one o'clock sharp. You know how Willard hates people walking in late, says the distraction causes him to lose his concentration."

"Well, we wouldn't want that, now, would we?"

"What's that mean?" Nate asked.

"Oh, nothing. It's just that ever since the company bought into the latest fad in management styles that the consultant said would increase efficiency, all we do is attend staff meetings. I'd have had the Hanson building designed a week ago if I could stay at my desk and work on it. The staff wastes more time reaching a consensus on some ridiculous issue, like who's responsible for cleaning the break room than they do working." Dan had never been one to hold back his opinion.

"Just be there, okay?" Nate walked off without a big smile and definitely no thumbs-up. No way was he going to criticize the bosses' new way of managing the company. He'd worked too hard to become Willard's lapdog, and with only four years to retirement, Nate wasn't about to risk falling out of the vice president's favor.

Dan had worked for Just Right Engineering for twenty-five years. He had seen it grow from only three employees to thirty-five. Initially, the job was rewarding, designing small commercial buildings and serving as the resident engineer monitoring construction. Now it was strictly a desk job. One of the three field engineers handled the on-site work, leaving Dan in the office to design one project after another. Although the work remained challenging, he'd tired of being chained to a desk. Dan looked forward to retiring from the company and spending more time with his wife at their western Maine camp.

At 12:55, Dan left his desk and headed for the conference room at the end of the hall. He assumed Willard had called the meeting to tell the staff that the company had taken on another client and to explain how it would fit alongside all the other priority work Just Right Engineering had on the books.

"Come in, Dan; please take a seat," said the vice president, doing his best to represent the caring face of management.

Dan glanced at the others sitting at the conference table. Ted and Mike from drafting, and Rose, the secretary for the engineering design team. Now Dan was uncertain what was up. It wasn't the usual cast of characters that met to review a new job. And why would Willard Harriman take the time to meet with four company "pee-ons"? Nate typically handled new work assignments, unless it was an exceptionally large job that meant buckets of profits for the company. For those clients, the company's president made the announcement.

"Welcome, everyone," Nate began. "Glad you could find the time for our little meeting."

As if attendance were optional, Dan thought to himself.

"Let's get right to it. Mr. Harriman has important news he would like to discuss with you. Go ahead, Willard. The floor is yours."

"Thank you, Nate. Well, folks, I have good news and bad news. Friday, Just Right Engineering completed the purchase of the Ramsey Engineering Company in Brewer. As you know, Ramsey has been a significant competitor for the past ten years. They have a stable of excellent young structural and civil engineers who have designed several exceedingly impressive structures throughout New England. We're pleased that we are now on the same team. Because of the merger, we will close the Brewer office and bring everyone here."

Dan felt he knew what was coming next. You don't bring another fifteen employees into a building that's already maxed out on space without significantly reorganizing.

"Now, because of this acquisition, we have a degree of overlap in several departments. To remain competitive, we need to bring personnel back into balance with the company's expertise."

Here it comes, Dan thought, taking a quick glance at the others. Everyone focused like a laser on Willard, waiting to learn their fate.

"To do this, we need to eliminate several positions. Now, I don't want any of you to think you are being let go because of shoddy work. You are four of the most capable and hardworking members of our team. All of you have been excellent employees, always willing to go the extra mile to complete the job on time, professionally, and with a smile."

Cut the bull and spit it out, Dan wanted to tell him. Just tell four of your most valued employees they've been fired.

Willard Harriman was known around the office as Hatchet Man. Willard did the dirty work when an employee needed to be let go, which kept the company president above the fray regarding personnel issues.

"Now that we have acquired Ramsey, we have a surplus of draftsmen, structural engineers, and secretaries," Willard said, glancing at Rose Merchant, who had worked for Just Right Engineering since the beginning. "I know this will be hard on you and your families. However, engineering firms from here to Portland want to eat our lunch. We need to keep the company lean and mean to get our share of the pie," he said, staring at the back wall to avoid further eye contact with the axed employees.

Willard's announcement shocked everyone in the room. Even Nate, who had miraculously escaped the same fate each time there had been a reorganization. He especially couldn't understand letting Dan go, one of Just Right Engineering's most competent engineers.

"Each of you will receive severance pay of one thousand dollars for each year you've been with the company. Questions?"

Mike Snow raised his hand. "How long before we're done?"

"May thirty-first will be your last day. That's a forty-five-day notice and fifteen days more than the state requires," Willard answered, sounding like the company had bent over backward to accommodate the soon-to-be-terminated employees. "Are there any other questions?"

Everyone was too overwhelmed to think of questions. "If not, the meeting is over. Dan, would you please stay for a minute? Nate, you can leave as well."

Willard waited for the door to shut before speaking. "Dan, letting you go wasn't easy for the company. You've been with Just Right for a long time and are one of our most valued design engineers. However, Nate tells me you've mentioned you'd be retiring in a year or two, so as it turns out, your future plans fit in with ours. Don't get me wrong, Dan, letting you go has nothing to do with age. It's just that Just Right Engineering is top-heavy with design engineers. So knowing your intention is to retire, it seemed logical that your position would be the one we'd eliminate," Willard said, trying to tap-dance around the fact that Dan's age was the reason for his termination.

"You can count on us to give you a top-notch recommendation if you should decide to work for another engineering firm."

"All I can say, Mr. Harriman, is that this is not how I planned to leave the company."

Willard put his arm around Dan's shoulder and guided him toward the conference room door.

"Good luck to you, Dan, and please let me know if there is anything I can do for you."

Dan and his wife sat on the couch having their usual drink before dinner. After he downed his second coffee brandy, he summoned the courage to tell her that he would be out of work in six weeks.

"How do you feel about it, Dan? I know you planned to work two more years so we could pay off the mortgage before you retired," Kathy asked. She knew her husband rarely acted on impulse. Everything needed to be carefully thought through and evaluated before making important decisions. A part of the genetic makeup of an engineer, she reasoned.

"It's funny, Kathy. When I got back to my desk, I was mad as hell. I've given twenty-five years of my life to the company, going into the office on weekends and working late to finish a job on time. It was like a stab in the back after doing my part to help the company succeed. I considered filing an age discrimination complaint. But why? Can you imagine what it would be like to work two more years in that toxic environment even if I won? Then I thought, maybe being let go isn't so bad. It gives us two extra years to do all the things we like to do. As they say, staying healthy is one big crapshoot. I thought of Joe Wentworth, working until he was sixty-seven. He had a head full of ideas about what he would do in retirement. The day after Joe hangs it up, he plays a round of golf and drops dead on the ninth green. Some retirement. Do you know what else I've been thinking, Kathy?"

"Why don't you tell me."

"I think we should do what we've discussed for the past five years. Sell our house and move to the Portland area. You know, to be closer to Hazel and Tom. I could even look for a part-time job with an engineering firm."

"Now, that would be great! Do you think we could afford to buy a place in southern Maine? Property is way more expensive than it is around here."

"With the twenty-five thousand in severance pay I'll get from the company, I think we can. Plus, the mortgage on this place is nearly paid off. So we'll have a good chunk of change to put down on a new home."

"Say no more, you have my vote. Let's do it."

"The only stipulation is that we need to sell this place first to know how much of a house we can afford in Portland."

"That's fine. I assumed that would be how it would work."

The plan to move closer to their daughter and her husband was set in motion. The next day, Kathy called a Realtor. Two hours later, the eager agent stopped in to do a walk-through. She told Kathy that a home as lovely as theirs would sell fast, so she should start packing—a comment Kathy suspected she told all her clients to reassure them that they had picked the right broker.

Kathy couldn't wait to move. She and her daughter had always been close. They would talk on the phone several times a week, keeping each other updated on what was happening in their lives. Once a month, Kathy and Dan drove to their daughter's home in Westbrook for a visit. Dan and Tom got along equally as well. Each fall, they hunted ducks together on the Penobscot River, and in the summer, they took several trips to Baxter State Park to camp and hike.

The next day, news of Dan's departure spread throughout the office. Besides the design staff, few said anything to Dan directly. Most only gave him quick sad looks when they passed him in the hallway. Nate eventually stopped at his desk.

"Have a minute, Dan?" Nate asked, dragging a chair beside Dan's desk.

"What's up, Nate?" Dan said, punching numbers into his calculator.

"Dan, I just wanted you to know that I had no idea why Willard called the meeting yesterday. Five minutes before it started, he told me about the reduction in force because of the acquisition."

"No problem, Nate. I never thought you had anything to do with it."

"So what are you going to do? I mean, once you're done working here."

"Well, Kathy and I decided to make the most of it. We'll sell our home and move closer to our daughter in Westbrook. I might even look for a part-time job with an engineering company, or we may just spend more time at camp. I'm more concerned about the others that got laid off. I've enough time as a professional engineer to have a decent retirement income. Still, I'm not so sure about the others, especially Rose. I don't expect her pension will go far, although with her abilities, she should be able to find a decent job with another firm."

"Yeah, you're right about Rose. That leads to my next question: How do you feel about a retirement party? The others are in favor of it. We'd do one big get-together for the four of you."

"Do it. Just one thing, though. Make it fun and not a downer because I'm being let out to pasture."

The sales agent was right. The first couple to look at their home made an offer. Kathy waited at the front door, eager to tell Dan the good news as soon as he stepped inside.

"Dan, you're not going to believe this, but we had an offer on the house," she said before he had barely set down his briefcase.

"Really? How much do they expect us to drop the price?" he asked, assuming the people would lowball their asking price, hoping for a bargain.

"Just the opposite. The buyer will give us five thousand more than what we're asking! On top of that, they didn't ask us to paint the upstairs bedrooms, as we had thought we would have to do. The only thing they want is a decision on whether or not we accept their offer by noon tomorrow."

"They must want the place bad."

"They do. The broker told me they both have jobs at the university and begin work on July fifth, and they want the housing situation settled before they start. I don't know if it's just a game the broker is playing or not, but she also said they're looking at two other houses and plan to make an offer on one of them if we don't accept their offer."

"I say sell it. What do you think?"

"You'll get no argument from me. I'll call Joan and tell her we will sell as is for what they offered."

Later that evening, sitting in the living room, Dan brought up the move to southern Maine. "You know, Kathy, I've been thinking."

"Yeahhh," Kathy said suspiciously, unsure if she would like what was coming next. It seemed that nearly every time Dan started a sentence with "I've been thinking," it was a precursor to another wacky idea. He didn't disappoint.

"I really hate being rushed into buying a house, and I don't want to be in a position like the couple buying our place and have to offer more than a home is worth just to be in a new home by fall."

"So what are you saying exactly?"

"Well, you know how we've always talked about spending a winter at the pond. I thought this would be the perfect time to do it. We can still take trips to Portland to look at houses and visit the kids. If we find a home that we like, we'll make an offer and see what happens. In the meantime, we'll enjoy cross-country skiing and snowmobiling. What do you think?"

"That you're nuts."

"Why? Even you have said that spending a winter at camp would be fun."

"I said it would be fun to do knowing that we weren't actually going to do it."

"Well, think about it before you make up your mind," Dan said, knowing it was best not to push Kathy for a quick answer that might end any chance of spending the winter at their cabin in northwestern Maine. He checked his watch. "It's time for the news. Let's check what's happening in the world," he said, and reached for the remote.

"God, do we have to? All they seem to talk about is that nut case in North Korea stirring up trouble."

Dan flipped the channel to the national news. As Kathy predicted, the news anchor was in the middle of a report about North Korea's latest test firing of a long-range missile over the Sea of Japan. The reporter went on about U.S. concerns that firing the rocket was a prelude to launching a ballistic missile with a nuclear warhead capable of reaching America's western coast.

"See? What did I tell you? That guy is starting to scare me," Kathy said as the screen showed the contrail of the North Korean missile screaming across the Sea of Japan.

"Don't take the news so seriously. The whole thing is nothing more than the television network's attempt to increase viewership. There's a competition to see who can put the most fear of God into us so that we'll stay glued to their channel for more doom and gloom. North Korea has launched missiles into the Sea of Japan for the past five years, and none of them made it five hundred miles.

"Well, this one traveled fifteen hundred miles. Either switch the station or turn the damn thing off."

The next evening, Dan revisited the idea of spending the winter at their cabin.

"So have you thought any more about living at Skyler Pond for the winter?"

"No," she said, thinking that would put an end to the idea.

"We'll be missing a once-in-a-lifetime opportunity to do something different. Think of all the nursing home memories we'll collect."

"Funny. By that time, we won't even have enough marbles between us to know what time of day it is, let alone remember how we froze our butts off at Skyler Pond."

"Well, I'll tell you what. If you agree to spend this winter at camp, come April, we'll take that two-week trip to St. John you always wanted."

"Just so there is no misunderstanding, you mean St. John, Virgin Islands, and not the St. John valley in Aroostook County, right?"

"You slay me, Kathy. Do you really think I would do something that low?"

"No comment. Actually, I have been thinking about spending one winter at the pond. If we're not going to rush into buying a house, it does make sense to do it now. We wouldn't have a monthly mortgage payment and no heating bill. Plus, we'll take that trip to the Caribbean in April, as you just promised. One more thing, Mr. Dan: This would be a one-time thing. Don't think I'll cave and agree to do it again next fall. There are too many places around

Portland to eat and shop. One winter of eating venison and onions will be it for me."

Dan and Kathy had owned the cabin on Skyler Pond for twenty years, located in a forested township of the same name twenty miles south of the Canadian border. A large landholding company owned the entire twenty-four-thousand-acre township, minus several dozen camp lots scattered along the shoreline of some of the remote trout ponds.

Three brothers from Vassalboro, Maine, had built the cabin in 1940 as their base for trapping beaver and muskrat on backwater flowages. Each January, Adrian, Clarence, and Bart Bridges spent the month at Skyler Pond tending their traplines.

It was during Dan and Kathy's first trip to Kingston for supplies that they learned a piece of the history of their cabin on Skyler Pond. At checkout, Kathy told the hardware store clerk, who happened to be Bart's nephew, that she and Dan owned a cabin at Skyler Pond, once owned by the Bridges family. Knowing that, the enthusiastic young clerk was only too happy to give Kathy and Dan an abbreviated account of the family's forty-year stay at the pond. What happened to Clarence and Adrian Bridges at Skyler Pond became permanently etched in Kathy's mind.

On a cold late afternoon in mid-January, Adrian and Bart returned to the cabin after a long day of tending their traplines. Clarence was always the last one back to the log cabin, so the brothers weren't concerned when he didn't show up for supper. Two hours after they had eaten, Clarence still hadn't returned. Now the two became worried. Adrian glanced at the thermometer, eight above zero, not a night to be lost or hurt somewhere in the frigid darkness. Ten minutes later, they were outside the cabin strapping on their snowshoes to search for their missing brother.

The two trudged through the woods all night, following the track Clarence had made that morning leaving camp. At sunrise, Adrian spotted a pack basket sticking above the snow on a frozen stream nearly five miles from Skyler Pond. They had found Clarence. He lay facedown in the snow, his outstretched hand clutching a metal ice skimmer as if about to clear the ice from the hole he had chopped with the ice chisel. Together, they rolled their brother's frozen body onto his back. Clarence's terrified eyes stared up at Adrian and Bart. His frozen hand clutched the skimmer in such a position it appeared as if poor old Clarence was about to strike at Adrian and Bart. They loaded the frozen corpse onto Clarence's toboggan and pulled him back to the cabin, his upstretched hand still attached to the ice skimmer. Adrian and Bart were devastated after losing their brother to a heart attack. They could only hope he had died instantly and not lain on the ice, slowly freezing to death.

Not long after Clarence's death, Bart sold his share in the cabin to Adrian. Adrian continued to trap alone until trudging through the deep snow lugging his trapping gear became too much for the seventy-year-old man. His trapping days ended, but he never lost his enthusiasm for hunting and fishing at Skyler Pond.

In late November 1960, his son-in-law walked to Skyler Pond for a week of deer hunting with Adrian. Harold could see smoke rising from the chimney as he approached the cabin. He rapped on the door and hollered to Adrian, but Adrian didn't come to the door. Figuring that he must have overslept, Harold opened the door and called. The kitchen was in shambles. Overturned chairs and dishes cluttered the floor. At first, Harold thought vandals had trashed the place, until he spotted Adrian dead on the kitchen floor. Death by choking, the coroner's report read. A chicken bone lodged in Adrian's throat while he ate supper. Panicked, he thrashed about the room, attempting to free the bone until he collapsed from the lack of oxygen. At camp, Kathy often thought of Adrian gagging and flailing about her kitchen before dropping onto the floor. She shivered each time she looked at where she imagined he had collapsed.

The cabin remained vacant for several years. Finally, a grandson of Adrian's bought the property to use as a family retreat for hunting, fishing, and snowmobile trips. As time passed, interest in going to Skyler Pond waned. Floyd Bridges' children had discovered that they preferred playing video games at home rather than getting up at four to tramp around in the woods all day looking for a phantom monster buck. After that, the cabin exchanged hands several times until Dan and Kathy purchased the property.

Dan and Kathy learned that the Skyler Pond property was for sale only by chance. The family had been driving north on the Dam Road for a weekend camping trip near the Canadian border when Dan spotted a man tacking a real estate sign to a tree at the entrance to the Skyler Pond Road. He and Kathy had often talked about buying property in the area, a place to spend weekends and vacations. Curious about what might be for sale, they turned around and returned to talk to the man, who was about to drive off.

The real estate agent told them about a log cabin on Skyler Pond, four miles west of the Dam Road. There was no running water or power, and the road to it was barely passable, unless you had four-wheel drive. The price was $26,000.

Dan asked how find the cabin if they decided to look at it. "Just follow the road to the pond, and continue along the east shore a half mile, and you will be staring at it," the man said, giving Dan his business card. Dan thanked him, and both vehicles went their separate ways, except Dan and Kathy went only a mile before they turned around and parked next to the tree with the green-and-white real estate sign.

"Let's hike in and take a look at the place. We'll take the tent and spend the night on the shore," he said, knowing they would never be able to get back to the car before dark. With five-year-old Hazel safely secured to her mother's back and Dan carrying the camping equipment, the three struck out to find the cabin.

Once Kathy and Dan saw the remote trout pond and the idyllic log cabin nestled among the spruce and pine trees overlooking the water, they knew they wanted the property. It was precisely what the two had dreamed of since they married. This property had it all, including a pair of loons patrolling the shoreline and a large bull moose feeding on pond lilies at the swampy end of the pond.

The following day, Dan disassembled the tent they had erected in front of the cabin, anxious to drive to Waterville to place a deposit on the property before someone else beat them to it. As Kathy and Hazel got into the car, Dan detoured to the For Sale sign nailed to the maple tree, and with one sharp pull, he ripped it off the tree and tossed it into the car's trunk. "No need to leave the sign up now that the property is sold," he said, smiling at Kathy.

Before Kathy would agree to buy the property, she'd insisted on a piped-in water supply and that the two-holer be replaced with an inside flush toilet. Dan knew that the cost of hiring a contractor to drive a backhoe to the pond to dig a well and install a septic system would not be cheap. However, he would do nearly anything Kathy asked to get her to agree to buy the cabin.

Thirty days later, the Simmons family became the proud owner of a secluded vacation cabin on Skyler Pond. That first year, Dan, Kathy, and Hazel spent most weekends at the cabin until the first significant snowstorm prevented them from driving to the property. By the end of the following year, the camp had been wired for electric lights fed from the new solar system, indoor plumbing, and a remodeled kitchen. Their dream vacation cabin was complete.

Hazel and Tom drove to Bangor to attend Dan's retirement party. They were about to leave for the event when Dan told his daughter about their plan to spend the winter at Skyler Pond. Hazel didn't have time to process what her father had just told her about living in a township with no year-round residents and a fifty-five-mile drive to the closest store.

While having drinks before the ceremony, Dan told several of his former coworkers of Kathy's and his plan to spend the winter at their cabin. Nate, the MC for the send-off, made a mental note to work Dan's retirement plan into his roast.

After the last coworker finished telling stories about working with Ted, Mike, and Rose, Nate turned his attention to Dan.

"For those who haven't heard, Dan and Kathy are selling their home in Hampden and heading for the hills to live as Mr. and Mrs. Hermit among the pine trees and moose. I even overheard Kathy say she's sewing sheepskins together so they can keep from freezing to death this winter," Nate told the audience. "Maybe Dan can tell us if that is true."

"Thanks, Nate. That is not true about the sheepskins. It's imitation rabbit pelts she's been hand stitching," he said to the crowd, giving a laugh of approval to his comeback. "Yes, we plan to spend the winter at our cabin on Skyler Pond. It's something we have always wanted to do. Isn't that right, Kathy?"

Another round of laughter erupted as Kathy used her index finger and drew it ear to ear, pretending to slash her throat. Dan concluded his remarks by thanking them for his memorable years at Just Right Engineering. He told them to come anytime to Skyler Pond to visit. One of his friends yelled back, asking if he would have to sleep on fir boughs. Dan laughed and told him no, just bring a sleeping bag and a folding cot.

As the party ended and people gave their final well wishes to Kathy and Dan, Art Simpson, one of the company's engineers, stopped to talk to Dan.

"I'm going to miss you, Dan. You're a damn good engineer. The company is making a big mistake letting you go."

"Thanks, Art. I appreciate you saying that. However, as they say, change is the only constant thing in life."

"Dan, I do wonder one thing about your plan to spend the winter at your camp. I mean, it sounds like a great experience and all. Still, the way the world is right now, don't you think it's a little risky being alone and so far away from, well, everything if we should go to war with North Korea?"

Art was a guy who worried about the possibility of anything and everything going wrong. That's why Dan liked having Art work on his projects. Other engineers saw him as a complete worry-wart, continually checking and rechecking his work almost to a fault. Dan thought of Art as a conscientious professional engineer who made sure that when a client received a final design, it was accurate, right down to the type of thread on the bolts.

"I know what you're saying, Art. Things are a little crazy right now. However, when has the world been perfect? I'm not going into this thinking that World War Three is a foregone conclusion. First of all, it's not going to happen, and second of all, we all go around only once in this life. I'm not going to end up in a nursing home someday and whine to everyone who visits about how I should have done this or that when I had the chance. Screw that!"

"Well, Dan, you're a better man than me. I like the security of knowing the hospital is five miles from my home and that I can call nine-one-one if I should catch my toe on a rug and fall flat on my face with a broken hip." Art continued, "Don't get me wrong, Dan. I admire you and Kathy for doing this. It's just the difference between people, I guess." Art shook Dan's hand, wished him well, and rejoined his wife.

Later that evening, after the four of them returned home, Hazel brought up what her father had told her about moving north for the winter. She had overheard the conversation between Art and her father. What Art had said about living near a hospital caused her to realize just how far away her parents would be from getting help if something should happen.

"Dad, you know if something happened to you or Mom, it would be nearly impossible to get help. The nearest rescue service is fifty miles from camp. You both would be dead before help arrived."

"I think we're pretty well covered on that one, Hazel. We have a landline, and I've contacted the Northern Skyler County Ambulance and Rescue in Kingston to let them know we'll be at the pond. All we need to do is call nine-one-one, and they'll be on their way."

"They may be on their way, but it's an hour's drive from town to the camp road and another twenty minutes to the cabin. If there is a lot of snow, they will need to reach you by snowmobile," Hazel argued.

"Don't forget, we'll have one vehicle at camp and the other one parked at the Dam Road. If we should get a sudden snowstorm and can't get out with the pickup, we'll snowmobile to the car."

"Tom, you tell my father spending the winter at the cabin is absolute craziness. It's one thing to live there for the summer, but not when it's twenty below zero, and there is three feet of snow on the ground. It's too reckless for them to do that at their age."

"To tell you the truth, Hazel, I think your father has all the bases covered. They'll be fine as long as they have plenty of gas for the generator and the snowmobiles. They certainly have plenty of wood to keep from freezing to death. I say they should go for it."

"Well, you're no help. I should have known you would side with my father." She turned to her mother. "Mom, how do you feel about living up there for six months?"

"At first, I was reluctant, but the more I thought about it, the better the idea sounded. It's not like we're being sent to prison for six months with no chance of parole. We can go to town anytime we want, and if the weather is bad one day, we will wait until the next good day. Don't forget, we plan to drive down for a visit every so often, and I assume you two will come up a few times to go sledding. Best of all, at the end of the rainbow is a three-week trip to St. John," she said, looking at Dan for a reaction.

"Wait a minute. I said two weeks. We need to get back for the spring fishing," Dan said, taking the bait.

"Well, I still don't like it," Hazel said. "It seems to be a little much for you two now that you're getting older."

"You don't have to be politically correct with us. It's okay to say that we're old. I'll tell you this, your mother and I are in better shape than half the people your age. The most physically fit part of their anatomy is their two thumbs, continually getting exercised playing on their smartphones."

"Okay, okay, don't get all bent out of shape. I didn't mean anything by it. Go ahead, spend the winter at the cabin. Just be sure you call us every couple of days, so we know you're still alive. Now can we all just call it a night? Tom and I need to be back in Portland tomorrow morning for a smartphone user group meeting."

"What! Don't tell me you're going to waste a Sunday on that foolishness," Dan exclaimed.

"Just kidding, Dad. We'll see you in the morning."

On September 6, the Simmonses became full-time residents of Skyler Township. They wasted no time preparing for the long winter ahead. A new woodshed needed to be built closer to the back door for easier access to the firewood on bitterly cold days. The water pipes in the crawl space needed to be wrapped to protect them from freezing, and the perimeter of the cabin draped in plastic to help keep the winter winds from sweeping under the cabin's pine floor. The big question was whether the waterline between the well and the cabin would freeze, as the ledge lurked only a few inches below the sandy soil. If the line froze, they would need to pump water from the pond into a hundred-gallon plastic storage tank on the second floor. Either way, there would be water to flush the toilet and shower.

Dan teased Kathy, telling her living at Skyler Pond was no different from being in the big city. Kathy's usual response was to tell her husband not to push his luck.

Oddly, the cabin did have a landline phone. The single black wire split from the main line at the Dam Road and followed the Skyler Pond Road, strung tree to tree. Dan had never asked the broker how the phone line came to be. He assumed that the Bridges brothers somehow coerced the phone company to run the line to the pond. The main phone line continued north along the Dam

Road to a flood control dam built in 1950 to protect the Kennebec River Valley from spring floods.

The camp line provided telephone service, and a satellite dish delivered the internet and television. Unfortunately, the nearby mountains blocked any cell phone service. Dan and Kathy would be safely tethered to the outside world as long as a fallen tree didn't break the wire and the satellite signal didn't fail.

Dan and Kathy's camp was one of three scattered around Skyler Pond and the only one accessible by vehicle. The other two cabins were reachable only by boat, launched from the landing located where the Skyler Pond Road met the pond before it continued to Dan and Kathy's property. The two seasonal camps were simple one-room log structures, used a few weeks a year as a home base to fish and hunt. Dan rarely saw the owners. The only giveaway that somebody was at the cabins was the near constant blasting of guns from across the pond. Target practice, Dan supposed.

The first week of October brought pleasantly mild days and frosty nights. The foliage at its peak set the mountains on fire with color; best of all, it was partridge hunting season. The two spent most days riding the logging roads in Dan's new Ford pickup, looking for the elusive bird. Kathy acted as a spotter, trying to see one feeding in the understory at the edge of the road. Retirement was going as planned.

Bird hunting stretched into November, and Kathy and Dan continued their daily trips riding the logging roads. On November 11, they parked at a scenic overlook for lunch. Dan turned the radio on to get the noon news.

"Well, let's see if we're at war," he kidded Kathy, turning the knob on the radio. No war, but the news was not good.

The newscaster reported that North Korea had test-fired another intercontinental ballistic missile. The latest one had traveled forty-one hundred miles, halfway across the Pacific Ocean, crashing into the ocean five hundred miles off the coast of

Hawaii. The reporter told listeners it was the hermit state's most provocative action since the Korean War.

"Jesus, that's not good," Dan said, looking at Kathy.

Kathy motioned for Dan to be quiet and raised the radio's volume.

The feed switched to a reporter standing outside the White House. The reporter read from his notes that the president had called an emergency meeting of his National Security Council to review the situation and decide on a response to what the White House press secretary called an "act of war." In the background were chants of "No war" from a group of antiwar activists, afraid that the United States would be drawn into a nuclear confrontation with North Korea. The president would address the nation tonight at seven.

Kathy turned off the radio. "This sounds really bad, Dan. Do you suppose we'll launch some kind of a strike against North Korea?"

"No, at least not for a while. I think President Carlisle is more pragmatic than that. My guess is that he'll try to defuse the situation in some way before retaliating. We'll watch tonight and see what he has to say."

Dan and Kathy continued riding the roads, looking for partridge. Neither of them spoke about what might happen between the two countries. Instead, they stared blankly out the truck's windows, their thoughts far away from spotting a bird for Saturday night's meal.

At seven, they turned on the television to hear the president.

My fellow Americans. This morning at nine forty-five a.m. eastern time, the Democratic People's Republic of Korea fired an intercontinental ballistic missile from the Punggye-ri test site north of North Korea's capital, Pyong-yang. The modified Hwasong-17 ballistic missile flew over the sovereign country of Japan, crashing into the ocean five hundred miles off Hawaii's western coast, a distance of forty-one hundred miles. A United States Navy submersible drone located the wreckage and positively identified it as a North Korean missile. Fortunately, it was not armed. This provocative action by the North Korean government was initiated after Supreme Leader Jeong was warned that firing an intercontinental ballistic missile toward the United States would not be tolerated. If North Korea did so, there would be a swift and decisive response by the United States. Supreme Leader Jeong disregarded this warning.

The president went on to tell the nation that this was a dangerous turn of events and that the country had the right to take whatever action was needed to protect the country and its people.

We have filed a complaint against North Korea with the United Nations and asked the United Nations Security Council to condemn this action. We will work with our allies to initiate further monetary and economic sanctions against Korea's Democratic People's Republic. However, to Supreme Leader Jeong, let it be clear that another flagrant act against the United States or its allies will not go unanswered. This administration will do whatever is needed to protect this great nation from any outside threat. However, we will not be drawn into a conflict without first exploring every means to resolve this unacceptable situation.

"Wow. That was one stupid move firing that missile," Dan said, shutting off the television.

"God, what do you think is going to happen?"

"Nothing except what the president said: more sanctions to squeeze the life out of that little Hitler. Jeong needs to know the full wrath and fury of the United States will come down on him if he keeps this up."

"I don't know, Dan. Maybe we should have kept our home in Hampden. What if there is all-out war while we're alone at the cabin fifty miles from the nearest town?"

"There's not going to be any war. Any retaliation will be on specific targets, like Jeong's nuclear research facility or one of his launch sites, to teach him a lesson not to do something this asinine again."

"I hope you're right."

"By the way," Dan said, wanting to turn the conversation to something more pleasant. "Did you see the email from Hazel? They'll be up for the long Thanksgiving weekend. I thought Tom and I might do a little deer hunting behind the cabin. Maybe we'll get lucky and get a deer. You know how much I like deer heart and liver."

"Oh boy, deer heart and liver. Yum. You can have my share. I plan on eating roast turkey, thank you."

Tensions between the United States and North Korea appeared to cool after the president's warning. North Korea was told by the United States and through back channels that there would be hell to pay if Jeong launched another rocket toward the United States. North Korea's rhetoric remained belligerent, designed for the consumption of the home crowd. The North Korean leader needed to convince the masses that the regime wasn't afraid of the capitalist warmonger.

Kathy had relaxed somewhat as well. No longer thinking war was inevitable, she focused on preparing for Hazel and Tom's Thanksgiving visit. Dan drove out to the Dam Road on Thanksgiving Day morning to meet them.

Hazel and Tom loaded their bags into the truck, then settled in. "So how's Mom doing out here in the willy-wacks?" Hazel asked, gripping the door's armrest as the truck bounced over the rocks driving back to camp.

"Fine. I haven't heard any complaints yet, but you can ask her yourself. She's been doing a lot of sewing—Christmas gifts, I guess. She doesn't tell me what she's making, and I don't ask."

"God, can you slow down a little? I just hit my head on the roof," Hazel said, rubbing the top of her head.

"See what I have to put up with, Dan? Complaint after complaint," Tom said, grinning at his wife.

"So, Dan, have you heard about the big snowstorm we're supposed to get Sunday? They're saying up to a foot down our way. It looks like an early start to the winter."

"Really? It must be a coastal storm. I checked the weather this morning. Up here, the National Weather Service is predicting one to three inches," Dan said, yanking the steering wheel hard to the right to avoid a large rock.

"Anyway, Hazel and I need to keep an eye on the weather. I want to be sure I'm sitting on the couch at home when it hits and not driving through a blizzard, unable to see a damn thing."

"Here we are. I'll back in. It will be easier to unload the food you brought, and I'd hate to see one of you drop the pumpkin pie."

During Thanksgiving dinner, the conversation turned to the news. "I suppose you've been following the mess we're having with North Korea?" Tom asked, taking a second slice of Kathy's pumpkin bread.

"It's kind of hard to miss. It's all they talk about on the national news. You can't get away from it," Dan responded.

"So have you thought about what you would do if things got hot?" Tom asked. "What I mean is, if there is an all-out war, surely you wouldn't stay here."

"Why not? We have plenty of wood to keep from freezing to death. I've six cords dry and split. It only takes two and a half cords to heat this place. I'd be more concerned if we lived downstate and only had oil for heat. No one can keep their furnaces running if the supply is cut off. Anyway, that's just a hypothetical question. As I've told Kathy, there will be a lot of bluster on both sides. Jeong will eventually blink, knowing it would be the end of him and his country if he pokes us in the eye with another one of his missiles.

"We've had these situations before, long before you kids were around. In the late fifties, during the Cold War, everyone was scared shitless that Russia was going to unleash its nuclear arsenal on the United States to try to wipe us off the face of the earth. And if they did try, the U.S. would lob hundreds of nuclear bombs on their cities. They called it guaranteed mutual destruction.

"My parents even had a fallout shelter. It was a windowless room in the basement under the concrete garage floor. I remember boxes of survival food lining the outside wall and gallon jugs of water. Once a month, I'd replace the old water with fresh. There were monthly air raid drills at school, and everyone hid under the desks to protect themselves from flying debris after the bomb dropped. It was silly to tell kids to duck and cover to protect them from something that wasn't survivable.

"Then there was the Cuban Missile Crisis in 1962. Surely you two studied that in high school. The United States discovered that the Soviet Union was assembling medium-range ballistic missiles in Cuba capable of hitting Washington, D.C., with a nuclear warhead. Talk about a tense two weeks. I remember photos of surface-to-air missiles along the beaches in the Florida Keys, ready to destroy any Soviet bombers that might invade our airspace. President Kennedy blockaded Cuba to stop more ballistic missiles from being delivered there.

"So what happened?" Tom asked.

"Russia blinked and removed the missiles. Although Kennedy agreed not to invade Cuba and secretly agreed to remove our missiles from Turkey.

"So you see, we have been a lot closer to being attacked by an enemy with nuclear weapons than what North Korea threatens. Sure, we should take the pompous ass seriously, but he will be the one that ends up on the short end of the stick if he starts anything.

"Well, that's today's history lesson. I think Tom and I should take a walk out back to see if we can cut a deer track."

Dan and Tom returned to camp late afternoon without a deer. After warming up next to the woodstove, Tom asked to turn on the television to get the latest update on the predicted snowstorm.

The meteorologist had upped the forecast to fourteen inches of snow along the coast and two to four inches in the mountains.

"Well, that does it," Tom said, looking at Hazel. "We better leave in the morning after breakfast to get home ahead of the storm."

Kathy dreaded seeing her daughter leave so soon. She had expected them to stay until Sunday. "The weatherman is probably way off on how much snow you'll get. I bet it will be closer to three inches than fourteen. It's too early for a major storm. It's not even winter," she said, hoping Tom would reconsider leaving the following day.

"I'd like to see them stay until Sunday as well, but they're the ones driving toward the storm, not us," Dan said. "When I picked you up at the Dam Road, I noticed that you hadn't put the winter tires on your Honda. Those compact cars aren't worth a crap in the snow without them," he told Tom.

"That's another reason I want to get back early. I want to be at the garage Saturday morning and have the tires changed over, along with everyone else."

"So, Dan, are you going to move the truck out to the end of the Skyler Pond Road before the storm hits?"

"Not when the prediction is two to four inches. I don't want to go through the hassle of walking four miles back to the cabin. Then later, walk out and drive the truck back to the pond. I'll check the weather in the morning before taking you two to your car. If they're still saying the same, I'll leave it here. Besides, we need to go to town Tuesday for gas and groceries."

The following day the forecast remained the same, so Dan decided to take his daughter and son-in-law out to their car and drive back to the cabin. Before leaving, Hazel promised they would be back up for Christmas. Dan said he and Kathy would find a Christmas tree and have it up when they arrived. After another round of goodbyes, the door shut. Kathy stood at the kitchen window, waving as the pickup drove off, already wishing for Christmas.

An hour later, Dan returned with news bound to please Kathy.

"Just before the kids left, I had a brainstorm."

"Now, there's a first. What is it?"

"I told them we'd drive to Portland for a weekend to do some Christmas shopping. They thought that was a great idea and said we could stay with them. What do you think?"

"Great! But where would we sleep? Their condominium only has one bedroom. Maybe we should stay at a hotel instead."

"No. We'll stay with them. Tom said they would sleep on an air mattress for the two nights, and we could have their bed. I told him that sounded good to me as long it was them and not us on the floor."

"You didn't say that, did you?"

"Sure, I said it. They don't want us old folks struggling to get off the floor to go to the bathroom during the night. I told them we would be down the second weekend of December."

Later that evening, just before going to bed, Dan checked the weather forecast. The weather bureau now predicted four to six inches of snow for the mountains, but still of no concern. He shined his flashlight out the kitchen window. The light's beam cut through the darkness, exposing large snowflakes gently floating to the ground. *The weatherman got it wrong again*, he thought. If it kept snowing at this rate, there would barely be an inch or two by morning. Confident he had made the right decision to leave the truck at the cabin, Dan went to bed.

Dan woke to the wind rushing through the trees next to the cabin. He squinted, trying to determine the time on his wristwatch; it was one thirty. The cabin creaked in protest each time a gust slammed against the outside walls. During brief periods when the wind slackened, he could hear Kathy's heavy breathing, oblivious to the storm raging outside their bedroom window. Dan stared at the ceiling, having second thoughts about not taking the truck out to the Dam Road. Perhaps the snowstorm was more severe than what the weatherman had predicted.

Too wired to sleep, Dan grabbed the flashlight from the nightstand and quietly shut the bedroom door. He needed to know how much snow had fallen. The flashlight's beam reflected off the living room windows as he made his way toward the kitchen. A shroud of wind-driven snow encased the windows. He turned the knob of the outside door, but the door wouldn't open. He gave the door a stiff pull, breaking the icy seal that had frozen the door shut. When the door swung open, the two feet of snow propped up by the door fell onto the entryway floor.

What happened? he thought. *How could the weatherman have screwed up the forecast this bad?* He picked up the phone. They still had a dial tone. Still curious about how much snow was on the ground, Dan turned on the end table lamp and grabbed the small brush he used to sweep the ashes off the woodstove's hearth. Slowly he lifted a window, brushing the snow outward as he went. Suddenly a gust of wind drove the snow back into the cabin. Dan slammed the window shut. He'd wait until daylight to find out how much had fallen.

Now wide awake, there was nothing to do until daylight except to sit in the dark and kick himself for being so foolish as to not move the truck to the end of the road. The Ford pickup would remain trapped at Skyler Pond until spring if the snow didn't melt before the next snowstorm.

At six thirty, Kathy came out of the bedroom. Barely awake, she staggered past Dan, sitting in the recliner.

"Good morning."

"My God! You scared me. I thought you were still in bed. How long have you been in the recliner?"

"Since three. Take a look outside."

Kathy walked to the window over the kitchen sink. "I don't believe it!"

"My thoughts exactly," Dan said, standing by her side, peering into the blowing snow.

"How much do you think is out there?"

"Hard to tell the way the wind is blowing. But guessing, I'd say at least eighteen inches, maybe even two feet."

"What are we going to do?"

"Nothing we can do, at least for a while. We'll just have to wait until the storm ends and see how much actually fell. We'll likely have to wait a couple of days for it to settle. There's no way we can run the snowmobiles until it does. They would be stuck before we drove them twenty feet." Just then, the phone rang.

"Hello," Dan said, sure Hazel was calling to check on them.

"Dad, are you and Mom okay?"

"We're fine. Although we do have a lot of snow on the ground," he said, purposely holding back how much they actually had. "How much did you get down your way?"

"Enough so that they called off work for both of us. The weatherman said a foot in the Portland area. North of Augusta, close to two feet, and even more in the mountains. I was worried you might be snowed in."

"Well, there is a lot. We'll wait a day or two before we snowmobile to the car. But don't worry about us, we're warm and have plenty of food. We could stay here the entire winter if we had to," he said, glancing at his wife, who was shaking her head, signaling to Dan that wouldn't happen.

"There is one more thing. Have you seen the news this morning?" Hazel asked.

"Not yet. Should we?"

"Yes. Things don't look good between us and North Korea. North Korea shot another rocket toward the U.S. that crashed three hundred miles off the California coast."

"You have got to be kidding! How stupid can they get?"

"Well, they did it. Now it sounds like there will be a retaliatory attack on North Korea. One network said the president might even use nuclear weapons. It's pretty scary. I don't like having you and Mom so far away and alone, not with everything happening."

"Hazel, we're fine. I'm sure things will settle down. They always do. We'll be down in a couple of weeks. Tell Tom we'll take you both out to eat Saturday night. Tell him all he has to do is pick up the tip. He'll get a laugh out of that." Dan thought for a moment. "Hazel, we might lose the phone because of the storm. Being the only ones up here with a phone, the telephone company will be in no hurry to fix the line if it goes down. So don't panic if you can't reach us. We'll communicate by email using the satellite internet connection. Now here's your mother. She wants to say hi. We'll see you a week from Friday, and don't worry about us," Dan said, holding the receiver out to Kathy.

While Kathy talked to her daughter, Dan turned on the television. All the networks were carrying live coverage of the latest confrontational action taken by North Korea. The news was pretty much as Hazel had told him. A second intercontinental ballistic missile crashed in U.S. territorial waters, barely three hundred miles from the United States mainland.

An emergency meeting of the National Security Council was in progress, which included key members of Congress to ensure political buy-in to whatever the president's response to the crisis might be. After a time, the anchor started repeating the same story, marking time while waiting for the president's meeting to end. Dan turned off the television and walked to the living room window to see if the storm had ended. It hadn't. If anything, the snow was falling harder than before. He looked at the outdoor digital thermometer display sitting on the stereo: twenty-four degrees. Dan wondered if the temperature would plunge once the storm ended.

By early afternoon, the ghostly image of the sun broke in and out of the thinning overcast. The wind calmed, and the temperature began to drop, as Dan had expected. Three hours of daylight remained to get the snow off the deck and a path shoveled to the woodshed. The wood box needed to be full for what looked like an unusually cold night for the last week of November. Right now, the priority was keeping warm. Worrying about what was going on in Washington would have to wait.

Kathy watched from the kitchen window as Dan attempted to clear the snow far away from the door so that they could both shovel without being in each other's way. Twenty minutes later, the eight-by-ten-foot deck was clear. Dan began to rough out a path to the woodshed while Kathy went inside to check the fire and prepare something to eat. The sun had set when the last armload of firewood dropped into the wood box.

"I need a drink," Dan said, falling into the recliner.

"One glass of water coming up," Kathy said, reaching for a glass.

"Not water. A real drink, like a double whiskey and light on the ginger ale."

"Actually, I might have one myself. I think we both deserve one after all that shoveling."

"Why don't you, me, and Johnnie Walker sit back and watch the evening news," he said, anxious to hear the latest developments on a potential war with North Korea.

"Let's you, me, and Johnnie sit back and relax for a while and not watch the news."

"We'll only catch the headlines, and then I'll turn it off, I promise."

"Sure you will," she answered, knowing that wouldn't happen. "Go ahead and turn the damn thing on if you have to."

The lead-in to the seven o'clock news began with a blank screen with dramatic militaristic music in the background. Seconds later, a full-screen graphic appeared: "The North Korean Crisis, What Will America Do?" The over-the-top introduction looked and sounded like the opening of an epic Hollywood war movie.

"My God, now what?" Kathy said, setting her drink on the table, bracing herself for the worst.

Dan and Kathy hung on to every word the anchor said.

"Good evening. We start tonight with a summary of where we stand on the North Korean crisis. This morning, North Korea launched a second ballistic missile toward the United States at three am Pacific time. Like the one fired toward Hawaii on November second, this missile fell within the territorial waters of the United States, three hundred miles off San Francisco, California." The screen showed both missiles' trajectories, with the impact points indicated by two large *X*s.

"The president has been in meetings with his cabinet and the National Security Council all day. He also had a closed-door meeting with Secretary of State Bingham and Secretary of Defense Sidelinger. After the meeting, the two secretaries held a joint news conference on the White House's back portico. We will broadcast their complete statement later in the newscast. First, a summary of what the two men said." The next graphic flashed onto the screen, and the news anchor read each bullet point:

- *State Department asks China and Russia to help defuse the situation*
- *Seventh Fleet sent to the Sea of Japan*
- *Anti-missile batteries deployed along the Pacific coast*
- *NATO forces activated*
- *Canadian and U.S. bomber and fighter squadrons deployed to three bases in Japan*

"The secretary of defense also stated that other defensive and offensive weapons are being deployed as well, but he refused to elaborate on what those might be."

The newscast continued with interviews with politicians and nearly anyone else with an opinion on the U.S. response to the crisis. One of the Senate's leading hawks told a reporter, without using the words "nuclear bomb," that the United States needed only to send one plane with one bomb over Pyongyang. This action would end any future problems with North Korea.

A seasoned adviser to the past president urged caution. Negotiate with the regime rather than employ a tit-for-tat approach. Any rapid escalation might draw the Chinese and Russians into the fray.

Dan and Kathy had seen enough of the pontificating by the so-called experts.

"So what's next?" Kathy asked her husband as she hit the off button on the remote.

"I think we're going to war. I don't see how the president can ignore a second missile crashing off the West Coast. If one of those things can fly fifty-two hundred miles, they sure as hell can send one fifty-five hundred miles. It could wipe out San Francisco, Los Angeles, or other West Coast cities. What about you?"

"I think it's going to happen. I'm scared, Dan, not so much for us but for Hazel and Tom. Maybe we should move in with them; that way, we could at least be together."

"How would that work? They have a small one-bedroom condo, barely large enough for two people, let alone four. We would be stumbling over one another. If you want to get under somebody's skin, stay in their home for a couple of weeks. I understand your concerns for the kids, but moving in with them wouldn't solve anything. The best thing for us is to stay put until we see where this mess is going. We'll give the snow a day or two to settle and then snowmobile out to the road and drive to Kingston to get gas and groceries. By then, we'll better understand what's happening between us and North Korea."

"I suppose. But I still don't like living so far from our daughter."

"Hey, you'll see her in a couple of weeks, right? Tomorrow morning, I'll shovel the sled shed out and start the generator so we can charge the batteries. Once we've cleaned up around camp, I'll make a track out to the car."

Shoveling a path forty feet to the storage shed after a typical snowstorm wasn't a major chore, but this was not a regular storm. Dan struggled for an hour to rough out a path to the front door of the snowmobile shed. He lifted the thumb latch to go inside, but the door wouldn't open. He pushed against the door. It wouldn't budge, bound to the floor by the weight of the snow on the roof. Finally, he rammed the door with his shoulder while lifting the door by the handle. Grudgingly, the door scraped across the spruce floor.

Dan waited for his eyes to adjust to the dark inside the window-less building, not wanting to trip over one of the snowmobile skis. The sled shed was a converted bunkhouse from when the Bridges owned the property, now used to store the snowmobiles and house the generator. With doors on opposite sides of the building, he and Kathy could drive the two machines in one double door and out the other.

He unlatched one set of doors and pulled them inward. In front of him, a wall of snow drifted nearly to the edge of the roof. The snow had to go, at least enough to drive the snowmobiles in and out without hitting his head on the top of the doorframe. It was exhausting work. Dan took a break and started the 3,000-watt generator to charge the solar batteries in the building next to the woodshed. One sharp pull of the starter cord and the reliable Honda roared to life. Dan smiled. He had never known a single time that the generator didn't start with one yank. No sooner had he had the thought than the generator began to sputter and then quit. The red fuel-level indicator showed three-quarters full. Dan pulled the starter cord repeatedly, but the generator would not start. Without the generator and the solar panels buried beneath three feet of snow, he could not charge the batteries. The cabin would be without lights once the batteries went flat.

Frustrated, he rechecked the fuel gauge. Dan did a double take when he saw no sign of the red indicator. The fuel tank was empty. The float inside the tank had stuck. Dan figured it must have jarred free when he slid the generator sideways to access the side panel to check the engine's oil level. With a full charge of fuel, the Honda was quickly up and running and sending thirty amps of power into the waning batteries.

Dan should have stopped work for the day. He knew better than to attempt to ride one of the machines before the snow settled. However, anxious to make a packed trail around the cabin, Dan was willing to risk that the snowmobile might get stuck.

Dan used Kathy's machine to make his run, the lighter of the two and the easiest to dig out if he happened to get mired. The old Polaris Classic fired after repeated pulls on the starter cord, skipping and coughing as oil-rich exhaust billowed from under the machine, filling the shed with a thick blue haze. Dan coaxed the engine to smooth out by gently playing with the hand choke while trying not to suck the fumes deep into his lungs.

Both vintage snowmobiles were designed to be ridden on packed trails, not to break through deep, loose snow. However, by letting the snow settle after each storm, they were dependable transportation between camp and the Dam Road.

Dan pulled the snowmobile helmet over his head, dropped the visor, and reminded himself to stay low so he wouldn't whack his head on the door's header. He revved the engine, the centrifugal clutch engaged, and the machine rumbled toward the open door. As the skis touched the shed's threshold, he punched the throttle. The Polaris rocketed up the steep ramp of snow with only the top of Dan's helmet grazing the doorframe. For one full second, Dan defied gravity as the snowmobile went airborne. Abruptly, the flight was canceled. The three-hundred-pound machine crashed back to earth, burying itself deep in the soft snow and sending Dan flying over the handlebars headfirst into the snowdrift. Kathy had witnessed the launch from the kitchen window and ran outside to see if he was hurt.

She couldn't see Dan over the pile of snow they had shoveled off the deck. Unless her husband needed help, she did not intend to wallow through the waist-deep snow to help him.

"Dan, are you okay?"

Dan had rolled onto his back by then, making a mental check to determine if he had broken anything. "I'm fine, I guess. But my glasses went flying," he yelled back to Kathy, scanning the area for them. "You had better get my extra pair from the top bureau drawer."

Without glasses, Dan was legally blind. They could be three feet in front of him, and he wouldn't be able to see them. Kathy returned to the cabin, and Dan rolled toward the path he had shoveled to the woodshed, mad at himself for foolishly thinking he would plow through a four-foot snowdrift and not get stuck. Tomorrow he would dig out the snowmobile.

Sitting in the recliner sipping a coffee brandy, Dan remembered that there were ten gallons of gasoline in the storage building, not fifteen, as he had first thought. He'd used the other five gallons to fill the generator. Still, it was enough if they needed to delay their trip to Kingston for a couple of days because of the weather.

After eating, Dan returned to the recliner, telling Kathy he'd nap until the national news. She was about to wake him up at six thirty but decided to let him sleep instead. She didn't need to listen to more threats and counterthreats of war between North Korea and the United States. She was sick of it. The only thing it would accomplish was to get them both stirred up and worried over something they couldn't control. They could watch the morning news. Tonight, she just wanted to shut the conflict out of her mind. While Dan slept, she went into the den to finish sewing pajamas for Christmas gifts for Hazel and Tom.

Early the following day, Dan attempted to extricate the stuck snowmobile. The job could take minutes or drag on for an hour if the snowmobile refused to budge from the depths of its snowy prison. He first packed the snow around the machine and then made a loop to the doorway on the opposite side of the shed.

Dan gave the machine just enough throttle to cause the track to tighten. He knew if he gave the snowmobile too much gas, the track would spin, and the machine would dig itself deeper into the hole. At the same time, he pushed on the snow machine's handlebars for all he was worth. Slowly the Polaris pulled itself out of the chasm. Once free, he rode on the packed trail and into the sled shed. Their trip to Kingston would have to wait for a few more days.

Dan filled the snowmobile with gasoline, pleased with himself for how easily he had freed it. The feeling of satisfaction was short-lived.

Kathy hollered that the phone was dead and the satellite dish had no signal. He returned to the cabin, wondering how the telephone and satellite could be down simultaneously. This was the first time this had happened since moving to Skyler Pond.

Dan disconnected and reconnected wires, hoping to isolate the problem. He could understand the phone being dead. The telephone line stretched thirty miles alongside the Dam Road, strung to dozens of pathetically small telephone poles that pointed in every direction except vertical. A single strand of insulated copper split from the main line and followed the Skyler Pond Road for three miles, draped tree to tree, supported by small white porcelain insulators. A fallen tree could easily break the line at any point along the line's route. Dan knew repair crews were likely to prioritize work with a better return on their effort rather than worry about one customer living at the end of the line in the middle of nowhere.

Before moving to Skyler Pond, Dan knew that the phone line was vulnerable to going down. Without it, there would be no contact with the outside world in an emergency. His first choice was cell phones, but the mountains blocked cell service. Dan installed a satellite system for the internet and television—a system that worked flawlessly except during extreme weather events.

As Dan fiddled with the connections to the satellite receiver, he remembered the day the satellite dish installer followed him into camp and how his van got stuck in one of the bottomless water holes dotting the Skyler Pond Road.

The installer wasn't happy about spending the entire day on one satellite system and was less pleased when a rock put a small hole in the van's oil pan on the way out, the same rock Dan had pointed out from the truck's window for the installer to avoid.

SNOWBOUND

"Turn on the radio," Dan told Kathy as he continued to check the connections. "We might as well listen to the news and get the weather while waiting to get the signal back."

Kathy pushed each preset button for the stations they usually listened to. This time there was only dead air. She rolled the tuner slowly to see if another station came in, but there was still no signal. It was like turning the dial with the radio unplugged. As she was about to tell Dan nothing was coming in, she picked up a weak signal. It emitted a sound different from the typical commercial radio station. The odd noise reminded Kathy of a similar sound when she was a child. Her mind flashed back to how she sat beside her grandfather nearly every Saturday morning, listening to children's radio shows. A weird, unnatural sound would interrupt the story. It began and ended with a series of short annoying blats sounding like a foghorn, followed by a distant and somber voice. The voice sounded as if it emanated from a coat closet three houses down the street. Her grandfather told her it was to inform the country what to do in case of an emergency so that people would stay safe.

Now Kathy realized what the annoying sound coming from the FM radio meant. She held the radio close to her ear, listing for someone to speak.

After several seconds of the annoying but attention-getting din, a computer-generated male voice spoke: "This is an

Emergency Alert System transmission. This is not a test. You are advised to shelter in place until the situation has stabilized. Stay tuned to this emergency radio network station for a prerecorded announcement by the president of the United States at seven this evening, November 31, eastern standard time, and rebroadcast every fifteen minutes thereafter." The obnoxious pulsating noise resumed.

"Dan! Come here! Something awful has happened," she yelled, still holding the radio to her ear.

Dan dropped the screwdriver he had used to tighten the connectors on the satellite receiver and hurried to see what had upset Kathy.

"What is it?"

"Listen. Listen to this announcement," Kathy told him. "There's been some kind of national emergency, and the president will speak to the nation at seven tonight. My God! Dan, do you suppose we are at war with North Korea?"

"Don't be ridiculous, Kathy. We can't already be at war. It's likely just a test of the Emergency Alert System. Or, at worst, perhaps a massive storm has wreaked havoc with the power grid, and the president wants to calm people down and tell them what's going on."

"It's no test. The voice said so. The message just keeps repeating 'shelter in place,' and the president is going to speak. This is the real thing. I think we've been attacked."

Kathy set the portable radio on the kitchen counter. They stood there, staring at the radio, waiting for someone to speak. Dan expected to hear the announcer say "This is only a test of the emergency network. If this was an emergency, an official message would have followed the tone alert. We now return you to your regular programming." The same verbatim message he and everyone else had heard countless times. Instead, the robot-sounding voice cut in and repeated the announcement Kathy had heard.

Kathy and Dan looked at each other in disbelief. Both had the same thought but were afraid to say it. At last, Kathy spoke, "I think there's been a nuclear attack on our country," she said, barely above a whisper. Dan grimaced, nodding his head in agreement.

"Hazel. What about Hazel? We have no way to find out if she and Tom are okay and tell them we're all right. She's probably making herself sick worrying about us. Dan, we have to leave here and let them know we're safe! We have to go now!"

"Kathy, calm down. We can't leave, at least not yet. There's too much snow. We'd never make it out to the car. Besides, we don't even know for sure what is going on. We need to listen to the president and decide what to do. Maybe it's not as bad as we think it is."

Dan's words did little to relieve Kathy's anxiety about their daughter and son-in-law's safety. However, she realized they couldn't ride or walk the four miles to their car, not with nearly three feet of snow. They needed to let the snow settle before they tried.

Dan looked at his watch. One o'clock, six hours before the president addressed the nation. He didn't feel like lunch, not even a drink. His mind whirled with numerous scenarios of what might have happened to cause this apparent national emergency. He supposed losing the satellite signal had something to do with it, but what? Did the North Korean military destroy America's communication satellites with missiles? Or perhaps our government shut down all the satellites, not wanting the enemy to know the damage they had inflicted on the country. He needed to go outside before he drove himself crazy, speculating about what might have happened. Dan didn't want to upset Kathy any more by telling her his dark thoughts. He told her he needed to check the solar batteries and fill the generator with gas.

Kathy welcomed her husband leaving the cabin. He had been pacing the floor, unable to sit for more than two minutes, and it wasn't making it any easier for her to keep what was happening in perspective.

Thoughts of Hazel and Tom filled her mind, wondering if they were safe. And there was Tom's sister living in Florida. Karen had married a career Air Force officer stationed at Tyndall Air Force Base assigned to the 601st Air Operations Command Center.

Kathy wasn't sure what he did other than what Tom had told them. She struggled to remember how he had described his brother-in-law's job. Something about if there were ever an attack on the country, the command center would be responsible for coordinating the Air Force's response. Just knowing that much convinced her he would be in the thick of any retaliation against North Korea.

In the corner workshop of the barn, Dan killed time putting away tools he had used on his last project, unable to clear his mind about what the president might say to the nation. He fretted about not taking the extra gas cans on their previous trip to town.

Now Dan doubted that Kingston's only gas station had gasoline. Once the locals heard that the country was preparing for war, everyone would have topped off their vehicles and filled every gas can they could scrounge. There must have been a run on the town's only grocery store as well. All the shelves empty, sucked clean by panicked customers who needed to provide for their families during the emergency. Who could blame them? Dan wanted to think he'd be above hoarding food, but deep down, he knew he'd do the same for his family.

Driving to Kingston would accomplish nothing other than needlessly burning five gallons of precious gasoline. That same amount of gas could run the generator for another ten days.

One way to prolong power to the cabin without starting the generator would be to shovel the snow off the solar panels. Even on the shortest winter days, four hours of direct sunlight on the six south-facing panels would be enough to keep the small battery bank charged. However, every day needed to be sunny; if not, the generator would be required to charge them. Although Dan had bought new batteries five years earlier, they had already started to lose their charge. Still, he thought he could get another year out of them before buying new ones. Instead, he would buy extra gasoline to keep the old batteries charged. His decision had made perfect sense at the time. Only now, he had no way of obtaining the gas for the generator to prevent the tired batteries from going flat. Two o'clock. Three hours of daylight remained. Enough time to drag the ladder out of the building, climb onto the roof, and remove the snow from the panels, hoping that tomorrow would be sunny.

During supper, there was little conversation, only an occasional glance at the kitchen wall clock, wondering if seven o'clock would ever arrive. Kathy and Dan went through the mechanics of eating, each absorbed in their own thoughts, wondering what was happening outside their snowbound world. It was depressing enough to just speculate about a war, and spending energy discussing something they barely knew anything about seemed unnecessary. There'd be plenty of time for talk after the president's address.

Just before seven, Kathy and Dan moved to the living room. Kathy placed the radio on the small pine end table between the two recliners. She set the dial to the emergency broadcasting station to hear the network's obnoxious warning tone, followed by a recorded announcement that the president's address to the nation would begin in four minutes.

Dan turned off the cabin's light and lit a Coleman lantern to extend the life of the batteries. The scene seemed surreal to Kathy. The two of them sitting beside a hissing gaslight, the radio blasting out an annoying whine to alert listeners of a pending catastrophe while waiting for the president of the United States to likely tell them that the country is at war. At precisely seven o'clock, the alert stopped. Seconds later, without introduction, the president began his long-awaited announcement.

My fellow Americans, I bring you grave and tragic news about our incredible country. Today, at 9 a.m. eastern time, the United States of America was deliberately attacked by the Democratic People's Republic of Korea. This unprovoked act of war by North Korea has had a devastating impact on our land and its people.

This attack came after the government repeatedly warned North Korea to stop firing ballistic missiles toward the United States. Twice these missiles have landed within this country's territorial waters. Our State Department warned the Supreme Leader of the Democratic People's Republic of Korea that the United States would not tolerate this aggressive behavior. If these actions continued, the United States would take appropriate and definitive action.

At the time of the attack, Ambassador Wainright was meeting with Supreme Leader Jeong in Pyongyang to defuse the situation through direct talks. As these talks were underway at Jeong's palace, North Korea launched nineteen intercontinental ballistic missiles armed with nuclear warheads from underground silos hidden in the Nangnim Mountains.

The Air Force's anti-ballistic missile batteries destroyed seven of these missiles. Two detonated in the desert in western Nevada. However, I'm sad to report that ten found their targets: the city of Tacoma, Pearl Harbor Naval Base, Hickman Air Force Base, Navy Base San Diego, Naval Air Station North Island, Naval Base Coronado, Elgin Air Force Base, and the Tyndall Air Force Base.

"My God! Tyndall! That's where Tom's sister lives!" Kathy cried.

And, I'm sad to report, New York City. The tenth missile, intended to hit Boston, detonated east of its target. The explosion triggered a massive tidal wave that caused significant damage and loss of life to Boston's waterfront.

Three minutes after North Korea launched missiles toward the United States, our military launched nineteen ICBMs against North Korea, including Pyongyang. This action neutralized the North Korean armed forces' effectiveness and eliminated Jeong's regime.

The war has ended, and our enemy has been defeated. However, the United States has suffered significant harm. Your government will do all that is necessary to assist those affected by the devastation. I've instructed all but critical military to provide immediate assistance to all states affected by this unprovoked attack. I urge all Americans to remain calm. Your government is doing all that is possible to help you and rebuild our country.

We did not provoke this despicable act, but be assured that North Korea will never again launch another weapon toward our country. We rightfully protected our land and her people with our might. We fought to preserve the United States Constitution, which has served us so well for two hundred forty years. Tyranny did not win.

Thank you, and God bless the United States of America.

The announcer then informed the listeners that in thirty seconds, the lead climate expert at the National Weather Service would speak.

The climatologist began her presentation by describing the effects of nuclear detonations on the long-term weather patterns in the western United States. Dust and smoke would reduce solar gain from the sun by 10–20 percent. The average daytime temperature for states west of the jet stream would decrease by five to eight degrees, with nighttime temperatures as much as fifteen degrees below the average. Las Vegas, Nevada, was already reporting a temperature of thirty-three degrees, compared to an average daily high of fifty-one degrees for this date. The decrease in sunlight had activated streetlights in several major western cities. Crop production could decrease by 40 percent, resulting from prolonged drought and lower average temperatures. The abnormal weather would last six months to three years.

Kathy and Dan listened intently to Dr. Mathews, anxious to hear what weather changes the detonations would bring to the eastern United States. At last, she switched her climate forecast to the East Coast. Kathy and Dan shifted to the edge of their seats to be closer to the radio, not wanting to miss what she had to say.

According to the scientist, the climate prediction models indicated that smoke and dust from the west would combine with the atmospheric dust in the east and travel north along the stationary jet stream.

This would bring prolonged rain and flooding in the mid-Atlantic states and near continuous snow in northern New England, worse in the higher elevations of Vermont, New Hampshire, and Maine, where temperatures would remain below freezing. The extreme weather would last several months to a year, depending on how long the smoke and dust remained in the atmosphere. The National Weather Service predicted that by two a.m. tomorrow, the first of the effects of the changing weather patterns would reach the northeastern United States. Kathy turned off the radio. She had heard enough. Only the sizzle of the gas lantern interrupted the quiet. Kathy finally spoke.

"Tell me this is a bad dream, Dan. Tell me it isn't happening."

"I wish I could. The whole thing seems like one horrendous out-of-control nightmare. Why would that crackpot do anything so stupid?"

"Who knows? And right now, I don't care. I only want to know what *we're* going to do."

"Nothing. There's nothing we can do. We need to stay put. There's enough propane to last until spring."

"Spring! What are you talking about, enough propane to last until spring? My God, that's five months away. We'll starve to death before spring gets here."

"I didn't literally mean spring. I meant to say we have enough to last a long time," Dan told her, trying to backtrack.

"What's the difference? We'll still run out of food if we don't get out of here!"

Kathy walked to the window overlooking the pond. The full moon was halfway above Bates Mountain, appearing as a giant orange ball against the horizon. She had witnessed dozens of moonrises since they owned the cabin, a scene she never tired of seeing. This time it seemed different. Perhaps knowing it might be the last moon they would see for a long time if the meteorologists were right about the coming changes in the weather. She watched the moon become smaller as it rose above the mountain, its orange color softening to a pale shade of white.

Kathy sobbed. "Dan, we're all alone here. There's no one to help us. There's not a house for fifty miles. What will we do if one of us gets sick or hurt? We can't get out with all this snow, and we don't even have a place to go unless we can make it to Westbrook and stay with Hazel. My God! I forgot about her and Tom. We can't even call her to tell her we're okay."

"Kathy, listen to me. Hazel and Tom will be fine. I'm sure everyone in their building will look out for one another. I'm positive this whole crazy mess will end sooner than the woman on the radio told us," Dan said, doing his best to console Kathy.

Kathy didn't believe a word. However, she was in no mood to argue. Instead, she turned back toward the window and gazed at the moon. A lone cloud roared past it, interrupting the narrow beam of light that shot across the snow-covered pond and into the cabin. The moon reappeared briefly and then was obliterated by a bank of clouds driven by a southerly wind. The branches on the two large pines beside the cabin began to sway. Kathy felt a sudden chill and sat in the rocker next to the woodstove, still lost in thought about her daughter's safety and the well-being of the rest of humanity.

Dan woke during the night, unable to sleep, thinking about what the president had told the country earlier. He checked his watch: three thirty. Perhaps if he read a while, he might get drowsy and catch an hour or two of sleep before Kathy woke up. Dan started toward the couch and then detoured to the entryway, curious to see if it had snowed during the night. With his head pressed against the glass, he cast the flashlight's beam into the blackness.

"I don't believe it!" He said aloud, staring at the wall of fresh snow that had fallen since they had gone to bed, whipped by the wind into a drift halfway up the door. He looked toward the storage shed. A five-foot-high snowdrift against the swinging doors resembled an ocean wave, its crest about to break against a ledge. It was hard to estimate how much had accumulated, with the wind driving the snow horizontally across the yard. All he knew for sure was that their long-awaited trip to the Dam Road would remain on pause.

Dan stepped back into the kitchen, amazed by the amount of snow that had fallen in the past seventy-two hours, nearly four feet, he estimated, and it was still snowing. Suddenly, a loud snap and a burst of light filled the cabin. He looked out the kitchen window toward the woodshed just as the sky lit a second time. The flash lasted only a second or two but long enough for Dan to spot a large animal running inside the tree line beyond the woodshed. The sudden boom and the burst of light perhaps startled a coyote. Then another rumble followed by an even brighter rush of light. In that instant, Dan saw what he thought to be the same animal sitting next to the woodshed facing the cabin.

Kathy flew out of the bedroom. "Dan, what is happening?"

Dan didn't answer. He continued to peer out the window straining to see if the animal was still there. The sky erupted again, not as brilliant as before but vivid enough for Dan to see the corner of the woodshed. Whatever he had seen had disappeared.

Now he wondered if there had even been an animal. Perhaps his imagination had gone wild from the stress of worrying about the war and the bizarre weather. There wasn't any need to upset Kathy over something that may have only been an illusion.

"Dan, did you hear me? What are you looking at anyway?"

"Oh, nothing in particular. I'm just trying to tell if it's still snowing. Thunder snow, they call it. It happens when cold air slams into the slightly warmer air, just like in the summer."

"I've never seen a thunderstorm in the summer this intense. Do you think it has anything to do with the nuclear attack?"

"Yes. I think that the snow falling is the result of the new weather pattern, as the climatologist said. She indicated that the Northeast would begin to feel the effects of the nuclear strike during the night. I also believe all the snow we received up until this storm resulted from a series of early winter storms, uncommon for sure but caused by normal weather patterns. A perfect storm scenario, three feet of snow from the unusual early winter weather and another foot from the nuclear attack. Perhaps the thunder and lightning signal the arrival of the colder air from all the dust and smoke shot into the atmosphere by the explosions."

They walked into the den and looked out over the pond. A rapid series of booms rattled the cabin's windows, followed by several bolts of lightning that seemed to strike randomly on the opposite shore. The thunder and lightning lessened as the storm moved east and eventually disappeared.

"Well, there's no sense going back to bed. It'll be light in a couple of hours. I'll turn on a light and start the coffee." Before he did, Dan checked the battery meter on the den's wall. Twelve volts; the batteries were nearly flat. Not wanting to drain them lower, he lit the gas lantern and placed the coffee pot on the woodstove.

Dan took a writing tablet from the desk and sat in his chair. It was time to take stock of what they had for supplies to get them through the weeks and possibly months ahead. They had plenty of propane to run the gas stove and refrigerator for months, and no worries about keeping warm, what with six cords of dry split hardwood in the woodshed. What they didn't have much of was food.

Dan told Kathy they needed to take inventory of what they had on hand for groceries. Kathy picked a file card off the coffee table and handed it to him.

"Here's the list. I checked all the cupboards yesterday while you were shoveling. Everything is there, all the food we have left, including what's in the freezer."

"Well, you're on the ball."

"I try to be," she said, forcing a smile.

Dan scanned the list. "There's one thing you don't have written down."

"What'd I miss?"

Dan grabbed his flashlight and went out to the storage room. Kathy could hear him shuffling pots and pans inside one of the cabinets and then a loud metal clang as one hit the pine floor. She just shook her head. Finding anything in a cabinet had always been such an undertaking for Dan. Things would be much easier and quieter if he just bent at the knees and methodically looked for a pot. Instead, it was like an undeclared war between him and anything stainless steel. Dan returned carrying a gallon glass jar.

"You forgot my jar of Pete's Premium Pickled Polish Sausage."

"I thought I'd thrown those out. We agreed that those sausages are cancer in a jar, with all the nitrates, nitrites, and whatever other toxins they use to keep the meat from rotting."

"You did toss them. But luckily, I found the jar before I threw the trash into the hopper at the transfer station the last time we went to Kingston. I'll add them to the list. We'll be glad we have them."

The two reviewed what Kathy had inventoried, mostly canned goods, mixes, and pasta. Lots of pasta. Dan scratched some numbers on the tablet.

"Well, the way I look at it, if we cut back as much as practical, we should have enough food to get us through the third week of December, about three weeks. Of course, it would be longer if I could shoot a few partridge or maybe a rabbit or two."

"Then what? I mean, what happens once we run out of food?"

"Let's not even go there now, Kathy. We'll tackle one problem at a time. Who knows, maybe the snow will melt by then."

"God, Dan, you can be a regular Pollyanna at times. Let's just be realistic in figuring out our options, okay?"

Dan ignored Kathy's comment and moved on.

"We have an idea where we stand on food. The next big issue is keeping the lights on. There's one full five-gallon can of gas in the shed and another half full. Also, I hadn't considered the gasoline in the truck. I had thought we'd need it to get to town, but now with all that's going on, that isn't going to happen. I remember the gauge reading about a quarter full, maybe a little more. If I can siphon the gas from the tank, that would add another five gallons. So we have around twelve gallons of fuel to run the lights and pump water." Dan did more scratching on the notepad.

"That should last us three weeks as well, if we limit the use of the generator to no more than two hours each day. After that, it'll be spending the evenings sitting in the dark and hauling water from the pond. Also, there's about a half gallon of fuel for the Coleman lantern. We'll keep it in reserve and use it as a last resort."

"Aren't you forgetting something?"

"I don't think so."

"How about the gas in the car? We can siphon the gas out of that as well."

"Actually, I did think of it. However, if I did that, we wouldn't have gas once we could leave. I thought we'd wait. We can always change our minds."

BARTLETT HAVEN

As Dan and Kathy confronted the problems they faced being stranded at Skyler Pond, twenty miles south three families struggled to survive as well, unable to escape from their cluster of trailers set back a half mile from the Dam Road.

Dan and Kathy had seen the narrow chained lane on countless trips to their cabin on Skyler Pond and the overabundance of crudely made No Trespassing and Keep Out signs nailed to the trees on either side of the barrier. They had assumed they were directed at would-be trespassers to keep away from some remote hunting cabin, not the secretive entrance to a backwoods family compound.

Frank Bartlett, now deceased, founded Bartlett Haven thirty years earlier. Frank had been a loner, preferring his own company to that of his family. He lived deep down inside his head, a place where only his dog and occasionally his son Frankie were allowed to visit, but only briefly. At one time or another, Frank Bartlett had been accused of stealing, trespassing, buying alcohol for a minor, being a drunk, and being a deadbeat when it came to paying his bills. The one thing he hadn't been accused of was being mentally stable, and to those not family, he could be downright scary.

Frank had once owned a fifty-acre dairy farm in Litchfield, Maine, a small town south of Augusta. It was a subsistence operation with insufficient land or cows to make it a financial success.

However, operating the dairy farm provided an independent lifestyle that matched Frank's lone-wolf personality.

After the Maine Turnpike Authority constructed a new spur to the town of Gardiner, a quarter-mile north of the Lazy Bird Dairy Farm, everything changed for Frank. The peace and tranquility of country living were replaced by the constant whine of trucks and cars zooming up and down Maine's newest four-lane highway. Each speeding vehicle dug a little deeper under Frank's skin. He spent hours on the farmhouse porch rocking back and forth, downing one beer after another, listening to the drone of the traffic. The more he drank, the more incensed he became about how the State of Maine had royally screwed up his once tranquil life.

The four-lane toll road wasn't the only issue that haunted Frank. Buying the farm had put him deep in debt. If it hadn't been for the bank of last resort—the federal government—he would have filed for bankruptcy years earlier. Now, even the lending arm of the United States Department of Agriculture had stopped loaning him money and threatened foreclosure if he missed another payment.

Frank had had enough. He sold his milk herd of twenty worn-out Jerseys to a Vermont cattle dealer and the farmland to a couple from New Jersey who planned to raise llamas and make a living by knitting sweaters from the animals' fiber, an enterprise that Frank thought only a person from away with more money than brains would dream up. Checks for both cattle and land were made payable to the U.S. government. If it hadn't been for the side sale of the farm equipment he'd hidden at a friend's house, far away from the prying eyes of the farm credit agency, Frank would have realized nothing from the liquidation. However, the money he received for the equipment was enough to buy one hundred acres of cutover woodland in northwestern Maine.

Frank's lifelong dream job was one without any hours, without any boss, and without any responsibility. As he wasn't destined to become a writer, Frank decided to move to the woods and live off the land. Three days after signing the papers, Frank, his pregnant wife Louise, Frank Jr., and one ugly German shepherd named Bubba—a dog that would just as soon bite a stranger as look at him—struck out for their new home in Skyler Township: population three, including the Bartletts. They would live off the land, growing their own food and cutting their own firewood to keep them warm during the long cold Maine winter. For money, Frank planned to cut pulpwood during the winter to help feed the Madison Paper Mill. His intention to work came with only one qualifier—that a workday didn't conflict with his favorite pastime: drinking Pabst Blue Ribbon. Louise had their second son, Dick, a month after moving into a quickly improvised bungalow, which most people would call a shack. She delivered another boy the following year, whom they named Josh.

The Bartletts were a strange lot, sticking to themselves but rarely getting along. None of the Bartlett boys had attended public school. Frank had told his cousin the first and only time he visited Bartlett Haven that he and Louise homeschooled the three boys. Back in Litchfield, the cousin told his wife that if Frank taught the boys all he knew about reading and writing, they'd be lucky to know how to spell their own names. Unfortunately, that turned out to be the case.

As teenagers, Dick and Josh developed a hankering to meet girls. The boys had overheard a logger who cut wood with their father talking about the monthly Saturday night dance in Shuman Falls, a two-hour drive from Bartlett Haven. They begged their father to let them go, but Frank refused to drive them, afraid they would get in with the wrong crowd. In truth, it would have been more likely that the other parents would worry about their children getting involved with the likes of the Bartletts. At last, the boys caught their father in a rare good mood, or perhaps a mind clouded from downing too many beers, and Frank relented. However, he refused to drive his sons to Shuman Falls. Frank appointed Frank Jr. driver. It didn't matter who took them; no one in the family had a driver's license.

That Saturday, the Bartlett boys arrived at the dance in their father's overripe Ford pickup. Frankie pulled up to the front door of the community center long enough for Dick and Josh to jump out of the pickup and then drove off to look for a place to park. Dick and Josh stood under the flickering outdoor security light listening to the sound of music and dancing feet permeating the walls of the rambling three-story building. They gave each other a quick smile. They bolted up the granite steps into the vestibule without waiting for Frankie to return. Suddenly, the boys from Skyler Township lost their nerve.

Until that moment, the outside world for the Bartlett family began at Bartlett Haven's property line. Rarely had the boys interacted with anyone from the outside other than the occasional hunter they happened upon during deer season. As for neighbors, there were none. The five Bartletts were the only year-round residents in the twenty-four-thousand-acre township. The nearest family lived in Fraternity Township, thirty miles south. Even if a family had lived nearby, Frankie, Dick, and Josh's upbringing would have been the same. In Frank's mind, it was the Bartletts against the world. And to instill this warped philosophy, Frank demanded absolute authority. He banned ventures outside the Haven's confines to avoid any outside influence. The boys were restricted to the hundred-acre property to hunt and fish the stream that divided the acreage. The same house rules applied to Louise. Unbeknownst to Frank, she had once walked along the Dam Road to admire the fall foliage. Two hours later, Frank found her. With a bit of oral and physical persuasion, she learned the hard way about the consequences of leaving the family compound without permission.

On rare occasions, Frank allowed the boys to accompany him on trips to the grocery store in Kingston. The three would follow their father up one aisle and down the other as Frank chose only those items he couldn't raise or shoot at home. While Frank shopped, Frankie, Dick, and Josh would quickly glance at the other customers' children. They were desperate but afraid to find friends beyond the chain that separated the Bartlett clan from the rest of the world.

On this night, the Bartlett boys found themselves sixty miles from home and, for the first time, away from the dictates of their heavy-handed father. As good as it felt to be free of Frank's authoritative rule, he did provide safety and security from any perceived or actual threats. The immediate question for Dick and Josh was whether to enter a room full of dozens of strangers hooting and hollering, flying around the hardwood dance floor, or to go look for Frankie to take them back to Bartlett Haven.

Dick cracked open the door so they could peek inside, the boys needing to know what they were getting into if they stayed. In front of them were people of every shape and size spinning by the door, each couple seemingly making up their steps as their partner twirled them around. To the side of the door, a middle-aged woman sat at a card table, tapping her fingers to the beat of the music. A large roll of red tickets lay next to a closed metal cash box with a white sheet of paper with "$2" printed in large black letters taped to the lid.

"Dick, we have to pay to get in!" Josh said in a loud whisper.

"Of course we do, Josh. You didn't think that band plays for free, did you?"

"But we ain't got any money," Josh whined.

"Sure we do," Dick said as he pulled a five-dollar bill out of his pants pocket. "It was on the kitchen floor. I seen it fall out of Father's shirt pocket when he stuck his head into the refrigerator, looking for a beer. I just scooped it up."

Josh gave his brother a big grin. Dick and Josh regained their confidence and went inside the dance hall with all the swagger that two backward boys from Skyler Township could muster.

They paid the four dollars and then stood in front of the card table, scanning the dance hall for a place to sit. Dick spotted two young girls sitting alone at one of the tables. They sported similar hairstyles and wore identical dresses with a large flowery print that would better suit much slender women. One of the girls noticed Dick and Josh looking their way and smiled. Dick nudged his brother with his elbow. That was all the encouragement the boys needed. The two worked their way along the edge of the dance floor, dodging dancers twirling by to the music of off-key fiddles and five-string guitars, neither knowing what they'd say to the attractive, slightly overweight girls.

The brothers just stood at the table, waiting for the other to speak. The girls giggled at the two shy boys, and then the brunette broke the ice.

"Hello, my name is Darlene. This is my cousin, Wendy. Care to sit at our table?"

From that simple introduction, a flame quickly ignited between the two local girls and the boys from Bartlett Haven.

As Dick and Josh were getting to know the first girls they had ever talked to, Frankie was doing a little hustling of his own. As nervous as a mouse trying to stare down a cat ready to pounce on its next meal, he had worked his way to the back of the dance floor to a girl standing alone with her back against the wall. It didn't go so well for Frankie. As he was about to introduce himself, she gave him an odd look and walked away. Frankie struck out before he'd even made it to the plate. Frankie, who acted like his father when things didn't go his way, took her rebuff as a personal affront. The initial embarrassment quickly turned to anger. Frankie stomped out of the building and sat in the pickup until the dance ended.

Dick and Josh continued to travel to the monthly dance to see Darlene and Wendy. The girls even got the boys on the dance floor, attempting to teach them how to dance to the catchy rhythm of the country band.

Frankie had been stung once trying to talk to a girl, and his hurt ego wasn't ready for another try just yet. Instead, he'd spend four hours in the parking lot learning to smoke cigarettes, starting with the pack he'd stolen off the kitchen counter. He also developed a taste for Pabst Blue Ribbon, finding a six-pack someone had left in the parking lot.

At the April dance the following spring, Dick and Josh asked Darlene and Wendy to live with them at Bartlett Haven. It was an easy yes for both girls, who were willing to do just about anything to be able to quit school and get away from their overbearing parents. Living with Dick and Josh in Skyler Township, a place they had never heard of, seemed like the perfect escape from Shuman Falls.

Dick and Josh dreaded telling their father that Darlene and Wendy were going to live at Bartlett Haven. Both boys had assumed he would explode even at the mention of having nonfamily living at the compound. Frank didn't. He didn't exactly welcome the girls with open arms, but he accepted their presence as more of a matter of course. Frank knew the day would come when his sons would marry. Although Dick, at age seventeen, and Josh, sixteen, shacking up with two teenage girls wasn't quite what Frank had visualized. One thing Frank did know was that there was no way the four would live under his roof.

Frank knew that the logging company he occasionally worked for was shutting down operations in Bingham Pond Township. The worn-out trailers the men stayed in during the workweek were to be hauled to Waterville and shredded. Frank convinced his boss to save the cost of moving them the ninety miles and deliver three of the better-conditioned well-used mobile homes to the Haven. One of the twelve-by-forty-foot-long Titan trailers would be for Dick and Darlene, another for Josh and Wendy. Frank would use the third trailer for storage. However, when Frankie found himself a woman, it would be his, he told Louise. As it turned out, Frank would soon have more room in his shanty to share than he had thought.

Louise dreaded living in the way outback. Life at the compound seemed unnatural, with the family's constant bickering and constant threats. The squalor made the situation worse. No one seemed to care if the garbage piled up around the trailers or the sewage seeped onto the lawn from under the shared privies.

Life for Louise when they'd lived in Litchfield hadn't been easy, but it was tolerable. There were marital problems, primarily arguments over money and Frank's refusal to take Louise out, other than the weekly trip to the grocery store. Louise spent most weekends at the farm while Frank drove to Gardiner for an extended drunk with his friends. When life at the farm became unbearable, she could count on her siblings, who lived three miles down the road, to help her until things calmed down between her and Frank.

Ever since Frank hit her the day she went for a walk on the Dam Road, Louise had waited for the opportunity to escape from Bartlett Haven. Frank had changed since leaving Litchfield. He'd never been easy to get along with, but he was never abusive until they moved to Skyler Township. Louise had grown up in an impoverished home with its own family drama. However, her parents had taught her that hitting a woman was wrong. As an adult, Louise refused to play the part of the victim.

One evening, as Frank slept on the couch, she gathered her belongings and slipped out the back door. Louise knew he would come looking for her when he stumbled into the bedroom and realized she wasn't in bed. So she hid in the woods about a mile south of Bartlett Haven. The following morning, she flagged down a pulp truck driver and rode to Kingston, where she called her brother to come pick her up.

Frank made the boy's mother out to be the villain for deserting the family to the point that he turned Frankie, Dick, and Josh against her. It wasn't until years later that Dick and Josh figured out that their father had driven her away. The two tried to locate their mother, but it was too late. A motorist had struck and killed Louise while she was walking along the gravel road near her brother's home. Frankie stayed on his father's side until the day he died, blaming his mother for tearing apart the family, just as Frank had told him.

Six months after Frank had filled the third trailer with everything from worn-out snowmobile parts to assorted screws and bolts, he moved all of it into one of the tar paper storage sheds behind his house. Frank Jr. had found himself a girlfriend.

Frankie considered the people who attended the Shuman Falls dance a bunch of jerks, a generalization based solely on his treatment by the girl who'd given him the brush-off the first time he and his brothers went to the dance. After Dick and Josh brought their live-ins to the Haven, Frankie decided to set his sights on the monthly dance in Madrid, a hamlet in nearby Franklin County. Frankie would go to the dance with a six-pack and low expectations of meeting somebody special.

It was Beatrice Morgan and her cousin's first time at the Madrid Barn dance hall. Beatrice had recently been through an ugly divorce and moved in with Alice while trying to piece her life back together.

When Frankie saw the two women sitting alone beside the dance floor, he managed to find the courage to ask if he could join them. To his great relief, Beatrice said yes. Frankie plunked his beer on the table and sat between Beatrice and Alice. The rest of the evening, the three made small talk as they watched the dancers twirl around the sawdust-covered floor.

Neither Beatrice nor Frankie had made much of the chance meeting other than as an opportunity to share some company for an evening. Frankie returned to the Madrid Barn the following Saturday night and sat with Beatrice and Alice again. He made a half dozen more trips to the weekly dance during the summer. In September, Frankie attempted to raise the relationship to another level: he asked Beatrice to live with him at Bartlett Haven. Frankie braced himself for another rejection, half expecting her to laugh, thinking the idea of moving in with him after a few casual encounters was ridiculous. She didn't. Frankie seemed like an all right guy. Besides, Beatrice needed to find a permanent place to live. Frankie Bartlett had made the right offer at the right time. Without hesitation, Beatrice said yes.

Frankie and Beatrice lived in the trailer next to his father's bungalow, Dick and Darlene in the middle trailer, and Josh and

Wendy in the third. The thirty-foot separation offered little privacy. The families were still close enough to hear the conversations next door through the mobile homes' paper-thin walls. In the next seven years, Bartlett Haven's population ballooned to eleven, with the addition of Dick's and Josh's four children.

Frankie was twenty-eight when his father died. Lung cancer, the family supposed, likely brought on by Frank's forty-five-year habit of smoking hand-rolled Bugler-filled cigarettes. He never went to a doctor the whole time he was sick. Instead, he spent his days hacking and coughing between drags on his sticks until one night, the cough became so violent that he choked on his own blood. Frankie found his father on the floor next to the couch with a half-empty pack of cigarettes beside him. After his father died, Frankie became the patriarch of the backwoods clan, just as his father had instructed at a family meeting three weeks before his death.

The Bartlett families were unaware of the nuclear exchange between the United States and North Korea. When Josh and Wendy's television lost its signal, they assumed there was a problem with the TV or that somehow the outage was related to the strange weather. Even if they hadn't lost the television signal, Josh and Wendy still wouldn't have known about the nuclear attack. They were interested in game shows, not national news. The three families were aware of the threats and counter threats between North Korea and the United States listening to the radio. Still, the Bartletts dismissed the news as something that didn't affect their lives. Like the television, they blamed it on the weather when the radio stations went static. For the Bartletts, the seemingly never-ending snowfall was just a weather oddity they needed to deal with.

"Jesus, Frankie, I've never seen so much goddamn snow!" Dick shouted, charging into his brother's trailer, slamming the door shut to keep the blowing snow at bay. "There must be three feet of the shit, and it's still snowing," he said, grabbing one of Frankie's beers from the refrigerator.

"What's the matter, Dick? Afraid you'll have to do a little shoveling? By the way, help yourself to one of my beers."

"Thanks, I will, and no, I'm not afraid of shoveling. I'm just saying that we've got more snow now than we get in a normal winter. Worse yet, no one's working in the woods until the crap settles. I need nine hundred dollars to fix the transmission in my pickup, and now it looks like it'll be spring before I get the friggin' thing running if the weather don't improve. Oh, I almost forgot, I need five gallons of gas to fill up my sled. Okay if I grab a can of yours? I'll replace it once I can get to town."

"You keep your goddamn hands off my gas. You haven't replaced the last can you borrowed, you cheap bastard."

"Hey, I forgot, all right? Big deal, I'll buy ten gallons when I go to town—once my truck's fixed."

"I'll be dead and buried before you get that piece of shit back on the road." Frankie thought for a minute. "Okay, take five gallons. Just pay me now, and I'll replace it myself next time I go to town."

That wasn't what Dick wanted to hear. "Come on, Frankie, I'll replace it like I said. I'm a little short right now. Just give me the gas, and I'll pay you when I get my check from Milligan."

"Dick, you seem to be losing your hearing. I said if you want the gas, pay me for it."

"Goddamn you, Frankie. Here's your friggin' money." Dick reached into his pants pocket, pulled out a twenty, and tossed it onto the kitchen table.

"That's for the five gallons you took two weeks ago. Now I want another twenty for today's allotment."

Dick pulled out another twenty. "There's your goddamn money! Be careful not to choke on it," he shouted, and stormed out of Frankie's trailer.

Life among the Bartletts was a near state of constant chaos. At times, the brothers could barely tolerate one another. Once tensions reached the breaking point, the three families would avoid one another until things blew over. Even the kids paid the price for the adults' rows, not being allowed to play with their cousins until the ruckus ended. A truce generally lasted a week or two before another silly argument sent the Bartlett compound into a new state of turmoil.

Frankie downed the half-empty beer bottle Dick had left on the counter when he stormed out of the trailer. Forgetting his winter coat, he headed outside to the old beater pickup that he used to plow snow. Perhaps if Frankie had been sober, he would have realized his worn-out half-ton pickup would not move three feet of snow. However, Frankie was determined to plow the half-mile-long driveway to the Dam Road.

After a considerable amount of cursing and fist-pounding the dashboard, the engine of the F-150 grudgingly turned over and then roared to life. As soon as the kids heard the rumble of the muffler-less truck, they gathered around the green Ford, yelling to Frankie to make the plow go up and down. Frankie lifted and dropped the plow and swung it left and right as Dick and Josh's kids clapped and begged him to do it again.

"All right, now. You kids get back out of the way," he barked, swallowing a fresh beer that he steadied between his legs. "Once I get rolling, I ain't stopping until I get to the Dam Road." Frankie chuckled to himself for coming up with such a clever pun.

The children hoot and hollered, encouraging their favorite uncle. He gave them a big toothless smile, raced the engine, tooted the horn, and let out the clutch. The pickup surged three feet ahead before the snow rolled over the top of the plow and into the truck's grill, stopping the vehicle dead in its tracks. Frankie slammed the shift lever into reverse to back the truck up to give the wall of snow another wallop, but the truck wouldn't move backward or forward. Frankie was hopelessly stuck. It didn't take much of a headwind for Frankie to become unhinged.

"You goddamn son of a whore!" he yelled and again commenced pounding on the dashboard. The children waited for their uncle to make another try until he stuck his head out the window.

"What are you little shits looking at?" he hollered. "Get to hell out of here!" Scared that Frankie would come after them, they wallowed through the drifts to the safety of the nearest trailer as fast as their short legs would carry them.

Three days after the plowing incident, Josh snowshoed to the Dam Road with his .22, hoping to catch a rabbit hopping across the road. Josh never saw a bunny, but he did discover that the Dam Road hadn't been plowed, and hurried back to tell Frankie and Dick. Not believing Josh, they jumped on their snowmobiles to see for themselves. The brothers had assumed that once they cleared their driveway of snow, they could drive to Kingston to buy gas.

"Jesus," Dick said, amazed that the road hadn't been broken open by the state plow truck. "I've never seen a time the Dam Road wasn't plowed after a storm. The truck must have broken down somewhere down the road."

"Either that or the state pulled the truck out of here to help clear roads down country. As usual, we get screwed so the people in town can have their roads all cleared and tidied up," Frankie said, spitting into the snow.

"I'll tell you two jokers one thing," Frankie continued. "We've got about ten gallons of gas to keep that gas-sucking generator running. After that, it's no more lights. And there's no way we can get to town to get more gas until they plow the friggin' road. We'd have another ten gallons if shithead here hadn't wasted it joyriding on that sled of his," he said, staring at Dick.

"Look, Frankie, how to hell did I know we'd get this much snow and I couldn't get to town? Besides, you're the genius who got the plow truck stuck. Any half-wit would have known there was no way that pantywaist truck of yours would push that much snow."

Frankie bristled at the pointed remarks and got into Dick's face. "Why you—"

"Boys, boys, calm down," Josh ordered, trying to defuse the situation before Frankie and his brother started going at it.

"Frankie, how much gas is there in the plow truck? We could drain the tank and keep the generator going for a while longer."

"Next to none. I had to put a couple of gallons into the tank just to get the fuel gauge to read the upside of empty."

Josh's comment about siphoning gas out of the plow truck got Dick thinking. "I know where there's gas. Free for the taking."

"Yeah? Where exactly would that be?" Frankie asked.

"Twenty miles up the road. Parked right next to the Dam Road. Every time I ride with Milligan to the woodlot we're cutting in Bowtown, I see it."

"See what?" Frankie demanded.

"The car that's parked there. It's a fairly new Chevy Impala. It's been there for the last month. Milligan told me it belongs to a couple from up around Bangor. They're spending the winter at Skyler Pond."

"What makes you think it's full of gas? Maybe the guy left it there because he didn't have enough to get to town to fill it up," Frankie said, unsure that his brother knew what he was talking about.

"I know so. I rode into town with Milligan to get diesel for the skidders a while back. When I went inside to get cigarettes, the boss struck up a conversation with the husband, who was filling up a shitload of gas cans. The man told him he'd just retired, and he and his wife were going to spend the winter at Skyler Pond, just to say they'd done it. Milligan said he seemed nice enough but appeared to be kind of an L.L.Bean type in how he dressed and carried on. You know, he likely had good book sense but hadn't a clue how to use a can opener. Anyway, he told Milligan they would leave the car at the head of the Skyler Pond Road in case there was a big snowstorm and they couldn't get out with their truck. The car probably has a twenty-gallon gas tank, *and* I bet it's full."

Now Frankie had caught up to Dick's thinking. "Twenty gallons," he repeated. "That's enough to run the generator for two weeks, maybe three if we stretch it."

"Let's go back to the house and get the gas cans. We can be there in a half hour," Josh said, about to pull the snowmobile's starter cord.

"No. There's a chance we might come face to face with the plow truck coming back down the mountain. Once the driver got to the Skyler Pond Road, he'd see our tracks around that car and figure we were up to no good. I know Darryl, the little weasel. He's friends with the sheriff's deputy and would love to go running to him and tell him about us. Besides, it would be just our luck that the guy who owns the car would stumble out of the woods about the time we're sucking on the siphon hose. We'll wait till dark."

"With this amount of snow, I doubt if there is a chance in hell Darryl will be plowing the Dam Road anytime soon. But you're right about not knowing when the car's owner might come out to check on it," Dick said.

Frankie had good reason to be cautious about stealing the gas. All three of the Bartletts occasionally worked cutting wood. However, most of their money came from breaking into seasonal camps scattered along the shoreline of the area's lakes and ponds and then selling the bounty to an acquaintance of Frankie's living in Portland. The county sheriff was sure the Bartletts were doing the break-ins but could never catch them in the act. He and his deputy had made several unannounced visits to the family compound, hoping to spot some of the stolen goods. The Bartletts weren't the brightest lot, but there were none better when it came to stealing and covering their tracks.

While the brothers were at the Dam Road planning their trip north to steal the gas from Dan's car, Darlene sat at the kitchen table drinking coffee, enjoying her time alone. Since the bizarre weather began, she rarely had any time for herself. Unable to work outside, Dick spent most days hanging around the trailer with Frankie and Josh, who were constantly barging in to talk to him. What they could find to talk about, she hadn't a clue. If it wasn't one of the brothers making a nuisance of himself, it was five-year-old Jacob whining about something. Four people crammed into the twelve-by-forty-foot-long trailer was stressful enough during normal times. Now it was nearly unbearable.

Darlene took her last sip of coffee when she heard Jacob running down the hall.

"Mommy, Mommy! A man is talking on the radio."

"That's nice. What did he tell you, Jacob?" his mother asked, setting her cup in the sink, thinking the boy was exercising his imagination.

"He said it would snow for a long time, and people were shooting bombs."

Darlene scooched down. "Jacob, what are you talking about?"

"The radio, Mommy. Come and see."

Jacob grabbed his mother's hand and pulled her down the narrow hall toward her bedroom. When Darlene was sitting in the kitchen, Jacob had entered his parents' bedroom and turned on the portable radio she kept on the nightstand. He had accidentally picked up the emergency broadcasting station while playing with the dial.

Darlene had no idea that the station even existed. She sat on the bed listening to the announcer update the situation between the United States and North Korea, followed by the weather forecast for northern New England. Darlene couldn't believe what the man was saying.

"Jacob, you stay here. I need to get your father. And don't touch the radio. Understand?"

Jacob said he wouldn't and hopped onto the bed, listening to the announcer repeat the news.

About to grab her winter coat and go outside to find Dick, Darlene spotted him and his brothers standing next to the snowmobiles in front of Frankie's trailer.

"Dick! Come in here quick!" she called from the trailer door.

Dick ran toward the trailer, with Frankie and Josh close behind. Dick knew something was terribly wrong by the sound of Darlene's voice.

"What is it?" he asked, out of breath from his sprint to the trailer. "Did something happen to one of the kids?"

"No. The kids are fine. Come into the bedroom. You need to hear this."

Dick, Frankie, and Josh followed Darlene into the bedroom.

"Just listen," she ordered, turning the radio's volume up. "It's horrible!"

Everyone crowded around the radio, listening to the news about the nuclear war and the wild winter storms.

"No wonder the weather's been so screwed up," Dick said. "We could be snowbound for months."

"What are we going to do?" Darlene asked.

"Survive," Frankie answered. "It won't be that hard for us Bartletts. The old man said that one day it would come to this. Just be thankful we're here and can do for ourselves and not living in the city, having to fight like rats for our next meal."

Frankie had been waiting for this moment since his father told him that society would crumble one day and only the fittest would survive. Now that time had arrived. Frankie felt destined to lead the Bartletts through the chaotic times ahead.

Frankie glanced at Dick and Josh and said, "Just another reason we should collect all the gasoline we can find," referring to their clandestine raid on Dan and Kathy's gasoline supply.

At ten that night, the brothers told Darlene, Wendy, and Beatrice that they were taking a short snowmobile ride and would return in a couple of hours. The women knew from experience that when the three left together after dark, they were up to no good, but they had learned a long time ago not to ask questions. Each time the men returned from their late-night excursions, there seemed to be less room in the storage shed.

"We'll take two machines. No sense in using more gas than we need to. Josh, you ride on the dogsled behind Dick. That way, you can keep an eye on the gas cans in case they decide to dance off the sled. I'll go ahead and break trail."

"Why do I have to ride on the sled? I don't want to stand on the back and try to keep my balance for twenty miles," Josh complained.

"Because I said so, Josh! Dick's machine has more power than your clunker, and we'll need that power to pull the loaded sled. If it makes you feel better, I'll ride on the sled coming back, and you can drive my machine. There, are you happy now?"

Josh didn't say a word. Instead, he flipped his brother off and stepped onto the snowmobile sled's narrow platform. Frankie had no intention of letting his brother drive his snow machine on the trip home. Still, it was a convenient ploy to appease Josh temporarily.

The two machines flew over one drift after another, riding north on the Dam Road. It began to snow lightly, and minutes later, the flurry morphed into a full gale with near-whiteout conditions. The wind-driven snow beat against Frankie's face, forcing him to stop and dry his eyes. While Josh and Dick waited for Frankie to continue, Dick looked back at Josh and gave a thumbs-up. Josh returned the gesture. Frankie refused to wear a helmet with a shield, telling his brothers only sissies wore them. This time, Josh and Dick didn't mind being branded unmanly.

Frankie estimated they'd gone about halfway when he stopped to let his machine cool and to have a quick smoke.

"Where the hell is Josh?" he asked Dick as he walked back to talk to his brothers.

"What?" Dick asked, not able to hear his brother.

"For Christ's sake, take that goddamn helmet off so you can hear me! I said, where is Josh? Him and the sled ain't there."

Dick flipped up the helmet's visor and looked behind him. "I don't know. The pin must have come out of the hitch."

"Didn't you realize the snowmobile wasn't working as hard without the sled?" Not waiting for Dick to answer, Frankie slapped Dick's helmet with his hand. "Turn this piece of shit around and go back and find him!"

Frankie grabbed a beer from the snowmobile's storage compartment and stood by his machine, waiting for the two to return. Ten minutes later, Dick's headlight reflected off the snow as he rounded a curve a half mile down the road. Not waiting for the two to catch up, Frankie hopped back on his machine and made the final dash toward the Skyler Pond Road turnoff.

Frankie scanned the parking area looking for the Simmonses' car, finally spotting the outline of the car's roof sticking above the snow. He then made several tight circles around the buried Impala, packing the snow to make it easier to conduct business. Frankie had just taken the hammer from his backpack when Dick and Josh pulled up behind him.

"Grab the shovels and clear the snow off the trunk and then dig down deep enough so we can siphon the gas," he ordered. "I'm going to spring the trunk and see what might be of interest inside."

While the brothers followed orders, Frankie used the hammer to smash the driver's-side window and reached inside the car to pull the trunk release lever.

Inside the trunk, he found a bright orange toolbox. "Well, lookie here, boys; this is one of the most complete set of tools I've ever seen. Even has both a metric and standard set of sockets." Frankie lifted the box out of the trunk and set it next to the sled, telling the others the extra tools would come in handy for projects back at Bartlett Haven.

"There's a full two-gallon can of gas as well. Normally, I wouldn't waste my time for two gallons of gasoline, but these ain't normal times," Frankie told his brothers, setting the can next to the toolbox. "I'll tell you boys one thing, the dude that owns this car is one organized person. Not very bright leaving all these goodies in the car, but organized."

Dick had been right about a full tank of gas. They siphoned four five-gallon cans of Dan's gas in twenty minutes. Ready to return home with their booty, Frank called out to the others.

"Watch this, boys!"

He circled back until he was thirty feet behind the car and stopped. Frankie hesitated briefly and then hit the throttle. The engine gave out a high-pitched whine, and man and machine bolted toward the target. The Polaris shot up the car's trunk onto the roof and then went airborne before crashing onto the Impala's snow-covered hood. It was all Frankie could do to keep from being thrown over the handlebars. As he flew past Josh and Dick, he gave out a blood-curdling scream and disappeared down the Dam Road.

Three days after the Bartletts stole gas from the car, Dan went outside to clear the path to the woodshed. He looked at the snow-covered solar panels and then at the sky. *No gain for the batteries today,* he thought. They'd been using far more gas than Dan had calculated, causing him to have second thoughts about leaving the full tank of gasoline in the Impala. Perhaps it made more sense to siphon half of the gas to keep the generator running a while longer. That would still leave plenty to get off the mountain when they did leave Skyler Pond.

Kathy urged Dan to get the gas as soon as possible and said she would go with him and try calling Hazel. The first opportunity to make a cell call after leaving camp was at the junction of the Dam Road and the Skyler Pond Road. Tomorrow they would go out on one snowmobile with the dogsled and bring back the gasoline.

This morning Dan would snowshoe out to the Dam Road to set a track and pick the best route to avoid downed trees, telling Kathy there would be less chance of the snowmobile getting mired down in the soft snow. Minutes later, Kathy stood on the deck, watching Dan tighten the bindings on his snowshoes. When he stood, she handed him his pack and poles, telling him to be careful and to be back before dark. Kathy watched him trudge out of the driveway and onto the woods road. He turned and raised his ski pole for a final goodbye and then disappeared among the trees for what would be a three-hour slog out to the car. Inside the cabin, Kathy checked the wall clock in the kitchen, Eight thirty. Dan should be back in six hours with daylight to spare.

After five minutes, Dan knew snowshoeing the three miles would be exhausting. With each step, his snowshoes sunk deep into the fresh snow, and it wasn't long before his legs began to burn with each lift of his legs. As time passed, progress slowed as his breaks became more frequent. Dan realized that snowshoeing in the deep snow was better than a workout on the StairMaster he had bought while living in Hampden but rarely used.

He told himself just to take it slow and easy, and he would make it. The thought of having a heart attack in the middle of nowhere convinced him to follow his own advice. Dan eventually discovered a rhythm that kept him from becoming exhausted. Walk fifty paces, stop for thirty seconds and suck wind, repeat.

During one of his breaks he noticed a large dark-colored object lying on the road a hundred yards ahead. At first glance, the odd shape appeared to be the top of a broken tree brought down by the high winds, its stubby branches pointing skyward. Dan continued down the road studying the strange form. At fifty feet, he realized it wasn't a tree but a large bull moose, and what had looked like branches were actually the tines of the dead animal's massive horns.

Dan stopped to study the animal. Its long tongue protruded from its mouth, resting on the snow. Tracks stained with blood and hair led to and from the dead animal. *Coyotes*, Dan thought to himself. A pack of coyotes must have run the animal to exhaustion, likely feeding on the moose as he lay dying after giving up the fight. He bent down for a closer look at the pathetic animal and ran his hand across the coarse brown hair. He felt something move on the animal's skin. He parted the hair, revealing dozens of engorged winter ticks. Dan checked several other areas along its back and found countless ticks swollen with moose blood. Coyotes undoubtedly brought down the big bull, but they had help from thousands of ticks, which had sapped him of any energy to resist his pursuers.

Dan glanced at his watch. He needed to pick up his pace to be home before sunset.

It was a long steady climb from the pond to the height of land, a distance easily covered in five minutes by snowmobile. An hour later, a biting north wind greeted him as he tipped over the last knoll to begin the downhill stretch toward the Dam Road, still another agonizing mile and a half away. Even though gravity was with him, it became harder to lift his feet. His thighs ached with each step. Dan was running out of steam.

At last, only a short steep grade stood between him and the car. As he reached the crest, the dome-shaped pile of snow that entombed his vehicle came into view. He hadn't thought of how much shoveling it would take to dig the car out and clear a narrow channel to the Dam Road. However, shoveling out the Impala was a nonissue, seeing the road hadn't been plowed. Dan snowshoed to what he thought was the center of the paved road and looked down the long straight stretch to the south. The road appeared as a thin ribbon of white, divided into small pastures by toppled trees and telephone poles. He snowshoed to the green-and-white Skyler Pond Road sign the county had put up several years earlier to identify the way to Skyler Pond in case of a medical emergency. The metal sign barely showed above the snow, its eight-foot post buried deep under the snow. Dan comprehended for the first time how much snow had fallen in the past weeks.

He turned his attention back to the buried Impala. There was something odd about the side of the snowbound car, a dark void on the driver's side just below the roofline. As he approached the vehicle, he realized the window had no glass. His first thought was that someone had broken into the car looking for valuables. Dan looked through the opening. Everything seemed to be intact. Even the new set of tire chains he had left on the rear seat was still there.

Since nothing appeared to be stolen, then somebody must have vandalized the car. Perhaps before the storms hit, a passerby with too much time on his hands decided to get his kicks by smashing the car's window. Dan decided to shovel around the car to check for more damage hidden beneath the snow. He reached over the back seat, feeling for the snow shovel he had left on the floor the day he and Kathy parked the car for the last time. Finally, his fingers grasped the shovel's handle. Gingerly he lifted it from the floor, over the back of the seat, and through the blown-out window. Already it was one thirty. He'd work until two o'clock and then head back to the pond. It would be tight, but he could still reach the cabin before dark. The last thing he wanted was for Kathy to worry and come looking for him.

Dan worked along the driver's side of the car, careful not to scratch the paint with the shovel's metal edge. While clearing the back of the vehicle, he uncovered two deep grooves on the trunk's lid, the channels made by Frankie's skis jumping the car. He cursed the lowlife who had damaged his vehicle. Dan had seen enough and slid the shovel back through the window.

Before leaving for camp, he tried his cell phone. A No Service banner popped up on the screen. Not having a signal made no sense. They always made calls from here after leaving camp. The cell tower was only twenty miles west. You could see it on a clear day with binoculars.

Returning to Skyler Pond was much easier, as he benefited from the hard-won track he had set on the way out. Dan thought about Kathy and how she would react knowing that the Dam Road hadn't been plowed and their car had been vandalized. Kathy had seemed so upbeat, knowing that tomorrow she would finally be able to call their daughter. He wouldn't tell her there wasn't cell service, not wanting to drop another disappointment on her. She'd find out for herself in the morning.

Now he realized his idea that the road crews would soon have the Dam Road cleared of eight feet of snow was ridiculous. No plow truck made was large enough to push that much snow. The only way to clear the road would be by using bucket loaders, which would take days, if not weeks. A terrifying thought popped into his head. Maybe the state had no intention of opening the Dam Road. No one lived north of Fraternity Township, and even if they plowed the road so that loggers could haul wood, the snow was too deep in the woods to cut it. He and Kathy could be stranded for weeks. That revelation he would also keep to himself.

The clouds thickened as another storm threatened to roar down from the mountains. Darkness would descend earlier than Dan had planned. He stopped long enough to take the flashlight from his pack. Already the blowing snow had erased the track he had set a few hours earlier. A twig snapped to his left, then another, the cold causing the trees to contract, he supposed.

Dan felt comfortable in the woods. He often walked the abandoned logging roads on moonlit nights, listening and watching for wildlife. Perhaps to hear the call of a distant owl hooting for its mate or to catch a glimpse of a deer on the move, looking for its next meal of twigs and buds. *Nothing in the woods will harm you*, he had told Hazel as a child when she was scared that a bear might eat her or that a monster lurked in the dark forest, waiting to jump out and grab her. However, this night felt different. Dan became overwhelmed with the same fear Hazel had when she was five. He didn't know why he sensed that something terrible was about to happen. All he knew was that he needed to get to the safety of the cabin as quickly as possible.

A hundred yards separated him from the dead moose. If the coyotes had returned to continue feeding on the carcass, they might not be in any mood to share the road with a passerby. He tried to pick out the dark form of the dead moose with the flashlight, but the distance was too great for a two-cell light. He kept walking, first shining the light into the woods on the right side of the road and then on the left, hoping the beam would scare off whatever might lurk in the shadows. Finally, his light picked up the moose carcass fifty feet ahead. He scanned the area around the moose, expecting to see a coyote slinking back into the woods. Nothing.

Relieved, he walked past the moose without looking down at its remains. Dan began to relax, thinking he had let his imagination get the better of him. Only five hundred feet separated him from the cabin. Soon he'd be sitting next to the woodstove with a tall drink, telling Kathy about his exploits on the Dam Road. A hundred feet past the moose came snarls and growls between the camp road and the pond. Likely coyotes having a major disagreement over a piece of moose flesh that they had dragged downhill. He flashed the light toward the ruckus, but the flashlight's beam barely reflected off the nearby hardwoods. Dan quickened his pace, only four hundred feet to the cabin door.

An odd sensation of being followed came over Dan. He knew he was being silly and forced himself to keep walking. However, the urge was too great. He spun around, waving the light up and down the road. As far into the night as his light would reach, the beam locked onto three silhouettes. He held the light on the shadowy objects, his hand shaking, wondering what would come next. The vibrating light caught the reflection of six small dots, each the size of a quarter. He was being stalked. Dan let loose with the loudest shout he could muster, hoping the animals would retreat into the woods like deer or bear do when startled by a strange booming sound. His holler failed to impress the animals. The creatures maintained their same slow and steady advance. He wanted to run but was afraid he might stumble and fall, allowing the night hunters to rush him and make him unable to fend them off. Through the falling snow, he could see the faint glow of the gas light coming through the kitchen window. Dan quickly looked over his shoulder, hoping the coyotes had given up trailing him and returned to feed on the moose. They hadn't. Instead, they had closed the distance by half. The animals seemed intent on chewing on something other than moose flesh.

Dan couldn't hold back any longer. Hoping he wouldn't fall, he took off in a frantic dead run toward the cabin. He had no idea if the coyotes had given up the chase or were about to latch onto his leg, and he wasn't going to look behind him to find out.

He ran as tight as he could run, hoping for the best. As his first snowshoe landed on the deck, the door opened. Kathy had been watching from the kitchen window for any sign of Dan when she saw the erratic movement of his light as he ran toward the cabin. She opened the door to greet him. Her timing could not have been better. Dan never broke stride. He flew across the deck and through the open door into the entry, catching a snowshoe's tip on the door's threshold. His out-of-control stagger ended when he collided with the clothes washer.

"Shut the door! Shut the door!" he screamed, struggling to get to his feet.

Slam! Kathy closed the door so hard that the whole cabin shook.

"My God, Dan, what is it?"

Dan was too winded to speak. He grabbed his shotgun from behind the door and reached for the box of 12-gauge buckshot he kept on the shelf above the coatrack.

"Get back into the kitchen and shut the inside door," he ordered, shoving three shells into the semiautomatic weapon.

Dan pressed his face against the glass, his hands cupped to his head to reduce the glare from the lantern, half-expecting to see the coyotes on the deck. He saw only the dim glow of his flashlight, which he had dropped when making his mad dash toward the open door. He grabbed a second flashlight he kept next to the shotgun shells. Dan slowly cracked open the door. Armed with the light and the shotgun, he cautiously stepped onto the deck, scanning the yard for any sign of the animals. Next to the deck were three sets of tracks. Dan guessed the coyotes must have cut off the chase when he went inside the cabin and kept running past the side of the building. Dan let loose with three quick blasts hoping that if the coyotes were lurking nearby, the gun's report would drive them back into the woods.

Hearing Dan fire his weapon, Kathy became even more baffled about her husband's strange behavior. Rarely did Dan become rattled. Typically, Dan calmed her through stressful situations, making what was happening all the more bizarre.

"What was that all about? Why did you shoot your gun?" she demanded to know as soon as Dan stepped back into the kitchen.

"Let me sit down a minute, and I'll tell you," Dan replied, still out of breath from his run.

"Here, drink this. It might help calm your nerves," she said, passing Dan a rum and coke.

He took several gulps, paused, and then finished the drink. He started with when he left the cabin early that morning to make what had just happened tie together. Dan told her about the dead moose killed by a pack of coyotes a short distance from the cabin, the Dam Road not being plowed, and the vandalism to their car. Finally, he recounted being stalked by the three coyotes.

"Coyotes! You were chased by a pack of coyotes? Did you see them?"

"I saw their eyes when I shined the flashlight on them just before I took off running. I heard them yipping and growling over which one would eat the next hunk of moose flesh."

"I've never heard of coyotes chasing a person." Kathy wanted to believe Dan, but the story of being chased by three bloodthirsty predators seemed a little over the top. In all the years they'd owned the Skyler Pond property, the few coyotes she had seen were when they were riding the woods roads while partridge hunting. Then they slipped into the woods as soon as they spotted the vehicle.

"Well, all I know is there were three of them, and they chased me back to camp," Dan said, annoyed that Kathy seemed to think the run-in with the animals was a product of his imagination. "We'll go outside, and I'll show you the tracks next to the deck," he told her, proving he wasn't making up the story.

Dan grabbed the flashlight, and they stepped onto the deck. Kathy watched Dan wave the light back and forth across the snow. "They were right there, three sets. The blowing snow must have covered them," he said, knowing that without them, Kathy would never believe that he was the intended target of a pack of coyotes.

Kathy didn't say a word. She went inside the cabin while Dan frantically waved his flashlight across the snow, searching for the animal's tracks. She feared that the isolation and anxiety brought on by the war were taking a toll on Dan's mind. Finally, Dan gave up the search, and he took off his boots and parka and dropped into his recliner. Several awkward minutes later, Kathy spoke.

"Did you try your cell phone?" No matter what else happened, her first concern was reaching Hazel.

"Yes, twice. I couldn't get a signal," he told her, blowing his plan to let Kathy find out for herself in the morning.

Kathy looked out the window nervously, twirling her hair with her index finger as she often did when worried. "What are we going to do?"

"We'll do just what we had planned. First thing tomorrow morning, we'll snowmobile out to the car and siphon the gas. I figure what's in the tank will keep the generator running for another week or so. Certainly enough to last us until the roads are plowed."

"How long do you think that will be?"

"No way of telling. It won't be long if we don't get any more snow. Regardless, we'll be fine with the extra gas," he said, leaving out his theory about the state diverting the plow trucks to other areas.

Dan couldn't help thinking about his encounter with the coyotes. He knew what Kathy had said about the animal's wariness of humans to be true. So why would three typically shy coyotes track him back to camp? After Kathy went to bed, Dan picked up a reference book on mammals from the bookshelf. Curious, he looked up the description of coyotes. What he read didn't square with what he had witnessed: "Coyotes usually feed on smaller animals like rabbits and birds. On average, they are four feet long from the tip of their nose to the tip of their tail, and when running, their bushy tail hangs low."

He thought back to the morning he had caught a glimpse of what he'd thought was a coyote running near the woodshed.

Even though he saw the animal for only a split second, he remembered thinking that it seemed large compared to other coyotes he had seen driving the woods roads. Dan flipped to the section on wolves: "Larger than a coyote, five feet long nose to tail, and holds its tail high when running. Feeds on larger animals like caribou and moose." Dan thought back to the animal running along the tree line. Its tail was up, not down. What he had seen the morning of the lightning storm was a wolf, not a coyote. Why were these large predators here? They'd been eradicated from the state a hundred years ago. The only plausible answer was to find food. Perhaps Canada was having the same freakish weather as here, and the animal's native prey had become scarce. Maybe to survive, they had migrated south into Maine, and for unknown reasons, this particular wolf pack had taken up residence around Skyler Pond. Dan read further. "Wolves tend to be more aggressive than coyotes, especially when running in packs." When Dan passed the moose carcass, the three wolves saw him as an easy meal. All they needed to do was shadow him and wait for the opportunity to take him down.

The next morning, Dan told Kathy that three wolves had tracked him, not coyotes. That clarification failed to impress Kathy. His remark reinforced her concern that her husband was suffering from an overly active imagination, saying wolves and not coyotes wanted to eat him for a late-night snack. To humor Dan, she told him it must have been terrifying having a pack of wolves chase him. Anxious to end any further conversation about the alleged wolf attack, Kathy suggested they leave for the Dam Road.

While Kathy put on her snowmobile suit, Dan went to the sled shed to warm up the Polaris. Opening the cabin door, he stared at the foot of fresh snow that had fallen overnight. Dan shook his head, wondering if these snowstorms would ever end.

Kathy soon joined him. The two dragged the steel dogsled up to the machine, strapped on four plastic five-gallon gas cans, a short piece of plastic tubing to siphon the gas, and Dan's chainsaw, in case the wind had toppled a tree into the road during last night's storm. Kathy sat behind Dan, wrapping her arms tight around his chest so as not to fall off. Dan pushed the snowmobile's thumb throttle, and the underpowered Polaris grudgingly moved forward.

He slowed down when passing the bull moose, so Kathy could see the animal, now covered in a mantel of fresh snow. The wolves had rolled the now frozen carcass ninety degrees, so all four legs pointed skyward, creating a grotesque scene. Kathy stared at the dead moose, thinking what a protracted, painful death it must have been for the animal, being eaten alive by the pack of starving animals. Mangled moose parts were scattered about the carcass, evidence that fierce, strong killers had ripped the animal apart. The carnage made Dan's story of being chased by wolves more believable. She felt guilty for doubting him and gave Dan a hard squeeze as she peered into the woods, uneasy, wondering if the vicious predators would come out to protect their prize.

The ride out the Skyler Pond Road was fast and furious, plowing through deep drifts and bouncing over downed trees partially buried in the snow. Dan knew if the snowmobile lost momentum, it might bury itself in the dry snow, causing them to lose precious time digging out the machine. They pulled into the parking area twenty minutes later, stopping beside the car.

"My God! What a ride! My back is killing me. Did you have to go so fast?" she complained.

"Hey, if the machine had gotten stuck, your back would ache even worse from trying to pull it out."

"I doubt that," she muttered under her breath.

While Dan dug a hole in the snow to set the first gas can, Kathy snowshoed onto the Dam Road. Like Dan, she marveled at all the snow and debris littering the road. As far as she could see, were fallen trees and telephone poles snapped by the impact of large maple and beech trees crashing through the phone line. Her thoughts drifted back to all the times they had driven up the Dam Road, anxious to get to camp for the weekend. Turning onto the

Skyler Pond Road seemed like they were entering another world, able to leave the interstate, malls, and impatient motorists behind for a few days. Kathy peered back down the Dam Road. It looked so desolate. No one would be coming to rescue them.

Kathy took her cell phone from her down parka and called Hazel. A second later, the No Service message appeared on her screen.

When she returned, Dan had already threaded the plastic tubing into the throat of the fill pipe. Thinking the siphoning hose was well into the gasoline, he took a big pull, ready to spit out any gas he might suck into his mouth. Instead, all he managed to pull from the hose was a mouth full of fumes. He pushed the hose farther into the tank, and again he sucked out only air.

"Third time is a charm," he told Kathy, pushing the hose so far that he barely had enough slack to reach the five-gallon can once the gas started flowing. He gave another big pull, resulting in nothing but a lot of air mixed with a teaspoon or two of gasoline.

"What to hell is going on?" He asked aloud, getting up off his knees. Dan reached through the window and turned on the ignition. The dash lit up, but the gas gauge never moved. The tank was empty.

"Son of a bitch! Those bastards drained the gas tank!" Dan bellowed. "If I find out who did this, I swear, I'll kill them."

"Maybe we should make a run for it on the snowmobiles. Load the dogsled with what gas we have and go down the road until we find someone to help us. We can use the chainsaw to clear the way."

"We could do that, but we have no place to go. We can't live with strangers, and we certainly can't drive the snowmobiles to Westbrook and tell Hazel we're moving in with her and Tom. The only thing we can do right now is to stay put and wait until things improve. There's enough gas for a while longer. We'll just have to be careful how we use it."

Kathy couldn't argue with Dan's logic. As much as she wanted to jump on the snowmobile and head south, she knew it wasn't worth the risk.

"There's a two-gallon can of gas in the trunk. It was for the gas-powered chain saw, but I forgot to take it out when we returned from town. At least that will buy us an extra day or two using the generator."

Dan reached through the open car window and pulled the lever to release the trunk, but it didn't open. He went to the back of the car and tried to open the trunk by repeatedly pushing down on the lid.

"Damn it! The release mechanism must have been damaged when those creeps vandalized the car. To hell with it. We might as well go back to camp."

They slowly walked back to the snowmobile for the long quiet ride to camp, discouraged that they had no extra gasoline and no prospect that the Dam Road would be plowed anytime soon. Kathy and Dan would have to remain at their cabin until the Dam Road was plowed or someone came to their rescue.

That evening, Dan and Kathy revisited their initial plan to conserve fuel. Instead of running the generator twice a day, they would use it only in the evening for an hour to fill the water tank, run the lights, and listen to the latest updates from the emergency radio network.

At seven, Kathy turned on the radio. The Defense Department spokesperson reported that the military had made significant progress in distributing food and water to those hardest hit by the devastation. Additional food and medical supplies were beginning to arrive from the United Kingdom and most European countries.

It all sounded encouraging until the meteorologist for the National Weather Service read the extended weather outlook for the northeastern United States. The Climate and Weather Prediction Center's revised computer model predicted temperatures colder than initially expected. A full degree and a half colder, thanks to more dust and smoke in the atmosphere than the experts first estimated. What hadn't changed was the projected historic snowfall for New England as pulses of moisture from the Gulf of Mexico traveled along the permanently stalled jet stream. The climate experts saw no improvement in the atmosphere for the next ninety days.

Neither their food supply nor the remaining gasoline would last two months, no matter how frugal they tried to be. The revised weather forecast raised the possibility of starving to death if they remained stranded at Skyler Pond.

"This changes everything," he told Kathy. "I really thought that with a little luck, we could stretch the food and gas until this weird weather ended."

"Maybe the camp owners on the other side of the pond left some gas when they closed up their camps for the winter."

Dan sat up in his chair. "You're right. I bet they did. I remember Ed Collins telling me he and his friends like to come to the pond a couple times a winter to ice fish. I know he has a small generator. I can't imagine him trucking gas in to run it. I bet he left at least five gallons. There's likely food there as well: cereal, pasta, and the like. We can get that too."

"Wait a minute, Dan. That's stealing. Wasn't that why you were so mad about someone draining the gas out of our car? If you took Mr. Collins's gas and food, you would be no better than whoever stole our gas."

"This is different. Old man Collins won't be up here this winter with all the snow. Besides, I'll replace everything we take once we get to town. I'll even give him a little extra money as well. Hell, if he was stuck here instead of us, I'd welcome him to take whatever he needed to survive."

"I understand what you're saying, Dan, but breaking into a neighbor's camp to snoop around to see what to take still isn't right. At least wait a few days to see if the Dam Road gets plowed before you do it."

"Kathy, you know as well as I do that no one is going to plow the Dam Road. The state won't touch it until the storm's end—whenever that might be. I'd feel a lot better knowing the food and gas Collins has at his camp resided at ours."

"Okay, fine, I get it. So what's your plan?"

"I think I'll go over and check the cabin out tomorrow. Since there's no road to either of the two camps, I'll cross the pond."

"On the snowmobile? Maybe I should go with you in case you get stuck."

"No. I'll go alone. I'll be pulling the dogsled, so once I get going, it's going to be a fast trip across, so I don't get bogged down.

"Then pack a trail using your snowshoes, like you did to the car. That way, you won't have to worry about getting stuck."

"It's not worth it. The wind has blown all the loose snow to the pond's south end, and what's left is wind packed. If I snowshoed across, I'd barely make a track. What I don't want to do is break through the snow and get bogged down in any slush that might be sitting on the ice."

The next morning, Kathy watched Dan from the den window snake the snowmobile through the trees and onto the pond. In a typical winter, it would have been an idyllic winter scene. A winter postcard of fir boughs weighed down with gobs of snow as a steady snow fell in the calm of a late December morning, with Dan's red parka adding a splash of color.

Once on the ice, Dan walked back to the sled. He checked each bungee cord, ensuring his shovel and backpack were secured to the sled for the fast, bumpy ride across the pond. Before he sat back down on the snowmobile, a sharp wind barreled across the pond. In seconds, the gently falling snow was whipped sideways, obliterating the opposite shore. Still, Dan knew the general direction to the Collins cabin from the numerous times he and Kathy had passed it when trolling for brook trout. The snowmobile started forward and quickly disappeared into the blowing snow.

Kathy lifted the window to listen to the engine's whine. The din stopped and then started again. Dan must have stopped to readjust his course once he could see the outline of the shoreline, she presumed. A minute later, the engine noise stopped. Satisfied he had made it to the Collins camp, Kathy shut the window and sat by the woodstove to write an entry into the camp log.

The Collins cabin sat back from the water, barely visible to anyone boating by. Dan strapped on his snowshoes, slung his cedar backpack over his shoulders, grabbed his shovel, and struck out toward the cabin. The top of a large spruce tree rested on the snow-covered camp roof, snapped off twenty feet above the ground, another victim of the relentless wind that accompanied every squall. He ducked under the tree and trudged to the storage shed forty feet beyond the cabin. He reasoned that if Collins had any gas stored, it would be in the shed.

A padlock secured the shed, with a closed hasp covering the screws. Dan took a screwdriver from his pack and removed the two hinges, allowing the door to drop, and then shoveled away enough snow to slip into the building. Inside, he panned the floor with his flashlight looking for a can of gas. Dan quickly spotted three red containers in a corner beside Collins's ice fishing gear. He thought he had hit the jackpot. Fifteen gallons of gasoline would carry them another two weeks. He lifted each can. The first felt full. However, the other two were empty.

Satisfied with the one full five-gallon can, he lugged it back to the main cabin and shoveled enough snow away from the door to expose the doorknob. Unlike the storage building's entrance, this door had concealed hinges. About to ram the door with his shoulder, Dan noticed a plaque nailed to the cedar shingles of two running deer, with the corny caption, "Welcome to Dear Camp." He peeked behind the plaque, and as he had suspected, the cabin key hung on a nail. He smiled, thinking how most camp owners hid the spare key behind a welcome sign, under the doormat, or in a magnetic key holder under the propane tank lid. The most obvious places a would-be robber would think to look. Dan slipped the key into the lock and turned the knob. The door dragged across the pine floor, depressed by the roof's snow load. Inside, he scanned the cabin's one room, thinking how stark a vacant cabin looked in the winter. The lack of day-to-day clutter, the windows cloaked by frost, and the furniture covered with sheets made the Collins cabin appear abandoned. Not the imagined picture of a cozy, welcoming cabin with a crackling fire and doors opening and closing as people came and went, doing what they do at camp during the other times of the year.

There were two cabinets in the kitchen, one on either side of the chipped porcelain sink. A hodgepodge of dishes and drinking glasses filled the first cabinet. The other cupboard held what Dan was looking for: a half-full box of cornflakes, two one-pound packages of spaghetti, and a jar of frozen peanut butter. Dan had hoped for more, but Ed, a widower, had no reason for a large food stockpile. As he turned to leave, Dan noticed a small cone-shaped pile of snow in the middle of the cabin floor. Above the snow, two large limbs from the fallen tree protruded through the busted roof boards. He told himself that when they did escape Skyler Pond, he would contact Ed to let him know he had a problem and offer to help repair the roof next summer—if there was a summer.

Dan thought about checking out the cabin about a quarter-mile down the shore, but decided to wait and make a second trip. Chilled by cold sweat after busting a path through the deep drifts to look for the gasoline, he was anxious to return to the cabin and sit by the fire. The snow had stopped, and with the improved visibility, Dan could see their cabin nestled among the pine and spruce on the opposite shore. A three-minute snowmobile ride and he'd be home. Or so he thought.

Halfway across the pond, the snow turned from a solid white to a light gray, a sure sign there was water lurking below the surface. The sheer weight of the deep snowpack had depressed the ice enough that water had seeped up through cracks in the ice and saturated the overlying snow. The track he had made earlier that morning had become soft and slushy. As Dan glanced left and right to see if he could go around the wet area, he felt the Polaris slipping into the slush before it regained purchase. Dan was confident that the ice under the slush was solid; his fear was sinking into the mush and becoming hopelessly mired in the middle of Skyler Pond.

Dan hadn't noticed the discolored area when he crossed the pond two hours earlier. Then he remembered: it was a whiteout when he left camp, and he was so intent on keeping the snowmobile in line with the Collins camp that he missed the telltale signs of the wet snow.

Dan punched the throttle and held the handlebars with a steel grip, hoping he didn't break through the thin veneer of dry snow and slip into the watery soup.

Inside the cabin, Kathy heard the high-pitched whine of the snowmobile speeding across the pond. She watched Dan through the den window, still a quarter mile from shore. The snowmobile looked incredibly small, flying across a sea of white, its heavy metal skis shooting spray into the air. Behind the snowmobile, a rooster tail of heavy wet snow curled up from the track, filling the dogsled's plywood deck.

Dan felt the snowmobile begin to slow. Unknown to him, the snow thrown up by the spinning track added more weight to the sled than the Polaris could pull. A hundred feet ahead, the snow was white. Dan would be out of the slush and safely back on dry snow if the snowmobile made it that far.

Only fifty feet left, and the machine slowed to a crawl. Dan jumped off the seat and pushed on the handlebars while keeping the throttle wide open. Removing the weight helped, but only slightly.

He cursed and pleaded with the struggling snowmobile. "Go, you son of a bitch. Go! Don't stop here! Please, just a few more feet, just another twenty feet."

The machine half cooperated. The skis made it onto the drier snow, but the rest of the snowmobile and sled came to a halt in the slush. Dan stood beside the snowmobile in the frigid knee-deep water assessing the situation. Kathy had seen the process play out. Knowing Dan was hopelessly mired, she put on her snowshoes and went to help. Halfway to the stuck snowmobile, she called to him.

"Are you okay?" she yelled, trying to keep her balance, hurrying as fast as she could through the soft snow.

"I'm fine. I can't say as much for this piece of shit," Dan replied, kicking the cowling with his foot.

"Do you think the two of us can pull it out?"

"Not with the sled attached," Dan said, discouraged by the situation.

"So unhook the sled."

Dan went to the back of the machine and pulled the linchpin. He grabbed a strap that he kept for such situations from the snowmobile's storage compartment and attached it to the tip of each ski. Then he tied a rope to the center of the harness for Kathy to hold on to.

"Okay. We'll give it a try. Tighten the rope. When I give the word, pull but don't overdo it and hurt your back. If it does come free, get out of the way fast, or you'll get run over."

Dan started the engine and braced his feet against the underlying ice. "Are you ready?"

Kathy nodded, keeping the rope taut, waiting for Dan's command to pull. Dan pushed on the handlebars and, at the same time, gave the snowmobile enough gas to hold tension on the track. Too much throttle and the track would spin, ending any chance of freeing the machine from the slush. The obstinate snowmobile inched forward. He gave it a little more gas, and the snowmobile crawled a few more inches toward the shore.

"Pull harder and be ready to get out of the way!" he hollered to Kathy while keeping an eye on the snowmobile track.

"I'm pulling as hard as I can!"

Kathy kept tension on the rope and slowly backed up as the snowmobile tried to extricate itself from the mire. Suddenly, the track gained traction on the drier snow and bolted forward, leaving Dan standing in the water. Kathy dropped the rope and jumped off to the side, just missing being hit by one of the skis.

The satisfaction of freeing the snowmobile was short-lived. Before they could celebrate, the dogsled needed to be retrieved as well. This time, things didn't go so well. Even after shoveling the heavy slush off the deck of the sled and removing the five gallons of gas, they could not budge the dogsled. It was as if an invisible force under the ice refused to let go of the sled.

"Screw it! We'll leave it. No sense blowing out a back pulling on the damn thing."

"You can't just leave it. We have to get it back to camp. Let's get more rope and use the come-along to get it out."

"That won't work. We're about five or six hundred feet from shore. I might have a hundred fifty feet of rope, tops."

Dan attempted to shovel the slush from under the steel sled's plywood bottom, hoping to break the dogsled from the suction of the slush. Then he hit upon an idea of how to do it.

"We'll let the slush freeze for a day or two. Then I'll use the ice chisel to free the runners," he said to Kathy, who was not totally convinced his scheme would work.

"Now let's get back inside before we freeze to death," Dan said, heading toward the cabin.

Back at the Bartlett homestead, the daily turmoil persisted. There seemed to be one blowout after another. Each accused the other of letting the generator run out of gas. Dick claimed that Josh intentionally ran over his daughter's cat with the snowmobile. Frankie accused Dick of sneaking into his house and stealing his supply of freshly wrapped cigarettes while he was outside feeding his beagles. Although in the case of the cigarettes, Frankie later found them on the floor, wedged between the counter and the propane stove, apparently landing there after being knocked off by the mountain of kitchen counter clutter.

The Bartletts weren't the kind of people who let outside events dictate how they lived their lives. However, these were not ordinary times. It wasn't the country being at war that concerned them. The three brothers had no doubt that eventually, the good old U.S. of A. would annihilate every one of those rice-propelled commies, as Frankie called them, a reference to his contempt for the North Koreans and every other person of Asian descent. The immediate concern was the eight feet of snow that stopped them from working in the woods and earning money to go to town to buy beer and cigarettes. There was even an occasional hint of concern about having enough food to last until the state plowed the road and they could get to the store.

Two weeks after their late-night raid on Dan's car, Dick and Josh were having a beer in Frankie's cluttered workshop, watching their brother attempt to weld the broken frame on Josh's oldest son's snowmobile.

"So, Frankie, when do you think the snow will end?" Josh asked his brother.

"How to hell do I know? Who do you think I am, the weatherman?" Frankie told him, trying to clamp the two parts needing welding.

"Well, I just thought, seeing you're so goddamn smart about everything else on the planet, you'd know when this goddamn snow would stop. Seems to me that would be an easy question for a man of your intellect to answer," Josh answered.

"Keep it up, Josh, you asshole. If you were half-smart, you would know how to weld George's sled instead of acting like the complete nitwit you are. Now get your ass over here and pass me my leads," Frankie ordered, dropping his face shield and beginning to weld.

While the three brothers argued, Josh's dog got up from his spot next to the woodstove and stood at the shed door, whining to go outside. Everyone was so engrossed in hurling insults that no one noticed Stalin until the dog approached the acetylene tank and started lifting its leg.

"No!" Josh yelled, grabbing Stalin by the collar and ushering the dog out the door and into the cold night air.

"If that dog pisses in my workshop, it will be the last leak he ever takes," Frankie told Josh, not taking his eyes off the weld.

A few minutes later, Stalin scratched at the entrance to be let back in, and he was soon back on his blanket, fast asleep.

"If you two clowns are through having a lover's spat, I have something serious to discuss," Dick said, tossing the empty beer bottle into the trash can.

"What's on your mind, Dicky boy? Got some kind of rash on the pecker you want to talk about?" Frankie shot back as he struck another arc with his stick welder, drawing a bead across the two pieces of broken metal.

"No. But you'll be the first to know if I do. Anyway, I don't know about you two, but Darlene and me are running pretty tight on supplies. I don't mean we're going to starve or anything like that, but both of us and the kids are getting sick and tired of rabbit pie and moose burgers, and that's almost gone. About the only other things we've got left are a half dozen cans of soup and a shitload of spaghetti."

"Jesus, Dick, you are one hell of a survivalist. Do you remember why the three of us stayed here after the old man died? Let me remind you. We were all of like minds, wanting to live by our wits and avoid all the other millions of assholes in this country who answer to everyone else except themselves. Now you're bellyaching that you don't have any greens to eat, and your orange supply is exhausted. Jesus, Dick, you're turning into one big-city crybaby. We do what we've always done. We shoot a deer or a moose when we need meat and go fishing when we want fish to eat. Sure, if we go to town and have enough money after buying gas, we buy stuff, but we don't depend on it."

"Lighten up, Frankie. Dick's right. The wife and I are getting low on food too. He's only saying if we're going to be stuck here for God knows how long, we need more to eat than moose, deer, and squirrel."

"Well, boys, it's funny that Beatrice and me don't have any problem with our food supply. Do you suppose it has to do with her canning twice as much as Darlene and Wendy?"

"That's bullshit, and you know it, Frankie!" Dick shot back. "Everything from that friggin' garden last summer we divided into thirds. If you have more canned goods than Josh and me, then it's because you haven't been eating nothing but meat. No wonder you keep saying you haven't shit for a week. You know what I really think, Frankie?"

"No, Dick, why don't you tell me."

"I don't think you have any more food left than me or Josh does. I think you want us to believe you're the great white hunter, and the leader of the pack doesn't want to admit he's no better off than us."

Before Frankie could retaliate, Josh stepped in. "Look, I don't give a sweet shit how much food Frankie has or hasn't got stockpiled. All I know is Wendy and me are getting low, and I've got to do something about it."

"So what's your plan, Josh?" Frankie asked, knowing his brother seldom thought beyond his next meal.

"I think we need to check out some camps north of here. I bet the owners left enough food when they closed up camp this fall to keep us going for months."

"Josh, I've got to hand it to you. That is one of the most brilliant ideas that ever came out of your mouth."

"Gee, thanks, Frankie. I'll see if I can top it sometime."

Over the years, the Bartletts had made out handsomely breaking into unoccupied camps around the remote ponds near the Canadian border. The generator that powered the three trailers had been one of their better finds. Frankie had told his brothers it would cost four thousand dollars to buy one of that quality. Frankie never considered taking what they wanted as stealing but rather as being on permanent loan to the family.

Frankie lowered the repaired snowmobile onto the concrete floor, opened the workshop door, and grabbed a beer bottle out of the snow. He placed the edge of the cap against the steel workbench and gave the bottle a quick downward snap, sending the bottle cap flying toward Dick. Frankie downed half the beer and then sat on the snowmobile, staring at the nude photo of Miss July hanging over the workbench. Dick and Josh watched their brother, waiting to hear his plan. Finally, he gulped down the rest of his Pabst.

"Okay, this is what we're going to do. Tomorrow we'll take a ride into Boundary Pond and check out the cabins. There are four camps on the east side of the pond and one on either side of the outlet. On the way back, if we've got time and aren't loaded down with too many goodies, we'll run into Skyler Pond and see what we can find."

"Isn't that a little risky, Frankie? We know there's someone in there. We stole his gas, for Christ's sake. He would see us," Dick said.

"Dickie, don't you think I know that? I was with you when we borrowed the gas, remember? Look, I know the two old farts that own the two camps on the east shore of Skyler Pond. I ran into them once rabbit hunting. That leaves the one camp on the west side of the pond, which has to be the asshole that owns the car. But if it makes you feel better, we'll take the Crossover Road when we leave Boundary Pond. About a mile out, an old haul road strikes off to the west that dies just behind those two camps. All we have to do is snowmobile a couple hundred yards through the woods, and we're there. Whoever that person is across the pond won't have a clue as to what's going on. We'll take three machines and the two dogsleds. If I'm right, we'll need both sleds to haul everything back to the Haven."

Boundary Pond was six miles north of the Black Falls Dam and one mile from the Canadian border. To reach the pond, they needed to travel north on the Dam Road, past the Skyler Pond Road, and then follow a paper company road to a spur leading to Boundary Pond, a thirty-mile trip by snow sled.

The Bartlett boys were teenagers when their father decided they were old enough to learn to get what they wanted without having to work for it. Boundary Pond was where the three received their initiation into thievery. After the elder Bartlett died, the family continued to make forays to other ponds, doing quite well at the expense of the waterfront property owners.

Because the ponds were remote, camp owners expected their properties to be broken into from time to time. To avoid having their toys stolen, most camp owners shuttled outboard motors, boats, and other valuables back and forth from home. However, a few camp owners felt they could outfox thieves by hiding their valuables where no one could find them. Unfortunately, most of them never found the perfect hiding place.

The thirty miles to Boundary Pond typically took about an hour by snowmobile, but dozens of downed trees needed to be cut wide enough for the snowmobiles to squeeze through. Two and a half hours after leaving Bartlett Haven, the three machines pulled onto Boundary Pond.

"We'll work our way around the pond, hitting each camp as we go," Frankie told the others. "Dick, you check out all the outbuildings. Josh and I will go into the camps and take a look around. If you find any gas, grab it. I don't care if it's a two-gallon can or a five. We can use it all. Let's go!" Frankie punched the throttle and took off toward the first camp, with Josh and Dick close behind.

Two hours later, with the sleds loaded with loot, they were ready to leave Boundary Pond.

"That's it, boys, time to head back to the ranch. I think we did good, real good. It appears to me we got us nearly thirty gallons of gasoline and five totes of grub, not to mention the two gallons of Old Grand-Dad," Frankie told the others, as pleased at finding the whiskey as the food.

Frankie made an abrupt stop rounding the last point of land before cutting across the pond to where they came onto the ice. Unable to brake in time, Josh bumped the back of Frankie's snowmobile. Under different circumstances, Frankie would have blown a gasket and berated Josh for hitting him. However, Frankie was so engrossed in what he was looking at that he barely felt the collision.

"Look!" was all he could say, pointing toward shore.

"Jesus Christ, where did that come from?" Dick asked.

Sitting high on the point of land nestled among the pine was the largest, fanciest log cabin the brothers had ever seen.

"Man, I knew some people built fancy places, but I always figured it was on Sebago Lake or the coast, not up here in the middle of nowhere," Dick said, staring at the expansive glass front of the house.

"You know what this means?" Frankie asked.

"Yeah, some son of a bitch has a shitload of money to build a place like that," Josh answered.

"That too. It also means we just hit the jackpot. I bet that place is full of stuff we can use." Frankie squared up to the steep bank and blasted his way to the top.

Frankie picked up a stick of firewood from the neatly stacked tier of wood next to the entry door and busted the glass out of the entry door. Careful not to cut his arm on the jagged pieces, he reached through the opening and unlocked the door. Inside, they wandered room to room, amazed at what some people called a camp.

"Do you think whoever owns this place would be interested in an even swap for our palace?" Josh said.

"Maybe. But before we make the offer, we need to spend a night or two here, just to be sure it's a fair trade," Frankie answered.

"What do you mean by that?" Dick asked.

"I'm saying it's going to be dark in a couple of hours, so why not spend the night here and head back in the morning."

"Frankie, what's the use of staying? We can't fit anything more on the sleds," Josh complained.

"Because I said so, that's why, Josh. Who knows what we might find hidden in this place. If we find stuff we want and can't fit on the sleds, we'll pile it in the living room and come back in a day or two to get it. Maybe we'll even take a ride into Skyler Pond on the same trip."

Josh and Dick knew there was nothing gained in arguing with their brother. They could only grumble and accept that they would spend the night at Boundary Pond and not at home with their families.

"Okay. But if we're spending the night here, we need heat. I'll start a fire in the fireplace," Dick said, heading toward the door to bring in an armload of firewood.

"Screw the wood fire! Just turn on the propane furnace. The thermostat is on the wall behind you. Turn it up to eighty. We're not paying the fuel bill. If we're going to live in a castle, then we might as well act like royalty," Frankie said, giving one of his toothless grins.

While waiting for the cabin to warm up, the three split up to search for anything of value. As Frankie and Josh checked out the kitchen, Dick went into the cellar. A short time later, he yelled for someone to turn on a light.

Josh reached for the wall switch to the kitchen ceiling light. "We've got lights!" He hollered down to Dick.

Dick had stumbled upon the battery room for the camp's solar system. Throwing the main breaker sent power throughout the cabin. They had no idea how long the battery reserve would last, but for now, it was like home, only better.

Soon the cabin had warmed enough to take off their winter coats, and they turned their attention to the variety of whiskeys in the well-stocked liquor cabinet. As soon as the first fifth disappeared, they opened a second. All the while, their voices became louder until they were practically yelling over one another.

Frankie had been right about the cabin holding the mother lode. There was more of an assortment of food than in a corner grocery store. Aside from the needed provisions, Josh discovered two shotguns and a .357 revolver still in its original box hidden in the back corner of a bedroom closet. High-end weapons, not the mass-produced Winchester and Remington firearms the Bartletts' owned.

"Boys, this has to be the best haul we have ever made. Each of them Italian over and under shotguns has to be worth a couple of thousand. And I know damn well this .357 Ruger Redhawk will bring a grand downstate," Frankie told the others, spinning the cylinder of the never-fired handgun.

"That may be, Frankie, but who in the hell is going to buy them with this freakish amount of snow? People can't even get to the grocery store, let alone drive around the country to look at a gun. Not only that, but as far as we know, we're still at war with the North Korean commies. Half the people in the country might be dead already, for all we know," Dick reminded Frankie.

"That's precisely why the guns are so valuable—because there *is* ten feet of snow and because we *are* in some kind of nuclear war. Dick, people need weapons to survive. If they can't get food, they get desperate, and when they're desperate, they'll take from those that have. This little Redhawk is just the persuader they need to keep their family from starving to death."

"You mean like we're doing, Frankie?" Josh interjected.

Frankie glared at Josh. "Yes, Josh, people like us. Only we're survivors, not victims. Remember that."

"Like I was saying before shithead here interrupted me, there's likely anarchy in the cities; no food to be had, no power, maybe even no water. Whether it's because of ten feet of snow shutting every-thing down or a bunch of nukes going off, it doesn't matter. The point is, people need weapons to defend their families and their property. Why, I bet when we do get to Kingston, we'll have people begging us to sell them these weapons. And the longer it is before we can get to town, the more desperate they'll be for a gun and the more willing they'll be to pay the price we ask. Boys, we'll have 'em right by the short hairs."

The next morning, the brothers went from room to room, grabbing anything that might have value. Frankie would offer what they didn't want or need to his fence in Portland once the weather straightened out. They tossed what they collected in a pile on the living room floor, planning to return in a few days with empty sleds to shuttle the swag back to the Haven. The exception was the three weapons. No way Frankie was leaving them behind. He carefully wrapped each in a blanket and secured them to one of the dogsleds.

Frankie and Dick sat on their idling snowmobiles, waiting for Josh. Finally, he appeared.

"What to hell were you doing in there? You're worse than an old woman when it comes to getting going in the morning," Frankie complained.

"I turned off the furnace and made one final walk around to see if we overlooked anything."

"Go back in there and turn that friggin' furnace back on! I don't want to have to come back to a cold cabin," Frankie commanded.

Once Josh reappeared, they were ready to leave. As usual, Frankie led the way. He went about twenty feet, stopped, and walked back to speak to the others.

"Did either of you check out that storage shed?" he asked, pointing to the nearby log-sided building.

Dick and Josh shook their heads.

"Well, don't you think it might be a good idea if we did? Come on. We'll do it now."

Fifty feet behind the main cabin sat a storage building the size of a small barn, with windowless roll-up doors on both ends. The snow reached the top of the side entrance door. The only way inside was through the building's one window. Frankie busted out the pane with the same hammer he had used to break into Dan's car two weeks earlier. He ordered Josh to crawl through the narrow opening and tell them what he found. Josh dropped to the cement floor with a light thud.

"It's darker than the inside of a boot in here," Josh whined.

"See if there is a light switch. I imagine Money Bags had the building wired for electricity off the solar system," Frankie hollered through the broken window.

The inside of the building lit up like a Christmas tree. "What'd I tell you? Old Frankie knows how rich people operate. They want all the conveniences of New York City or where in hell this dude is from, and they've got the money to do it."

"Frankie! You're not going to believe this, but there are two snowmobiles in here, and they look brand new."

"Really. Anything else?"

"Yes. Five gas cans, and they're all full."

"Okay. We need to get in to get the gas. Look for a snow shovel so we can start digging out the overhead door."

"Here," Josh said, passing two shovels through the opening.

"While Dick and I shovel, take a closer look at the snow machines and tell me the make. Also, look around to see if Money Bags left the keys to the ignitions hanging on a nail near the door."

"Frankie, they're in the ignition."

"Now ain't that convenient. Money Bags shouldn't have done that. Some local lowlife might come along and steal them."

After much shoveling, Dick and Frankie had cleared enough snow away from the overhead door so that Josh could raise it from the inside.

"Well, lookie there, those are two fine-looking snowmobiles," Frankie said, sliding down the massive mound of snow onto the concrete floor.

Frankie studied the machines. "These are mountain sleds. Look at the size of the paddles on those tracks! You could climb Everest with one of these things." He sat on one of the machines and turned the key. The big Arctic Cat sprang to life. "Four-stroke too. I've always been concerned about saving the environment. Here's the chance to ditch our overripe, gas-guzzling two-strokes and save us gas and the planet at the same time. Boys, we need to trade two of our old clunkers for these two fancy machines."

At first, Frankie was going to hook the two dogsleds to the new machines and leave the old snowmobiles where they sat. Then he had second thoughts. It would be nearly impossible to tie the snowmobiles back to the Bartletts, as none were registered with the state. However, Frankie knew if the local warden eventually showed up to investigate the theft, he might recognize them as belonging to the family, which could mean big trouble for the clan. Instead, Frankie ordered Josh and Dick to drive their machines to the far end of Boundary Pond, ride them into the woods, and abandon them. He would follow along on one of the new machines, and all three would squeeze onto the long track for the ride back to the cabin.

After a minor blowout over which brother would ride the other new snowmobile, they left Boundary Pond with their treasures. Josh came out on the stick's short end as usual and continued riding his outclassed 340 Polaris. Their acquisition included two new snowmobiles, three valuable firearms, a significant gasoline supply, and enough food to last the three families several weeks. As well as the swag that remained at the cabin to be picked up later.

Meanwhile, life at Skyler Pond had settled into the same monotonous routine. Each morning Dan rose before dawn and slipped out of the bedroom, careful not to wake Kathy. He'd check the outside thermometer and then open the entry door to see how much snow had fallen during the night. He'd be pleasantly surprised if less than four inches had accumulated on the deck. Rarely was Dan surprised. Most mornings, he'd confront six or more inches of fresh wind-driven snow piled against the cabin.

Next he'd turn his attention to the woodstove, stirring the near-dead coals and adding several pieces of kindling to bring the flames back to life. Dan always filled the wood box before dark, haunted by the memories of the episode with the wolves. He still wondered if the animals' strange behavior that night was a onetime occurrence, provoked by the draw to the moose carcass, or something more sinister, perhaps their sensing the vulnerability of a person walking through their domain after dark.

Kathy had her own morning routine. Once drawn from the bedroom by the aroma

of freshly brewed coffee, she'd check the temperature and open the outside door to see how

much new snow had fallen overnight, the same as Dan had done an hour earlier. Habitually, Kathy would pour her coffee, then walk over to the wall phone and lift the receiver, hoping to hear a dial tone but never expecting one. She'd then sit in the chair next to Dan, placing her coffee on the stand between the two recliners, and silently wait for the room to brighten so she could write in her journal.

The weather also had its own daily routine: a constant overcast with calm winds and temperatures in the mid-teens, typical winter temperatures for the western Maine mountains. At times, the odd weather that had held the Simmons captive for nearly two months seemed to improve. The clouds would thin to reveal the sun's white halo, bright enough to cast faint gray shadows across the wintry wooded landscape. Then, as quickly as the sky had brightened, the clouds would thicken and start snowing. Giant flakes floating gently to the ground in the calm wintry air, the kind of snow that flies from a person's hand with a single puff. However, the idyllic winter scene would be short-lived.

At least once a day, something ominous stirred deep in the woods. It started as a barely audible rumble, like a freight train barreling around a distant bend. At first, tree branches would dance to the rhythm of the freshening wind. Seconds later, the runaway whirlwind would tear down the mountain toward Skyler Pond, a tempest on a mission. The wind would stiffen to a gale, tree branches snapping under the stress of the tormenting squall. What a few minutes earlier had been a placid winter scene turned into a raging blizzard. As the wind's velocity exploded, temperatures plummeted, often twenty-five degrees in mere minutes. A pleasant twenty-degree winter day would quickly disintegrate into a bone-chilling five below zero.

The phantom storms erupted without warning and offered no clues as to when they would end. Whiteout conditions could last a half hour or drag on for half a day. The only constant was that another violent storm would happen. Afraid of being caught in the teeth of a freak microburst of blowing snow and plummeting temperatures and unable to find their way back to the cabin, Kathy and Dan stayed close to home.

Kathy had kept a camp journal for twenty-five years, each entry packed with the family's adventures at Skyler Pond since Hazel was five years old. Dan joked that every minute of their life at the pond was accounted for in that journal. After seven weeks stranded at Skyler Pond, her entries had trailed off to only a few lines consisting of the most basic information, much like an engineer's field notes.

7 am. Minus eight, cloudy. No wind. About seven inches of snow fell overnight. Today we need to fill the water tank and do laundry. We'll have wet clothes hanging over every chair and from every rafter.

2 pm. Another squall, horrific winds. A falling limb from the big sugar maple next to the cabin hit one of the apple trees Dan and Hazel planted when she was ten. We'll have to cut it up for firewood in the spring—if there is a spring.

Each journal entry ended with the same thought:

I do hope Hazel and Tom are okay. It will be so nice to see them again.

Like Kathy's diary entries, their conversations had also dwindled. Both were weary of talking about when the snow would stop, how the food supply was holding out, and how long the generator would run with the remaining gasoline. Their lives had spiraled downward to the point that their existence revolved around staying warm, pumping water, and shoveling snow. The monotony of the endless cloudy days of snow and windstorms had worn them down to the point of despair. The strain was especially tough on Kathy. Unwillingly sequestered in their twenty-four-by-twenty-eight-foot cabin, she slipped into a state of melancholy.

"Dan, I just went through the camp log. We haven't seen the sun for seven weeks."

"Only seven weeks? It feels like seven months," Dan said, pushing back in the recliner with his eyes closed.

"Do you know what I miss the most, other than not seeing Hazel?"

"What would that be?"

"I miss not seeing the blue sky, the shadows of trees dancing back and forth in the yard, rocked by a soft, gentle breeze, and the butterflies flying from one flower to the next in our garden. I miss it all," she said wistfully, staring out the living room window. "I would give anything to look up and see blue if only for a day, just to know there is hope that things will get better."

Dan flipped the handle on the recliner and sat up straight, looking at Kathy. "You'll see the sun again. Everything will go back to the way it used to be. It will just take a while. I bet this crazy weather will straighten itself out in time to plant the window boxes with the marigolds and geraniums, just like you always do."

"Do you really think so, Dan? Or are you just telling me that so that I'll keep my spirits up?"

"No. It's going to happen. All that dust in the atmosphere has to settle out first. Once that happens, the sun will appear, the days will turn warmer, and all the snow will melt. Everything we've gone through will be just a distant memory, although, I will admit, an unpleasant one."

"I hope you're right, Dan. Do you want to hear what else bothers me? You'll probably think it's foolish, but I think about it a lot," she said, staring at a chickadee sitting on the mound of snow covering the window feeder.

"Tell me. I'm listening. I promise I won't laugh."

"I think about all the wildlife, like that bird at the feeder, and how this senseless war has messed up their world as well as our own. Collateral damage is what military types call it. The sad part is that they struggle to go about their business of living, not having a clue about what humankind has done to the planet. It's their world as well as ours, you know."

"Maybe it's best they can't understand what has happened. Sometimes I wish I didn't know what a mess we've made of things."

"You're probably right. They shouldn't know. If they did, every animal in the forest would cry," Kathy said, still staring at the lone chickadee.

"Well, enough of that. Right now, we can only make sure we survive until spring to see the sun again. Let's have breakfast. What will it be, oatmeal or oatmeal?"

Kathy lightened up. "Make mine oatmeal, please," she said, watching the chickadee fly into the woods.

After breakfast, Kathy announced that she was going outside to clear the snow off the deck.

"Have at it. To tell you the truth, I'm sick of all the shoveling. I'd like to get up one morning and look outside and see that it hadn't snowed one inch during the night. But before you go outside, sit down for a minute. I need to tell you what I've been thinking."

What now? Kathy thought to herself. It must be serious if she had to sit down to hear what Dan had to say. "Okay. What is it?" she asked, almost dreading hearing what scheme Dan had devised.

"You know, there is still another cabin across the pond that we haven't checked."

Kathy sensed the direction Dan was headed in. "You aren't thinking about snowmobiling across the pond to see what might be there that we can use, are you?" Without giving Dan a chance to respond, she continued. "You know what happened the last time you crossed the pond. If that snowmobile had become mired twenty feet farther back from where it did, it would still be there. As it was, it took you two hours to chisel the sled out of the ice. If you tried that again, you could end up stuck in the slush in the middle of the pond. Then where would we be? We'd never get it to shore. We need that snowmobile to get us out of here once this snow ends and the road's plowed."

"Hold on. I wasn't thinking of going across the pond. I'd pull the toboggan along the shore wearing my snowshoes. That way, I'd stay on top of the snow and out of the soup."

"God. That would take you forever, following the shoreline. You could do all that walking and not even find a frozen can of beans."

"True. Or I could find five pounds of frozen lobster meat or a thick porterhouse steak," Dan said, trying to calm things down. "Look, all I'm saying is that we could use more gas and food. No, that's not true. We *need* more gas and food to make it until this friggin' weather changes."

As much as Kathy didn't want her husband to attempt to walk to the far side of the pond, she secretly relished the opportunity to have a few hours to herself. They had been together constantly for nearly two months. Before the strange weather started, the cabin had been adequate for two people. Now the home felt like an oversize dollhouse that was shrinking by the day. They had become inmates inside a log-walled prison, and along with the isolation, so came the common irritability.

Each night, after Dan turned the generator off and went into the bedroom, Kathy sat in the dark, wearing a headlamp writing to Hazel, an evening ritual since becoming snowbound. She didn't intend to mail the letters; they simply expressed her inner feelings about being trapped at the Skyler Pond cabin. And if fate worked against them, the letters would provide a chronology of what she and Dan had gone through while being isolated at Skyler Pond.

At first, her writings offered hope that eventually the snow would melt and they would be reunited with Hazel and Tom. However, as the days and weeks dragged on, the tone of the letters became less optimistic, to the point where she began to doubt if either of them would survive the nightmare. Kathy worried that they both would starve before they escaped their wintry prison.

No matter how depressing her writings became, each one ended the same. She told Hazel how much she loved her and longed to see her again. And that if they didn't survive, she should stay strong, go on with her own life, and always remember Dan and her as they were before the world fell apart. When she was finished, she'd quietly creep into the bedroom and add the letter to the others hidden beneath her sweaters in the bottom bureau drawer, away from prying eyes.

Kathy was torn between taking a chance to go for help and staying at the cabin, as Dan wanted to wait for the horrible weather to end. If they left, at least they'd be attempting to save themselves rather than just remaining at camp, staring out the window and hoping for the best. What held her back from pressing Dan to leave Skyler Pond came from a reoccurring nightmare. Kathy dreamed a ferocious snowstorm overtook them, leaving them to flounder helplessly in the waist-deep snow before the bitter cold took its toll. She visualized Dan and her dying in each other's arms, their backs pressed against a large rock outcrop. Her spirit watched as a ravenous pack of wolves tore their dead bodies apart. As horrific as the gory scene was, the scariest part of the nightmare was Hazel not knowing what had happened to her parents. Kathy imagined that rabbit hunters discovered their remains years later after one of their beagles returned carrying a bleached white bone: her leg bone.

"Dan, I still don't think you should do this," Kathy told him as he swung his backpack over his shoulder, about to leave for the east side of the pond. "I have a feeling something will happen while you're away."

"Don't worry, Kathy. I'll be fine. I'll follow the camp road to where it leaves the lake and get on the ice there. I'll never be more than fifty feet from shore the whole time I'm gone. Plus, I have the two-way radio. If I get into trouble, I'll call you. Just keep your receiver on channel one and we'll stay in contact."

"Big deal. So you get into trouble and call me. What do you expect me to do if you're hurt; walk five miles looking for you and then carry you back to the cabin?"

"Jesus! Nothing will happen to me for the umpteenth time," Dan shot back, annoyed with Kathy's needless worrying.

"All right. I'll shut up about it. But promise me just one thing, Dan."

"What?"

"Call me when you reach the cabin. Then I'll know you haven't broken through the ice and drowned."

"Okay. Now I've got to get going, or I'll never be back before dark. By the way, what's for supper?" Dan asked, trying to make light of his daylong trek.

"Don't worry about what's for supper. Just show up to eat it," Kathy said, giving her husband a long tight hug.

She stepped onto the deck, watching Dan adjust his snowshoe bindings, and then passed him the plastic sled's rope. Dan traveled about fifty feet when he glanced back toward the cabin to see Kathy watching him. He couldn't resist tormenting her one more time. "Let's have a steak on the grill!" He yelled, sporting a wide grin. Kathy shook her head and waved him off.

The day before Dan's trip to check out the cabin on Skyler Pond, Frankie, Dick, and Josh returned to Boundary Pond to claim the booty they had left behind. The brothers could have easily returned home to their families the same day. However, part of Frankie's secret master plan was to spend the night at the lakeside cabin, the perfect opportunity to get away from Beatrice and enjoy another evening sampling the variety of spirits in the owner's liquor cabinet.

"Now, boys, tell me I had a great idea to leave the heat on when we left last time. Why it would be as cold in here as a witch's broom if we hadn't," Frankie said, locking the leather recliner back in the most horizontal position. He continued, "You see, that's an example of why I'm the leader of this pack and not one of you boneheads. The captain always has to be looking ahead, you know, to keep the ship off the rocks."

Frankie held his empty tumbler out. "Dick, be a good host and fill my glass with more J&B, would you? Oh, and break off one of those icicles hanging from the entryway eave. A good whisky always goes down smoother with a little ice."

"Sure, Frankie, anything you say. Do you want me to turn the blanket down for you as well, your most royal pain in the ass?"

"Whoa there, young feller. Sounds like junior has some kind of grievance with management. Care to explain to Josh and me what's troubling you, boy?"

"I'll tell you what's troubling me. You! You and your pompous attitude."

"Pompous? Where did you ever come up with such a fancy word? Have you been watching *Jeopardy* again?"

"That is exactly what I mean, Frankie. You can't talk to me or Josh without putting us down. You think we're your friggin' lackeys, and all you have to do is tell us to jump, and we're going to ask you how high. Well, you're not King Frankie. You're a backwoods hick, just like Josh and me. And I'm telling you now, you keep up your shit, and you'll live to regret it."

"Why, Dick, I never knew you were so sensitive."

"I'm warning you, Frankie, keep it up," Dick said, glaring at his older brother.

"Josh, you feel the same as Dick?"

"Yeah, Frankie, I feel the same way, and so does Wendy. She even thinks we should leave the Haven and find a place where we can live by ourselves."

"You mean where you can get away from me?" Frankie said, looking at Dick and Josh.

"Yeah, that's what I'm saying," Josh answered, staring at his drink.

"Why, you two ingrates! If it wasn't for me telling you what to do, you both would be on the state or, worse yet, pushing up daisies in the pauper's section of the Kingston cemetery. I don't say things to be mean. It's just sometimes you boys need a little guidance. You know, so you get things done. Sometimes you don't tend to stay focused on what's at hand and end up making mistakes. Like when Josh put gas in the generator while it was still running. He might have been incinerated if that machine exploded or burned down the shed. Lucky for you, Josh, I stepped in just in time and turned it off.

"Or you, Dick, remember the time you were cutting down that maple in front of your trailer? You never saw that dead limb about twenty feet over your head, ready to come down and crush your skull as soon as the tree started to fall. You'd have been deader than a red squirrel trying to beat a loaded log truck across the Dam Road if I hadn't seen what was going to happen and yelled to look up. Boys, I just want to make sure both of you make it to old age. That's the only reason I sometimes offer instructions."

"Oh! So that's why you want me to fix you another drink while you sit on your skinny ass in the recliner—so Josh and me will live to be eighty."

"Dick, you asshole. I'll get my own drink. I wouldn't want you to do your brother a favor," Frankie said, releasing the recliner and staggering off to the liquor cabinet.

Soon Frankie returned with a glass in hand. He settled back into his chair, sipping his drink while chewing on a cold sandwich Beatrice had packed for him. Dick and Josh sat in the overstuffed leather chairs, still stewing about Frankie forcing them to spend another night away from home. Ten minutes passed, and no one spoke.

Dick glanced at Frankie. Frankie looked like a deer caught in a car's headlights, staring blankly at the cabin's wall, holding his whisky glass in one hand and the half-eaten sandwich in the other.

Dick watched the muscles in Frankie's throat flex as if struggling to swallow. Before he could ask Frankie if anything was wrong, his brother let loose with a long string of hiccups, topped off by a frantic round of self-induced belches.

"Christ, Frankie, do you think you're going to live?"

Frankie didn't say a word. He sat his drink and sandwich on the side table, rested his arms on his legs, and continued to stare straight ahead, his torso ever so slightly rocking back and forth.

"Have you something caught in your throat again?" Josh asked.

Frankie touched the point above his stomach where Beatrice's sliced venison sandwich hung up.

"Don't throw it up in the cabin. Get outside!" Dick ordered.

Frankie struggled to his feet, careful not to hit his drink, and then staggered to the front door, holding his hand over his mouth.

"And don't puke in front of the door! Get off to the side. I don't want to step in half-digested chunks of venison when I get up during the night to take a piss," Dick hollered, looking at Josh, both enjoying a good laugh at Frankie's predicament. It felt good to hurl a zinger at Frankie and not have to listen to his self-righteous rebuke, even if it was only temporary enjoyment.

After several rounds of uncontrollable retching to clear the obstruction, Frankie returned to the recliner and resumed downing his sandwich.

"Frankie, why don't you go to that clinic in Kingston and see if they can open up that sphincter? What's the sense of going through all that gagging and puking if they can do something to help you?"

"He's probably worried they might open up the wrong one," Josh interjected. Both brothers started to laugh.

"You clowns, just keep it up. I'm not seeing any goddamn horse doctor and have him pound a half-inch piece of rebar down my throat. It's Beatrice's fault that the food won't go down. I'd be fine if she'd cut the goddamn meat into smaller slices."

"You mean like they do for old people in nursing homes?" Dick said, initiating another round of laughs.

"Both of you can go to hell."

After another round of drinks and now fully recovered, Frankie got down to business.

"We'll stop at Skyler Pond and check out the two cabins on the way back to the Haven," Frankie announced, staring at the moose head mount perched over the cathedral windows. "We'll go the way I told you. We'll take the Crossover Road and follow the skidder trail to the back of the cabins. That way, whoever's staying at the old Bridges place won't have a clue we're even in the neighborhood."

"I don't think I can get through the woods without getting stuck. The track on my machine is too narrow, and I'll end up sinking in the soft snow," Josh told Frankie.

"You go third. Just stay in our tracks. And remember, I'm not going to get a double hernia yanking on that poor excuse for a snowmobile of yours," Frankie declared, still staring at the moose.

"As you remember, Frankie, I'm riding that "poor excuse for a snowmobile" because you and Dick ditched your two relics and took the Mountain Cats for yourselves. I never had a say in who would use the new machines."

"Hey, being older has its privileges. Just don't get stuck."

THE BARTLETTS VISIT SKYLER POND

The next morning, the brothers loaded the sleds. Frankie planned to check out the two cabins at Skyler Pond, backtrack to the Crossover Road, and then retrace their route down the Dam Road back to the Haven.

The first camp they hit was the Collins cabin, the one Dan had searched two weeks earlier. It didn't take long for the Bartlett boys to realize that there wasn't anything of value, and they blazed their way through the woods to the second cabin. There they had better luck. The brothers worked fast, something their father had taught them at an early age: "Get in and get out before you're found out" was the senior Bartlett's guiding principle when breaking and entering. Fifteen minutes after smashing the cabin's side door, they returned to the Crossover Road with two cans of gasoline and a small tote packed with goods they had stripped from the kitchen shelves.

An hour after Frankie, Dick, and Josh left for home, Dan stood on the ice in front of the vintage hunting camp. He reached for the two-way radio, remembering Kathy telling him to call her when he arrived. He ran his hands around his belt, searching for the walkie-talkie. Before leaving Skyler Pond, he knew he had attached the holster to his belt. Then it came to him what had likely happened.

The clip must have slipped off his belt when he bent down to adjust his snowshoes about an hour after leaving camp. He'd find it on the way back. A black case against a white background should be easy to spot—as long as it didn't snow. He could only hope Kathy wouldn't panic when he didn't call. Worse yet, she couldn't reach him in an emergency at the cabin. Dan snowshoed toward the camp, anxious to complete his mission and start for home.

Back at the cabin, Kathy enjoyed her time alone, going through a box of old family photos while listening to her favorite CDs on an old Walkman she had bought decades ago. She stopped when Fleetwood Mac's "Don't Stop" began to play, leaned back in the recliner, and listened to the lyrics. *Oh, how I wish it were true. A better tomorrow has come soon,* she thought, as tears ran down her cheeks. After listening to the song a second time, she checked her watch. Dan should be calling anytime now. She could call him but told herself she wouldn't be a pest. She'd wait for his ring.

Two hours had passed, and still no word from him. It was a long walk to the other side of the pond following the convoluted shoreline, but still, he should be there by now. Whether Dan thought she was being a pain or not, Kathy couldn't wait any longer; she needed to know he was safe. She pushed the ring button on her two-way and waited for Dan to answer. She pressed the button again, expecting to hear Dan's voice. Why didn't he answer? Kathy convinced herself that the radio was out of range, even though the Belanger cabin was less than two miles in a straight line. Dan would call on his way back. She pushed play on her portable Walkman and continued looking through the old snapshots, trying to keep her mind off what might be happening on the far side of the pond.

At the time Kathy was trying to reach Dan, the Bartletts were screaming south down the Dam Road, heading for home. As the three sleds flew past the Skyler Pond Road, Frankie glanced at Dan's car, buried in snow so deep that only the shape of the roof gave a clue that there might be a vehicle under the mountain of snow. Unexpectedly, he clamped onto the hand brake, causing Dick and Josh to take evasive action to avoid a three-snowmobile pileup. Luckily, Dick swerved to the left as Josh yanked his snowmobile to the right.

"What to hell are you doing, Frankie? Trying to get the three of us killed?" Dick yelled at his brother.

"You two idiots shouldn't have been following so close," Frankie shot back.

"Anyways, I just had a thought about the people who own that car. I don't think they're staying at Skyler Pond. I think they left before the snow closed the road."

"What makes you think that?" Josh asked.

"Well, think about it. Look at the snow over it. No one's been near that car since we drained the gas tank."

"There's been so much snow, maybe their tracks got covered up," Josh theorized.

"Maybe, but I doubt it. Dick, you said you saw the two when you rode to Kingston with Milligan for fuel. How old do you think they are?"

"I only got a glimpse of the woman sitting in the cab, but I'd say mid-sixties. He looked a few years older than his wife, although it's hard to tell after a man goes bald."

"What did he drive for a truck?" Frankie pressed.

"A fancy Ford F-250, maybe a year or two old."

"That's about what I figured. Here's what I think. The guy retires. He wants to live his dream of spending a winter at his camp before he gets too old, just to say he's done it. One of them stupid bucket list things that people come up with when they have too much time on their hands. Anyways, he convinces his wife to go along with his harebrained idea. The only problem, once the two are snuggled into their cozy little cabin on Skyler Pond, they find out the country has been attacked by the North Korean commies.

"On top of that, they freak out hearing how all them nukes will change the weather. The weather girl on TV predicts a 'snowmageddon'; they panic and hightail it for home with the pickup leaving the car behind, thinking they'd be back once things improve. So you boys know what that means?"

"We take their car and sell it as soon as the snow melts?" Josh answered.

"No, you idiot. It means they left a whole winter supply of food and fuel behind when they cut and run, and it's ours for the taking."

"I don't know, Frankie. You're just guessing. Maybe they're still in there waiting out the weather," Dick said, knowing from experience that Frankie's reasoning power could be short on reality.

"No. They're gone, all right. No old fart is going to take a chance of having a heart attack shoveling ten feet of snow or risk his wife falling and breaking a hip with no way to get to the hospital. I say we leave the dogsleds here and ride in to check the place out for a future procurement trip," he said, smiling. Frankie could see that Dick and Josh weren't convinced that riding back to Skyler Pond to see if the strangers were holed up in their cabin was a wise move.

"Look, all we'll do is make a run past their camp. We'll know I'm right if we don't see the pickup. In a few days, we'll come back and see what they left behind. Maybe even spend the night the same as we did at Money Bags camp. What could be simpler than that?"

"What if the truck is there? Then what?" Dick asked.

"Same thing. We ride by the cabin and sneak a look. If the truck's there, we turn around and fire back by so fast that no one will get a look at us. We'll be a mile down the road before they step outside to see what's going on. Simple."

Dick and Josh thought their brother's plan made sense. What could possibly go wrong with taking a ride by the camp for a quick look? Frankie ordered them to unhook the two loaded dogsleds, and the three Bartletts raced down the Skyler Pond Road.

Dan made his way to the back of the cabin. He was astonished to see three sets of snowshoe tracks leading to and from the rickety porch. He bent down to take a closer look, wondering who had made them and where they led. There was no indication that anyone had snowshoed to the cabin from the pond. Like a blood-hound, he followed the imprints into the woods, where he found part of his answer. Three snowmobiles had traveled through the woods and stopped just out of view of the pond. But why would they have come through the woods? The logical way to reach the cabin would be to ride in on the Skyler Pond Road and then snowmobile along the edge of the pond to the camp, as he had just done, only walking.

Dan snowshoed back to the hunting cabin. It was then that he noticed the partially open door. Robbers. He slowly pushed the door open and peeked inside, not knowing what to expect. The kitchen was trashed. The contents of the drawers and cupboards were thrown into a heap in the middle of the floor. Dan made his way to the combination bedroom and living room; every-thing seemed intact. Fluorescent hunting clothes were still on the hangers, and an old 20-gauge shotgun stood against the wall next to the woodstove. Whoever busted into the cabin had one purpose: to steal any food Belanger had left when he closed camp at the end of hunting season.

Dan decided to check the storage shed, a tarpaper shack fifty feet beyond the Belanger cabin in desperate need of repair. As he approached the building, he could see the crudely built door lying in the snow, apparently ripped from its flimsy hinges. Dan slid down the steep snowdrift through the doorway, where he was abruptly confronted by a disgusting odor. The overwhelming smell reminded him of his cousin's chicken coop after it hadn't been cleaned out for three months. He scanned the window-less structure with his flashlight and locked on to the source of the obnoxious smell. The storage building also served as the outhouse, and whoever broke into the shed took the opportunity to use the facility.

Dan knocked the cover down with his boot to reduce the stench. Holding his breath as best he could, he waved the light around the inside of the shed. A hoe, a shovel, and a coil of rope hung from several nails driven into the studs. If there had been anything of value, it was gone now. As he turned to leave and get a breath of fresh air, his light picked up something odd. He looked closer. The perfect snow-free imprints of two containers were in the thin veneer of snow that had blown through a crack in the door. Gas cans, Dan assumed. Somebody had taken whatever food and gas old man Belanger had stored just a short time before he'd arrived. Discouraged and mad at himself for not checking out the camp weeks earlier, he would return home empty-handed. Just as Kathy had warned him three hours earlier.

As Dan retraced his route back to camp, his thoughts returned to the intruders. Why did they approach the cabin from the north? Access to the region was from the south by way of the Dam Road. The pavement ended at the dam, five miles farther north of the Skyler Pond Road. Beyond the reservoir was a network of woods roads that extended to the Canadian border. Perhaps the interlopers were Canadian and had snuck across the border to loot the scattered seasonal camps that dotted many lakes and ponds in northern Skyler County. It never occurred to Dan that they might be locals that bypassed the Skyler Pond Road to avoid being seen by him and Kathy.

Still absorbed in thinking about the thieves beating him to the food that might have carried Kathy and him until they could leave the pond, Dan failed to notice the dark clouds settling over the distant mountains. Light snow began to fall, unnoticed by Dan, who was still lost in thought, staring at the tracks ahead. Then, in the distance, a deep, barely audible rumble. Before the war, the sound would likely be a distant airliner passing over Skyler Pond en route to Europe. Dan knew this wasn't an airliner carrying passengers on holiday. He rushed for the protection of the shore, finding shelter beneath a large pine hanging over the pond. He pulled his knit cap over his ears and tightened the strings on his hood. Then lifted the sled and drove it into the snow in front of him to help break the relentless wind and snow that was certain to slam into him any second. He crouched between the sled and the trunk of the pine, watching and waiting for the inevitable. What seconds earlier had sounded like a distant plane had suddenly morphed into a squadron of fighter jets all racing toward Dan. The squall line raced across the pond, ripping the snowpack from the ice and obliterating all visibility. Dan was in a hurricane, only instead of driving rain, it was blowing snow. The first gust slammed into him so violently that he nearly lost his balance. Snow swirled around him, sticking to his eyebrows and beard. He felt incredibly cold. Dan wrapped his arms around his chest to maintain his body temperature as his fingertips tingled from the brutal penetrating blast of cold air. It was as if someone had opened the door to a freezer locker and tossed him inside. All he could do was hunker down and wait for the storm to pass.

Dan prayed that this storm would be short-lived. After thirty minutes, the wind slackened, and the air temperature slowly moderated. The snowfall eased as well, now falling in sudden short bursts. Believing a storm had passed had fooled Dan before, forcing him to seek shelter again as another front barreled out of the mountains, reigniting the wind, cold, and snow.

He needed to take the chance that this squall had passed, having no desire to be on the ice after sunset and have a chance encounter with a pack of wolves searching for their next meal. Dan stepped from behind the tree and brushed the thick coating of snow off his jacket. Sporadic gusts of wind whipped the snow across the pond. He needed to keep the shoreline in sight, knowing he could easily wander off course and become lost in the swirling snow. The wind and snow slackened enough to catch a glimpse of the tops of the swaying spruce trees lining the shore. Each time the visibility improved, he moved ahead, stopping when another gust of blowing snow blotted out the trees.

Five hours had passed since Dan left their cabin. Now Kathy was sick with worry. She knew the storm would cause him to seek

shelter. However, he should have been home by now, even account-
ing for the time lost. She had lost interest in listening to her music
and slid the cardboard box of the old family photos back under
the bed. It was two-thirty by the kitchen clock. In two hours, it
would be dark. Kathy paced back and forth, looking out the den
window at the lake, hoping to see Dan making his way along the
shore, and then out the kitchen window to see if he might be
snowshoeing down the camp road. Worry caused her imagination to run wild, and all the "what-if" scenarios overwhelmed her
mind. What if Dan had broken through the ice or maybe became
lost in the snowstorm and was wandering aimlessly on the pond?
Or, the most disturbing thought, he had fallen prey to the same
pack of wolves that had stalked him a few weeks earlier. The possibilities were endless, but her options to help him were few.

Kathy was looking over the pond when a strange noise on the
roadside of the camp caught her attention. Her first thought was
the rattle of the diaphragm pump bringing the captive air tank up
to pressure, as it did several times a day. Low battery voltage could
cause the pump to sound a little strange. She walked back to the
storage room to check. The pump was off. Kathy dismissed the
odd sound as perhaps the wind rustling the tree branches next to
the cabin. As she shut the storage room door, she heard the sound
again and rushed to the kitchen window in time to see the back
end of a snowmobile whiz past the cabin.

Kathy couldn't believe it. A snowmobile meant rescue. Thinking they probably didn't realize anyone lived here, she grabbed her
parka to run outside and flag down the strangers before they left.
She became so excited that their days of seclusion were over that
she nearly lost her balance stepping into her boots. Ready to open
the door, another sled went by. This snowmobile was louder, more
like Dan's old Polaris.

Frankie stopped at the end of the camp road, waiting for his
brothers to catch up. As soon as Josh pulled up behind Dick, he
jumped off his machine and ran up to Frankie.

"Frankie! There's someone in the cabin. I saw smoke coming from the chimney. The truck is there, too, the canoe rack sticking out of the snow. We got to get out of here before they come out to stop us," Josh yelled.

"For Christ's sake, Josh! Relax, I know they're there. I'm not blind. We went by so fast that they never saw us. The old coots were probably napping or filling their pill cups."

"Let's just get out of here. I knew this was a dumb idea from the start," Dick shouted to the both of them, sitting on his snowmobile, revving its engine.

Josh and Dick waited for Frankie to lead them back to the Dam Road, but Frankie just sat there smoking his cigarette. He wanted to make a statement that he wouldn't be intimidated into leaving Skyler Pond just because some old person might stick their head out the cabin door.

Finally, Frankie tossed the cigarette butt onto the snow and clamped down on the throttle, lifting the skis off the snow. In a flash, he was out of sight. Dick flipped down his tinted visor and bolted after his brother, leaving Josh struggling to start the old Polaris. The engine refused to fire. He pulled and pulled, but nothing happened. Josh went into panic mode and started cursing the twenty-year-old machine when he noticed the kill switch in the off position. He pulled out the small red button, gave one strong snap on the starter cord, and took off in hot pursuit of his brothers.

While the Bartletts were having their discussion about a quarter-mile away, Kathy had managed to put on her snowshoes and start to make her way toward the camp road. She knew that whoever these people were, any chance of rescue would go with them once they passed the camp. With only twenty feet to go, she heard the whine of Frankie's machine. She tried to run, but with each stride, the tips of the snowshoes sunk into the snow, nearly tripping her. Out of breath, she could only wave her arms and yell for the man to stop. Frankie blew past her full throttle without making eye contact.

Kathy wondered how he could not have seen her as she watched the snowmobile's red taillight disappear from view. There was no time to dwell on why the scruffy-looking man didn't stop. Another snowmobile was fast approaching.

Dick saw Kathy nearing the camp road. He hesitated momentarily, not knowing if he should slow down if the woman stepped into the road. He made his decision. No way he would stop. She would have to take her chances of being hit. The Mountain Cat accelerated, missing Kathy by inches as she stood on the edge of the camp road, waving her arms for Dick to stop.

Kathy spun around, yelling after Dick, "Please help us! Come back—please, come back!"

Kathy could not understand why neither of them would stop. She couldn't believe anyone would be so cruel as to not even stop and ask if she needed help. Kathy was so mad at the two strangers that she had forgotten about the third machine. She had turned to return to the cabin when she heard the whine of the two-cycle engine and then raced back to the camp road to flag him down. This time the snowmobile *will* stop, Kathy told herself. She stepped into the middle of the snowmobile track facing the oncoming machine, holding both arms high so there would be no misunderstanding of what she wanted the driver to do.

Josh couldn't believe anyone would stand in front of a snowmobile traveling thirty miles per hour. He took one hand off the handlebars and motioned to Kathy to get out of the way. Kathy held her ground. Desperate for someone to help, she was willing to put her life on the line. Kathy's refusal to move rattled Josh. The only way to avoid hitting her was to swerve left, thread the machine between two large trees, and then pull back onto the road. Barely twenty feet separated them when he turned the skis hard left and then back to the right. He might have made it if the half-buried fir sapling hadn't become wedged between the track and a ski. The machine's abrupt stop caused Josh to go airborne, hitting his head against a large beech before he landed in a heap five feet from the snowmobile. Even though the helmet saved him from serious injury, his head spun from the impact.

Once he regained his bearings, Josh wallowed back to the disabled machine. First taken aback by the man's misfortune, Kathy snowshoed into the woods to confront Josh, who was fighting to dislodge the sapling.

"We need help!" She pleaded, watching Josh trying to free the stubborn fir from the track. Josh kept pulling, pretending he didn't hear or see her.

Kathy was relentless. "I said we need help. We need you to take us to Kingston. We will pay you to take us there." Josh continued to ignore her and fought his way in waist-deep snow to the other side of the machine to try freeing the limb from a different angle.

A quarter-mile down the road, Frankie and Dick had stopped to wait for Josh to catch up.

"Where to hell is he?" Frankie asked, disgusted that Josh had gone missing.

"We better go back and check. Maybe he's got engine problems," Dick said, looking back toward the cabin, hoping to see Josh's headlight coming toward them.

"He'll have problems, but it won't be with his snowmobile. You can always count on numbnuts to screw things up; it happens every time," Frankie bitched.

"Come on, Frankie—cut Josh a little slack. We're riding twelve-thousand-dollar machines, and he's on a piece of useless crap not worth a hundred dollars on a good day. Let's just go back and see what happened."

The two reversed course and headed back down the road to find Josh. In the distance, Frankie spotted him off the trail, struggling to free the stuck machine. Next to him was a woman who appeared to be talking to Josh.

"You've got to be shitting me," was all Frankie said and sped toward the stuck machine.

When Kathy noticed Frankie, she walked back to the trail to convince him to help her and Dan. Frankie was not in a conversational mood.

"My name is Kathy Simmons. This is our camp," she said, pointing toward the cabin. "We are nearly out of food and need to leave. Please help us!"

"Go back to your cabin, lady!" he ordered, looking at the disabled machine, trying to figure out what had happened.

"Why won't you help us? We'll pay you to take us to Kingston."

Frankie had heard enough from the woman. He unzipped his parka, reached inside, pulled a revolver from his shoulder holster, and held it in the air for Kathy to see. "You! Go back to the cabin now!" Frankie ordered, glaring at Kathy.

Kathy started to speak, but Frankie cut her off.

"I said now! I won't tell you a third time," Frankie said, lowering the .45 until it was level with Kathy's chest.

She put up her hands. "Okay, okay, I'm leaving," she said and retreated to the cabin, but not before giving Frankie a long hard look.

Frankie turned his attention to Josh's stuck machine. "Dick, help genius pull that branch out so we can get out of here."

Kathy watched Josh and Dick work to free the track from behind the kitchen window curtain. She took particular notice of the man without a snowmobile helmet who had threatened her with the weapon in case they should cross paths again. Soon Josh's machine was back on the trail, and the trio disappeared down the camp road.

"Where are you, Dan?" Kathy spoke aloud, looking at the kitchen clock. Already it was three thirty. In another half hour, it would be dark. Kathy was at a loss for what to do. Stay put and wait for Dan to return or go looking for him. Scary thoughts raced through her mind. Maybe the three thugs on snowmobiles had met Dan and done something terrible to him. Maybe beaten him for his money—or worse. Perhaps they figured his cabin was nearby, and that's why they happened to show up when they did, hoping to break in and steal what they wanted. Kathy was terrified, thinking something sinister had happened to her husband. She needed to find him. She decided to walk the camp road to where Dan began his trek following the shoreline to the Belanger cabin, hoping to meet him along the way. Kathy grabbed the flashlight from her nightstand and scribbled a note to Dan should he return while she was gone.

LOST

The late afternoon air was cold, but Kathy had been outside in much colder temperatures. The forms of the hardwood trees were melding together in the final minutes of daylight. Standing on the deck, Kathy agonized over whether she was doing right by leaving the cabin's security to look for Dan in the dark.

She recalled the story of Clarence Bridges and how he didn't return to camp one cold mid-January evening after tending his trapline. And how Bart and Adrian found their brother's frozen stiff body next to a beaver set the following morning. Kathy struggled to think of today's date. Finally, it came to her. It was January 15. Clarence might have died on this very night. That did it. It was too much of a coincidence; she would stay at camp and wait for Dan to return.

Kathy hesitated, her hand poised to turn the cabin's doorknob. She couldn't just sit inside the cozy cabin waiting for Dan to return because of Clarence's demise decades ago. She could never live with herself if she waited until morning only to find Dan's frozen body on the road just beyond the camp. As Kathy continued to procrastinate, it began to snow.

Back to the original plan: she would snowshoe the half mile to where Dan stepped onto the pond and return home if there was no sign of him. It would only take an hour. Her reasoning made it feel like not such a big deal, being away from camp, after dark, alone in a snowstorm.

Her dithering had cost precious daylight. In January, darkness descends quickly in the north woods, and even quicker when the sky is cloudy. Kathy had walked this section of road dozens of times and knew every curve and grade. This time it felt different, strange somehow. Everything seemed so dark without the moon and stars, a scary nothingness, a black void where she was the only object in the universe. With the flashlight pointed at the snow ahead, Kathy wandered from one side of the road to the other, unable to see the adjacent trees to keep her on course.

Her mind was consumed with thoughts of Dan and all the possibilities of what might have happened to him that she had forgotten the moose carcass lying next to the camp road. Kathy pointed the light at what appeared to be pieces of a broken tree limb scattered in the snow. She gasped. The intact seven-hundred-pound bull moose of two weeks earlier was now nothing more than a scattering of chewed body parts and hair. The wolves had eaten everything other than the hide and head.

Kathy didn't intend to stare at the moose. Still, she was drawn to the grotesque head's half-eaten tongue resting on the snow and the black recessed sockets where there had once been brown eyeballs. She had seen enough, anxious to leave the moose's remains far behind.

She dreaded passing the animal when she returned to the cabin. It wasn't so much the moose that concerned her. It was the wolves. She would be offering them an easy one-hundred-thirty-pound appetizer as she snowshoed past their favorite restaurant. The thought of becoming fresh raw meat to a pack of vicious predators was more than unnerving.

At last, she reached the point where the Skyler Pond Road left the pond. She stepped onto the snow-covered pond and peered into the nothingness, slowly waving the light back and forth, hoping Dan might use the glow to guide him toward shore. The light's beam cut a narrow path into the falling snow but could not penetrate the blackness. No way would Dan be able to see the ray of light from the pathetically underpowered flashlight.

Discouraged, Kathy was ready to return home. First, she would snowshoe to the small point of land blocking the view of the northern half of the pond and wave the flashlight for no other reason than to satisfy her that she had done her best to locate Dan.

After a few minutes of probing the blackness with her light, Kathy turned back toward the cove. She feared snowshoeing past the moose, not wanting a run-in with the wolves. Then she had an idea. Walk the shoreline back to camp and avoid the camp road altogether, along with a chance encounter with the pack of wolves.

Kathy knew every twist and turn of the shoreline from the dozens of times she had kayaked Skyler Pond. Once she reached the camp lot, it was a quick two hundred feet to the safety of the cabin. All she had to do to stay safe was to stick close to shore and avoid any suspicious areas that might be slushy.

Huge drifts ran deep into the woods, built by the gale winds accompanying the sudden storms. The massive mounds of windblown snow completely changed the landscape. Nothing looked familiar. The farther she snowshoed, the more worried she became that she would not be able to recognize the needed landmarks.

It was a painfully slow slog, up one side of the giant drifts and down the other. Her stops became more frequent, trying to pick out features she recognized. At last, she came to a massive pine with a double top that leaned over the pond, the distinctive tree she had used numerous times as a target crossing the pond in her kayak. Seeing the pine buoyed her spirits. The camp was only a short distance ahead. Kathy exhaled, relieved knowing she would be sitting next to the woodstove in twenty minutes.

The only missing piece to the puzzle was exactly where to leave the pond. Knowing when she was at their lot would be easy without the massive drifts. But with all the snow, she wasn't so sure. Everything looked the same. Then she remembered the wooden float she and Dan dragged out of the pond each fall and tied against a large yellow birch. Surely the top of an eight-by-eight-foot float would stick above the snow.

Suddenly, everything went black. She gave the back of the flashlight two good whacks with her wrist. The bulb popped back on, although not as bright as before. Without the light, Kathy wouldn't be able to see the float or any other landmark. Her life depended on the light working.

Kathy considered cutting through the woods to the camp road. However, if the course she chose was too far to the north, she might come on to the road before the moose carcass, something she'd rather not do. Worse luck would be to intersect the road at the exact spot where the predators might be feeding on the moose. If she unknowingly traveled too far on the pond, she would be beyond the end of the camp road and could become hopelessly lost in the uninterrupted forest. The best option was to locate the cabin before the flashlight batteries played out.

Kathy's head filled with stories of people becoming lost in the wilderness and sometimes dying before being rescued. She thought of the five snowmobiles flying across a Maine lake late at night, going too fast to see the open water ahead. One after another, all five plunged into the murky depths of Horsecollar Pond. She trembled, thinking about their last seconds struggling in the icy water, knowing they didn't stand a chance of saving themselves.

Then there was the woman hiking the Appalachian Trail, not twenty miles from Skyler Pond, who left the marked trail to relieve herself and couldn't find her way back to the well-worn footpath. Game wardens found her remains two months later. Kathy had often wondered how people could be so careless as to allow themselves to become victims of such needless tragedies. Yet here she was, snowshoeing alone on a frozen lake in the middle of the night, uncertain how to find the cabin, with a flashlight barely as bright as a candle.

The farther she walked, the more her mind was filled with self-doubt that she had made the right decision to follow the shoreline back to camp. Now the camp road seemed like the obvious choice. If she had just returned to the cabin the way she came and not worried about the wolves, she would be sitting in front of the woodstove with her hands hugging a hot cup of coffee. Instead, she faced the real possibility of spending the night huddled against a tree, trying to survive until daylight.

Her mind focused on the immenseness of the area. Tiers of mountains and ridges spread out in every direction. Dan had told her that nearly a million acres of forest surrounded Skyler Pond. As she snowshoed along the shore, she wondered about the distance to the nearest house. It was perhaps thirty miles to the south, but even that was a guess. To the north and west, the nearest town was in Quebec, and in between, there was a huge nothingness of trees dissected by hundreds of logging roads and twitch trails. She felt insignificant, shuffling along on her snowshoes in the dark. She and Dan, wherever he might be, were likely the only humans for dozens of miles. Nature's rules prevailed, and the natural world could be ruthless. The weight of the all-encompassing wilderness was nearly more than she could bear.

Another five minutes passed, and still no trace of the float tied to the tree. White pine was numerous along the shoreline. Perhaps the big pine wasn't the landmark she had thought. She kept going, looking for anything that looked familiar. At last, the faint light locked onto an enormous boulder protruding into the pond. Kathy immediately recognized the rock. Each summer, she caught several fat trout on her fly rod in the deep hole in front of it. She also knew the boulder was a fifteen-minute paddle from camp, which meant she had snowshoed a quarter mile beyond the cabin. How could she have walked past the lot and not realized it? This was becoming too much. To have any chance of saving herself, Kathy needed to retrace her steps. Even then, she might still not be able to find the exit.

Kathy considered snowshoeing back to the landing and following the camp road. However, the light would never last that long. Without it, she might wander away from shore and become hopelessly lost on Skyler Pond. She could only pray the batteries lasted long enough to find the float protruding above the snow.

A distant rumble caught her attention. She frantically snowshoed toward the large boulder. Kathy released the binding on one of her snowshoes and used it as a shovel to rough out a cavity next to the rock she could use to escape the onslaught headed her way. She had just crouched against the boulder as the freight train barreled down the mountain, breaking limbs and uprooting trees, roaring onto Skyler Pond.

It hissed as it tore by her, rattling the branches of the nearby yellow birch and young maples. The unnerving racket sounded like a hundred drummers, each playing to a different beat. And with its fury came the driving snow and plummeting temperatures. She pulled her head deep into the parka and tugged at the zipper until only her nose and eyes were exposed to the howling wind and snow. Kathy cupped her ears to mute the sound of falling trees and snapping branches, praying an errant limb ripped from one of the tall spruces wouldn't impale her. As suddenly as it began, the wind and snow abruptly stopped. Finally, something was going right for Kathy. The storm could have lasted all night. Luckily, this one lasted only minutes.

Seconds later, the storm slammed into the opposite shore with the same ferocity. Kathy stayed in her fetal position, listening to the distant trees snap and moan as the limbs danced to the rhythm of the wind. At last she stood, listening. The night calm had returned, as if the raging storm had never happened. The unexpected squall added another dimension to an already dire situation. She needed to find the cabin before another blast raced down the mountain, one that could hold her captive on the pond for hours.

Kathy began the trek back toward the cabin, repeatedly telling herself to stay calm and not panic. However, her mind had other plans. Unconsciously, her pace quickened and soon built to a fast walk, intermingled with short bursts of running. She couldn't help herself. Kathy was consumed with the fear that she wouldn't make it off the pond.

Bizarre thoughts rushed through her mind. She visualized her body stretched out on the snow. She felt terribly cold, a cold unlike any she had ever felt. She could not feel her limbs. She was freezing to death. As Kathy waited for the end, she heard dogs yipping. *No one at Skyler Pond owned dogs*, she thought. The yips and howls seemed to be coming closer. *Wolves! Wolves are going to tear me apart, and I'm not even dead!* Kathy could see the three animals circling her body, the rings becoming tighter with each pass. Two beasts took positions on either side of her as the biggest of the three predators stood over her head. They just stood there, looking down, growling, the low deep growl a dog makes when protecting its bone. Then, in concert, all three wolves lunged at her body.

Kathy yelled, scaring herself back to reality. At the same time she screamed, she caught the tip of her snowshoe under the crust, staggered forward, and fell facedown into the snow. Lying there, she realized it had all been her out-of-control imagination. She needed to concentrate on getting to the cabin and put the nonsense of being attacked by a pack of wolves out of her mind, or she would die on the pond.

Using her poles, she lifted herself to her feet and resumed walking, desperate to find her way off the pond. The night was silent. Only her labored breathing interrupted the stillness until a tree branch snapped no farther than fifty feet into the woods. Kathy froze. Using her ski poles to keep her balance, she leaned into the darkness, straining to catch a glimpse of whatever had caused the branch to break. Another snap—the noise was barely inside the tree line. This can't be happening, she told herself, wolves stalking her, waiting for the perfect opportunity to take her down. She broke into a run, her lungs burning from sucking in the cold night air. After twenty yards, she stopped, barely able to catch her breath. Gasping for air, she heard another crack. It was as if every predator in the forest had joined the chase. Then, a limb broke in a large maple tree overhanging the pond.

Kathy looked up, expecting to spot the eyes of a large wolf staring down at her, hunched and ready to jump. Suddenly, reality set in, and Kathy relaxed. The sounds were not from wild animals giving chase but from the trees contracting in response to the plunging temperature brought on by the storm. She had heard the same noises dozens of times, standing on the cabin's back porch on bitterly cold nights while listening to the owls hoot to one another high up the mountain. She should have known better than to think it was anything else. Kathy knew that if she got out of this mess, everything that had happened this night would be best left imagined and not told.

Out of nowhere, a story she had read in one of Dan's outdoor magazines popped into her head about a deer hunter who had gotten lost in the deep woods of Aroostook County. Several days after his wife reported the hunter missing, a search party found his naked frozen body lying at the base of a large maple. The would-be rescuers were at a loss as to why the man had no clothes. The man appeared to have panicked when he became lost and started to run, trying to escape the woods before dark. For whatever reason, he began to shed his clothes. The search party found his rifle and plaid hunting coat a quarter mile from the body. A hundred yards further were his pants and shirt, and then his underwear caught on a limb barely two hundred feet from where they found his corpse.

The newspapers reported that the panicked man had scared himself to death. Lost his mind, as most locals told the story. The medical examiner determined that a heart attack had killed him, likely brought on by the fear of being trapped in the seemingly never-ending wilderness. Wardens theorized that he stripped off his clothes as he became increasingly delirious. Kathy promised herself no one would find her undergarments hanging in the trees, no matter how desperate she became.

Forty-five minutes later and there was still no sign of the float. A sense of hopelessness replaced what little confidence Kathy had remaining in finding the cabin. Just when she thought she might actually die on the ice, her flashlight caught an odd-look-ing snow-covered sapling high up on the bank. She stepped closer to get a better look. It sprung from the snow taut and straight and ended at a yellow birch tree. She reached out with her ski pole and gave it a tap. The thin sheath of snow dropped, revealing a white nylon rope. The rope Dan had used to secure the float to the tree in November.

At last she'd found what she had been so desperate to locate. Her spirits soared; she wouldn't die on the ice after all. Only two hundred feet separated her from the cabin's safety and the fire's warmth.

Until that moment, all her thoughts had been about survival, her survival. Kathy had been so engrossed in saving herself that she had forgotten about Dan. Suddenly, she broke into tears, realizing she might never see him again. *What happened to him?* she wondered. His plan to reach the Belanger cabin to check for supplies seemed reasonable and safe. He had a flash-light, the two-way radio, and promised to be home before dark. Maybe he had become lost in a squall and wandered away from shore or fell through a thin spot in the ice. Or perhaps he had unknowingly stepped onto a soft area of snow and sunk deep into the underlying slush, unable to fight his way out. That was as far as she would allow her imagination to take her. Kathy didn't need to torture herself thinking of Dan's demise when she didn't even know if he was dead. Once it was daylight, she would continue to search for her husband. However, she still needed to make it to the cabin before she could be confident of her own survival.

Kathy studied the bank for the easiest way off the pond. Just as she grasped a red maple branch to help pull herself up the bank, she sensed she wasn't alone. She turned her head just enough to see a form standing motionless a hundred feet from shore.

Wolf. Frantically she tried pulling herself up the bank, but it was no use. The deep soft snow would not support her weight. It was as if she were marching in place, unable to get one snowshoe ahead of the other. She fell forward into the snow, struggling to crawl the way to the top, grabbing onto every branch and tree within reach to pull her along. Halfway up the bank, Kathy needed to stop to catch her breath. A twig snapped behind her, sending her scrambling for all she was worth to escape whatever was coming up behind her.

"My God, my God, no! No! Please don't let this happen!" she cried.

Something latched onto her ankle, and with one hard yank, the steel grip dragged Kathy back down the bank onto the frozen pond. There was no struggle left in her. She lay facedown in the snow sobbing, expecting the excruciating pain of razor-sharp incisors ripping into her body.

"Kathy! It's okay. It's me. Dan. You're okay," said the familiar voice.

Kathy rolled onto her back and looked up at the shadowy figure standing over her. "Dan, I thought you were an animal. I thought I was a goner. Why didn't you say something?" she asked, her voice cracking with emotion. Dan held out his hand and helped Kathy to her feet.

"Kathy, I was as scared as you," Dan confessed. "All I saw was a large shape moving along the shore, or at least I thought I did. I froze to see what would happen next, hoping whatever it was didn't notice me. When you started up the bank, I inched my way closer. Then I thought it was you but didn't dare to yell, afraid I'd scare you out of your wits, so I pulled you back down the bank before you got out of reach."

"Well, if there is ever a next time, yell. I'll take a chance of having a heart attack instead of thinking I would be ripped apart alive." She paused to catch her breath.

"What happened to you? Why didn't you come home before dark like you promised?"

"I'll tell you everything when we get to camp. I don't know about you, but I'm frozen. I need to sit next to the woodstove and thaw out."

Dan helped Kathy reach the top of the bank. Ten minutes later, they were huddled around the wood fire. Finally, the two had warmed up enough to remove their parkas.

"Why weren't you back before dark? I was worried sick," Kathy demanded to know, staring at the flames through the glass door of the woodstove. Kathy wanted to tell him about the three snowmobilers who appeared while he was gone but decided to hold back and listen to Dan's story first.

"I became lost on my way back from Belanger's cabin. I saw the clouds tear down the mountain, so I rushed to the shore to find shelter and wait out the storm. When things finally improved, I started out again, sticking close to shore in case of another storm— that is, until I reached Mud Cove. I knew it would be dark in a couple of hours, so I cut across the cove to save a little time. When I started, I could see Black Point. I couldn't see how anything could go wrong in that short distance. But it did. I was halfway across the cove when the sky turned dark, and it began to blow. The wind whipped the snow off the pond, blotting out the opposite shore. I didn't dare to keep going, afraid I would get all screwed up, so I turned back."

I could see the point of land where I had started. Two seconds later, it disappeared as well. I could have sworn I was going in a straight line. Still, I must have drifted off toward the middle of the pond. I didn't know it then, but I made one big half circle. When I finally reached shore, I was standing in front of Belanger's camp, exactly where I had started two hours earlier. I went inside the camp to wait for the wind to die down. Once that happened, I struck out again.

"It was dark when I reached the point just before the landing. It was there I spotted your tracks."

"How did you know they were mine?"

"Who else's would they be, since there is no one else within forty miles?" Dan said, stating the obvious. "Anyway, once I got to the landing, I saw where you stepped onto the pond. I assumed you snowshoed to the point to look for me and then, for whatever reason, followed the shoreline toward camp rather than walk back the camp road. Care to tell me why you did that in the dark?"

"No. Not now," Kathy said, embarrassed to tell Dan it was because of the dead moose and her being scared the wolves might attack her.

"I knew something was wrong, so I followed your tracks, knowing eventually I would find you at the end of them. Then that damn squall hit. Like a fool, I didn't head for cover, thought I'd tough it out, and wandered off course after the snow filled your tracks. By a stroke of luck, I reached the shore as you were trying to get up the bank. You know the rest."

"Why didn't you call on the two-way and tell me what was happening? We could have avoided all this mess."

"I lost the phone on the way to the cabin. I hoped to find it on the way back and call you, but the snowstorm changed everything. I never did find the damn thing."

"I'll tell you this, Dan: you picked the wrong day to leave me here alone," Kathy began.

"What does that mean, the wrong day? Did something happen while I was gone?"

"You might say that." Kathy recounted the events of earlier in the day, when the three snowmobilers had ridden by and, after she flagged them down, had refused to help. Dan came to a rapid boil when Kathy told him about the man who appeared to be the pack's leader, threatening her with a handgun.

"What a bunch of lowlifes! If I'd been here, I would have—"

Kathy cut him off. "You would have done what, shot them all? There were three of them. You, or both of us, might have wound up dead if you confronted them. The one with the weapon really scared me. He looked like he was capable of just about anything. You might have reasoned with the other two, but not the one toting the gun. He looked and acted pure evil."

"I bet it was the same ones who broke into the cabin. From what I could tell, they were only an hour or two ahead of me. Somehow they found a way to the pond other than the Skyler Pond Road."

"Well, these three rode in and out on the Skyler Pond Road. When I went looking for you, I saw remnants of their snowmobile tracks going up the hill headed toward the Dam Road. Maybe there were two groups of creeps."

"I doubt it. That would be too much of a coincidence that two sets of thieves would choose the same day to burglarize camps on Skyler Pond. No, I think it was the same three. I don't understand where they came from. I had thought perhaps from Canada, but now I'm unsure."

After the run-in with Kathy at Skyler Pond, the Bartletts headed home. Dick and Frankie arrived ahead of Josh, who could not keep up on his outclassed snowmobile. Dick hit the kill switch on his Mountain Cat and bolted from the machine. He ran over to Frankie, still sitting on his snowmobile, and grabbed his arm. Frankie reeled to see Dick standing over him. He stood up, and the pair went nose to nose.

"Don't you ever grab me again, Dick!" Frankie roared. "If you do, it will be the last time you touch anything. Do you understand?"

"Frankie, why did you threaten that woman with your gun? What was the purpose?" Dick hollered, throwing his helmet onto the snow, ready for anything Frankie might try.

"Because she wouldn't shut up and go back to the goddamn cabin like I told her, that's why, little brother."

"You do realize she can ID you if she goes to the cops."

"Goes to the cops?" Frankie repeated. "The country is at war. We're living in the mother of all natural disasters with this never-ending snowathon. For all we know, the country is in total chaos, and it's every man for himself. The last thing the cops give a shit about is me raising a gun to scare an old woman. That is, if there are any cops still on the job and not held up in their homes trying to fend off an army of anarchists."

"Maybe, but there will come a time when all this happy horseshit will end. And when things do get back to normal, there will be one big friggin' housecleaning of the people who broke the law. You know, like breaking and entering, grand theft, threatening a person with a firearm, things like that," Dick shot back.

"Bullshit! No one knows what we've been up to. And as far as that broad back at Skyler Pond goes, she won't remember what we look like, for Christ's sake. She ran back to the cabin like a scared rabbit."

"Not Josh and me, she won't. We had our visors down. She doesn't even know if we even have faces. It's you she'll finger, you idiot. The macho man thinks wearing a helmet is for girls. Your ugly face she'll remember. Didn't you see her stare at you before she turned around? She was counting every hair of your filthy beard." Dick hesitated, knowing what he was about to say would come with a price. "I suppose you could sled into Skyler Pond and take care of her like you did Floyd Carsley."

Frankie became enraged. He shoved Dick in the chest, knocking him backward onto the snow. Dick attempted to stand and Frankie pushed him a second time. This time Dick stayed put, knowing his brother was so angry he would have no chance to defend himself.

"Shut up, Dick. I told you a long time ago never to bring up his name," Frankie said, standing over Dick with his fists clenched. "That little prick had it coming. He thought he was so goddamn smart, thinking he would hold me at gunpoint until the cops arrived. Well, that didn't work out so good for him, now did it?" In an unintended moment of truthfulness, Frankie had confirmed what Dick and the other Bartletts had suspected all along: Frankie had murdered Floyd Carsley.

"All right, forget Carsley. I'm just sayin' that you're too stubborn for your own good. You seem to think you can do anything you damn well please and get away with it. Well, one of these times, you're going to screw up royally. And when you get caught, just make sure you don't drag me and Josh down with you."

"Anything else you have to say?" Frankie demanded.

"That's it. Just try thinking for once before you go off half-cocked," Dick said, brushing the snow off his snowmobile suit and heading toward his trailer.

Frankie called after him, realizing what he had blurted out about the murder. "I have one more thing to say to you, Dicky boy. You don't tell anyone what you just heard. I don't care if you are my brother. You say anything, and you're history. You got that, Dicky boy?"

Dick ignored Frankie's ultimatum and kept walking. Dick could barely stand his brother in the best of times, and those times were rare.

Frank had always favored Frankie, partly because he was Frank's firstborn but mainly because they shared the same outlook on life: take what you want and to hell with the next guy.

It had always been a love-hate relationship, one full of resentment and mistrust, and yet beneath all the arguments between Frankie and his father, there was an unspoken bond not shared with Josh and Dick. When Frank started to show increasingly worse signs of being sick, Frankie got scared he would soon lose his father—feelings he didn't share with Beatrice, and certainly not with Josh and Dick. Frankie's escape from dwelling on his father's condition was to stay inebriated as often and for as long as possible. It's much easier to cope with the inevitable when you can't remember the day of the week.

When his younger brothers became distraught about their father's pending demise, Frankie played the role of a tough guy. He told Josh and Dick that their father should have known better than to smoke cigarettes for forty-five years. His cancer was payback for being so stupid—a statement neither of his brothers quite understood, as Frankie had been smoking up a storm since he was fourteen. Adopting a cavalier attitude about his father's terminal illness was Frankie's way of avoiding having to reveal his emotions about how much he cared for the old man. The last thing he wanted was to break down in front of his brothers in a moment of emotional weakness. His father had beaten it into Frankie's head to not get all teary-eyed when things go wrong; just deal with it—a philosophy he had preached to all three boys ever since their mother had walked out on the family.

Three weeks before Frank died, he called his three sons to his bedside. It was a short meeting reminiscent of a change in leadership of an organized crime family. Frank knew he had only a short time to live and wanted his sons to know his wishes. His breathing had become labored, and his voice weak. The three brothers crowded around the bed to hear what their father was about to tell them. Frank wanted Bartlett Haven to continue after he passed. The Haven would be the safest place to live once society broke down. When that happened, they'd understand why they had lived as survivalists. Frank's arm shook as he feebly pointed at Frankie. He told the three brothers in a barely audible voice that Frankie was to lead the Bartlett clan, and Dick and Josh were to listen to him. To ensure there was no misunderstanding about who would be in charge, he asked Dick and Josh if they understood what he was saying. Hearing Josh and Dick agree, Frank closed his eyes and slept. The meeting ended, as did Frank's campaign to rule from the grave.

Frank knew that of the three, Frankie had the toughness to keep the family together and wasn't afraid to ride roughshod over his brothers. Frankie's domineering personality mirrored his own. Dick was too easygoing and eager to compromise, not wanting hard feelings within the family. Frank wanted his successor to stand on principle and not be swayed by what others thought. As for Josh, Frank knew early on that his youngest had limitations. A slow learner and easily manipulated, Josh was a follower. The only choice to head the family was Frankie.

A SHOOTING FATALITY

The weeks leading up to Frank's death brought more sullen changes in Frankie's behavior. The more he drank, the less predictable his actions were. He ignored everyone, including Beatrice, who was constantly after him for lying around doing nothing. Beatrice threatened to leave him if he didn't straighten out, but her constant complaining caused Frankie to drink all the more.

Frankie spent his days lying on the living room couch in a self-induced drunken stupor, getting up just long enough to take a whiz over the back porch before grabbing another beer from the refrigerator. Beatrice had had enough of Frankie's immersion in self-pity. After a week, she had reached her boiling point.

"Frankie, get to hell off that couch and do something! You've been lying there flat-ass drunk for a week. I'm sick of it," Beatrice bellowed, towering over Frankie, who was staring at a spider making its way to a fly struggling to free itself from the web in the corner of the nicotine-stained ceiling.

"Go to hell," Frankie shot back, fumbling for the half-empty bottle of Pabst sitting on the coffee table, not taking his eyes off the spider.

"Come on, Frankie. This place smells like a brewery and looks like the town dump with all the goddamn potato chip bags and empty beer bottles you've thrown wherever you damn well please. Get your skinny ass off the couch so I can clean up this pigsty."

"I'll get up when I'm damn good and ready. And right now, Beatrice, I'm not ready. So take your urge to beautify our lovely home into the bathroom and clean the toilet if you need a project," Frankie told her, sitting up long enough to gulp down the beer. "And before you do, grab me another beer out of the refrigerator. I'm working up a terrible thirst lying here wondering what you're going to make for supper."

"Jesus, Frankie, you sure make a person feel like shit. I don't know why I put up with your friggin' bullshit. Some days I just want to leave this poor excuse for a life like your mother did when she left your father. The only reason you asked me to move in with you was to cook and keep you in clean clothes so you'd have more time to get shit-faced. And now you seem to think it's my responsibility to take care of your father."

"You leave my father out of this. As for your leaving, you let me know when you're ready, and I'll help you pack," Frankie told her, reaching under the couch for a three-year-old issue of *Penthouse* he had a habit of hauling out each time he and Beatrice argued.

"Frankie, I know why you're drunk half the time. It's your father, isn't it? You can't stand the thought of him dying, so you get smashed just to avoid thinking about him. Admit it."

"You don't know shit about anything, Beatrice, and you sure as hell got it wrong how I feel about the old man. He brought it on all by himself, him, with his goddamn smoking. And for your information, Einstein, I drink because I like the taste of beer and nothing more. So quit trying to play psychiatrist!"

"Well, I may not be the smartest person in the room, but I know I'm right on this one. You're just not man enough to admit it, Frankie."

"Ah, go to hell. I can't stand any more of your preaching. I'm out of here," Frankie said, struggling to get off the couch.

"Where are you going, Frankie? You told Josh and Dick the three of you were going deer hunting up on Green Ridge this afternoon."

"Yeah? Well, they're just going to have to go without me. I'm going into town."

"More beer?"

"What of it?" Frankie said as he staggered into the kitchen to grab the last one from the refrigerator to keep him company for the twenty-mile ride to Kingston.

Beatrice watched her husband zigzag across the yard toward his Ford pickup when Stalin, Josh's eight-month-old German shepherd, spotted Frankie and took off on a dead run to greet him. The dog came up behind him, brushing against the back of Frankie's legs. Any sober man would have quickly recovered from the glancing blow. However, it was more than Frankie in his inebriated state could handle. He staggered forward, straight into the rusted fifty-five-gallon drum the three families used to burn trash. Frankie bounced off the barrel and fell backward into the snow, the beer flying out of his hand. Beatrice started for the door to call out to see if he was hurt, but she was so mad she decided to watch, hoping his collision with the barrel would smarten him up. It didn't.

Frankie used the garbage barrel to pull himself up and immediately scanned the area for his beer bottle. Finding it empty, he hurled it as hard as possible at Stalin but missed and instead managed to smash the bottle against the metal wheel of one of the junk ATVs that littered the yard. Frankie let out a string of curses Beatrice heard through the closed door and continued his erratic course across the yard.

The engine revved, and blue smoke poured from the exhaust pipe. Frankie flew down the driveway toward the Dam Road, narrowly missing Dick's two youngest boys coming up the driveway on an ATV. Beatrice cringed at how close her husband had come to hitting them. She muttered aloud, "Idiot," and turned away from the window. At last she was rid of him for a few hours, time enough to clean the living room.

Just outside Kingston, Frankie remembered that Riverside Market closed at six on Saturdays. Frankie checked his watch, but each time he tried to focus on the dial, his pickup wandered across the centerline, much to the ire of the oncoming drivers. He turned on the radio, frantically punching the seek button, hoping to catch the time. Out of frustration, Frankie beat on the dash with his hand, shouting at the radio to give him the friggin' time. Finally, the disc jockey said it was five forty-five. The thirst for a sixteen-ounce Pabst was too great to take a chance the supermarket might close before he arrived. Reluctantly, he decided to stop to buy beer at Carsley's, a convenience store a mile ahead.

He had two reasons for not wanting to stop at Carsley's: he would have to pay twice as much for a six-pack, and his intense dislike for the store's owner. Each time Frankie entered the store, he felt Floyd Carsley watching his every move, as if he thought he might steal something. However, with his intense thirst for a beer, being followed from aisle to aisle was not reason enough to prevent him from pulling into the empty parking lot. The door opened just as Frankie was about to enter.

"Store's closed," Carsley said, recognizing Frankie.

"Closed? How can it be closed? It's only a quarter to six. The store's open every night until eleven!" Frankie said, his finger shaking as he pointed to the sign on the door's window.

"Because I say it's closed, that's why," the owner shot back, pointing to a handwritten sign taped to the glass that read "Closing at 5:30, Nov. 6—anniversary." "That notice has been on the window for a week. I'm already late getting home."

"How about opening up just long enough for me to buy a couple of six-packs? It won't take five minutes," Frankie pleaded.

"No! Go to Riverside Market and buy your damn beer," Carsley said, sticking his key into the lock. "Now I've got to get going," and brushed by Frankie heading for his car, parked in the far corner of the parking lot.

"Asshole!" Frankie yelled. Carsley ignored him and continued toward his car.

Frankie watched the big blue SUV pull onto the highway and disappear down the road. Frankie was ripped. Out of beer, the store closed, and not having enough money to buy gas to drive the fifteen miles to Dudley, the next closest town, it didn't take long to figure out what he would do. He'd find a way inside to get his beer.

Frankie drove to the back of the store. There was still enough daylight to find his way around inside. All he needed to do was get into the building. Five minutes inside, he would have what he wanted and be on his way home, rehydrated, and Floyd Carsley would only be out two six-packs.

He hoisted himself onto the loading platform and tried opening the door to the storage room. It was locked, but not tight against the jamb. Frankie could rock the door back and forth. He smiled. A door installed this sloppily was only to keep out the honest people. Grabbing the doorknob, he rammed the door with his shoulder. The wood splintered, and the door burst inward, taking Frankie with it.

Frankie worked his way toward the double swinging door that opened into the main store. About to go through the doorway, a bottle smashed onto the concrete floor. Startled, he pivoted to see a cat jump down from a shelf and run outside. A mouser, Frankie assumed, making a mad dash to freedom from the windowless room. "Make a run for it, cat. This is your chance to get away from shithead Carsley," Frankie called to the cat.

Frankie walked straight to the lighted beer cooler, grabbed the two six-packs, and headed back toward the storage room. He pushed the door in and stepped through the threshold, then froze. Floyd Carsley was standing in front of him, holding a revolver at his side.

Frankie just stood there, one of the rare times he'd ever been lost for words.

"Now put the beer down and step back into the store," Carsley told him, motioning Frankie back with the weapon. "I don't want your arms to get tired, waiting for the sheriff."

"Come on, Carsley, it's only two six-packs. I'll pay to have the door repaired. Just put the gun down before somebody gets hurt."

"I don't think so. Everyone in town knows you Bartletts are no-good thieves. Well, this time, one of you bastards got caught red-handed. Now get back inside like I told you."

That caustic comment was all Frankie needed to hear to touch him off. No one, not even a person holding a handgun, gets away with slamming the family. With one violent swing of one of the six-packs, he caught Carsley in the groin, driving him back into one of the metal shelves and then onto the floor, reeling with pain.

Frankie dashed toward the loading ramp only to trip over Carsley's flailing legs, falling to the floor alongside him. Carsley had recovered enough from the blow that he turned the gun on Frankie, barely three feet away. Frankie grabbed Carsley's arm and forced it over his head. The handgun fired. The bullet hit the metal shade of the storage room's only light, snapping the bulb's filament. In the dark, the struggle continued.

Frankie rolled Floyd onto his stomach and started beating his head against the floor, yelling for him to drop the revolver. Carsley managed to slide his arm out from under his belly and twisted the gun, trying to point the barrel at Frankie. Frankie felt the steel barrel touch his arm. Struggling to pry the gun from Carsley's grip, the weapon discharged. It was over in an instant. Frankie felt Carsley's body go limp. He had bent Carsley's arm enough that the gun pointed at the back of Carsley's head. The .45-caliber Smith and Wesson blew a crayon size hole into the base of the store owner's skull.

The loading dock's dusk-to-dawn security light began to flicker. Each burst of energy jumped through the open door that led to the loading platform, lighting the storage room with an eerie glow. And with each flash, Carsley's body lit up like a black-and-white neon sign. Frankie gawked at the blood oozing from the bullet entry hole in his skull. It looked black, more like writing ink, most likely caused by the pulsating security light, he imagined. He stared at Carsley's body, trying to convince himself the shooting had been an accident. After all, he didn't pull the trigger. Carsley shot himself. Nevertheless, Frankie knew a defense that lame would not impress a jury. He needed to get away fast in case a neighbor heard the shot and called the police.

Just then, the loading dock light snapped on. Frankie spotted the two six-packs and grabbed them off the floor. He gave the dead body one final glance and left the store, careful not to leave any trace that he had been there.

Frankie's mind whirled at what had happened during the twenty-mile ride back to the Haven. He'd done many things in his life that would have prevented him from receiving a Good Citizen award. Still, he had never killed anyone—until now. He debated if he should tell his brothers about the shooting. Certainly not Beatrice. She would fly off the handle, leave the family compound, and walk the fifty miles to her cousin's in Madrid if she had to. On that point, Frankie thought her leaving wouldn't be all that bad, but still probably not a good idea to tell her about Carsley's demise. He decided to keep the events of the past two hours to himself, convinced that saying nothing and acting dumb about the incident was the best strategy for staying out of prison. He downed one of the newly acquired beers, tossed the empty onto the pickup's floor, and turned the radio to his favorite country-western station.

When Frankie arrived home, he resumed his horizontal position on the couch, staring at the ceiling. Frankie had two things to consume him: his dying father and Floyd Carsley's murder. Beatrice walked into the living room, saw Frankie sprawled out on the couch, and resumed her incessant badgering. She told Frankie he had turned into one useless slug and demanded he get off the goddamn couch and find something to do outside.

"Beatrice, there's something you need to know. You assume the person you're talking to gives a rat's ass what you have to say," Frankie said, holding the empty beer bottle out. "Now, if you want to be helpful, take this empty, and bring me a cold one from the refrigerator."

"I'm touched by your show of affection, Frankie. Really touched. You jackass!" She grabbed the bottle out of his hand, tempted to implant it into his skull.

Frankie tried to go after Beatrice, but as he struggled to get off the couch, the room began to spin violently. He collapsed back onto the couch and slept until morning.

Several days passed before the rest of the Bartletts learned of Carsley's murder. Frankie had let Josh use his pickup to drive to Kingston to pick up groceries at Riverside Market and to stop at Carsley's to buy cigarettes. At the counter, Josh noticed a large portrait of Mr. Carsley draped in black crepe paper on the wall behind the cash register. The young female clerk cried when Josh asked about the sullen painting. Between sobs, she proceeded to tell him about her boss's murder. Josh couldn't believe it. Other than the clerk at the NAPA Auto Parts store, Floyd Carsley was the only person in town that knew Josh by name, and Floyd was one of the few adults the shy Bartlett dared to talk to. Even though he had a total disdain for Frankie and Dick, Floyd had taken a liking to Josh and always found time to speak with him. He knew Josh was a little slow and felt bad about how Frankie treated his younger brother each time they entered the store.

The Carsley killing shocked the tight-knit community of Kingston. The last homicide in Skyler County was in 1962 when Fred Clough went berserk and killed his father with a baseball bat during an argument over what year the former Boston Braves baseball team moved to Milwaukee.

Josh couldn't wait to get home to tell his brothers what had happened to poor old Mr. Carsley. He raced up the driveway blowing the pickup's horn and scattering the chickens in every direction. Soon, the doors of the three trailers flew open, and everyone rushed toward the truck to see the cause of the commotion. Even Frankie was curious enough to pry himself off the couch. He took the time to open the bedroom door to check on his father. Frankie watched the bedcovers slowly rise and fall as his father slept. He quietly shut the door and stumbled outside to join the others. Everyone had crowded around Frankie's pickup, waiting for Josh to tell them what had excited him.

"It's Mr. Carsley. Someone shot him dead! Executed him," Josh bellowed as he jumped out of the truck.

"Executed him?" What do you mean, Josh, executed him?" Dick's wife asked.

"Well, that's what Sarah told me when I stopped in to get cigarettes for Frankie. Oh, by the way, Frankie, they're on the seat in the truck. You owe me twenty dollars for the four packs. Can I have my money now?" Josh asked, often having a problem staying focused on the issue at hand, although rightly concerned about being stuck paying for Frankie's two-pack-a-day habit.

"You'll get your goddamn money when I'm ready to give it to you. What else did Sarah tell you?" Frankie asked, trying to appear relaxed and calm, only interested in Carsley's murder from the perspective of an innocent bystander.

"Like I said, he was killed execution-style. Forced to stand facing the beer cooler and then shot in the back of the head."

"Is that what she said?" Frankie asked, knowing that wasn't exactly what happened.

"Well, not in so many words, but how else would you execute someone if they didn't stand facing a wall?"

"Jesus, Josh, where do you come up with your wacky ideas? Anything else?" Frankie asked, still probing to discover what rumors were circulating around town about the murder.

"Sarah told me the state police have a couple of leads they're working on. Seems like half the town saw a black Honda with New York plates parked in front of the store on the day of the murder. The cops think maybe whoever it was came back later to rob the store, and somehow Mr. Carsley caught them in the act and killed him."

"That's likely what happened. A whacked-out cocaine junkie passing through town needed money to buy drugs and thought breaking into Carsley's store was a quick way to get it," Frankie said, eager to promote the narrative.

"When was the murder?" Darlene asked.

"Three days ago. The cops figure someone killed him after the store closed late Saturday. Mrs. Carsley found the body when she went looking for him when Mr. Carsley didn't show up after work. It was their anniversary, and they'd planned to go to Waterville for supper to celebrate."

"Well, that's an anniversary surprise she will never forget," Dick said.

"That's not very nice, Dick. The man is murdered, and the wife finds the body; have a little sympathy, okay?" Darlene told him.

"Yeah, maybe for her, but I never could stand that asshole husband of hers. Just because he owned a business, he thought he was King Shit. Every time we went into the store, he watched us like a hawk. It was as if he was a second lieutenant in the Gestapo, ready to pounce if we tried to steal a roll of toilet paper or a bottle of ketchup."

Frankie nodded in agreement, knowing he had taken care of that minor annoyance.

For three nights, Floyd's homicide had been the lead story on the news channels. However, Josh and his wife, Wendy, owned the Haven's only television, and neither watched television news. "Too much competition from the game shows; besides, you can learn a lot watching *Jeopardy*," Josh had told his wife.

The last television Frank owned was while living in Litchfield, twenty-five years earlier. Five-year-old Frankie never forgot the day his father carried the TV out of the farmhouse.

The farm had sold, and the Bartletts had moved most of their possessions out of the rickety farmhouse. One of the last items to go was the RCA tabletop television. Young Frankie assumed it was going in the truck body for the four-hour ride to its new home in Skyler County. Instead, his father stepped off the porch carrying the television and set it in front of the woodpile. Frankie watched his father walk to the pickup, turn on the truck's ignition, hit play on the CD menu, and jack the volume to full power. Out screamed Frank's favorite tune, "A Country Boy Can Survive." He then grabbed the 30-caliber carbine from the gun rack on the back window and slipped seven cartridges into the magazine. He walked past Frankie without saying a word, dropped to one knee, and took dead aim at the RCA. In rapid succession, seven bullets blew through the 21-inch screen. Frank remained crouched, staring at the annihilated television, satisfied with his aim and its destruction. He slowly stood and glanced at his bewildered son staring at the shattered television, holding his hands over his ears.

"How'd you like that for shooting, Frankie boy? Not bad for someone who hasn't fired a rifle since deer hunting season," he said with a grin.

"Why did you do it, Dad? Why did you shoot the TV? I thought we were taking it to our new home," Frankie complained, baffled by his father's actions.

"I'll tell you why, son." The two walked back to the pickup and sat on the tailgate, Frankie stopping long enough to turn off the pick-up's ignition.

"You might not understand everything I'm going to tell you, Frankie, but you will when you're older." Frank reached into his shirt pocket and pulled out a cigarette. Frank always carried his smokes lose. His cigarette addiction was too great for him to take the time trying to coax one out of a full pack.

"You hear those cars zooming up and down the highway over there?" he asked, pointing over his shoulder toward the newly built turnpike. Before Frankie had answered, his father continued.

"Well, before it was built, I could sit on the porch on a warm June night and listen to the peepers down by the marsh work themselves into a frenzy. Why they would get so loud, you couldn't hear yourself think. And before I cut hay in the summer, you could listen to the bobolink sputter away as it flew from stem to stem, staking out its territory. Well, all of that's gone. The state filled the marsh and, in the process, drove out the frogs and every other critter that lived there, all to build a highway for people to race here and there doing nothing important. Most of the birds disappeared as well. It's hard for a bird to build its nest when its home is under eight inches of hot top. And most of those who managed to raise a family got splattered against some out-of-stater's grill.

As for the bobolinks that relocated, you couldn't hear them if you wanted above the whine of the traffic or an irate trucker blasting his air horn at the car in front of him. Well, they got their brand-new road, and us farmers got the shaft. Nearly every farm for twenty miles of here went out of business. All because the state took their land for pennies on the dollar and then split it in two to build that goddamn four-lane monstrosity of a road. Why the whole process stunk so bad that old Bert Hemingway couldn't take it anymore. Hung himself. His wife found him swinging from the hayloft." Frank looked at his son, hoping he could comprehend what he was telling him. Unfortunately, Frankie had not heard a word his father had spoken to him. He only wanted the answer to one question.

"So why did you shoot the TV?"

"Because of what it represents."

"What does that mean?"

"It means people have gone numb watching that poor excuse for a babysitter. Nobody thinks for themselves anymore. They just sit and stare night after night at the box, expecting to be entertained, and if one channel doesn't do it for them, they flip to the next until they find a show that does. I swore if I ever sold this place, I would do it cold turkey and leave behind all the happy horse shit of today's society. I'd blow up the TV, throw away the newspapers, live in the woods, raise a big garden, and hunt for our own meat. Live off the land as folks used to; to do that, you can't sit around wasting time watching television. Do you understand what I'm telling you, Frankie?" he asked, pulling another cigarette from his shirt pocket and lighting it with the barely burning stub.

"No. I just wanted to take the television with us," Frankie whined and then jumped off the tailgate and sat inside the pickup, mad at his father for demolishing the television. Frank sat alone on the tailgate, shaking his head, puffing on his smoke. As Frankie became older, father and son became similar in thought and deed, but at this moment, all the boy wanted to do was watch cartoons.

After Josh told all he knew about the murder, Dick, Darlene, Josh, and Wendy started back to their homes when Beatrice asked Frankie a question. One that caused the four to return to the pickup to hear Frankie's answer.

"Frankie, wasn't last Saturday when you went to Kingston for beer?"

"Yeah, what of it?"

"It was late Saturday afternoon, as I remember."

"Yes, Beatrice, it was late Saturday afternoon. Wait a minute! You're not thinking I killed Carsley, are you?"

"No. But I do think it's quite a coincidence that you were at Carsley's store just before he was murdered." Beatrice didn't know if he had gotten his beer at Riverside Market or Carsley's, but she would soon find out.

"That's all it is, Beatrice, a coincidence. I grabbed two six-packs out of the cooler, and Carsley rang them up. He mumbled something about it being his anniversary and closing early. I paid him for the beer and walked out of the store. That's all there was to it," Frankie said, sounding confident in his actions.

Beatrice continued to press. "Was anyone else in the store at the time?" The others stepped closer to hear his response.

"That's enough, Beatrice! I know what you're trying to do."

"What am I trying to do, Frankie?"

"You want everyone here to think I was involved in Carsley's murder," Frankie said, pointing at the others. "You're trying to plant the seed, so they'll wonder if I'm the killer. I did not kill Floyd Carsley! It was those druggies looking for cash, just as the police said," Frankie bellowed, avoiding eye contact. By the expression on the other Bartletts' faces, Beatrice had achieved her objective.

"Don't any of you ever bring up Carsley's name again. Got that?" Frankie ordered and stormed back into the house, slamming the kitchen door.

Usually Beatrice came out on the short end when dealing with her husband. However, this time she'd gotten the best of Frankie. He knew she was on to him and had the others speculating on his guilt as well. The adult Bartletts knew Frankie was capable of nearly anything, so the possibility he might be involved in Carsley's murder was not out of the realm of possibility. As time passed and there was no arrest for Carsley's murder, it appeared more and more likely that Frankie had done the crime. However, none of them spoke of the slaying again until several years later, when Dick dropped Floyd Carsley's name after the run-in with Kathy at Skyler Pond.

LEAVING SKYLER POND

After their near-death experience being lost on the pond, neither Dan nor Kathy was interested in wandering far from camp. Dan's excursions outside took him as far as the woodshed and the sled shed to fill the gasoline generator. Kathy confined herself to the twenty-four-by-twenty-eight-foot cabin, staring out the windows at the ever-growing mountain of snow, wondering if the nightmare would ever end.

Ever since she was a child she'd had a penchant for reading. It didn't matter the subject, she just enjoyed reading for reading's sake. During the past three months, Kathy had reread all the books she had brought from Hampden and had no interest in reading them a third time. She remembered how she had looked forward to going to Portland before Christmas to shop with Hazel, planning to buy her reading material for the winter at one of the city bookstores. If only she had that pile of new books to help her get through the days of nearly unbearable monotony.

Kathy constantly thought about her daughter. Was she safe? Did Hazel have heat and electricity? Most importantly, would she ever see her only child again? Her eyes teared each time she thought of Hazel. Often, she'd glance at the phone, wishing it to ring. She only wanted to hear Hazel say "Don't worry, Mother, I'm fine. See you soon. Love you," just ten little words that would allow her to keep her sanity.

One afternoon during a squall, Kathy turned from the window to Dan, sitting in the recliner, reading.

"You know, Dan, I've been thinking a lot lately about all the crazy weather. I know this might sound a little strange, but what if all the snow and freak storms we've been having for the last three months have only been here at Skyler Pond."

Dan set aside his book. "Only at Skyler Pond? What are you talking about?" he asked, giving her a questioning look.

"Well, maybe not just here, but only in the mountains. What if there is no snow in other parts of the state, and everyone is going around doing what they've always done? You know, just going on with their lives, like working, taking the kids to school, going shopping," Kathy said, turning back to the window, thinking wistfully about what it would be like to return to everyday life.

"That's silly, Kathy. Of course the whole state is in the same mess as us."

"How do you know that, Dan? We have no TV, no radio, and no newspaper. Since Hazel and Tom were here for Thanksgiving, we haven't talked to anyone."

"All of that's true, Kathy. However, you forget a few critical details, like why haven't the roads been plowed. Seems to me the state would have every plow truck from Portland to Bangor out clearing the back roads if they weren't needed downstate. And what about Hazel? If everything was sunny and bright in Westbrook, don't you think Hazel would attempt to find out how her parents are making out in the backwoods of Skyler County and send someone by snowmobile to check on us?"

"No, I'm sorry, Dan, but this isn't real. We don't know if there is a United States of America anymore. Maybe we've been taken over by the North Koreans or perhaps the Chinese army for all we know. Either that or half the country has been blown to bits thanks to Edward Teller and his hydrogen bomb.

"I think it's fake, all of it. I bet a Hollywood movie was trying some new high-tech special effect that got out of control and screwed up the atmosphere, causing this nutty weather. To cover it up, the government told us North Korea attacked us. That's what I think," Kathy said in a barely audible voice, staring at the trees.

Kathy's off-the-wall reasoning stunned Dan. He moved from the recliner to the couch. "Kathy, come here and sit beside me."

Kathy sat close to Dan and began to cry. "Oh, Dan, am I going crazy?"

"You're not going crazy. This whole stinking mess is just wearing us both down. Making our minds go into overdrive, trying to reason what is happening to us. I know it's not easy, but we can't let it beat us. We need each other to get through this, and we will get through it. We just need to hang tough a while longer. The sun will shine again, and we want to be ready when it does," Dan said, putting his arm around Kathy and drawing her closer. Consoling Kathy, his eyes were drawn to the scribbling on the envelope lying on the coffee table. He wanted to tell her what the figures meant but was uncertain if this was the right time. Unknowingly, Kathy presented Dan with the opportunity he needed.

"Dan, isn't there anything we can do to get out of here? I don't think I can take much more of this, or I will go insane. Let's make a run for it. I'm willing to take the risk that we won't make it, but it's better than staying here and going stark raving mad."

Dan sat up, gently removing his arm from her shoulder. "Kathy, there's something you need to know."

"What is it?" she asked, drying her eyes on the sleeve of her flannel shirt.

He picked up the envelope. "We have about four gallons of gasoline left to run the generator. The way I figure it, if we cut back on the amount of time we use the lights, it will last another two weeks, tops."

"We only run it for a half hour in the evening now. How much less do we need to run it? Dan, I hate sitting in the dark."

"Fifteen minutes for the gas to last another fourteen days."

"My God, Dan. We might as well not run it at all if we have to cut back that much."

"I'm afraid there's more."

"What?" she asked, wondering what else could be worse than sitting in the dark for thirteen hours a day.

"I took stock of what we have left for food. There's basically nothing except for a half bag of sugar, three cans of soup, a couple boxes of pasta, and a jar of peanut butter."

"What about the ten pounds of flour you said you found in the corner of the storage room?"

"Oh, it was there, all right. Except a mouse ate a hole through the bag and decided to raise a family inside. The smell was enough to gag a maggot, so I tossed it out."

Kathy remained remarkably calm. "I told you to put it in the metal can for that very reason. Why didn't you do it?"

"Forgot, I guess," Dan said sheepishly.

"So where does that leave us? Do you have a plan, or will we just sit here until we starve?"

"I have a plan. It's to get the hell out of here. We'll have to risk everything and go south. We need to go now and take what food we have left. Eventually, we'll find someone that will help us. Maybe they'll have a phone that works, and we can call Hazel. She might know of a friend we can stay with."

"Yes. Let's do it. We'll leave first thing in the morning." Finally Dan had agreed to leave Skyler Pond, which Kathy had wanted to do since the first snowstorm three months earlier.

"No. We'll leave the day after tomorrow. This will be a one-way trip, no turning back if we forget anything, so we need to get it right. There's not enough gas for both snowmobiles, so we'll take mine. The 440 has more power to pull the loaded dogsled and us. In the morning, I'll drain what gas there is in the generator and your machine. We'll load the dogsled with our food and pack it tight with our warmest clothes. We'll take the little backpacking stove we use for camping to melt snow for water. Once we have everything we need packed and ready to go, we'll head out."

After a full day preparing for the long-awaited departure from Skyler Pond, it was finally time to go.

The snowmobile's fuel gauge read three-quarters full, enough gas to make it thirty miles down the Dam Road. The big unknown was how the weight of the loaded sled would cut into that distance. He fretted, remembering how he'd almost bought a new snowmobile before they moved to the pond, a high-end off-trail machine that would go just about anywhere and get twenty miles per gallon, but at the last minute had decided not to spend the money.

Dan grabbed a plastic snow shovel out of the sled shed and the battery-powered chain saw he used for limbing trees and strapped them to the rear of the dogsled. Kathy didn't notice him slip his 12-gauge pump shotgun and a handful of double-aught buckshot into his sleeping bag. Although buckshot was a little excessive for killing rabbits or squirrels, it was the perfect load for holding off two-legged vermin.

Steering the snowmobile would be difficult, with both of them riding on the machine. Dan needed room to negotiate snowdrifts and dodge downed trees. Kathy agreed to sit on the sled wedged among the extra clothes and supplies. Dan wondered if the snowmobile had enough power to break trail while pulling Kathy, him, and all their gear. Once they were underway, he needed to maintain his speed to keep the machine from bogging down or risk overheating the engine or blowing a drive belt. If that happened, it would mean a long slow trek on snowshoes to reach civilization, an undertaking fraught with its own dangers.

It was a typical cloudy sky. The sun's ghostly image periodically showed through the clouds, wanting to break through the overcast but lacking the power to make it happen. Kathy and Dan readied to leave the cabin for the last time. There was little conversation. Both knew what they were about to do had risks, but staying at Skyler Pond meant certain starvation. At least they had a fighting chance to make it to safety, wherever it might be.

Nearly to the snowmobile, Kathy and Dan stopped. The sky turned black as midnight, and the wind began to howl. The threat of another snowstorm forced them back inside the cabin. They silently stood at the window in their snowmobile suits for nearly an hour, watching and waiting for the wind and snow to end.

At last, the storm sped across the pond, and Dan pronounced it was safe to leave. While he went outside to start the snowmobile, Kathy searched for an extra pair of gloves she had forgotten to pack.

Dan stood by the idling snowmobile, impatient for Kathy to return. Finally, she appeared on the deck, closed the door behind her, and trudged up the snow-beaten path. Dan helped Kathy climb onto the sled and get situated on the plywood floor. With her back propped against the sled's rear panel, he packed the plastic bags filled with clothes around her to keep her warm on the long trip to somewhere. Dan couldn't help but think how odd she looked stacked among the supplies, with only her eyes and nose visible under the snowmobile helmet. They traded weak smiles and gave each other half-hearted thumbs-ups.

Blue smoke from the overly rich mixture of gas and oil poured from the old snowmobile as Dan pressed the throttle. The machine revved, the drive belt engaged, and the snowmobile jerked forward for twenty feet and stopped. Dan walked back to tell Kathy that he had forgotten the extra box of wooden matches on the kitchen counter and went back to the cabin, leaving her wedged among the bags of supplies.

Dan rechecked the rooms, ensuring he had locked the windows and the wood fire was out. Even though their future was uncertain, Dan hoped to one day return to Skyler Pond, and when he did, he wanted to return to a camp that was still standing and secure.

Satisfied he had left nothing to chance, he picked up the box of matches and headed toward the door when he noticed an envelope on the kitchen table wedged between the salt and pepper shakers. A folded piece of paper leaned against the envelope with two words in Kathy's handwriting.

"Please Read." The unsealed stamped envelope was addressed to Hazel Martin, 621 Orange Street, Westbrook, Maine. Dan couldn't help himself. He needed to know what Kathy had written and slipped the letter from the envelope.

To whomever reads this note: Our names are Kathy and Dan Simmons. This is our cabin. Since the start of the nuclear war, we have been stranded here, and now we have to leave. Our food is nearly gone, and we are using the last of our gasoline to leave Skyler Pond, hoping to find food and shelter. We want to live, but there are no guarantees we will find someone to help us. Please mail this letter. It's to our daughter, Hazel Martin. She must know what happened to us and that we love her.

Thank you.

Dan refolded the letter and placed it back into the envelope. He stood there, staring blankly at the kitchen table. Kathy was right. There were no guarantees they would survive the journey. Other than Kathy's brief encounter with the three hooligans who had threatened her, they hadn't had contact with anyone for three months. Maybe there was no law and order. Perhaps the three rogue snowmobilers represented a new hierarchy of marauding gangs that survived by taking what they wanted from those who couldn't defend their homes or themselves and, maybe, were willing to kill intruders accidentally entering their territory.

Dan's mind whirled with the many unforeseen hazards they might encounter, all more likely than to be killed by an imaginary band of bloodthirsty marauders. Freezing to death or starving were the first possibilities that came to mind. Nevertheless, they had to try. They were out of options.

Dan's mental wanderings were interrupted by the two-cycle snowmobile engine's steady hollow rhythm idling outside the cabin. He looked at Kathy's letter and then turned toward the door, noticing his cell phone on the counter next to the gas stove. He couldn't believe it. It was the last thing he needed to leave behind. He was sure he had tucked it in with his extra clothes last night. Dan slipped the phone into his down parka and zipped the pocket tight. Outside, he came up behind Kathy, struggling to get off the sled to see what was taking Dan so long.

"All set?" Dan asked, not mentioning the letter to Hazel. He helped her resettle on the sled and told her to yell if she wanted him to stop. At ten thirty on February 23, Kathy and Dan made their dash to escape Skyler Pond.

It was a wild ride out the Skyler Pond Road. Dan threw his weight one way and then the other, trying to keep the snowmobile from being sucked into the loose, drifting snow. With each lurch of the snowmobile, Kathy was whipped from side to side, all the time gripping the sled's rails to keep from being tossed off. At the Dam Road, Dan stopped to check on Kathy.

"You all right?" Dan asked, knowing Kathy must have taken a thrashing on the blazingly fast trip to the Dam Road.

"Yeah, I'm okay, although I should have taken a Dramamine before we started."

"From here on, it shouldn't be so rough. You should make out a lot better."

"If I don't, you can ride back here, and I'll drive."

Kathy looked around the parking area. "Dan, I don't see our car."

"It's right here." Dan grabbed one of the ski poles off the sled, walked off to the side of the snowmobile, and shoved the pole into the snow. At about two feet, it hit resistance. He looked at Kathy and smiled. "Believe it or not, that's the car's roof," he said, tapping the pole's tip against the metal.

"I'll have to believe it. It just seems impossible there can be this much snow. It has to be seven feet deep."

"I'd say closer to nine. Look at the Skyler Pond Road sign, or I should say where the sign should be. That signpost is close to eight feet high, and now it's buried. We need to get going before another storm hits," Dan said, sitting down on the snowmobile.

"Dan, I just thought of something," Kathy said, sounding concerned.

"What?"

"Where will we sleep tonight if we don't find anyone to help us?"

"We'll stop along the road and sleep next to the snowmobile. We can put one of the tarps we brought on the ground and pile fir boughs on top of it. Once we're in our sleeping bags and have the wool blanket on top of us, it will be just like being in bed at camp," Dan told her, trying to put the best face on a bad situation.

"Really. And suppose we get a storm during the night and are covered in a foot of snow. How are we to stay dry?"

"Simple. We will have the second plastic tarp over us. We will shake it a few times before we get up, and all the snow will slide off. We'll be as dry as we are now. Any more questions or concerns?"

"If I do, you'll be the first person I ask," Kathy snapped, ending the conversation. Dan always had an answer for everything. An annoying trait that she tried not to let get under her skin.

Dan turned south on the Dam Road. Their long journey into the unknown had begun.

The road wound out of the mountains through long flats separated by short steep descents. As bleak as their situation was, there was a marvelous beauty in the distant snow-covered mountains, a truly scenic snowmobile ride in ordinary times. However, times were far from ordinary. Although the ride was reasonably pleasant, nothing looked familiar. All the landmarks they had passed countless times driving to Skyler Pond were now buried beneath a mountain of snow.

Dan maneuvered the snowmobile through areas decimated by the ferocious winds dodging downed trees, massive limbs, and snapped-off telephone poles. Areas clogged with debris that couldn't be penetrated needed to be cleared wide enough with the chainsaw for the snowmobile and sled to slip through.

He had glanced at the odometer to see how far they had traveled since leaving Skyler Pond when a faint thumping sound came from under the cowling. A noise Dan chose to ignore. The noise became louder over the next mile, culminating in an explosive bang. Instantly the machine stopped. Dan lifted the cowling. The drive belt was in shreds. The heavy load had put more stress on the belt than it could handle.

"Son of a bitch! Everything was going so well, and then this had to happen!"

"What happened?" Kathy asked, pulling herself off the sled.

"The drive belt blew."

"So put the spare on. You have one, don't you?"

"I have the old one that I replaced. The problem is that it's three-quarters worn out and has a dead spot from when I tried to move the machine with the break on. We'll be lucky to get five miles out of it before that one explodes."

"Well, that's five fewer miles we'll have to walk. Just put it on and let's get going," she ordered, wanting to put as many miles between her and Skyler Pond as possible.

Five minutes later, with the replacement belt installed, they continued down the Dam Road. Dan eased up on the throttle, hoping that going slower would extend the belt's fragile life. No matter how he babied the machine, it was only a matter of time before the worn belt disintegrated like the first one.

Progress was slow, with frequent stops to clear a path through the fallen trees and woody debris and to recover the snowmobile when it bogged down in the soft snow. Now the enemy was the oncoming darkness only two hours away. Dan was looking for a place to spend the night when he spotted a softwood stand, precisely what they needed to make a mattress of boughs.

"Cozy, isn't it?" Dan asked after erecting their shelter for the night.

She studied the Rube Goldberg contraption her husband had erected. A corner of the blue plastic tarp was tied to the rail of the dogsled and then draped over a ridgepole held up by two cedar poles driven into the snow just beyond the snowmobile. Poles driven into the snow anchored the other three corners of the little shelter, all secured by the cotton rope Dan had grabbed from the sled shed before leaving camp.

"You're the engineer. I guess it will work."

Dan had hoped for a more enthusiastic endorsement of his handiwork, but he'd settle for what he could get.

After a meal of peanut butter spread on two stale granola bars, they sat in their sleeping bags on the fir boughs with their backs propped against the snowmobile.

"How far do you think we went today?" Kathy asked, too wired after the day's events to think about sleeping.

"If you believe the snowmobile's odometer, twelve miles."

"That's it? Twelve miles? My back feels more like I rode a hundred and twelve." She continued, "How far do you think we'll have to go to find someone to help us?"

"Who knows? We might get lucky and find someone at one of the old farmhouses once we get to Fraternity Township. Even that's another thirty miles."

"And if we find no one there?" Kathy asked, not really wanting to know Dan's answer.

"We keep riding until we do. We may have to go all the way to Deadwater. At least the odds should be in our favor in a town with a population of eight hundred." Dan neglected to tell Kathy that if they had to journey as far as the isolated logging town, it would be on snowshoes. Dan knew they would be lucky if they had enough gasoline to reach the first of the scattered homes in Fraternity Township.

"What was that noise?" Kathy asked, sitting up straight in her sleeping bag.

"I didn't hear anything. You probably heard a branch break under the weight of the snow."

"Maybe," she said, peering into the darkness. "There it is again! You must have heard it that time."

"I heard it," he said, sliding his arm inside the sleeping bag, searching for the flashlight. Dan pointed the light toward the noise as both strained to see the sound's source.

Another twig broke off to the side. "Dan, there's two of them," Kathy said, feeling as if something big was about to happen.

Dan leaned over Kathy and pulled the loaded shotgun from the sled. At the same time, Kathy continued to probe the darkness for any sign of movement.

"Just keep watching, and tell me if you see anything."

"See anything? I can hardly see my hand in front of my face," Kathy whispered.

As both of them stared into the night, looking for what might be watching them inside the tree line, the tops of the fir trees started to sway. They were so focused on what might be lurking in the woods that they hadn't heard the approaching storm. Seconds later, the squall hit. The temperature plummeted, and it commenced to snow.

"Of all the luck," Dan complained. "We'll never be able to hear it now," he yelled over the howling wind.

"Maybe whatever is out there will go back into the woods to escape the storm," Kathy shouted.

The wind beat on the tarp, causing it to flex inward and then outward in response to the gale. A blast of wind worked one of the stakes loose, and soon one corner of the tarp had ripped free. The half-detached tarp snapped in the wind until it collapsed and blew down the road until it was fetched up by the rope tied to the dogsled.

"I don't like this, Kathy. I've got a bad feeling that whatever it is, is still out there."

"Start the snowmobile! Maybe the headlight will scare it off," Kathy screamed.

Dan passed the shotgun to Kathy and lifted himself onto the Polaris. He repeatedly pulled the starter cord, but the machine didn't fire. Fumbling for the choke, he tried again. Nothing. Dan cursed and repeatedly yanked on the rope until he was exhausted. In his panic, he had forgotten to turn on the ignition switch. Dan ran his hand over the dash until he felt the key. A turn to the right, one more pull on the cord, and the engine snapped to life. The headlight began to glow, becoming brighter as the engine settled into its regular rhythm.

Dan searched the area illuminated by the headlight, not knowing what he might see. To his relief, there was only the snow-covered road littered with limbs and tree branches. He began to think he had overreacted to the sounds they had heard, trying to convince himself everything sounded different at night. Noises you would pay little attention to in the daylight tended to be louder and more mysterious after dark, particularly when surrounded by the deep forest. Still, Dan wanted to be sure they were alone and looked again, this time with the light on high beam.

The snowmobile's headlight penetrated the swirling snow and deep into the darkness. At the far edge of the beam, Dan saw what appeared to be the ends of two short logs lying next to each other. He struggled to confirm that they were, in fact, pieces of wood and not something more menacing. However, each gust of wind brought a temporary whiteout, making it impossible to see beyond the front of the snowmobile. Finally, after a break in the storm's fury, the two unidentified forms popped back into view. They seemed closer, but Dan rationalized that he must have misjudged the distance—that is, until the shadowy forms began slowly edging toward the snowmobile. It wasn't until they were in full range of the headlight that he identified them. Wolves! Two of them crouched low to the snow, inching toward the snowmobile.

Dan yelled, trying to scare them off. He flashed the snowmobile headlight, but they were on a mission, and that mission was devouring their next meal. Another blast of wind pelted Dan's face with snow. He quickly cleared his eyes with the sleeve of his jacket and refocused on the two approaching animals. At fifty feet, the smaller of the two broke off the hunt and disappeared into the shadows as the second continued to close the gap between it and Dan.

Dan was about to tell Kathy to give him his shotgun when the wolf charged the snowmobile. At eight feet, it sprang. Dan had little time to react to the large body hurtling toward him. Instinctively, he rolled off the machine to avoid the oncoming animal.

Above the raging storm, a single shot. Dan had no idea what had happened until he stood up and cautiously approached the snowmobile. He could see the windshield riddled with holes in the headlight's reflection. Dan looked back to see Kathy standing in the shadows, the butt of the shotgun still pressed against her shoulder, ready to fire again if necessary. Dan peered over the top of the cowling. The predator's head and front legs rested on the plastic hood below the headlight. Kathy stood next to him, shaking from what had happened.

"Is it dead?" she asked, not wanting to come any closer to her target.

"Yes, it's dead," is all Dan could say, still stunned by the incident.

Both stood there, not saying a word, staring at the dead animal. Finally, Dan spoke.

"Nice shooting. Thanks."

"I had to do it, Dan. It would have killed you," she said, having regrets she had shot the beast.

"Of course you did. You had no choice. It could have killed both of us."

Still shaken by the wolf's attack, Dan tried to lighten the situation. "I didn't know you were such a good shot. How come you refuse to shoot partridge in the fall? We would have a freezer full of birds."

"I never felt a partridge would fly up and rip off my face."

There was no way Kathy was sleeping so close to the dead animal. She insisted Dan move the bed of boughs farther away from the snowmobile. In the end, it didn't matter. Neither of them could sleep after the adrenaline rush from what had happened, wondering if the second predator would try for a free meal. Instead, they lay in their sleeping bags waiting for morning, anxious to get moving and put the nightmare behind them.

"Do you still think the wolves are acting normal, Dan? Or has the nuclear war changed their behavior? Maybe the radiation from all the bombs has affected their brains, and now they're programmed to kill people."

"That's ridiculous. No mad scientist is running around turning wolves into killing machines. And wolves aren't lapping up pond water laced with strontium 90, causing them to go stark raving mad craving human flesh."

"How can you be sure? We don't know what's been happening in the world for the last three months. Maybe it's turned into chemical warfare, and that's caused all kinds of bizarre things to happen. If not, why did those animals attack us? Wolves try to avoid people, not confront them."

"Normally, they do run off. It's just that these aren't normal times. The predators are starving, just as we are. To them, we look like two extra-large protein bars ready to be unwrapped.

"It's not just the wolves. All the wildlife is struggling. Did you notice we hadn't seen as much as one red squirrel around camp in the past few weeks? I think all the cones have been blown off the trees by the damn wind, and they can't find them under all the snow. How's a rabbit going to survive when all the shrubs are buried? I'm sure the deer herd has been decimated. There's no way they can browse in eight feet of snow, let alone walk through it.

"The day I went to Belanger's camp looking for food, I saw two pairs of snowy owls. It's rare to see even a solitary snowy owl in the entire winter. My guess is to survive they were forced to leave Canada to find new territory. There's not enough food to go around, so the owls, and other predators, will travel to where they can find it."

"Do you think we will ever see normal again?" Kathy asked, wondering if the world would ever be the same. "I don't mean whether governments will rise or fall. I mean, normal in the sense that this seemingly endless nuclear winter will eventually end."

"The planet has an uncanny ability to recover from all the shit we humans keep throwing at it. It will just take time for the atmosphere to shed all the crap that got sucked up by all the friggin' bombs that were detonated. I guess once the climate readjusts, wolves, owls, and every other species will return to their natural habits, and life will continue."

"Maybe, if there is any wildlife left. Right now, the idiots in Washington and North Korea have Mother Nature on the run, and hopefully they don't drive her over a cliff," Kathy said, disappearing inside her sleeping bag.

At daybreak, Kathy and Dan were ready to move on. As the snowmobile lacked a reverse, they first needed to drag the dead wolf off to the side. The two grabbed its tail and pulled the hundred-pound carcass away from the snowmobile. Kathy detested touching the animal. Once it was out of the way, she repeatedly wiped her mittens in the snow.

"Trying to get rid of the wolf cooties?" Dan said, attempting to get a rise out of Kathy.

"Funny. I was trying to get the wolf hair and whatever else might be attached to it off my mittens. I don't want to come down with the screaming meemies or be infected with some kind of canine parasite."

Dan smiled and shook his head.

Less than a mile down the road, what had been an annoying thump with every revolution of the worn snowmobile belt turned into constant pounding. With no remedy short of a new drive belt, all Dan could do was keep going until the belt broke. He didn't have long to wait. Soon a cloud of burnt rubber spewed out from under the chassis, followed by a loud pop,

"Well, that's it. From here on, it will be on snowshoes. Are you up for it?" he asked Kathy.

"What choice do we have? I sure don't plan to die next to a busted snowmobile."

"There's just one thing, Kathy. We have hardly any food left. If we really tighten our belts, perhaps enough for three days. After that, the odds kind of work against us. Do you know what I'm trying to say?"

"Yeah, I know what you're trying to say. We might not make it out of here alive. I've known that since we left the cabin. I'd rather take my chances trying to save ourselves than sit in the recliner waiting for the end. Besides, the likelihood of seeing Hazel again is greater as well. The way I look at it, every mile we go is one mile closer to our daughter, and that thought alone is enough to keep me going."

"Okay. I know we'll make it, but it won't be easy. I think I know where we are, and if I'm right, it's still two days to Fraternity Township by snowshoes. If no one will help us there, it's another day to Deadwater," Dan said, wanting Kathy to know what they were up against.

"Why don't we go to Kingston? It's closer."

"That's an option. Except it's thirty miles west. If we want to reach Hazel and Tom, we must go south toward Waterville."

"Then let's get going."

Dan unlashed the plastic sled and began to load the tarps, sleeping bags, and extra clothes. The remaining food and gear would be crammed into the two small daypacks.

"What about the chainsaw?" Kathy asked.

"Leave it. We won't need it. Everything we haven't packed stays."

"Shotgun?" Kathy asked, noticing it lying across the snowmobile seat. Figuring there was no way Dan would leave it behind.

"I'll carry the shotgun. This time I'll be ready for whatever we come across."

After three hours on snowshoes, Dan told Kathy to hold up a minute while he took a piss. Standing at the edge of the road, he gazed down the steep embankment and noticed a dome-shaped object sticking above the snow. Dan knew what it looked like but thought he must be mistaken. He continued to study the mystery object until he realized what was wedged among the hardwood trees.

"Kathy! Come over here! You won't believe this," he yelled.

Kathy stepped up beside him. "What?" she asked, expecting to see a carcass of a dead moose or deer.

"Down there. It's a car!"

Kathy looked to where Dan pointed. "Oh, I see it. It looks like it's been there a while, with all that snow packed around it."

"I'm going down and check it out," Dan said, starting down the slope.

"Don't be foolish, Dan. You'll break your neck trying to get down there. Let's just keep going. We can go another three or four miles before we have to stop for the night.

"Kathy, there might be something inside we can use, maybe a flashlight or blanket. Perhaps food."

"Okay, but I still don't like it. Just be careful. It would be a shame to have to wrap you in that blanket you expect to find if you crack your skull open on the way down."

Kathy barely got the words out of her mouth when the branch Dan was hanging on snapped. He fell and then rolled down the bank, bouncing off several trees and finally stopping against a six-inch maple twenty feet above the buried vehicle.

"Are you okay?" Kathy yelled.

"Yeah, I guess so, except my back is killing me."

"Come on up. It's not worth it," Kathy demanded.

"I'm down here now. I'm going to see what I can find," Dan hollered, using the maple to pull himself to his feet.

He brushed the snow off the vehicle's side window and, through cupped hands, peered inside. "Jesus, I don't believe it."

The man appeared to be in his mid-fifties and extremely obese. A hunter, Dan supposed, based on his clothing and the fluorescent vest and hat lying on the floor. Dan struggled to read the date of a newspaper lying on the seat next to the dead man. November 27. That would mean the man had been at the bottom of the ravine for about three months. Probably trying to reach deer camp for the final three days of deer hunting, hit an icy spot, and flew over the bank, Dan speculated.

Before telling Kathy about the body, Dan looked through each window for anything they could use. He spied the man's groceries in a heap on the back seat's floor. Food that could help fend off starvation, at least temporarily. Dan had an idea. Stay the night in the car instead of lying on a bed of boughs somewhere along the road.

"Kathy! I've found food and lots of it!"

"Great! Bring it up."

"There's something else."

"What?" Kathy hollered back, thinking there was more good news to come.

"There's a dead man in the car."

"There's a what in the car?" Kathy replied, thinking she must have misunderstood what Dan said.

"I said a dead man is on the front seat."

"Is he dead?"

"Yes. A dead man is usually dead," Dan shot back, unsure if Kathy couldn't hear him or was just being smart. "Come on down, and we'll get him out. We'll spend the night in the vehicle."

"Forget it! I'm not pulling on any frozen corpse. You sleep in the vehicle. I'm staying up here."

"Come on, Kathy. We'll be out of the wind. You can have the back seat, and I'll sleep on the front seat." Lying where the frozen hunter had been for three months didn't appeal to Dan either. Still, being able to sleep one night out of the cold and snow, he could tolerate most anything.

"I said no. You get him out. Better yet, leave him there, and you can sleep in the back seat."

"Maybe I'll do that. Don't forget to keep the shotgun handy when you crawl into your sleeping bag in case you have unexpected visitors."

After a long pause, Kathy answered. "Okay. I'm coming down. I'll roll the plastic bag with the sleeping bags down to you."

"Good. Bring the shotgun if you can."

While Dan used a snowshoe to shovel enough snow away from the door to get the man out, Kathy looked inside.

"My God, Dan, that guy is huge! We'll never get him out." Kathy said, staring at the frozen corpse.

"That's why we're going to pull him out the passenger door— to avoid the steering wheel," Dan said, working frantically to clear the snow away from the door.

After repeatedly ramming the door into the drifted snow to gain a few extra inches of opening, the fat man was ready for his exit.

"Grab a leg. When I say 'pull,' pull.

"Pull!"

The body didn't budge. They gave him another yank, but still, they couldn't move the dead man. Dan inspected the dead body, trying to figure out the problem as Kathy looked on, anxious to finish the disgusting job.

"Got it," he announced, leaning across the hunter's body to free his frozen arm wedged in the steering wheel.

This time, the man grudgingly slid several inches toward the door. After a half dozen more tugs, the body slipped through the open door onto the snow.

"Now what?" Kathy asked, hoping that would be the end of it.

"We'll drag him away from the door and then check out what's inside the car for food," Dan said, gazing at the body.

After they pulled the body off to the side, Dan got into the car. Resting his knees on the front seat, he reached into the back and passed Kathy the supplies the man had intended for his hunting trip.

An unopened box of graham crackers, peanut butter, a half-dozen cans of frozen soup, dry cereal, a box of 5th Avenue candy bars, and two bags of potato chips topped the list.

Ten minutes later, they were sitting in the front seat having a meal, compliments of the fat man's misfortune of sliding off the road.

"You know, Dan, I never did like Lucky Charms. But now it's my favorite cereal," Kathy joked, cramming handfuls of the colorful cereal into her mouth.

"Yeah, and thanks to our little camping stove, washing them down with a can of Hearty Tomato Soup is a treat too."

Kathy noticed the key in the car's ignition. "Try the radio."

Dan turned the key, never expecting the radio to actually work. He pushed the scan button, and the display ran through the frequencies searching for a signal.

"Well, I'll be. It does work." Dan sat erect, straining to hear even a hint of a voice.

On the third scan, it locked onto a station. Kathy and Dan pulled themselves closer to the speakers trying to hear what the crackly voice was saying. But it was no use. There was so much static. It sounded like the person talking was in a tunnel with firecrackers going off in the background. Then the crackly voice ended, replaced by the sound they both recognized: the annoying two-tone alert signal of the Emergency Alert System. Dan and Kathy anticipated that an announcement about the war was imminent and stared at the radio, waiting for the newscaster to speak. Suddenly, the radio quit. The car's battery went flat.

"What do you make of it?" Kathy asked.

"Since we only picked up the government's emergency system, I would say things are pretty much the same. I think the freakish weather backs that up. It hasn't worsened. The storms are about as intense as ever and seem to occur with about the same frequency, so on the bright side, I guess that's a plus. All we can do is get a good night's sleep and continue on in the morning."

Kathy didn't answer. She finished eating and started to crawl over the front seat, hoping to fall asleep and forget about their nightmare for a few hours.

"Wait." Dan ordered. "Let's have a drink before calling it a night."

"Have what drink? Does this car have a bar?"

"No bar, but it does have this," Dan said, holding up an unopened pint of coffee brandy.

"Where in God's name did you find that?"

"In the glove compartment. It looks like we have something in common with our dead friend. The three of us like Allen's Coffee Brandy. Let's have a sip to celebrate."

"Celebrate what? We're sitting in a car at the bottom of a ravine, half-starved, with a frozen dead man barely three feet from us. The world could be on fire for all we know, and you and I might be the last two people left on earth."

"That's even more reason to celebrate. Think of it, Kathy and Dan Simmons, the last two humans standing out of eight billion people."

"That's not funny, Dan. Just the thought is terrifying."

"Sorry, Kathy. But face it, it's all out of our control. None of this happy horseshit is of our doing. All we can do is do the best we can to survive, which means getting out of the mountains and finding someone to help us. So let's taste brandy and try to relax for a while. I guarantee you'll get a better night's sleep with Mr. Allen circulating through your veins."

Kathy sat back down next to Dan. He broke the seal and handed the bottle to her, putting his arm around her shoulder.

"You go first. You deserve the first pull for all you have been through."

Kathy put the pint to her mouth, took a long sip, and handed the bottle back to Dan. "I was just thinking, Dan, of all the times we've had a drink of coffee brandy before having supper."

"Yeah. I guess you'd call it a late afternoon ritual."

Kathy smiled. "Or an addiction." She continued, "You know what I want most?"

"Tell me."

"What I want most is for the four of us—you, me, Hazel, and Tom—to one day go back to the cabin, sit around the woodstove, and have one big drink of coffee brandy to toast our survival. Is that too much to wish for?"

"No, that's not too much to wish for. It will happen. We just need to keep going. And not give up hope. If we do that, we'll have that toast, guaranteed."

The next morning, Kathy awoke before Dan. Rather than wake him, she decided to let him sleep a while longer. Out of boredom, Kathy peeked out the side window, curious if it had snowed during the night.

Using the heat from the palm of her hand, she cleared the frost and then pressed her face against the opening.

Kathy screamed, thrust her back against the seat, and began hyperventilating. She had forgotten the hunter's corpse was lying next to the car, his body facing Kathy with his eyes frozen open.

What was most scary was the man's arm. It remained in the same frozen position as when it had been caught in the steering wheel. The fat man appeared to be waving to her.

Kathy's scream woke Dan. He fumbled for the shotgun, thinking someone or something was trying to break into the vehicle. Seeing nothing, he turned and looked at Kathy.

"What is it, Kathy? Are you all right?"

Kathy sat there, her eyes shut, gasping for air. Finally she was able to speak. "It's the

hunter. His eyes are open, and he waved. I think he's still alive," Kathy said, struggling to regain her composure.

Dan peered out the passenger-side window. "No, he's dead, all right. He's been frozen in that same position for three months. Just don't look at him."

"Let's just get out of here. This place gives me the creeps."

To ensure they hadn't missed anything, Dan felt under the front seat, groping for anything that might have become lodged there during the car's tumble down the incline. He touched something odd and definitely not edible.

He latched onto a leather strap and pulled out the hunter's rifle, a .308 Winchester, with a shoulder strap and a three-power scope.

Dan's dilemma was whether to take the rifle and leave the shotgun. The rifle would be much more suitable for defending Kathy and himself, having a longer range and more killing wallop than buckshot. Then again, the 12-gauge shotgun would be a better choice at close range, as he found out when Kathy shot the charging wolf. First, he needed to find the cartridges for the rifle. Dan rummaged through the car's interior again, finally finding an unopened box of ammunition lodged behind the seat's adjustment mechanism. He'd keep both weapons for now and decide which one to ditch later.

A TEMPORARY SANCTUARY

After two round trips up the steep slope, they left the fat man and the SUV behind and continued down the Dam Road, the shotgun stored on the plastic sled and the rifle slung over Dan's shoulder. The snowshoeing was painstakingly slow. Their thighs burned with each step, lifting their snowshoes from the fluffy snow that fell overnight. As the day progressed, Dan and Kathy spent nearly as much time resting as walking.

"I can't take much more of this," Kathy confessed. "My legs are killing me. Maybe we should stop here for the night and get a fresh start in the morning."

"Can you make it another mile or two? We need to go as far as we can before dark."

"I guess. Just let me rest awhile," Kathy said. "Give me ten minutes, and I'll be ready to go."

"Take your time. I can use a break too."

Kathy placed her hands on her hips, stretching her back, and looked down the road while Dan checked the straps on the sled, making sure the gear was secured.

"Dan, look behind you! A person!"

Dan whirled around. "Where? I don't see anyone."

"Down the road, near the dead pine tree on the right. He's wearing a red jacket." When she turned to look again, what she thought was a person had disappeared.

"Well, he was there. Maybe he stepped into the woods," she told Dan, searching up and down the Dam Road for any sign of what she had presumed to be a person.

"Why would anyone go into the woods with ten feet of snow on the ground?" Dan asked. "Besides, there aren't any houses for another twenty miles." He also knew enough not to dismiss what Kathy said she'd seen. "Let's walk down and see what we can find," he added, a diplomatic way of telling Kathy she likely imagined she saw a person walking on the Dam Road.

Snowshoeing toward the pine, they studied the snow for any tracks, animal or human. Only tracks in the fresh snow would validate what Kathy claimed to have been a person in a red hunting coat. The farther they walked, the more dubious Dan became that she had actually seen anything.

"This is the place. I know he was near that dead pine," Kathy said, pointing to the large needleless tree.

Dan scoured the snow for tracks. "Nothing here. Perhaps you saw a couple of trees that happened to line up just right to look like a person. It's easy to do, especially from that distance," Dan said, looking back up the road.

"I know what I saw, Dan. It was a person walking along the Dam Road. The tracks have to be here," Kathy responded, annoyed Dan thought she couldn't distinguish a tree from a human. "Let's just keep walking."

They had traveled barely twenty feet when Kathy found the proof that she hadn't hallucinated. "Right there!" she said, pointing straight down at the deep imprints in the snow. "There are the snowshoe tracks." She gave Dan a long stare, waiting for an apology for doubting her.

Dan took the hint. "Well, you were right. I should have known better than to doubt you," he said, studying the traveler's direction.

"It looks like whoever it is turned onto the old logging road." Dan thought for a second. "There can't be a house up there. We've driven by that woods road countless times and have never seen anyone coming or going."

"Apparently, someone's living there now. Let's go find out. Perhaps they will help us," Kathy said, walking toward the woods road.

"Wait up a minute, Kathy."

"For what? We want help, don't we? That help could be a short distance up that road," Kathy said, wondering why Dan was so hesitant.

"We have no idea what we might be getting ourselves into. These are crazy times, and I suspect a lot of otherwise ordinary people are so scared and confused about what's going on in the world that they don't know who to trust."

Kathy interrupted. "So what are you saying, Dan? We shouldn't take a chance to find these people?"

"No, I'm not saying that. I was going to say they might accept us like their long-lost cousin and be more than willing to help us. On the other hand, they may see us as vermin trying to steal their food and whatever else they have of value. We need to be careful about how we approach them."

"So, what's the plan?" Kathy replied, impatient to get going regardless of what Dan had to say.

"The last thing we want to do is knock on the door carrying a .308 Winchester. If they're armed and of the mind that we're a threat, it could get ugly. We need to show them we are defenseless and only want to talk. I think we should leave the two guns. Hide them before we go looking for whoever is up that road."

"I think you're making way too much of this, Dan, but if that's what you want to do, we'll hide the weapons."

"I'll wrap them in one of the tarps and bury them at the base of the dead pine. They should be easy enough to find—if we need them. Then we can approach whoever lives there as a married couple desperately needing help."

"How about we act like an *old* married couple desperate for help? That should evoke even more sympathy."

Plastered to the trees at the entrance to the narrow woods road were several crudely painted signs placing potential trespassers on notice not to go any farther.

"Keep Out, Private Property," Dan read. "Sound like real friendly folks."

"Maybe they're just to scare off traveling salesmen, and all others are welcome," Kathy quipped, not deterred from finding help.

"Yeah, right, just like they're going to feed us prime rib after telling them our last meal was a box of Lucky Charms."

Farther up the road there were more signs designed to ward off intruders. "Turn back; trespassers will be shot on sight" was the most disturbing.

"What do you think, Kathy? Maybe we are getting in over our heads. These people mean business."

"We'll have to chance it. I cannot imagine turning away two people needing help regardless of how they feel about outsiders.

"That's not what you found out when those three characters visited Skyler Pond and threatened you," Dan reminded her.

"Thanks for reminding me. I was trying to put that episode out of my mind. Besides, I can't believe everyone acts that way. Until I find out different, I'm going with the presumption there are still more good people than crazies in this world, like those three. But, if the people who live here give us a hard time, we'll just say thank you very much and walk away."

At the edge of the wooded tract, a final sign," Bartlett Haven," and beyond it, a clearing giving Dan and Kathy their first view of the Bartlett family compound.

The three vintage trailers were a sight neither could have imagined. Kathy's first thought was that if the trailers were in a city, it would be called a slum. Bags of garbage, junk cars, broken appliances, snowmobiles, and a dozen metal barrels full of who knows what surrounded the three mobile homes. Only the circular drive was clutter-free.

Kathy began to have second thoughts. She was about to tell Dan they should turn back and look elsewhere for help when a dog chained to its doghouse caught their scent and began to bark. Not a couple of curious woofs, but the growls and snarls of a vicious German shepherd. Chained, Stalin transformed from a playful family pet to a ferocious protector of the Bartletts and their property. Stalin repeatedly lunged at the intruders and, luckily for Dan and Kathy, was snapped back by its hitch chain. The commotion touched off two other dogs sleeping on the deck of one of the trailers. The two mongrels sprung from the deck, eager to investigate what had their canine friend so upset.

Kathy stood close to Dan, both prepared for what might be a nasty welcome. For an instant, Dan regretted not having his shotgun. However, even though the two mongrels sounded tough, the wagging tails gave them away as being all show. As soon as they ran up to Kathy and Dan, they stopped barking and began sniffing each of them thoroughly.

"Blackie! Fireball! Get the hell over here. Now!" came the raspy call of a woman standing at the door of the trailer on the right. The dogs were reluctant to leave their new friends and continued their olfactory inspection.

"Goddamn it! I said get your hairy asses over here!" This time she got their attention. The two took off on a dead run back to the woman with the loud, grating voice.

Hearing the ruckus, Darlene and Wendy stood on their decks staring at the two interlopers. Then, taking their cue from Beatrice, they followed her, with their four children close behind. The seven marched in a single line across the packed snow on a mission to learn why two strangers had entered their private world.

The shepherd's aggression intensified as the women and children made their way toward Kathy and Dan. Unable to get at Kathy and Dan, the dog muckled onto a grain bag and shook it violently, throwing slobber in all directions. While he was snarling and growling, the other two dogs, now tied, yipped and howled, watching their owners go off without them. Suddenly, to Kathy and Dan, the thought of being alone at their secluded cabin on Skyler Pond didn't seem so bad.

"Who are you?" Beatrice asked, as the others formed a semicircle around Kathy and Dan.

"My name is Dan, and this is my wife, Kathy."

"Do you have a last name?" Beatrice asked, always a stickler for details.

"Simmons. We have a camp on Skyler Pond."

"So, how'd you get here?"

"By snowmobile—until the machine broke down a ways back. We snowshoed the rest of the way," Dan replied.

"What do you want?"

Dan noticed the woman kept her right hand in her coat pocket. To keep her hand warm, he supposed. But when she took her hand out to zip up her jacket, Dan noticed the butt of a handgun. Beatrice played it safe, not taking any chances that he and Kathy might be up to no good.

"Our food ran out, and we had to leave our cabin. We hoped you might be able to help us," Dan said, seeing Beatrice slide her hand back into her coat pocket.

Beatrice studied the plastic sled mounded with their belongings and then at Kathy and Dan. She sensed the strangers were telling the truth and took her hand out and closed the pocket's flap.

"Where were you headed before you came here?"

"South. We need to get to Westbrook," Kathy replied, reluctant to give the woman too much information.

"Westbrook! That's a hundred miles from here. You'll never make it. Besides, what in Christ's name do you want to walk to Westbrook for anyway?" Beatrice asked, now thinking she was face to face with two people who hadn't a clue what they were up against.

Kathy felt compelled to answer. "Our daughter lives in Westbrook. We hope to live with her until the weather breaks and the war ends."

"What makes you think they're any better off than we are around here? They're likely a hundred people fighting over a loaf of bread, and that's if there's any left in the cities to fight over."

She continued to study the strangers. Beatrice could come on strong and cold, but she could also show streaks of kindness if she liked you. Dan and Kathy didn't appear to be a threat and could use a little help.

"You can stay here a night or two, but no longer. We aren't exactly overstocked with food ourselves. Darlene has a small room in her trailer you can use. That's all right with you, isn't it, Darlene?" Beatrice hollered, not taking her eyes off Dan and Kathy. Darlene responded with a weak yes, wondering how Dick would feel about it when he returned home.

"Tonight you can eat with us. Once a week, us Bartletts get together for supper. We call it family night. Weird, isn't it? We can't get away from each other 'cause we live so close. Yet once a week, we torture ourselves sitting ass to ass around a kitchen table shouting insults at each other." She continued, "Now go with Darlene. She'll show you where you'll sleep."

As the others turned to go back to their trailers, Darlene motioned Kathy and Dan to follow her. To reach Darlene's home, they needed to weave through a sea of junk in various stages of being buried beneath the snow. Dan followed Kathy and Darlene, pulling the sled. As he watched where he stepped, he noticed the top of a red gas can barely sticking out of the snow with the words "Property of D. S." printed on the top in bold black letters. It was his gas container, the one missing from the car's trunk. Dan's mind began to whirl. If that was his can, someone living at Bartlett Haven must have also drained the gas from the car. Dan hurried to catch up with the others, anxious to tell Kathy what he had discovered.

The inside of Darlene and Dick's mobile home was in the same disarray as the outside. Darlene moved through the clutter with ease, following the narrow route to the trailer's back end to what once was a bedroom, now used for storage. In the center of the chaos was a couch, barely big enough for one person to sleep on, let alone the both of them.

"You can stay here," she announced. The first words she had spoken to Kathy and Dan. "The pipes are frozen, so the wash water won't go down the drain. Toss it out the rear door if you use the washbasin. The outhouse is behind the trailer. Knock first unless you want to be surprised." Darlene turned to leave and added, "One of us will come and get you when it's time for supper."

Dan hesitated to speak to Kathy about the gas can with Darlene only a short distance down the hall. He motioned her to sit beside him on the couch and quietly told her what he had found.

"Are you certain it's yours?"

"Positive. I printed my initials on the can before Nate borrowed it to take on a camping trip for spare gas for his outboard. It was a reminder that the container had a home. Someone in this place stole it when they drained the car's gas tank."

"What are you going to do?"

"Nothing. There's nothing to be gained and probably a lot to lose by bringing it up."

"This place really freaks me out. Why aren't there any men around? There has to be at least one that caused all these children. Outside, the third woman never spoke at all, and I didn't think Darlene could talk until she brought us in here. What's with the one that did all the talking? She never told us her name. It's as if we're stuck in a weird Halloween horror movie minus the chainsaw."

"Actually, there is a chainsaw. It's on the counter next to the sink."

"Great. Dan, let's leave. I'd rather take my chances on the Dam Road than stay in this nut factory."

"Not just yet. Let's spend the night. Tomorrow morning we will tell them we have changed our minds and need to leave."

"Why wait?"

"It'll be dark soon. We wouldn't get a mile down the road before we stopped for the night. Besides, it would be nice to leave on a full stomach and maybe with extra food if they are willing to part with any. Quiet, someone's coming down the hall."

One of Darlene's children appeared in the open doorway. He stood there, staring at Kathy and Dan, holding a stuffed animal tight to his chest. The boy seemed to be around five, and likely Kathy and Dan were the first outsiders he had ever seen.

"Would you like to come in?" Kathy asked.

The boy barely stepped through the threshold.

"What's your name?" Kathy asked.

The boy didn't answer, just continued to gaze at the two.

"Cat got your tongue?" Dan asked.

The boy started to laugh. "The cat doesn't have my tongue."

"Well, let's see. Why don't you sit beside us so I can take a look?" Dan said, patting the cushion.

The boy ran to the couch and opened his mouth for Dan to inspect his tongue. "It's there, all right. The cat must have dropped it." The boy laughed.

"Now, can you tell us your name?" Kathy asked.

"Tommy." He continued, "My dad went hunting. He's going to shoot a big buck for us to eat. Uncle Frankie and Uncle Josh went with him, and they're going to shoot one too."

"Well, let's hope they all get a deer," Dan said.

"My mother said that too. She said we don't have much food left, so we need a big buck real bad."

"When are they coming home?" Dan asked.

Tommy was about to answer when he heard his mother call. He jumped off the couch and ran down the hall.

"Well, that was interesting. Now we at least know there are men around," Kathy said.

"Yeah. And we even know the names of two of them."

Kathy and Dan napped while waiting to be called for supper until they were woken by a man's voice at the other end of the trailer. They stood at the bedroom doorway, listening to the conversation between Darlene and the man they assumed to be Darlene's husband.

"Where did they come from? I didn't think there was anyone within fifty miles of this place," they heard the man say.

"I'm not sure. I heard Beatrice ask, but that goddamn dog of Josh's started barking and gagging, pulling on his chain, so I missed hearing what the guy told her."

"So you just invited the two to stay in our house?"

"I didn't invite them! Beatrice told them they could stay with us."

"Beatrice! What is wrong with that woman? She should know better than to invite two strangers to stay in *our* house."

"Well, they're here now, and Beatrice told them they could eat with us tonight."

"Jesus! I've got to have a talk with Frankie. He's got to put a muzzle on that woman. For some reason, Beatrice thinks she's queen bee whenever Frankie's not around." He continued, "I'm going into that bedroom and tell those two to get to hell out of here now."

"I'd wait on that one. Let Frankie deal with it. It will start another war if you get in the middle of this. Frankie is the self-appointed leader of the tribe, so let him do the dirty work," Darlene told him. "Here, drink this. You'll feel a lot better."

"By the way, speaking of the pain in the ass, I didn't see Frankie ride in with you and Josh."

"That's because he didn't. After we tromped around looking for deer sign for four hours and then spent three hours shoveling the cabin out enough to get in through the upstairs window to warm up before we started home, Frankie announced he was staying the night. Said he would check another area out for deer before heading home in the morning. Josh and I knew it was his lame excuse to get shit-faced and not have Beatrice harassing him about it. And just in case you're wondering, we never cut a track. I think every deer in Skyler County has starved to death thanks to this friggin' weather."

"Sounds like one big happy family," Dan whispered to Kathy, stepping back from the door.

"It also sounds like Frankie makes all the family decisions. I have a feeling it's best to avoid him. He could be a little off the wall if he's anything like the others. Let's get up early and be out of here before this Frankie shows up."

Darlene asked Dick to tell their visitors it was time to eat.

"I'm telling them nothing. Looking at two outsiders sitting at the dinner table will be bad enough. I don't want to see their faces more than I have to. You tell them. I'm heading over to Beatrice's. I'll see you there."

Beatrice's trailer was similar to Darlene's except for the addition Frankie had built to accommodate family meetings and the weekly meal.

Dick and the children were already at the table when Darlene entered the room, followed by Dan and Kathy. Darlene made it a point to sit Kathy and Dan across from Dick for no other reason than to watch him squirm each time he looked up from his plate. Only after the three had sat down did Dick look at the strangers. The instant he saw Kathy, he knew she was the woman Frankie had confronted at Skyler Pond.

Dick wasn't concerned about Kathy recognizing him or Josh, as both had their helmet face shields down at the time of the run-in. Still, he needed to alert Josh that she was here. The last thing Dick wanted was Josh blatting something stupid that would tie them to the incident at Skyler Pond.

As Dick was about to go into the kitchen to ask Beatrice why Wendy and Josh weren't at the supper, Wendy walked into the trailer.

"Wendy, where's Josh?"

"Thawing out the trap under the kitchen sink. It's the second time it froze this week. The friggin' sink looks like a cesspool. He'll be over in a while," Wendy said, sitting in the chair next to Dan.

"I'll go see if he needs any help," Dick said.

Dick intercepted Josh on his way to Beatrice's. "Josh, hold up a minute. There's something you need to know. Remember the woman at Skyler Pond that gave you a hard time when you got your snowmobile stuck?"

"Yeah, I remember. I thought she would never shut up."

"Well, she's sitting at the dinner table at Frankie's house."

"You've got to be joking! Wendy told me that a man and woman were staying at your place, but I never dreamed it was the woman from Skyler Pond. How to hell did she get here?"

"By snowmobile until it broke down and then by snowshoe. The man with her is her husband."

"Do you think she recognized you?" Josh asked.

"Josh, you and I had our face shields down, remember? It's Frankie she can identify."

"Oh, that's right. Wait until Frankie finds out. He'll shit his pants."

"You're right about that. Who knows what he will do when he sees her." Dick thought a minute. "Frankie said he wouldn't be back until tomorrow morning. We'll make sure those two are long gone before Frankie gets home. I'll tell them that we have barely enough food for ourselves, and they have to leave."

"That's not far from the truth."

"I'll even offer to give them a snowmobile ride a couple miles down the road just to be rid of them," Dick said. "God! I told Frankie he should never have pulled his gun on that woman."

Josh and Dick joined the others, already halfway through the meal. He decided it was a good time to bring up Kathy and Dan's leaving in the morning.

"You know," Dick said, continuing to eat, "if these were regular times, we'd be glad to help you two out. Before the freak weather set in, we had a freezer full of meat. But now that there's no game within a hundred miles of here, we've had to eat most of it. In fact, you two are eating the last of the stew beef we had from the steer we raised. I'm trying to say that we're a short step from running out of food ourselves. I'm sure you understand that family comes first. So Josh and me think it's best if you both leave in the morning, early.

"We'll give you what food we can spare. If you make it to Fraternity Township, I have a friend there that might help you. The name is Clement. Norris Clement. He lives on River Road. You tell him Dick Bartlett said he would help you." There was no Norris Clement. Dick had made up the name on the fly to give Kathy and Dan some added inspiration to leave Bartlett Haven.

Beatrice gave Dick a long disapproving stare. She didn't like him undercutting her decisions. As far as Beatrice was concerned, she was the one to decide when visitors had worn out their welcome. At least until Frankie came home.

"We understand. Times are tough for everyone. Kathy and I appreciate what you've already done for us," Dan said, thinking things were playing out just as they'd hoped. "We'll leave in the morning as soon as it gets light."

The conversation ended, and everyone went back to eating. Minutes later, the silence was interrupted by the clatter of metal hitting the floor. Everyone turned toward the kitchen.

"Probably the stack of pans I had sitting on the counter fell on the floor," Beatrice said and started for the kitchen. Beatrice was half-right. Frankie sat in the center of the clutter of pots and pans, looking confused, wondering how he'd ended up in Beatrice's kitchen. Seconds later, an uproar erupted.

"Frankie, you're flat-ass drunk!" Beatrice hollered.

"So what if I am?" Frankie slurred, barely able to string the words together.

Dick looked at Josh. They rushed to the kitchen to intercept Frankie before he stumbled into the dining room.

"Frankie," Dick asked, "I thought you were spending the night at the cabin?"

"Dickie, it's nice to see you as well. How about giving your brother a little boost off the floor?" Frankie asked, propped against the kitchen cabinet.

Dick and Josh lifted Frankie to his feet. "I thought you would be home tomorrow," Dick repeated.

"And miss our weekly family meal? Not a chance. I checked that deer yard out after you two left and then headed out just about dark. I'd have been here sooner if it weren't for that goddamn snowmobile running out of gas three miles back," Frankie said, holding on to the countertop to steady himself. Now, if you boys would assist me to the table, I'll join you for supper."

"The meal's over, Frankie. Everyone is about to leave. I'll help you to the bedroom, so you can sleep it off," Dick said, hoping to prevent Frankie from seeing Kathy and Dan sitting at the dinner table.

"I'm not going to bed, for Christ's sake. Who do you think you're talking to, a two-year-old? Get out of my way! I'm going to have supper with my lovely family."

"Frankie, I said the meal's over. Darlene and Wendy are getting the kids' coats on. They're going home," Dick told him.

"Like hell they are. We're going to have a family meeting before anyone leaves."

Frankie pushed Dick aside and staggered into the dining room. "Come on, everyone, get back to the table. We're going to have a family meeting," he ordered. "Darlene and Wendy, get on back in here. The children too. They're part of the family. We don't keep secrets from anyone."

Everyone inside the trailer had a problem with that statement, knowing how Frankie played everything close to the vest.

"Who to hell are those two?" Frankie said, spotting Dan and Kathy sitting quietly at the table trying to ignore the fiery exchange between Frankie and Dick.

"Beatrice! What are they doing in my house?"

"Calm down, Frankie. I told them they could stay here for a day or two." Before she could explain further, Frankie ripped into her.

"Who to hell died and made you queen? You had no right to allow two strangers to stay with us. How could you be so stupid, Beatrice?" Frankie yelled.

Kathy felt embarrassed, listening to the family quarrel. She could only sit there staring at the table as the two continued their verbal combat. The more Frankie ranted, the more certain Kathy became that she knew that voice. Finally, she looked up at the scruffy man going nose to nose with his wife.

That's him, she thought. The man who had pulled a gun on her when she refused to return to the cabin. Kathy looked at Josh standing off to the side, watching Frankie and Beatrice going at it. She remembered the one who got the snowmobile stuck was short and thin. *Then the other two must have been the ones with him*, she reasoned.

Kathy wanted to tell Dan who these men were but needed to wait until they were alone. In the meantime, she could only hope Frankie didn't recognize her.

At last, Beatrice retreated to the kitchen, knowing she couldn't win an argument with a drunk. Frankie plopped down in the chair across the table from Kathy and Dan. For nearly a minute, he stared at Kathy. Finally, he spoke.

"Don't I know you?" he asked, his elbow resting on the table, pointing at Kathy.

"I don't think so," she answered, trying to avoid eye contact.

"I think I do," Frankie said. "I've seen you somewhere. I just can't quite place where it was."

Frankie turned his attention to Dan. "You do know we can't allow you to stay here. In the morning, you leave. Do you understand?"

"We plan to. As soon as we're up," Dan answered.

"Good. Then we understand each other. Where did you come from, anyway? There are no houses within forty miles," Frankie asked, still having trouble focusing his eyes.

Kathy attempted to kick Dan's leg to stop him from answering Frankie, but it was too late.

"Skyler Pond. We've been there since the war began and became stranded with all the snow," Dan said.

Frankie's eyes darted back to Kathy, who was looking down at her plate.

Now he remembered why she seemed so familiar.

Dick and Josh watched, certain Frankie was about to erupt.

Frankie was about to speak but decided to hold off. His mind was lucid enough to realize she might not have recognized him from that day at Skyler Pond, and he didn't want to say something that might incriminate himself. Instead, Frankie hollered to Beatrice to bring him his supper.

"Are we still having a family meeting?" Josh asked.

"No, we're not still having a family meeting," Frankie replied condescendingly. "Meetings are for family, and those two ain't family," he said, pointing his fork at Kathy and Dan.

Relieved not to have to suffer through another long, agonizing family gripe session, the rest of the Bartletts quickly left the
trailer, with Kathy and Dan following close behind. Frankie sat
alone at the table, waiting for Beatrice to bring him his meal.

Sitting on the bed in Dick and Darlene's trailer, Kathy
whispered to Dan that Frankie was the one who threatened her
at the cabin, and that Josh and Dick were there as well.

"Do you think he recognized you?"

"Yes."

"I doubt if he will try anything. Anyway, by the time he wakes
up from his bender, we'll be long gone, and that will be the end of
it. We'll leave at daybreak."

Dan needed to use the outhouse before turning in for the
night. Dick's and Josh's families shared one facility, Frankie and
Beatrice the other. Upon knocking on the door, he was surprised
to hear one of Darlene's children say he would be out in a minute.
Dan excused himself and walked toward the second privy between
Dick's and Frankie's trailer.

He had no sooner stepped inside the privy when he heard
Dick's trailer door shut and the sound of boots squeaking on the
cold, dry snow. He couldn't make out the words over the generator
humming in the background but was sure it was the three Bartlett
brothers having an argument. The discussion continued as they
walked in the direction of Frankie's trailer. Then the three stopped
directly in front of the privy.

Barely thirty feet separated the three brothers and Dan. To
hear over the drone of the generator, Dan cracked open the privy
door to listen to what was being said.

"Let it go, Frankie. They'll be leaving in the morning," Dick said.

"There's something about that woman I just can't stand."

"Maybe it's because she's smarter than you?" Josh asked,
without thinking.

"Cut the crap, Josh. It's just that both times we've run into her,
she's caused problems, first at Skyler Pond and now here, wanting
a place to stay and to eat our food."

"I told you, Frankie, that you should have never pulled that gun on her," Dick told him.

"I'm not worried about it. She didn't act like she remembered me."

"She knew who you were, all right. The woman was just smart enough to keep her mouth shut," Dick told him.

"Maybe I ought to take care of her, and that worthless husband of hers like the druggies from New York did old man Carsley."

"Come on, Frankie, don't be a jerk. Killing someone just because you don't like them is crazy," Dick said.

"Well, maybe I'm just cracked enough to do it," Frankie said, reaching for the pint of Jim Beam inside his down parka.

Dan was terrified. Murder Kathy and him for doing nothing? It seemed like something nightmares are made of. No rational person would consider taking another person's life for anything so innocent as asking for help. Perhaps it was only the liquor talking, and Frankie was trying to act the big shot with his brothers, but Dan didn't dare to take the chance. He and Kathy needed to leave Bartlett Haven now in case Frankie decided to follow through on his threat. They would go tonight while everyone was asleep. Dan wanted to run back to Kathy and tell her what he had overheard but remained trapped in the privy until Frankie, Dick, and Josh left.

Kathy's analysis of the Bartletts had been correct. Life at the Bartlett compound was equivalent to residing in an insane asylum. Dan continued to listen to the conversation.

"Well, boys, I've about had it for the night. I'm going to use the shitter and then head for bed. I've got one pounding beer headache. Perhaps a good night's sleep will knock it down," Frankie told the others.

Dan could hear the snow crunch under Frankie's boots as he made his way toward the privy. When Frankie opened the privy door, they would be face to face, and Dan had no idea what Frankie might do when he saw him. He thought of bolting out the door and rushing past Frankie so fast he wouldn't have time to figure out who it was, but he decided that would be silly, as there were only four men at the Haven, and three were just outside the privy. All Dan could do was wait for the door to open and try to talk his way out of his predicament. Frankie was fifteen feet from the outhouse when Dick called to him.

"Frankie!"

Frankie turned in his brother's direction, unable to see him in the darkness. Dan used the seconds Frankie was distracted to escape the privy. He slipped out the door and disappeared behind the shanty, with Frankie none the wiser.

"What?"

"Think about what you told Josh and me. Don't do anything stupid. Okay?" Dick hollered, concerned Frankie might actually try to harm Kathy and Dan. Frankie didn't answer and continued toward the outhouse.

When Dan returned to the trailer, Kathy was asleep. He gently shook her shoulder.

"What?" Kathy exclaimed, startled from being awakened from a deep sleep.

Dan placed his finger to his lips and sat beside her. Barely speaking above a whisper, he told Kathy about the conversation he had overheard five minutes earlier.

"My God, what are we going to do?" she asked.

Just then, the outside door to the trailer opened. Kathy and Dan listened to Dick make his way to the bedroom and shut the door.

"We'll leave before dawn before anyone is awake," he whispered. "I don't think Frankie will try anything around the kids."

"Why wait?" Kathy asked. "If we go now, he won't realize we've gone until morning. By then, we'll be well down the Dam Road."

"Makes sense. Okay, we'll wait an hour to be sure everyone is asleep, then we'll get the hell out of here."

Finally, Dick's heavy breathing and the occasional cough from the kids' room were the only sounds inside the trailer. Kathy and Dan crept down the narrow hallway past Darlene and Dick's bedroom and into the kitchen. Outside, Dan used the flashlight he had taken from the kitchen counter to light the way to the storage shed, where they had left their sled and snowshoes.

They followed the circular drive toward the woods road leading them back to the Dam Road. The calm night air made the squeaks from their snowshoes seem loud enough to wake everyone in the trailers. Almost to the entrance to the woods road, all hell broke loose.

Stalin caught wind of them and commenced the same incessant barking as when they'd arrived. A light snapped on in Frankie's trailer, followed by lights at Josh's and Dick's. Kathy and Dan shuffled down the driveway as fast as they could on snowshoes until they were well concealed by the trees. Dan stopped long enough to look back at Bartlett Haven. Through the trees, he saw three light beams scanning the yard, searching for what had set Stalin off. Not seeing anything, Dan heard Frankie yell to the dog to shut up, and with that directive, the flashlights went out, and everyone returned to bed. Once at the Dam Road, they relaxed, believing the worst was behind them.

"God, I've never been so glad to get away from anybody as that crowd. I think they're all woods queer."

"Maybe, but if you took Frankie out of the mix, the rest might act halfway normal. Anyway, enough with psychoanalyzing the Bartletts. We need to put as much distance as possible between Frankie and us before he comes to realize we flew the coop. I have no idea who Carsley is or was, but from what Frankie said last night, I'm damn sure we don't want to end up like he did. You wait here while I get the guns. If Frankie does want to do us in, at least we'll have a fighting chance."

With the two weapons safely secured to the sled, they continued south. Dan set the pace. It wasn't long until Kathy fell behind, unable to match his stride.

"Dan, hold up a minute," she called between breaths. "I know we've got to move as fast as possible, but I can't keep up. You've got to slow down."

Dan waited for Kathy to catch up. He was about to say he'd try to slow down when a blast of wind shot through the trees, strong enough to free the bent boughs of the evergreens of their heavy snow load. Another storm was on its way.

Instinctively, Kathy started toward the woods, seeking shelter before they felt the full fury of the squall.

"No!" Dan called to her.

"What do you mean, no? We need to get out of the road before the storm hits."

"Not this time. We need to keep walking."

Kathy walked closer to Dan. "Dan, what's the matter with you? We won't be able to see where we're going once the snow starts. We need to get out of the wind. Now!"

Dan answered, trying to be heard over the howling wind. "Look, if Frankie does want to kill us, he has to find us first. The snow will cover our tracks. He won't know if we are hiding in the woods or somewhere down the road. While he's trying to figure out where we went, we'll keep getting farther away from him." If we stay between the trees on either side of the road, we'll be okay."

Dan took a short length of rope from his pack. "Here, hang on to this. The rope will keep us together."

The wind howled as the storm quickly morphed into a white-out. Dan and Kathy fought their way forward, trying to stay oriented. Backs hunched, heads down, they leaned into the wind, holding on to the rope that kept them together with one hand and protecting their faces from the driving snow with the other. Each sudden gust pushed them sideways, nearly knocking them off their snowshoes. Everything was white. There was no horizon to keep themselves oriented, and without objects to focus on, there was no depth perception.

They trudged along in silence as the wind whistled by them. Kathy felt a violent yank on the rope. The next thing she knew, she was lying on top of Dan.

"What happened?" she cried out over the howling wind.

"I ran into something," Dan said, struggling to untangle himself and Kathy from the rope.

"It's a snowmobile," he said, tapping the snow-covered cowling with his ski pole. "It must be Frankie's. He said it ran out of gas on the way back from the hunting cabin."

"Well, it doesn't do us any good. Let's keep moving or head for the woods until the storm blows over. I'm freezing just standing here."

As Kathy watched Dan use his hands to sweep the snow from the cowling, she asked, "What are you doing?"

"I'm going to make sure no one will be able to start it," he hollered.

Dan removed a glove, reached into the engine compartment, pulled the wire off the spark plug, and yanked the other end from the distributor. After doing the same to the second cylinder, he held the two wires up for Kathy to see and threw them into the woods, satisfied no one could start the disabled machine, no matter how much gas they put into it.

Darlene and Dick sat at the kitchen table at Bartlett Haven, waiting for Kathy and Dan to get up. Dick was anxious to get them on the road before Frankie stopped for coffee, a part of his daily routine. After downing his second cup, Dick announced he would make a quick trip to the privy.

"Darlene, what did you do with my flashlight?" he asked, expecting it to be on the counter next to the outside door.

"I didn't touch your flashlight. You probably left it in the living room."

"I always leave it next to the door. The extra batteries are missing as well. Goddamn it. If I find out one of those kids took it, I'll ring their necks."

"My God, Dick, it's light enough outside. You can find your way to the outhouse without a flashlight."

"That's not the point. When I came in last night, I left my flash-light on the counter, and now it's gone, and that pisses me off."

A short while later, Dick returned, still fuming about the missing flashlight. He poured another cup of coffee, looking down the empty hallway after each sip. Finally, he ran out of patience.

"That's it. It's time they get their lazy asses out of bed. They need to be out of here before Frankie walks through the door."

Dick stormed down the hall to roust Kathy and Dan out of bed. A minute later, he was back in the kitchen.

"They're gone!"

"How can they be gone? We've been sitting at the table since six."

"They must have left during the night. Why would they pack up and leave without saying a word, not even a note?" Dick bristled. "The ingrates!"

"I can't say I'm disappointed they skipped out. Now Frankie will have no reason to make an ass out of himself," Darlene said.

Although he wouldn't admit it, Dick was relieved as well. With the two gone, Frankie's threat to harm them was meaning-less. Dick downed a leftover slice of pizza while thinking that life for the three families had returned to normal with the uninvited guests gone. Unfortunately, returning to what was normal for the Bartlett clan was short-lived. Dick heard footsteps coming across the deck. Frankie barged into the kitchen, slamming the door behind him.

"Where are those two thieves?" he demanded to know.

"What to hell are you talking about?" Dick shot back.

"Those two lowlifes that have been eating our food and steal-ing my money, that's who!"

"Stealing your money?"

"Yeah, stealing my money," Frankie repeated. "I put two hundred dollars on the kitchen counter when I got back from camp last night. It was in the pocket of my snowmobile suit. I thought I had lost it. I got that money last winter cutting firewood for that idiot flatlander who bought the old Henson hunting camp on Otter Pond Mountain. Said he was going to use the place to commune with nature. Christ, he lasted until the end of May. Once the black flies came out, the pussy turned tail and ran back to wherever in hell he came from. Anyway, those two from Skyler Pond stole it."

"What makes you think those two stole the money?" Darlene asked.

"Who else would have taken it? The only others there were you two, Josh, and Wendy."

"Maybe one of the kids took it. Have you asked them?" Dick asked.

"No need to. Those kids know they wouldn't be able to sit down for a week if they stole as much as a dime from their uncle. It was those two from Skyler Pond, all right, and I'm going to get my money back."

At first, Dick couldn't believe that Kathy or Dan had stolen the money. At least one adult had been with them the entire time at Frankie's trailer. Yet his flashlight was missing as well. Maybe they took the two hundred, anticipating they might have to pay someone to help them or use it to buy food.

"I'm stayin' right here until those two stumble out of the bedroom. Then I'll get my money back one way or another."

"You're going to be here a long time. They've already left," Dick told him.

"Gone! How could they be gone? The sun's barely up. How long ago did they leave?

"No idea. Must have been in the night," Darlene said.

Frankie sat at the kitchen table staring out the window, stewing about the two from Skyler Pond stealing his money and skipping out. "They're not going to get away with it."

THE CHASE

"What do you plan to do?" Dick asked.

"I'm going after them. I want you and Josh to come with me. We'll take your snowmobile and track them down. Bring your rifle too. You never know what vermin we might see along the way," Frankie said with a sneer. He stood up and walked over to the door. "I'll go hook up the dogsled and you get Josh," he said and then went outside.

Dick looked out the kitchen window to ensure his brother was out of earshot.

"Jesus, I don't want to take my rifle. I know what he's up to, and I don't want any part of it," he told Darlene.

"Taking it doesn't mean you have to use it."

"Yeah, you're right. I'll take it just to shut Frankie up."

Frankie's plan was for him and Dick to ride on Dick's snowmobile and for Josh to ride on the dogsled. Once they gassed up Frankie's machine, Josh and Dick would ride together, and the three of them would set out looking for Kathy and Dan.

Frankie was confident it would only be a matter of time before they caught up with Kathy and Dan. A snowmobile traveling at thirty miles per hour would quickly overtake two people on snowshoes, even with a five-hour head start.

"Now, let's see if this cat is going to purr," Frankie told his brothers after he filled his snowmobile with gasoline. He turned the key,
expecting the engine to roar to life. Not as much as a sputter. He
pulled out the choke and tried again. The starter engaged, but the
engine wouldn't turnover.

It didn't take long for Frankie to explode. "What is wrong
with this goddamn friggin' piece of shit!"

While Frankie continued his tirade, Dick lifted the cowling.

"Frankie. It won't start because there are no spark-plug wires."

"Let me see," Frankie said, muscling Dick aside to get a better
look. "What the hell? Who could have done that?" Then he answered
his own question. "It was those two. They messed with my machine.
By the Christ, they're going to wish they'd never stopped at Bartlett
Haven." Frankie ordered Dick and Josh to get on the dogsled.

"Josh, you sit in the sled and watch the woods on the right side
of the road. Dick, you stand on the back and do the same looking
left. They might be hiding just off the trail, waiting for us to go by.
I'll go slow so we don't miss them."

After disabling Frankie's snowmobile Kathy and Dan continued
their slow slog down the Dam Road. Finally, even Dan had had
enough of marching through the storm. It was too difficult to talk
over the howling wind to tell Kathy that the plan had changed.
Instead, he tugged the rope and pointed toward a recently toppled
maple inside the wood line. Kathy nodded that she understood,
and the pair made their way to the side of the road. One step off
the packed trail, their snowshoes sunk deep into the loose snow. It
was a struggle, but finally, they made it to the downed tree. Dan
managed to unpack the blue tarps stored on the sled. Sitting on
one of the tarps with their backs against the tree's trunk, they
pulled the other over them to keep them dry. All they could do
was nap while waiting for the storm to end. It was an uneasy sleep,
interrupted by thoughts of Frankie closing in on them no matter
how hard they tried to stay ahead of him.

The sound of a distant limb breaking woke Dan. He had no idea how long they had slept, but the storm had ended, with only a slight wind now rocking the upper branches of the towering hardwoods. He snowshoed to the edge of the woods, curious if the snow had covered their tracks. Satisfied that there wasn't any indication they'd been walking along the Dam Road, Dan rejoined Kathy.

"Ready to leave?" Kathy asked, still in her sleeping bag, assuming they would continue down the Dam Road.

Dan studied the woods behind the fallen tree. "Kathy, see the woods road over there?"

"Yeah, what about it? It's just an abandoned logging road."

"Yes, it's a logging road, but look at its direction; it parallels the Dam Road. Let's follow it for as long as it continues south. The longer we do, the longer there will be no tracks for Frankie to follow."

"You mean if he's actually following us. Maybe it was just so much bluster telling his brothers he wanted to do us in. Perhaps we're overreacting to the whole situation. Besides, breaking a trail following that road would be near impossible."

"Maybe. But what if he is after us, and he sees our tracks? He could come up behind us and mow us down with the snowmobile. We wouldn't stand a chance. As far as snowshoeing goes, it will be tough going, but with no pressure trying to outrun Frankie, we can take our time and stop whenever we need a break."

Grudgingly, Kathy agreed to walk the partially overgrown road set two hundred feet from the Dam Road. An hour passed when Kathy and Dan stopped to rest. Leaning on their ski poles, they heard the distant whine of a snowmobile.

"Uh-oh. Sounds like we have company. Get behind the big maple beside you and don't move," Dan ordered, dropping onto his stomach.

Dan lifted his head off the cold snow to watch through the trees as the snowmobile slowly passed. Dan was surprised to see all three Bartletts. Dan had it in his mind that only Frankie was out to get them. At least that's how it seemed when eavesdropping on their conversation from inside the privy.

Frankie was driving, seemingly studying the road ahead for tracks. Josh peered into the woods on the right side of the road, but Dan didn't worry about being seen. Josh focused on the first fifty feet of woods, never once looking two hundred feet back, where he and Kathy hid. Neither he nor Kathy moved until the throaty sound of the four-stroke engine trailed off to nothing.

"Dan, there's three of them," Kathy said, stepping out from behind the tree.

"I know. I thought for sure Josh and Dick wanted nothing to do with Frankie's plan to get us. Anyway, now we have three pairs of eyes looking for us. We'll have to be all the more careful that one of them doesn't spot us."

"Maybe we ought to stay here until they go back the other way," Kathy suggested.

"We'll find another place to hide and then wait them out. They'll likely go south until Frankie's satisfied we can't be ahead of them, and then they'll double back."

A half-hour later, Kathy and Dan watched from their new position as the black-and-silver snowmobile slowly crept past, the three still scanning the woods for them.

"I think we've seen the last of the Bartlett boys," Dan told Kathy, watching the snowmobile disappear behind the trees. "There's no reason for them to keep searching for us after making two passes and not finding any tracks. We'll give them a few minutes to make sure they're well away from here. Then work our way to the Dam Road so we can make better time."

Frankie and his brothers returned to the family compound empty-handed.

"Well, that ends that," Josh said. "I thought my eyes would pop out of their sockets, staring into the woods for three hours."

"It ends nothing," Frankie declared. "We just didn't see them. There's no way they could have walked as far as we went before turning around. They were in the woods watching us, probably laughing the whole time, thinking how smart they were to give us the slip. Well, boys, no one laughs at us Bartletts and gets away with it." He turned to Dick. Dick, you pull two spark-plug wires off one of those junk snowmobiles out front. At the crack of light, we'll head out. First, we'll get my machine running, and then we'll go after those two. You two better bring plenty to eat 'cause we're not coming back until we find them and take care of business."

"C'mon, Frankie. This is getting ridiculous. Just let it go. Josh and I aren't going to waste any more time chasing those two, are we, Josh?"

"Nope. I've got wood needing splitting," Josh said in his own eloquent style.

Dick continued, "Frankie, listen to me. Why go looking for trouble? So they pulled the wires out of the snowmobile. Big deal. They only did it to slow you down from trying to find them. You wanted them gone from the Haven. Well, they're gone. Let them work their way out of the mountains. Why should we care? Just stay out of it."

"You don't understand, do you, Dick?"

"Understand what?"

"That people have always treated us Bartletts like dog shit. I've heard them talk when they didn't know I was around, like the time I was in the next aisle at the Riverside Market in Kingston. Telling how they could smell a Bartlett five minutes before he came into sight and how the whole clan is nothing but a bunch of backwoods inbreds. Those two from Skyler Pond are no different. Thinking they're the smart ones with two fancy vehicles and their cabin on Skyler Pond. Did you notice how the woman looked at us? It's like she's doing you a favor just to let you be in the same room with her. That four-eyed bald-headed husband of hers ain't no better. Well,

I'm sick of it. I'm going to show those two horses' asses that we Bartletts got feelings too."

"Jesus, Frankie! Why do you care what people say? We live at Bartlett Haven because we want to. We love living off the land. If we didn't, we'd pack up and leave. Not one of those people who like to shit on us could survive a week here. They'd starve to death waiting for Walmart to deliver their groceries. Just forget those assholes. We'll live how we want and screw the world," Dick told Frankie.

"Yeah," Josh chimed in. "We are what we are, and we ain't what we ain't."

Frankie and Dick looked at Josh. On rare occasions, Josh would come out with something profound, although often quite cryptic.

"Josh is right. We are who we are and don't need to apologize for that or how we live. So let them talk. They can live however they want, and we'll do the same."

"Well, that's the way you look at it. I'm not about to forget those two playing us Bartletts for a bunch of chumps. You and Josh, be ready to leave in the morning," Frankie told them, stomping off to his trailer.

Beatrice stepped into the kitchen, hearing Frankie rummaging around in the refrigerator. "Did you find them?"

"No, I didn't find them," he said, mocking Beatrice.

"By the way, look what I found in the garbage can," she said, holding up two crinkled hundred-dollar bills that Frankie had accused Dan and Kathy of stealing. "They were on top of the trash, probably blew off the counter when the kitchen door was opened."

Beatrice finding the money changed nothing for Frankie. They had still vandalized his snowmobile, and for that action alone, he wanted payback.

"There's what's left of the venison stew in a blue container on the top shelf. I'll warm it up for you," she said, trying not to antagonize her husband.

"I'm not interested in a watered-down venison stew," he answered, sliding the contents of each shelf around. "Here's what I'm looking for," he said, pulling out a sixteen-ounce bottle of Pabst hidden at the back of the refrigerator.

"Frankie, you're not planning on getting drunk, are you?"

"I just might do that. It's been a long day."

"Please don't do it, Frankie. Just go to bed and get some rest," Beatrice pleaded.

"For Christ's sake, Beatrice, leave me alone! I don't tell you how to live your life, do I?"

Frankie's comment was more than Beatrice could tolerate. "As a matter of fact, you do. You tell me nearly everything to do from the time I get up in the morning until I go to bed. You treat me like the village idiot. I feel worthless living in this dump you call Bartlett Haven. A better name for this place would be Bartlett's Hellhole. Cause that's what it's been like living with you here the past seven years.

"So why don't you pack up and leave?" Frankie shot back. "You remember, this hellhole, as you call it, goes both ways. It hasn't been exactly a picnic listening to you bitch every time I do something that doesn't meet your approval."

Beatrice had had enough. She ran into the bedroom crying, slamming the door behind her.

"Baa, I'd be better off without that crazy bitch," he said aloud, downing half the beer in one long pull. He went into the entryway storage room to find the six-pack he had stashed away for situations like this.

Frankie spent the night on the living room couch, floating in and out of consciousness. When awake, he could think only of Kathy and Dan and how they had given him the slip. He knew they must have passed by them going down the Dam Road. The more he thought about it, the more agitated he became. Finally, he bolted from the couch, went into the kitchen to put on his snowmobile suit, and grabbed his rifle from behind the door. Ten minutes later, Frankie cruised down the driveway on Dick's sled with a fresh bottle of beer locked between his legs. He would make another sweep of the Dam Road, hoping to find Kathy and Dan.

Dick awoke, hearing the snowmobile start. By the time he staggered to the kitchen window, all he could see was the red taillight of his snowmobile whizzing through the trees. He knew Frankie was on a solo mission to find Kathy and Dan. Dick ran to Josh's trailer to tell his brother what Frankie was up to and then ran off to see Beatrice.

"Frankie took off on the snowmobile. Did he say anything before he left?" Dick asked Beatrice.

"Nothing. All I know is he planned to get shit-faced. We had words, and I went into the bedroom. If we're lucky, he might wrap the snowmobile around a tree. That will take care of the problem permanently," Beatrice said, still emotionally bruised from the earlier confrontation. "Sorry, Dick, I know he's your brother, but at this point, that's exactly how I feel."

"That's okay, Beatrice. To tell you the truth, I've felt that way a few times myself. Darlene, Wendy, and Josh know you've had a rough time of it. I mean, putting up with Frankie's drunkenness. At times, he can be the perfect asshole, but he's still my brother, and I'll do what I can to stop him from hurting himself or anyone else.

"Josh and me are going after him to make certain he doesn't do anything stupid if he finds those two."

"I want to go with you."

"I don't think that's a good idea, Beatrice. We'll take care of Frankie."

"You mean I'd just be in the way."

"I don't mean that at all. It's just Josh's machine hasn't the power to handle the three of us. We can make better time with two. And time is what we don't have much of if Frankie is intent on harming them."

"I'm going with you," Beatrice repeated. "Perhaps I can convince Frankie to cool down."

Rather than waste time trying to convince Beatrice not to go, Dick relented.

"Okay. He's your husband, and I can't stop you, but I still think you should stay here. Get your snowmobile suit on. If we have another freak snowstorm, you're going to need it. While you're getting ready, I'll help Josh gas up and finish modifying the spark-plug wires so they'll fit Frankie's snowmobile."

Josh and Dick sat on the idling machine, waiting for Beatrice to arrive.

"Ready?" Dick asked when Beatrice finally appeared. "Hop on the back of the dogsled and hold on. It's going to be a fast ride." Dick hit the throttle, and the old Polaris bolted forward. Beatrice nearly fell off the sled, not expecting a jackrabbit start. Fifteen minutes later, they pulled alongside Frankie's snowmobile.

"Jesus, Dick! I thought we were in a race for the finish line at the Daytona 500," Beatrice said.

Dick laughed. "I usually don't baby it like that, but I didn't want to see you get hurt."

"Here goes nothing," Dick told the others, dropping the cowling after installing the new wires. He turned the key, and the machine sprang to life. "I'd say having a bunch of junk snowmobiles around the house comes in handy once in a while," he told Josh, standing next to him, amazed that their repair job had actually worked.

"Beatrice, you take Josh's sled. Josh and me will see if we can catch up with Frankie. Just follow our track." The brothers dropped their visors, and Dick punched the Mountain Cat's throttle, covering Beatrice in a veneer of snow as they tore down the Dam Road looking for Frankie.

Kathy and Dan had continued to snowshoe down the Dam Road, the walking made easier by the track Frankie and the others laid down earlier in the day. Still, after three hours on snowshoes, the two were exhausted and decided to stop for the night. Dan set up their shelter on the side of the Dam Road, too tired to traipse around the woods looking for a spot to set up camp.

Kathy tossed and turned, unable to sleep. She stared up at the blue tarp Dan had erected over their bed of boughs thinking of all they had been through since leaving Skyler Pond. A distant hum distracted her. At first, she felt the noise was only her imagination until the buzz turned into a high-pitched whine as it came closer and louder. Snowmobile! And it was approaching fast from the north.

"Someone's coming!" she said, shaking Dan.

Dan sat up, listening. As the snowmobile topped the grade, the beam from the headlight bounced off the treetops.

"Get up! Get up!" Dan yelled. "Take my hand!" Kathy reached out. He latched on to her and pulled her off the tarp toward the woods. The next thing Kathy knew, she and Dan were tumbling down the embankment into a snow-filled road ditch.

Frankie was driving faster than he could see ahead, unaware of the oncoming plastic shelter. As the snowmobile streaked by the campsite, it straddled one of the poles supporting the tarp. The broken pole fell away, and the tarp became tangled in the skis. Frankie had no idea what had happened. All he knew was that he had hit something, and whatever it was, was slapping him in the face, preventing him from seeing ahead. Before he could break, the snowmobile veered left and piled into a stand of alders.

Kathy and Dan watched from the ditch. The shadowy figure of a man sat on the machine, trying to figure out what had just happened. He reached for the flashlight in the storage bag strapped to the dash and shined it to see what had tangled in the skis. Frankie knew to whom the shredded tarp belonged. He remembered seeing it on Dan's plastic sled back at the Haven. Frankie got off the machine and looked up the road.

"I know you're there!" he shouted, his words echoing off the mountain behind Kathy and Dan. "There's no reason to hide. Just come out so we can talk." Frankie looked into the blackness, waiting for a response. "Do you hear me? I only want to talk to you. I've changed my mind. I want to help you get home."

"What are we going to do?" Kathy whispered.

"We've got to get out of here before he comes back. Do you have your pack?"

"Yes. I grabbed it just as you pulled me out of the road."

"Good. It's got most of the food. I need to find my pack. The ammo for the rifle is in it."

"What good is that going to do? The gun is on the sled, and we don't have the sled."

"We will if I sneak up the bank and find it before Frankie gets there."

Dan began crawling up the bank when Kathy whispered, "The snowshoes. We need the snowshoes." Dan raised his hand and crawled toward the tarp they had been sleeping on five minutes earlier.

Frankie slowly walked back toward where he hit the pole, scanning the woods with his light for any sign of the two. He abruptly stopped a hundred feet from the campsite and walked back to the snowmobile. He removed the rifle from the case he had strapped to the snowmobile's rear bumper. Staring into the darkness, Frankie slid six rounds into the weapon's magazine, the maximum rounds the weapon would hold, then retraced his steps toward Kathy and Dan's campsite.

Meanwhile, Dan slithered on his belly, searching for his pack and the sled. He quickly located the daypack resting on the ground tarp. However, he couldn't find the sled. Dan could see the beam from Frankie's flashlight combing the woods as he came closer. Just as he was ready to retreat back into the ditch, a stroke of luck. Frankie made a pass with his flashlight along the top of the bank. At the margin of the light's beam was the plastic sled pointed down the slope, held back by only a small branch. Dan rolled toward the edge of the road. As he passed the sled, he gave it a stiff push, sending it flying down the embankment, stopping just a few feet from Kathy. Dan quickly followed.

Standing next to the ground tarp, Frankie searched the area with the light. Thinking they couldn't have gone far, he walked to the edge of the road, scanning the bottom of the ditch. The light passed over the heads of Dan and Kathy, lying facedown tight against the snow. He was about to make another sweep of the ditch when he heard a snowmobile approaching. Seconds later, Josh and Dick pulled up beside their brother.

"Took you two long enough to get here," Frankie said.

"If you had told us you were leaving, we would have gone with you," Dick shot back.

"Anyway, this is where they camped," Frankie told his brothers, pointing the light at the blue tarp. "I think they're still around here, hiding in the woods."

While Frankie talked with his brothers, Kathy and Dan slipped deeper into the woods.

"Frankie, why not let them go and come back home with us?" Dick asked.

"Beatrice is worried about you. She's right behind us, riding Josh's machine."

"Now, there's a first. Beatrice concerned about my welfare. Look, you two can go back, but I'm going to see this through." Frankie hesitated. "Let me rephrase that. I'm telling you to get to hell out of here. Go back to Darlene and Wendy, and on your way, take Beatrice with you. Have you two got that? Now get to hell out of here! I don't need help from a couple of whiners."

"To hell with you, Frankie. Just remember, you'll have to live with whatever happens to those people," Dick said, sitting back down on his snowmobile. "Come on, Josh, let's leave Dr. Demento to play his little fantasy of Get the Flatlanders."

Frankie watched the snowmobile race up the road until it disappeared over the knoll. He then walked back to the edge of the road to continue scanning the ditch for evidence of Kathy and Dan. After several passes, his flashlight locked onto something suspicious.

"Well, I'll be damned," he said aloud, staring at two sets of snowshoe tracks leading into the woods. "Now we're getting somewhere."

Frankie often hunted deer in the area. He knew a logging road had been recently built a mile farther down the Dam Road. The new woods road ran west for two miles. To escape the mountains, Kathy and Dan needed to travel south. That meant they would either cross the woods road and continue south or use it to walk back out to the Dam Road. Either way, Frankie intended to be there waiting for them.

Blowdowns, soft snow, and steep drifts made the trek south difficult for Kathy and Dan. Dan sat down on a large fallen maple to catch his breath while waiting for Kathy to catch up. "I don't know about you, but this is almost more work than I can stand," he said as Kathy sat down beside him.

"You and me both," she managed to say between breaths. As her breathing eased, she asked Dan, "Do you think Frankie is following us?"

"Yes. I think the guy is obsessed with finding us. Although I can't imagine him being the type that would exert himself snowshoeing. He'd probably stop for a smoke and then drop dead of a heart attack if he tried following us through what we just came through."

"Maybe he's waiting for us to step out onto the Dam Road."

"That's possible, although it would be a wild-ass guess on his part to know where that might be. Regardless, we'll need to stay in the woods and avoid the Dam Road for as long as possible."

"Maybe we'll be the ones that die of a heart attack if conditions don't improve."

"We'll take it slow and easy."

"How much food do we have?" Kathy asked, trying to think of anything that would prolong their rest.

"I'm not sure. This is as good a place as any to find out."

Dan cleared an area of snow off the maple and laid out the remaining food. "Well, there it is," he said, looking at the pathetic pile of supplies.

"Oh, I almost forgot," Kathy said, reaching into her pack. "I did snitch a few items before we left."

"I'd say you did. Where did you get it?" Dan said, looking at the dozen packets of instant cereal.

"In one of the plastic totes in the bedroom. Apparently, the Bartletts use the room for storage between guests."

Dan smiled, "Other than for us, it must be used as a permanent storage room."

"There's one more item."

"I can hardly wait. What is it?"

"This," she said, pulling out an unopened pound box of angel hair pasta.

"Wow! Looks like we'll be eating Italian one night this week. Any more surprises?"

"That's it. Let's boil water and eat a packet or two of the cereal."

"I've got a better idea. Let's heat some water and eat all twelve packets," Dan said, rummaging for the burner from his pack.

Dan was repacking the backpacking stove when the treetops began to stir. "Uh-oh, looks like another storm is coming. We'd better stay until it passes."

They knew the routine. Dan used a snowshoe to dig a cavity behind the log large enough to accommodate Kathy, him, and their packs. After tying the sled to a sapling, they wedged themselves into the hole, their backs pressed against the maple log, quietly waiting for the wind to start ripping through the trees. They didn't have long to wait. It hit with a vengeance. This fast-moving squall seemed more intense than most, breaking tree limbs and sending the wooden projectiles in all directions.

"Keep your head down!" Dan screamed.

Kathy didn't answer. Her head was already touching her knees, and her hands covered her ears to mute the wind's fury.

Above the howling wind came a series of pops and snaps. Dan looked up to see a lone spruce among the hardwood start to wobble as a large seam shot up the spruce's trunk. There was no time to warn Kathy of what was about to happen. He wrapped his arm around her shoulders and pulled her tight against his body as the sixty-foot spruce broke from the stump. The tree's trajectory could not have been worse.

The giant spruce landed on top of the maple with such force that the tree's trunk shattered into two pieces. The downed maple saved them from being crushed, but the limby spruce held Kathy and Dan captive inside a thick nest of spruce boughs.

Kathy opened her eyes to a wall of green inches from her face. She tried lifting her arms to remove twigs, but the larger tree branches had pinned her arms to her sides. She called out to Dan, uncertain if he was alive or dead.

"Are you okay?" she asked, anxious for a response.

"I think my leg is broken. It hurts like hell."

"Can you move it?" Kathy asked, staring into the shroud of spruce needles.

"Barely. It about kills me to try."

"You wouldn't be able to move it if it was broken. It's probably badly bruised," Kathy said, attempting to put the best possible spin on Dan's condition. "Dan, I know you're hurting, but I've got to get out of here. I can't take being trapped. It's really freaking me out."

"See if you can break off some of the branches to make a hole so you can get out."

"I can't move my arms. They're pinned."

Dan reached over and worked down her arm to the spruce branches holding her left arm captive. He snapped each one until Kathy could pull her arm free. After releasing her other arm, she broke the boughs separating her from the outside. Out from under the tree, Kathy walked around the spruce to extricate Dan. Once she sprung Dan from his prison of the tangled web of broken branches and limbs, Kathy lifted the leg of Dan's snowmobile suit to look at the injury.

"Wow! That calf is going to be one massive black-and-blue bruise," Kathy told him. "You'll have to baby it for a while. Do you think you can walk on it?"

"Maybe, but I'll never be able to pull the sled and keep my balance. You'll have to do it."

"I don't know if I have the strength. The snow is too deep to break trail *and* drag the sled."

"I'll go first. I should stay upright if I take my time and use a sapling as a staff to help me stay upright. Just walk in my tracks as you have been, and you'll do fine."

Dan asked Kathy to get a dry pair of mittens from his backpack. As she dug through the pack, she didn't notice that one of the loose rifle cartridges had lodged between the two mittens. As she took the mittens out, the .308 shell fell onto the snow unnoticed.

The pair resumed their journey, Dan shuffling along on his snowshoes, favoring his good leg, and Kathy following a few feet behind, pulling the loaded sled. For the next hour, they barely made headway. Neither spoke, not wanting to waste energy on such luxury. They kept their heads down, scanning the snow ahead for any obstacles that might trip them up.

Dan was so focused on the next step he never saw the bank. Misjudging the drop-off, he lost his balance, tumbled to the bottom, and lay sprawled out on the snow, clutching his bruised leg. Kathy had seen Dan disappear and cautiously approached the pitch. The slope was too steep to go down pulling the sled. Instead, Kathy dropped the rope and let it speed down the incline, stopping at the far end of the clearing. Then sitting on the snow, she lowered herself to the bottom. They had stumbled upon a newly constructed haul road, that had been built by one of the paper companies to harvest wood.

"Where do you think it leads?" Kathy asked.

"No idea. But it must come off the Dam Road," Dan answered, still sitting on the snow, holding on to his leg.

"Why so certain?"

"Well, for one thing, it runs east to west, and the Dam Road runs north to south, so I assume they must intersect. And second, the snowmobile track we're standing on had to come from somewhere."

Kathy hadn't noticed the track. "My God, who made that?"

"Frankie Bartlett would be my guess. He must have known the road was here and rode in looking for us. Since there's only one track, he's still here, farther in, likely parked, waiting for us to stumble out of the woods."

Like Kathy and Dan, Frankie held up for the squall to pass before resuming the search for the pair. Satisfied the storm had ended, he turned onto the woods road, slowly making his way west, looking deep into the woods for any movement that might give away Kathy and Dan's location. The deep paddles on the wide track snowmobile made dodging downed limbs and trees easy. He smiled, thinking what a great find the snowmobiles had been and how he'd like to have been standing in the shadows to see the former owner's reaction when he discovered they were missing.

Josh and Dick met Beatrice three miles north of where they had last seen Frankie. Dick told her that Frankie was mad that they had shown up and had told them he didn't need or want their help. The three sat on the snowmobiles, debating what they should do.

"I think we should do what Frankie told us and go home," Josh told the others.

"We can't do that. What if Frankie does kill them, and we do nothing to stop him? How are we going to feel then? Not only that, but Frankie will go to prison. Our own brother could get forty years to life because of our unwillingness to stop him. I'm not going to let that happen," Dick said. "Beatrice, what do you think we should do?"

"I understand you want to protect Frankie. He's family. Now I will tell you what Frank Bartlett Jr. is really like as a woman who has put up with his self-serving bullshit for seven years.

"Frankie only thinks of himself. You two know what I'm talking about. He treats both of you like crap, especially Josh, always putting him down because Josh is no Einstein. Sorry Josh, but it's the truth.

"He treats me the same way, always saying I'm stupid and how lucky I was that he showed up when he did to take care of me. Sometimes, when he's drunk, I worry he will take care of me like he took care of poor old man Carsley. I've never told anyone this, but there have been times after he's gotten falling-down drunk when he beat me. Never around the face, so that any of you would notice, but on my legs and back, for no real reason other than to make sure I didn't forget who's the boss, I guess."

Josh and Dick cringed hearing Beatrice tell how their brother had assaulted her.

"So, why did you move in with my brother?" Josh asked.

"I've asked myself that same question every day for seven years. In a way, Frankie was right when he told me he'd take care of me. I'd just divorced my first husband. The creep promised alimony, but he never came through. I didn't have a penny to my name and needed a place to stay, so I moved in with my cousin living in Madrid. She wasn't much better off than me, so it wasn't long before I felt I needed to get out, not wanting to leach off her any longer than I had to.

"Alice and I went to a dance at the Madrid Barn one Saturday night to do something fun. That's where I met Frankie. Frankie was working in the woods and making good money at that time. We danced a few times. He sat at our table drinking when we weren't on the dance floor. He was a different person then, or so I thought. He seemed like a nice guy, but later I found out it was all an act. I should have picked up on it with all the booze he drank at the dances, but it never occurred to stupid me that what might be my meal ticket out of Madrid was nothing but a drunk—and an abusive one at that. Anyway, the following Saturday, we happened to meet again at the Barn. Before long, we saw each other pretty regular. Two months later, he asked me to live with him. As I said, I was flat-ass broke and needed a place to live, so I agreed. I guess it shows you some things in life you shouldn't do for money. Two days later, I moved to Bartlett Haven, where we were supposed to live happily ever after. The rest, you know.

"As far as what the three of us should do about Frankie? It's like I told you before we left Bartlett Haven, Dick. I don't care if the son of a bitch dies in prison or wraps himself around a tree on his snowmobile. I've had enough of Frankie Bartlett. The problem is him trying to harm those two from Skyler Pond. All those people wanted was a little help to get downstate, and from that simple request, they're being chased by a lunatic who wants to kill them. So if I have a say in family affairs, it's to go after Frankie, not to save Frankie from himself but to stop him before it's too late for two innocent people."

"Okay, that's what we'll do. Josh, did you bring your rifle?" Dick asked.

"No, I didn't think I needed one."

"Neither did I, but we should each have a weapon just in case."

"In case of what? You're not going to kill Frankie, are you?" Josh asked, uneasy about Dick's motive for wanting the weapons.

"Of course not. It's just that we need to be prepared for anything. If we should get separated, the other can signal their location," Dick told his brother. "Go back to the Haven and bring back both our rifles. And don't forget the ammunition. Also, grab the snowshoes out of the storage building. We may be in for some walking." Dick glanced at Beatrice. "And bring Beatrice's snowshoes too. We'll meet back where we left Frankie. And don't take all night, either, Josh. We need to find Frankie—and fast."

Dick and Beatrice rode to Kathy and Dan's campsite to look for clues as to the direction they traveled to escape Frankie. Dick walked to the side of the road and peered down the bank, where he saw a line of deep holes in the ditch, the kind a person might make struggling to walk in deep snow without snowshoes. Near where the holes ended, nearly obliterated by windblown snow, were the remnants of Kathy and Dan's snowshoe tracks leading into the woods.

Dick assumed Frankie must have also seen the prints and wondered why he hadn't followed them. Then he remembered the new woods road. "There's a new haul road two miles ahead.

My guess is Frankie followed it, looking to intercept them when they come out of the woods," he called to Beatrice, studying the remnants of the blue tarp still covered with boughs.

There was nothing for Dick and Beatrice to do except sit on the snowmobile and wait for Josh. Several minutes passed when Beatrice broke the uncomfortable silence.

"Dick, remember me telling you and Josh about the times Frankie would beat me when he got drunk?"

"Yes. I never thought even Frankie would do something that low."

"Well, I've never told anyone this, but there's more."

"Jesus, what do you mean, more?"

"No, no. It has nothing to do with Frankie, at least not directly. It's something that I go over and over in my mind. You see, I grew up in an abusive family. I watched my dad beat my mom. I never understood why my mother put up with it. When I was older, I kept telling her to leave him. All she said was, 'I can't.' I never knew what she meant. All she had to do was walk out the front door.

"I was sixteen when I met Merton. I was so anxious to leave home that I ran off with someone just like my Father. I hardly knew the guy when we married, although it didn't take long to realize I'd married an insecure loser who felt a lot better about himself after slapping me around. Fortunately for me, but not the girl he traded me in for, I got out of the relationship. Then what did I do? I turned around and hooked up with Frankie, who came from the same mold as Merton. I guess if you're raised by animals, you partner with wolves. And do you know what, Dick?"

"What's that?" he replied, staring into the woods, uncomfortable with what Beatrice told him.

"I finally figured out what my mother meant by telling me she couldn't leave my father no matter how bad it got for her. You hope that things will change after each beating, and you tell yourself if you just try harder, you can make the relationship work. But it doesn't work that way, and it just goes on and on.

"I figured out how to keep Frankie somewhat in check when he becomes belligerent. If I go on the attack verbally, Frankie usually backs down. He seems to be intimidated when I hold my ground. Don't get me wrong, I know enough to back off before he flies off the handle and comes after me. Though I think the beatings would be more frequent or worse if I cowered every time Frankie threw a tantrum.

"Now I don't care what happens to him. I want out. I don't have any money, but I'll get by. Thank God we never had kids. My scariest nightmare would be the girls ending up like me and my mother and the boys turning into monsters like Frankie.

"That's it, Dick. I just needed to say it out loud. Anyway, I can hear Josh coming."

Dick stood up and walked past Beatrice, briefly touching her shoulder.

"What took you so long?" Dick asked once Josh shut the engine off.

"Everything kept falling off the snowmobile, and I had to keep going back, picking the stuff up."

"Josh, next time, tie things down. It will make it much easier for you," Dick said, explaining the obvious.

"I'm going to follow the tracks. Josh, you ride down as far as the new woods road. Wait thirty minutes and then slowly start in on it. I should be on the road by then. I'll walk back toward you. Be on the lookout for Frankie, but try to avoid him. It'll be better if we approach him together."

"What do you want me to do?" Beatrice asked.

"Follow Josh. Just stay in his track so you don't get stuck. If we don't find them, we'll regroup and figure out what to do next."

Beatrice and Josh watched Dick disappear into the woods and then drove to the entrance of the woods road.

The storm dumped little snow, but the ferocious winds had nearly obliterated Dan and Kathy's tracks, making them nearly impossible to follow. After an hour and numerous times backtracking to find their route, Dick came upon the maple tree with the large spruce across it. It took a minute, but he figured out from the broken spruce limbs and tracks that Kathy and Dan had sheltered against the maple and then became trapped under the toppled spruce.

In the center of the trampled snow, Dick noticed something metallic. An unspent rifle cartridge. A .308-caliber cartridge lying on the snow in the middle of the woods made no sense. Kathy and Dan had no weapon at Bartlett Haven. However, one of them must have dropped it, as it was the only plausible explanation for the cartridge being there. If he was right, a weapon complicated everything. Dick could visualize a shoot-out between Dan and Frankie not ending well for either of them. Knowing that Dan was armed changed Dick's tactics as well. Until now, the objective was to catch up with the two and warn them about Frankie. Now he also needed to be alert to his surroundings should Dan decide to use his weapon on anyone who appeared to be stalking him.

The snowshoe tracks were crisp and clear. Dick estimated, based on his experience tracking deer, that they were only an hour or two old. He upped his stride while looking deep into the woods for any sign of movement.

As Dick gained ground on Kathy and Dan, they stood on the woods road debating their next move.

"We need to follow this road back to the Dam Road," Kathy told Dan. "It's the only sure way we can make any time."

"Too dangerous, Kathy. Frankie will see us from a mile away and be on top of us before we know it. We need to continue south a while longer before cutting back to the Dam Road. Maybe by then we'll be beyond where he expects to find us by then, and he'll have given up the chase."

"I doubt if that wacko will ever give up. I think he's obsessed with finding us. Think about your leg, Dan. It's taken us God knows how long to go a mile since we were nearly impaled by that tree. You've struggled to get that bum leg over every downed tree and branch. If we continue to stay in the woods, it will be more of the same. Eventually, you'll miscue and fall face-first into the snow or, worse yet, slam your head into the side of a tree or something. At least if we stay on the road, you'll only have the snow to contend with.

"Dan, we know Frankie is somewhere behind us. We'll hide in the woods as soon as we hear the hint of his snowmobile. Chances are he'll either be going so fast or be so drunk he'll never see us."

"Maybe he won't see us, but likely he will see our tracks. It's way too dangerous on the road."

"Sorry, Dan, you lose this time. We're sticking to the road. If you fell in the woods and got hurt bad, we'd both be screwed. We could freeze to death unless I decided to leave you."

Kathy could tell by Dan's expression that he wasn't sure if she was serious about leaving him behind.

"I'm just kidding. I wouldn't do that. That is, I don't think I would. Actually, Dan, I'd have to make that decision after knowing how bad you were injured." Kathy broke out laughing.

"Funny, Kathy. A regular stand-up comedian. This is serious. We've got a lunatic trying to kill us, and you're making with the funnies."

"I have no idea where that came from. I didn't mean it. It just popped out of my mouth," Kathy said, breaking into another fit of laughter. "Sorry. I'm okay now. But I was serious when I said we're staying on the road. I'll take my chances with Frankie out in the open. I refuse to risk you becoming so lame or injured that you can't make it through the woods."

"Okay, you win. We stick to the road. But I want my rifle handy just in case."

"I'll get it."

Dan slid six rounds into the magazine and one into the chamber. With his gun slung over his shoulder, they began snowshoeing west.

About the time Kathy and Dan started toward the Dam Road, Josh and Beatrice turned onto the woods road looking for them. Unknown to Dan and Kathy, they were being squeezed from the back and front.

Even with few obstacles to avoid, the going was still tough for Dan. Kathy stayed back to not pressure him to pick up the pace. Occasionally, she stopped to look back and listen for the sound of an oncoming snowmobile. A mile into the trek, she stopped to listen one more time. Kathy thought she heard the faint whine of a snowmobile. To be sure, she squared up to the road, removed her cap, and stared into the distance. It was real. Kathy couldn't see it but knew a snowmobile was bearing down on them from behind.

At the same time, Dan stopped and looked ahead. In the distance, he could hear a machine
coming toward them.

"Snowmobile ahead!" Dan yelled.

"Not ahead of us, behind us!" Kathy hollered back.

They looked at each other. "Dan! They're coming from both directions!"

It was a mad scramble to get to the woods before the machine traveling from the Dam Road rounded the curve. Kathy was in the lead when Dan gave out a groan. She looked back to see him lying in a heap just inside the tree line. Kathy went back to help, but it was too late. All they could do was lie flat and hope not to be seen.

Kathy lifted her head off the snow. "There are two machines!" Kathy said, barely above a whisper. "It looks like Josh on the first snowmobile, and the second person looks like...my God, it's Beatrice. What is she doing here? All of the Bartletts are after us!" she exclaimed.

"If Josh, Beatrice, and Frankie are after us, then Dick can't be far off," Dan said, clutching his bruised leg.

The two snowmobiles were fifty feet from where they had left the road. Kathy dropped her head, believing at any moment, Josh and Beatrice would spot the imprints of their snowshoes and stop to investigate. Instead, Josh turned and shouted at Beatrice. Kathy couldn't tell what he said, but both machines suddenly accelerated and disappeared down the road.

"I thought we were goners for sure," Kathy said, turning toward Dan to see the rifle pointing toward the road.

"I just wanted to be ready," Dan said, seeing Kathy staring at the carbine.

"Would you really have used the gun on Josh and Beatrice?"

"I don't know. I guess I would have to decide looking down the barrel, with one of them at the other end." Dan continued, "Right now, we have a more pressing problem. Now that we know three and likely four are chasing us, we must travel in the woods. One of them is bound to discover our tracks riding back by."

"What about your leg? You won't make it a mile."

"What choice do we have? We'll have to stick with it. If we stay here and do nothing, we're done for. We need to keep moving and eventually work our way back to the Dam Road as we planned, only farther down."

"Dan, I'm not sure we'll make it out of the mountains alive. It's hard enough trying to avoid Frankie. But with the four of them looking for us, it puts the odds in their favor that they'll eventually get us."

Josh had seen Frankie a half mile down the woods road, and the two raced to meet him, never noticing the snowshoe tracks Kathy and Dan had made crossing the woods road. Beatrice wondered what Frankie would do when they met.

"I thought I told you I didn't want your help," were Frankie's first words.

"We changed our minds. Dick and me and Beatrice decided you were right, so we came back to help you find those two. Ain't that right, Beatrice?"

Beatrice didn't answer. She and Frankie only traded glares. Frankie turned his attention back to Josh. "Well, it's about time you and Dick came to your senses. Speaking of Dick, where is he?"

"He's coming through the woods following their tracks. He started back where they camped—where the blue tarp is."

"I know where they camped, for Christ's sake," Frankie told him, conveying to his brother he didn't need help being reminded where Kathy and Dan spent the night.

"Did you see any sign of them?"

"Nope. Beatrice and me looked real careful riding in from the Dam Road."

"Then they must still be in the woods, working their way toward the haul road. We need to spread out so one of us spots them when they step onto the road. Josh, you go back down the road and wait. Beatrice, you stay here. I'll go back up the road a hundred yards or so. If either of you sees something, shoot a round into the air," Frankie ordered.

"I don't have a rifle," Beatrice told Frankie.

"Then just yell 'BANG.'"

"Always the smart-ass, aren't you, Frankie?" Beatrice answered with fire in her eyes.

Frankie ignored the comment, spun the snowmobile around, and powered up the logging road.

Having received his orders, Josh drove off in the opposite direction, taking a curve position to give him a good look in two directions. He had barely turned off the engine when he heard branches breaking off to his right. Josh reached for his rifle strapped to the snowmobile, still looking toward the sound. Whatever it was, it was coming closer. Snow fell from the tops of the hardwood sapling as it neared the road. Josh raised his weapon, not wanting to be caught off guard if something sinister stepped out of the woods. The front bead of his weapon wobbled in tiny circles trying to follow the motion of the swaying trees. At the same time, his index finger fidgeted on the trigger. Another ten feet and Josh would have a clear shot.

"Don't shoot!" Dick hollered, standing at the top of the bank and seeing Josh standing on the road, pointing the gun in his direction.

"Jesus, Dick. You scared the hell out of me," Josh said, dropping his weapon to his side. "I thought you were those two from Skyler Pond or a bear or something. Could you follow their tracks?"

"Yeah, I followed them," Dick said, cautiously working his way down the bank. "They came out right here," pointing the gun's muzzle at Kathy and Dan's tracks. "Looks like one of them fell down the bank into the road. Maybe one of them's hurt," Dick said, studying the snow for blood.

Dick could tell that Kathy and Dan had turned right toward the Dam Road, but that was it. Josh's and Beatrice's snowmobiles had obliterated the rest.

"You do realize you ran over their tracks?" Dick asked.

"No. I guess we were in such a hurry to meet up with Frankie that we didn't see them."

"Doesn't matter. We'll ride west and look for where they left the road. Their tracks should be easy enough to find."

"Beatrice and me already checked both sides of the road up to where we met Frankie," Josh said.

"We're going to check again. They had to leave the road at some point unless a helicopter came in and picked them up."

"Do you think that might have happened?" Josh asked.

"What?"

"A helicopter took them away?"

"No, Josh. No helicopter. I'm just saying that they have to be in the area. They didn't just disappear." Dick squeezed onto the snowmobile behind Josh. The two continued down the haul road to find where Kathy and Dan had retreated into the woods.

"Stop! Here's where they went into the woods. I'm going in after them. Wait here fifteen minutes, then go back and tell the others I'm on their track. That will give me a good head start—time enough to catch up with them before Frankie gets to them."

A half-hour later, Josh returned with Frankie and Beatrice. Frankie wasted no time strapping on his snowshoes, barking orders for Josh to go back to the Dam Road and ride south in case they tried to walk back to the road. He told Beatrice to slowly drive back and forth on the Dam Road, and if she spotted them to find Josh, who would fire two rounds to let him know, and he'd join them.

Meanwhile, Dick was in hot pursuit, confident Kathy and Dan were a short distance ahead. A branch behind him snapped. Dick turned to see Frankie making his way toward him. Whatever chance Dick had of warning Kathy and Dan vanished. Dick waited for Frankie to catch up.

"Any sign of them?" Frankie asked, gasping for air.

"No. I think they're long gone." Not wanting to encourage Frankie by saying they might be nearby.

"I don't. I think they're a couple hundred yards ahead. One of them is injured. I see where one had fallen in the snow, and the other had to help the hurt one stand. We should separate. Coming at them in two directions will increase the odds of finding them. You stay on their trail, and I'll swing wide right and try to get in front of them."

Before Dick had a chance to protest, Frankie was already in motion. The search was shaping up like one of their deer hunting trips, tracking a big buck. Frankie was always the one trying to cut the deer off while he and Josh acted as dogs, pushing the animal toward him. It dawned on Dick that Frankie thought going after Kathy and Dan was all about the hunt. Instead of outwitting a deer, it was to outsmart Kathy and Dan. A game that gave Frankie a rush greater than any drug, except this high might end with two people dead.

SHOWDOWN

Frankie's flanking maneuver worked. He saw the two snow-shoeing a hundred yards behind and angling toward him. He slipped behind a large yellow birch to wait and jump in front of them when they were about to pass by.

"Hold up! I need to take a break. My leg is killing me," Dan called out.

Kathy stopped. Waiting for Dan, she looked ahead for the easiest route. The woods were shades of browns and grays, except for a tiny patch of fluorescent orange.

"Dan," she said in a calm, soft voice, not taking her eyes off the yellow birch.

"What?"

"Keep your voice down. Someone is behind that large yellow birch straight ahead. I can see a piece of his hunting jacket."

Dan saw it as well. "Okay. Come back here and get behind a tree." Dan lowered himself to his knees, took the rifle from his shoulder, and then dropped to a prone position. He raised the weapon, took sight on the fluorescent patch, and then elevated the gun about two feet, the height of a man's chest.

Frankie wondered why they were taking so long to reach his position. He peeked around the tree to see where they were. Still unable to see them, he leaned out farther. Frankie assumed Kathy and Dan had veered off their expected course and disappeared into the hardwood. Confident they were gone, he stepped away from the tree. He had no idea that two hundred feet away, the front bead of a .308 lined up perfectly with the center of his chest.

Dan told himself he would not pull the trigger unless Frankie made a threatening move with his weapon.

Frankie stood in the open, panning the woods, trying to catch a glimpse of the two before they melted into the forest, regretting that he didn't shoot when he had the chance. The only way to determine their direction was to snowshoe to where he'd seen them last. He had barely started when something black sticking slightly above the snow caught his attention. Frankie knew exactly what it was, the top of Dan's wool cap. Frankie stepped behind the nearest tree, watching. He was in no hurry to shoot. The hunt was over, so why rush the kill?

"I see you there in the snow. Come on over and we'll talk."

Dan kept his gun aimed at Frankie's chest. "Why are you following us? We haven't done anything to you."

"Oh, I don't really know. I guess I like the chase." Frankie paused, then asked, "Do you hunt, Mr.... You know, I don't think I know your name." Frankie waited for an answer while scanning the woods for Kathy.

Dan didn't answer, keeping the weapon aimed at Frankie.

"You do have a name, don't you? I don't want to remember you as the man from Skyler Pond. That would make your death too impersonal."

"Dan. Dan Simmons."

"Well, Mr. Simmons, do you hunt?"

"Yes. I hunt."

"Do you enjoy the kill, Mr. Simmons?"

"Not particularly. It's part of hunting."

"Well, Mr. Simmons, that's the difference between you and me. As much as I like the hunt, I like the kill even more. A clean kill, of course. When I shoot, I shoot to kill." Frankie slowly raised the gun to his chest.

It was now or never for Dan. If Frankie got the first shot

off, that would end it. Yet he still had reservations about shooting another human being. His gun shook, trying to decide what to do. He remembered his instructor at a self-protection class telling him that if confronted by an armed person who means to harm you, you shoot to kill, not to wound. A wounded assailant can shoot you just as dead. The barrel went from Frankie's chest to his arm and back again, still reluctant to go for a kill shot.

Frankie took a bead on Dan's cap.

KAPOW!

The two explosions sounded as one. Luckily for Dan, a 2,500-feet-per-second projectile will beat one traveling 2,100 feet per second to its target every time. Dan's bullet ripped through the fleshy part of Frankie's upper right arm, causing it to flex upward as he pulled the trigger, sending the round harmlessly over Dan's head.

Frankie's arm stung, but he wasn't sure why until he saw blood drip from his coat sleeve onto the snow. While Frankie tried to piece together what had happened, Dan and Kathy slipped deeper into the woods.

Hearing the shots, Dick ran up to Frankie. "What happened? I heard shots," Dick said, winded from the sprint, then noticing the softball-sized patch of blood on the snow.

"The son of a bitch shot me."

"Who shot you?"

"The guy from Skyler Pond. He shot me for no good reason."

"How do you know it was him?"

"Who to hell else would it be? We're in the woods, remember? The only ones out here are you, me, and those two," Frankie said, avoiding telling Dick what led up to the shooting.

Dick knew there must be more to the story, but he let it slide. To challenge Frankie, you had better have a good reason or else suffer his wrath. Dick remembered he had forgotten to tell Frankie about the cartridge he had found in the snow. At this point, it no longer mattered.

"Let me look at your arm," Dick said.

Dick slid Frankie's arm from his coat. "For Christ's sake, be careful," Frankie yelled. "Don't take all day! How does it look?"

"Actually, it looks like you're going to live. The bullet missed the bone and artery, although it did take a hunk of flesh. It really needs stitches to close the hole."

"Well, that ain't going to happen. Cut a piece off my shirt with your knife to stop the bleeding. Then use my belt to hold it in place. We're going after those two."

Josh and Beatrice took the two rapid rounds to signal that Frankie or Dick needed help or perhaps someone was shot. Josh left his snowmobile on the Dam Road, grabbed his rifle, and headed in the direction of the gunfire. Beatrice was on the woods road when she heard the gun's report and rode back to where Dick and Frankie left the haul road to follow Kathy and Dan. She strapped on her snowshoes and went into the woods to find them.

Dick tried to persuade Frankie to stop his vendetta against Kathy and Dan.

"You're not going to start that again, are you? I told you once I didn't need your help. So either come along and keep your mouth shut or get out of here."

"I should have let you bleed to death."

Frankie got in Dick's face. "Well, you lost your chance, didn't you? So what is it, Dicky. Are you going with me or running home to Darlene?"

"Someday, someone will take a shot at you and hit more than your arm."

"That wouldn't be you doing the shooting, would it, Dicky? Because if you try it, you better make your first shot count 'cause you won't get a second."

"No, Frankie, it won't be me. I'll be second in line."

"Get out of here! Before something bad happens to you," Frankie said, raising his rifle to his chest.

Dick retreated, only far enough to stay out of Frankie's sight. He wasn't ready to give up on stopping his brother from harming Kathy and Dan.

Meanwhile, Josh aimlessly snowshoed through the woods, unsure of which direction to go to find his brothers. As hunters are taught, Josh fired a round skyward, hoping to hear an answering gunshot that would give him a direction to Frankie or Dick. Josh did right, but in this situation, it had unintended consequences.

Dan and Kathy heard the report of Josh's rifle. Dan knew Frankie was somewhere behind, but the gun's blast was ninety degrees to the west. There was no way Frankie could have traveled that distance so fast. "There must be two people chasing us," he told Kathy. "We need to continue south."

"Why? We agreed to work our way back to the Dam Road to make better time," Kathy responded.

"Whoever fired that shot is between us and the road. We can't take the chance of running into him. We'll walk another hour to try to outflank him and then turn west."

Dan sensed something around them was different. "I don't believe it, not now."

"What?"

"Look at the treetops."

Kathy looked up to see what had upset Dan. "We'd better find a place to hole up before the storm hits."

"We have to keep going. I don't think Frankie will follow us, but we can't be sure, and we need to put as much distance between us and whoever fired that shot."

"Dan, I know this isn't the best time to ask this, but I need to know. Why didn't you kill Frankie? You had the opportunity to end this nightmare once and for all. Now we don't know if he's still after us or not."

"You're right. This isn't the best time. The short answer is I couldn't bring myself to kill even a monster like Frankie. It didn't seem right that I should end someone's life. I didn't want to go through life knowing I'd murdered a human being."

Kathy wanted to tell Dan that taking the moral high ground might have cost them their lives. However, this was not the time for that debate.

"We better keep going," she told him and started forward, pulling the sled.

Frankie pushed himself as hard as he could with his wounded arm, but it was enough to gain ground on Kathy and Dan. As snow began to fall, only a hundred yards separated them. Dick continued to dog Frankie but kept his distance to avoid being seen. Beatrice was farther back, following their tracks, looking and listening for any clue that might signal Dick's or Frankie's whereabouts. Simultaneously, Josh continued to stumble through the woods, unknowingly toward his brothers.

The storm's intensity grew, forcing Kathy and Dan to seek shelter. Through the blowing snow, Dan made out a distant fir stand that would break the biting wind. Frankie caught sight of them nearing the cover of evergreens.

Frankie watched them disappear into the clump of trees and slowly advanced, shifting from one tree to another. Dick followed, still keeping his distance, not knowing his brother was setting another ambush.

Frankie positioned himself behind a large pine, using a stub of a broken limb to rest the gun he pointed at Kathy and Dan's green refuge. Frankie planned to wait for the storm to end and conclude his business when they exited. This time, he wouldn't waste time before taking the first shot. Confident that his plan was foolproof, Frankie only needed to wait.

Several minutes passed when Frankie caught a flash of movement off to his right. Without taking the rifle from the broken branch, he turned his head and cursed. It was Josh heading straight toward him. Frankie tried to wave him off, but Josh took his frantic hand gesture to mean to come to him. Frankie knew the instant he spoke, Kathy and Dan would know what was up and try to escape out the backside of the stand of trees. Josh was less than a hundred feet away, sporting a big smile, pleased that he had located his brother even though it was purely blind luck.

Frankie put a finger over his lips, hoping Josh would understand he needed to be quiet, and then used his good arm to motion him back the way he came. Finally, Josh understood, backtracked to a large yellow birch, and watched to see what would transpire.

Dick used the heavy snowfall as cover to steal closer to Frankie. Dick could see him braced against the tree, his rifle pointed toward the clump of firs. Not seeing Kathy or Dan, he surmised that the two were hiding among the trees.

Beatrice came up behind Dick, stopping fifty feet behind him, then worked her way off to the left and crouched behind a downed tree. Dick would not have known she was there if he hadn't glanced in her direction. Beatrice looked back and gave him the high sign with a quick hand raise. Dick pointed ahead toward Frankie.

Like snow-covered statues in a city park, Frankie, Josh, Dick, and Beatrice froze, waiting for someone to make the first move. Ten minutes passed and then the fir trees began to quake, releasing the fresh snow from the bent boughs. Seeing the snow fall from the branches, everyone watched and waited, knowing something big was about to happen. A head peeked out from one of the fir trees. It was Kathy looking to see if the storm had passed. She retreated inside the shelter and soon reappeared, pulling the plastic sled. Dan followed, his leg still stiff from the run-in with the spruce tree.

Frankie watched, waiting for the perfect time to make his move. Dick edged closer, knowing Frankie was preoccupied with watching Kathy and Dan. Beatrice also moved up as Josh watched the scene play out from behind the birch tree.

Frankie waited for Dan to put the rifle's sling over his shoulder, giving him the advantage if Dan went for his weapon. The two were ready to resume their trek. This was the opportunity Frankie had waited for.

"Mr. Simmons. Do you have a minute before you leave?" Frankie asked, the barrel of his rifle aimed at Dan's back.

Dan and Kathy spun around but couldn't see Frankie standing behind the tree.

"Over here behind the pine, just look for a gun barrel looking back at you," Frankie taunted.

Dick had no intention of letting anything happen to Kathy and Dan. He raised his rifle and pointed at Frankie. "Frankie put your rifle down. Now!" he ordered.

Frankie turned toward Dick. "What do you think you're doing, little brother? Don't you know you shouldn't play with guns? You could get hurt."

"You heard me. This foolishness is going to stop now. So put your gun down!"

As Frankie bantered with Dick, Dan slid the sling from his shoulder and quickly raised the weapon, taking a bead on Frankie. "You're in a tough spot, Frankie. You can only shoot one of us before the other kills you. So why not just put the gun down?"

Stalemate. Frankie kept the rifle aimed at Dan, trying to find a way out of the jam. His wound prevented him from spinning around to take out Dick. Even if he did get a shot off, Dan would have time to unload on him. One thing he knew for sure was that he wasn't dropping the gun. The namesake of Frank Bartlett Sr. cowers to no one. He'd rather go down with a bullet through the heart than surrender his weapon to his younger brother. He'd bank on Dick not having the guts to kill him.

Dick heard the faint click of Frankie's rifle safety turn off. "I'm warning you! Stop now. I will shoot."

The report of the explosion reverberated through the forest. Then the air went deathly silent. For nearly a minute, no one moved. Everyone was overwhelmed by what had happened. Dick and Josh slowly walked toward Frankie's dead body. Soon Kathy and Dan joined them. They stared at Frankie in disbelief at what had happened as large snowflakes drifted gently down, melting on his still warm face. Dan was the first to break the silence.

"I'm sorry, Dick. It has to be gut-wrenching to shoot your own brother."

Dick gave Dan a questioning look. "I didn't shoot him. I thought you did."

"I didn't shoot. I was going to, but I never got the shot off," Dan said.

The four of them looked at each other, bewildered as to who shot Frankie. Behind them came the steady rhythm of shuffling snowshoes. Beatrice stepped between Dan and Dick and stared at Frankie.

Dick caught a glimpse of something drop from Beatrice's hand. He looked down at the revolver resting on the snow.

"You? You shot Frankie?"

"Yes. I know you will hate me for killing your brother. But I had to do it. I couldn't let him go on hurting people. Seeing him ready to kill two innocent people was more than I could stand," Beatrice said, staring at Frankie.

Uncomfortable standing over Frankie's corpse, Dick led everyone to the side. Josh remained behind, sobbing, unable to pull himself away from his dead brother.

"I don't understand. Where did you get the gun?" Dick asked.

"I took it from the bureau drawer just before we left the Haven to look for Frankie. I don't know why I took it. It wasn't like I had planned to kill him. I just saw it in the drawer when I went after my gloves and took it."

"I didn't know you owned a handgun," Dick said.

"Frankie gave it to me shortly after I moved in. Said I might need it in case some weirdo showed up when he wasn't home. He took me target practicing a couple of times. After that, it stayed in the bureau draw except for a time or two I thought there might be trespassers messing around the trailers." Beatrice began to cry. Kathy stepped up and did her best to console her.

"What should we do?" Kathy asked, her arm around Beatrice's shoulder.

"Nothing," Dick answered. "We say nothing to no one. What's done is done. Josh and me will take Frankie back to the compound on the dogsled. There's an old toolshed our father built years ago up behind the trailers. Like most of his projects, he never did finish it, but it's animal-proof and watertight. We'll put Frankie inside. Once the snow melts, we'll bury him. He always liked the little stand of pine across the brook. That's where he'd go when he got down or had an argument with Josh or me. Father is buried there, as well. They can finally be reunited."

Dan and Josh constructed a crude stretcher out of pole-sized cedar, placed Frankie's body on one of Dan's tarps, and hoisted it onto the pole frame. Everyone paused to look at the scene of the tragedy for the final time. "Let's go," Dick told the others, and he and Josh lifted the stretcher and the solemn procession began the long walk back to the snowmobiles.

Once back to the haul road, everyone needed a rest. It was decided that Dick and Dan would continue carrying Frankie's body toward the Dam Road while Josh rode back to get the dogsled they had left where Kathy and Dan had camped. When Josh returned, the others had reached the Dam Road.

"You two are welcome to come back with us if you want," Dick told Dan and Kathy.

"Thanks anyway, but we need to keep going," Dan replied.

"Then take Frankie's snowmobile. Not much gas in it, but it will get you a ways down the road."

"What if it does run out of gas?" Kathy asked.

"Josh and I will ride down and take it back to the Haven once things settle down."

It was a brief farewell. Kathy approached Beatrice and gave her a long embrace. She told her how sorry she was for what had happened. Beatrice clung to Kathy, sobbing. After another parting hug, Kathy joined Dan.

"Are you familiar with the Morton cutoff?" Dick asked.

"Never heard of it. All the years we've been going to our cabin has been driving the Dam Road."

"It was a snowmobile trail, a shortcut to Fraternity Township until the landowner closed it off about ten years ago. You'd never know it was there unless you're looking for it. Do you know where Little Michael Stream goes under the Dam Road about ten miles farther down?"

Dan looked around, trying to get his bearings of where they were on the Dam Road. Everything seemed so different with all the snow. Finally, he recognized a tall gnarly white pine next to the road.

"Yes, now I know the stream you're talking about."

"Just before you cross the stream, you'll see a stand of young fir trees on the left side of the road. Bull your way through them. It's only fifty feet or so. On the other side are the remnants of an old county road. I was in there a few years back partridge hunting, so I know the road's still visible. Follow it for a mile, but not more than two. Eventually, you'll break out of the woods into an abandoned field. Although you won't recognize it as such, buried under ten feet of snow. Stay straight on the same course that you followed through the woods. In a half mile, you will come to a farmhouse on the left. An old man and his wife live there, or did the last I knew. They let me hunt birds in the apple orchard. They'll help you. If the place is abandoned, bust in. There's bound to be firewood in the ell and maybe food. That's the best I can tell you."

"Thanks."

Dan reached for the ignition switch. He hesitated and looked up at Dick.

"I just wanted to tell you I'm sorry it ended this way."

"It was bound to happen. Frankie battled many demons in his life, and eventually, one of them was bound to come out on top. He only cared about himself, oblivious to what anyone else felt or cared about. My brother was a stranger in his own life. After our father died, Frankie changed for the worse. I'm no psychiatrist, but I think there was an unspoken bond between the two of them, far stronger than any of us realized. He never accepted our father dying, and every day he seemed to fight to bring him back."

"And Beatrice, will she be okay?"

"I don't know. How does anyone be all right after killing a person? I don't blame her for what happened. Frankie was mean to her, perhaps crueler than we'll ever know. She's welcome to stay with us as long as she wants, but I suspect Beatrice will want to get away from us Bartletts and try to put this whole mess behind her, if she can.

"I worry about my brother. Poor Josh. It'll be hard for him. He always wanted to please Frankie, no matter how rotten Frankie treated him. Frankie couldn't make himself understand Josh was different. Different in the sense of being slower than most. Every time Josh screwed up, Frankie was there to tell him how stupid he was. The few times he did get things right, Frankie would still find a way to bring Josh down. With Josh, you have to have patience. That's a word Frankie never understood."

CURLS OF WOODSMOKE

Dan glanced into the snowmobile's rearview mirror for one last look at the Bartlett clan. The sight of Dick and Josh lowering Frankie's body onto the sled for his final ride to Bartlett Haven was now permanently etched in his mind. Dan slowly shook his head, knowing that none of this should have happened.

Neither spoke as the snowmobile wound around fallen trees and over giant snowdrifts. The memories of the past two hours were too fresh for Dan and Kathy to be conscious of their surroundings. Dan and Kathy replayed the tragedy in their minds, wondering if they had done things differently, maybe Frankie would still be alive.

Twenty minutes after leaving the Bartletts, the snowmobile sputtered and died. Dan cursed. He had hoped they would make it a few more miles before it ran out of gas.

"Hey, we knew it would run dry at some point," Kathy told him, unphased by the delay. "We'll snowshoe the rest of the way. It's not like we haven't done that before. Is your leg up to it?"

"Don't worry about my leg. I'll crawl the rest of the way if I have to."

An hour later, Dan spotted the stand of fir they'd been looking for. On the other side of the trees, Kathy noticed a weather-beaten sign nailed to a tree, its top barely sticking out of the snow. They pulled the rotted sign off the hemlock and stared at the faded black letters: Fraternity Township. Population 58. Kathy put her arms around Dan and gave him a squeeze.

"We did it, Dan! We actually did it!"

"Now we need to find someone to take us in," Dan said, knowing their ordeal wouldn't be over until they found shelter.

"We will. I'm positive we will. Nothing can stop us now!"

"I hope you're right."

"Of course I'm right. The people in the first place we stop will help us."

Dan smiled. "Then I guess we should get going. I don't want to be late for supper."

An hour later, there it was, just as Dick had told them. A farmhouse, barely visible above the snowdrifts a hundred feet from where they stood.

"Dan, look at the chimney."

"I see it. Let's go."

Curls of woodsmoke gently rose from the chimney before being grabbed by a gusty northerly wind. A cornice of snow curled off the roof, encasing the entire east side of the house in a huge impenetrable drift. The snow thinned at the top of one of the buried windows, revealing a warm glow of light emanating from inside the home. Dan snowshoed up the drift and peered through the top windowpane. An elderly woman sat on the couch by the woodstove, reading. A light rap on the glass got the startled woman's attention. At first, she was leery of the stranger scooching down in the snow, motioning her to the window. The woman seemed relieved when Kathy appeared next to Dan. They could hear her shoes striking the pine floor as she approached the window. Dan mouthed, 'Help us.' She smiled and pointed toward the rear of the building. Dan understood. He and Kathy snowshoed along the side of the house to find a partially shoveled path between the house's back entrance and a large woodshed. The door opened.

"Come in. come in," she repeated. "You two must be frozen."

Kathy and Dan removed their snowshoes and stepped into the hallway, dragging gobs of snow onto the floor. They were greeted by the warmth of the woodstove. A comforting heat they hadn't felt since leaving Skyler Pond.

"Hello, we're Kathy and Dan Simmons. We hoped you might be willing to help us," Dan said.

"Of course we'll help you. I'm Doris Olsen. Give me your coats."

Kathy and Dan followed Doris down the hall. Kathy gave Dan's sweater a firm tug and mouthed, "I told you."

"Bert, come here!" Doris shouted to her husband.

Bert, a slightly overweight, balding man, stepped into the living room, looking as if his wife had just woken him from a nap. At first, Bert only saw Dan. Thinking a stranger had broken into his home, he stepped back into the den and reached for the shotgun he kept behind the door, locked and loaded just for this kind of situation.

"No, Bert! It's okay. This is Kathy and Dan Simmons, and they need our help."

For the next hour, Kathy and Dan told the Olsens about leaving Skyler Pond and their adventures along the route, leaving out any reference to being chased through the woods by a psychopath.

"So where are you trying to get to?" Bert asked.

"Our daughter's home in Westbrook. We're so worried about her, and we know she must be worried sick about us. We haven't talked to her in three months—not since the war broke out," Kathy answered, her eyes starting to water. Somehow, saying aloud how long it had been since seeing Hazel made the separation more real and terrifying.

"That's going to be a challenge. Westbrook is more than a hundred miles from here. You know how bad the situation is right now," Bert said, assuming both of them knew what had been happening in the outside world since the start of the nuclear exchange.

"Actually, we don't. Our radio stopped working right after the attack. All we know from listening to emergency broadcasting before it quit was that the North Koreans attacked the United States with nuclear weapons. We did manage to hear the president say they hit a number of military installations around the country and that we retaliated. And we know the nuclear explosions caused the weather to do weird things."

"'Weird' isn't the word for it. Everything has gone nuts," Bert replied, his face tightening at the thought of how the war had caused the world to flip upside down.

"I'm afraid it was more than military installations that got hit. One of North Korea's missiles was on course to hit Boston, except three miles out, there was some kind of malfunction, and it crashed into the ocean. The bomb did detonate, creating an enormous tidal wave that wiped out nearly every building within a half mile of the waterfront. Some escaped, but most drowned.

"New York City and military bases in Florida and Norfolk Virginia took direct hits. Worse yet is on the West Coast. Closer to North Korea, I guess. Nearly every significant military base got it, along with nearby urban areas. As you said, those explosions messed up the atmosphere, causing this crazy weather. All that dust thrown into the atmosphere dropped the temperature enough that everything that usually comes as rain has fallen as snow, at least here in New England. We have nearly ten feet on the ground right here in Fraternity Township.

"As bad as the weather's been, the breakdown in society has been worse. Riots, looting, complete mayhem. Portland is one of the worst. No one dares to go outside, afraid they'll have nothing to return to if they leave their property unattended. That's one reason Doris and I live where we do. We have good neighbors, plenty of wood and food, and a loaded 9-millimeter beside the bed."

Hearing what Bert said about the anarchy in Portland scared Kathy. Westbrook is nothing more than an extension of the city. Whatever happened in Portland surely must have spilled over into the surrounding towns.

"Have things calmed down any? I mean, has law and order been restored?" Dan asked, thinking that selling their home in Hampden and moving to Skyler Pond was the right decision.

"Yes, somewhat. The police, backed up by the National Guard, are in control in most areas from what we hear on the radio. However, the state still has pockets that even the National Guard is afraid to enter."

"What about the weather? Is there any hope it will improve?"

"If you'd been here yesterday and asked that question, I would have told you the weatherman saw no end in sight. Just more of the same: freakish snowstorms, violent winds, bitter cold, and no sunshine. However, Doris and I heard on the morning news that the experts are now saying the atmosphere is starting to improve. Southern New England actually saw several hours of sun yesterday. The meteorologists now predict that the weather patterns should straighten out in a month or two, ending this weird weather. Hurrah for that!"

"Can we make it to our daughter's in Westbrook?" Dan asked.

"Like I said, Mr. Simmons, everything is in a state of flux right now, with the weather and turmoil in the cities and all. Besides, according to the news, other than the interstate south of Bangor, all the roads are snowbound, even along the coast, except parts of Route 1."

"Jesus, that's the last thing I wanted to hear."

"Look, I can't tell you what you should do, but here's something to consider. Why don't you two stay with us awhile? Let things calm down. As for tonight, you can sleep on the sofa bed in the den."

"I don't know, Mr. Olsen. We really want to see our daughter," Kathy said.

"I understand that. I'd feel the same way if I was in your shoes. But the fact remains it's near impossible to get downstate right now. The other thing, say you did make it to your daughter's. The news is full of stories of food shortages and the looting of grocery stores. That's if there's anything left to steal."

Kathy and Dan knew what Bert meant without coming out and saying it. Maybe there wouldn't be enough food for the four of them. The last thing they wanted was to worsen the situation by moving in with Hazel and Tom.

Bert knew from the look on Kathy's face that he had scared her. He attempted to walk back just how dire the problem might be in the cities. "Of course, every city is different; likely not all of them are that bad off." However, Kathy knew what he had told them was true. After three months of constant strife, all parts of the state must be suffering from food shortages.

"Bert, let the two discuss it alone. We can talk about it tomorrow. Right now, let's have supper. This is Saturday night. Bert and I have beans every Saturday. We grow our own beans, you know. Make our own maple syrup too. We ran out of molasses a month ago, so we use maple syrup to substitute for the molasses. I hope you folks like homemade baked beans and bread."

Dan's stomach growled just hearing Doris talk about food. "That sounds great, doesn't it, Kathy?"

It was all Kathy could do to keep from yelling, "Let's eat!"

The next morning, at the breakfast table, Bert approached Dan about staying with them. "Did you and your wife decide to stay here awhile?"

"We talked about it. We both agreed it's a nice gesture, but having two people move into your home wouldn't be fair to you and Doris. This is your space. The last thing you need is to have strangers move in and upset your lives."

"You needn't worry about that. It's not like you and Kathy would be sleeping on cots in our bedroom. You two would have your own space upstairs. You see, about five years ago, Doris's mother moved in with us. Before she did, I converted the upstairs into an apartment with a kitchen and bath. She passed two years ago, and the space has been closed off since.

"Another thing, it's not like you wouldn't earn your keep. I'm getting too old to lug firewood through all this snow. You'd take that job over and finish splitting what's left in the woodshed. And, if you really get bored, you can paint the downstairs ceilings. Doris has been after me to do it for the past two years," Bert said with a grin. "So I have my motives for asking you to stay."

Dan looked at Kathy for her thoughts.

"Bert, we'll take you up on your offer. We really appreciate what you and Doris have done for us already," Kathy said. "I'll try to do my part and help Doris in her kitchen—only if she asks for it, of course."

That night lying in bed, Kathy began to laugh.

"What are you laughing about?"

"Oh, I was just thinking how far we have come in our accommodations."

"Meaning?"

"We've gone from sleeping on a tarp at ten above zero and peeing in the woods to a storage room in a run-down trailer with a shared backhouse. Now we have our own apartment with a flush toilet. All of that in just one week. How's that for moving on up?"

"Good night."

Soon after settling into the apartment, Dan noticed Kathy spending much of her time writing at the small desk. Each time he walked past the desk, Kathy would shuffle the papers so he couldn't read what she'd written. Finally, curiosity got the best of him.

"What are you writing, Kathy? And why all the secrecy?"

"Oh, I'm just writing about our experiences since leaving Skyler Pond."

"You mean like an after-the-fact journal?"

"Sort of," she said sheepishly.

"What does that mean, 'sort of'?

"Well, I thought I would try to write about all we've been through since the war broke out. You know, trapped at the cabin, our escape, and the crazies we met while trying to get help. I suppose everyone has a story about how they survived the war; many are likely terribly tragic. I just thought our journey was different than most. I'm not saying I will actually do anything with it. It may be nothing more than a therapeutic exercise and end up in my bureau's bottom drawer. I only want to get it on paper before the memories fade."

"I don't think you need to worry about that. I have a feeling we will relive the nightmare more than once." Dan thought for a second and asked, "Does your story include everything, even what happened to—"

Kathy interrupted. "Yes, everything, including what happened to Frankie Bartlett. Only in my account, his name is Harry Daigle."

"Can I see it?" Dan asked, picking up the top sheet of paper.

"I'd rather you didn't. Maybe after I'm finished."

"Is this the title?"

"Yes."

"'Stranded,'" he said aloud. "Nice." Then he set the paper back down on the table.

EPILOGUE

Kathy and Dan were finally able to get a message to their daughter. The emergency radio network station for southern Maine read brief messages to and from family members isolated from one another. Bert's neighbor, a ham radio operator, relayed a message to the station. Three days later, a reply from Hazel came over the radio: "Dan and Kathy, we are well. Hazel and Tom." Those were the most satisfying words Kathy and Dan had ever heard.

Dan and Kathy stayed five weeks with the Olsens. During that time, society slowly regained its footing, and the rule of law prevailed. Citizens gained confidence that life would improve, and in the larger cities, goods started to flow.

Each morning, after Bert started the generator, the four sat in the living room, listening to the latest news on the radio. This morning, midway through the broadcast, an annoying ringtone competed with the newscaster's update. Everyone assumed it was a cell phone going off at the radio station's studio. Suddenly, Kathy realized it was her cell phone. The first time it had rung in four months. She frantically fumbled for the phone she kept in her shirt pocket.

"Hello," she said warily, not knowing what to expect. "Yes, this is Kathy Simmons." She began to sob. Unable to speak, she held the phone out to Dan.

"Hello, this is Dan Simmons. Hazel!" Dan started to tear up but managed to regain control. "My God! Hazel, it's so great to hear your voice. No, your mother is fine. She was just overwhelmed to hear your voice. Are you and Tom okay?"

Dan and his daughter talked for several minutes. At the end of the conversation, he told Hazel he would put her mother on, but Kathy waved him off. "Not now," she told him. "Ask her to call this evening."

After the call ended, Dan told Kathy and the Olsens what their daughter had said.

"Great news! Our daughter wants us to join her in Westbrook. She said the state runs buses from Bangor to Portland on the interstate every hour. Gasoline is in short supply, so there are no cars. Hazel said to call her along the way, and she'll meet us at the drop-off at the Maine Mall. Now all we need to do is get ourselves to that bus!"

Two nights later, everyone woke to a constant whine in the distance, similar to the sound a small plane makes going overhead. However, this noise was getting louder rather than fading away. Dan opened the bedroom window and stuck his head outside. A quarter mile down the road, two behemoth military-style trucks with front-mounted snowblowers clawed their way toward them. Their huge spotlights cut through the blowing snow with the intensity of an airport beacon. Kathy and Dan rushed to the downstairs living room for a better view. Soon Doris and Bert joined them. Everyone cheered. Four months of isolation was being blown away one foot at a time.

"Hurry! We've got to be out there before they go by again. We'll bum a ride as far south as they go," Dan hollered, scrambling to find their parkas and gloves.

Minutes later, they stood at the side door, ready to rush down the driveway to flag down the trucks. Kathy and Dan thanked the Olsens for their help and promised they would return one day.

Bert held out his hand. "Here, take this. It's the name and address of a friend who lives in Skowhegan. If you make it there,

contact him. He'll get you to Waterville by snowmobile if he has to."
Dan thanked Bert and stuffed the note into his parka.

"Hurry!" Kathy said. "They're coming back. I can see the headlights."

Dan stood in the half-plowed road waving his arms. The huge truck ground to a halt, and Dan jumped onto the running board.

"We need a ride. Can you take my wife and me with you?" Dan shouted over the rumble of the idling snowblower.

"One of you get in with me. The other will have to ride in the other truck," the operator barked. Dan helped Kathy into the cab and then ran back to the second truck.

The snowblowers engaged, and the two trucks jerked ahead. Kathy peered out the side window to see Doris and Bert waving flashlights at the open door. She rolled down the window and stuck out her arm, waving until the Olsens disappeared in the blowing snow.

Fortunately, they didn't need to contact Bert's friend for a ride. They rode to the state transportation garage in Sidney and then with a plow driver about to start his shift plowing the southbound lane of the interstate to Augusta. The bus rolled into Portland three hours later, where Hazel anxiously waited to meet them.

Two years passed before conditions improved enough for Kathy, Dan, Hazel, and Tom to return to Skyler Pond. Although life would never be the same, the country had survived the aftermath of nuclear war, and through it all, most Mainers learned to smile again.

"Well, there it is, still standing," Dan told the others with a sigh of relief as the cabin came into view. "Although I had my doubts with the weight of all the snow on the roof."

"I would hope it held together. You were the ace engineer who reinforced it," Tom said, ribbing his father-in-law.

Kathy didn't laugh. Seeing the log cabin brought back a tidal wave of memories of their ordeal two years earlier. She tried to force herself to reflect on their good times before the war. She remembered Hazel's excitement at seeing a moose and catching her first fish off the dock. She looked so proud holding that seven-inch trout. The photo still hung alongside other family photos on the den wall. There were wonderful memories of their times at their little cabin. However, no matter how hard she tried, the time she and Dan were sequestered at Skyler Pond bubbled to the surface.

Thoughts of the night when two starving wolves chased Dan into the cabin. The night she became lost on the pond, thinking she would never survive until morning, dying in the bitter cold. She remembered the day Frankie, Dick, and Josh flew past the cabin on snowmobiles and how she foolishly thought they would rescue them and put an end to the three-month nightmare of being isolated in their cabin. At the end of the driveway was where Frankie had pointed his revolver at her, his eyes cold and calculating. She shivered, remembering how he had threatened her.

Dan interrupted Kathy's thoughts. He asked if she and Hazel would go into the cabin and start a fire while he and Tom walked around the outside to check for damage. While Kathy fussed at the woodstove, trying to encourage the kindling to ignite, Hazel noticed a piece of folded writing paper resting on the kitchen table. Curious, she picked it up. In large letters were the words "Please read." Next to it was the envelope addressed to her. Hazel glanced at her mother, watching the flames feed on the wood as the cast iron woodstove cracked and popped, expanding to the heat.

Hazel sat at the table and read her mother's letter. She read it a second time, absorbed by each word. Her eyes watered. She knew her parents had endured a terrible ordeal stranded at Skyler Pond. Still, until now, she hadn't comprehended just how dire the situation had become. The thought of her parents lying in the snow, slowly freezing to death, caused her to tremble. She looked at her mother, studying the framed family photos on the den wall. *How did she do it?* Hazel asked herself. *How did a sixty-one-year-old woman survive being isolated for three months in the Maine woods?*

She walked over to Kathy with the letter and hugged her mother.

"What was that for?" Kathy asked.

Hazel held up the letter. Kathy read what she had written. She looked at Hazel, waiting several seconds before she spoke. "Looking back, the scariest day of my life was leaving Skyler Pond. I really thought we might not make it. We had little food and only enough gasoline to go partway down the mountain. If something did go terribly wrong, I wanted you to know what had happened to us."

Kathy reached for Hazel's hand and held it tight. "Soon you will know everything that happened. Even after two years, it's still too much for me to talk about. Writing down everything that happened here and our escape from the mountains has been easier. Once you've read about our journey, you will understand. I can tell you, Hazel, that it's a tragic story with a happy ending."

At that moment, Dan and Tom burst into the kitchen. "Other than a large pine resting on the roof, the place looks fine," Dan announced. "Now that we know our little cabin survived, we should have a drink to celebrate being back at Skyler Pond." Dan pulled out a fifth of coffee brandy he had stuffed into his backpack at the car.

"Kathy, do you remember what I promised the night we spent in the car at the bottom of that ravine?"

"Yes, I remember. And you were right, we did persevere. You open the bottle while I get the glasses."

The four gathered around the woodstove. Dan started to make a toast, but Kathy stopped him.

"Let me do it, Dan." She looked at Hazel and smiled. "A toast to the Simmons and the Martins. May our families always be together." As they downed their brandy, no one noticed Kathy drop the letter into the fire.

The Bartletts

After the shooting, Dick, Josh, and Beatrice returned to Bartlett Haven with Frankie's body strapped onto the dogsled. Wendy and Darlene were in the yard watching the children play when Dick rode up the driveway with Josh standing on the back of the dogsled watching over Frankie's body. Beatrice followed behind driving Josh's machine and then quickly disappeared into Frankie's trailer, unable to face Darlene and Wendy after what had happened. The women were stunned by Frankie's death, but they'd known the day would come Frankie would get into a jam he couldn't escape. Although they never dreamed his time would end with Beatrice shooting him.

As time passed, feelings toward Beatrice changed. Even Dick, who harbored no ill will toward Beatrice at the time of the shooting, became annoyed by her presence. Everybody understood why she had killed Frankie, but the fact remained he was Josh's and Dick's brother. The clan tolerated Beatrice's presence, but deep down they resented her for what she had done.

Beatrice wanted to leave the Haven as soon as possible. However, until the weather straightened out and the Dam Road was made passable, she remained secluded in the trailer, avoiding contact with the others.

The day the Dam Road was plowed, Beatrice asked Dick to drive her to Kingston to call Alice to ask if she could stay with her. No one at the compound made an effort to say goodbye. Instead, Josh, Darlene, and Wendy watched from the kitchen window as Beatrice stepped into Dick's pickup and disappeared down the driveway.

After a few weeks of living with Alice, Beatrice found an apartment on the outskirts of Madrid. It was a brief walk to the woodturning mill, where she worked the next twenty years packing endless boxes with mass-produced wooden novelties. Beatrice never knew happiness, consumed by the January day when she had taken Frankie's life. She was in her late fifties when life changed for the better. Beatrice met Mike, a widower, at the local church she regularly attended. Mike was the opposite of Frankie. Finally, Beatrice had found a winner, a man who cared about her and her about him. Mike and Beatrice married and moved to Farmington, where Beatrice worked at the shoe shop until her death at age sixty-nine.

Dick and Darlene stayed another year at Bartlett Haven before moving to Fraternity Township, where Dick worked sorting lumber at the local sawmill. They would have remained at the compound if not for the children. However, Dick realized that if they didn't leave, the two boys would grow up as he did, barely being able to read or write. Dick and Darlene often returned to the Haven to check on Josh and to visit his father and brother's graves in the little stand of pine beyond the brook.

Josh visited Frankie's grave daily, grieving the loss of his brother. He went through life never fully accepting Frankie's death. Wendy wanted the family to leave Bartlett Haven and move to somewhere their children could attend school and she could reconnect with her family. However, Josh would have no part of it. His bond was with the land and his desire to remain close to Frankie, at least in spirit. Wendy eventually left Josh and returned to Shuman Falls with the children. Even though he and Wendy had parted ways, every month, without fail, Josh sent a check to Wendy to help support his children.

Josh continued to work in the woods, eventually buying a well-used skidder. He lived alone at the Haven and, in his later years, was known locally as the Hermit of Skyler Township. Josh died at seventy-two working under his skidder, crushed when the machine slipped off the hydraulic jack.